THE MANDALAY PROTOCOL

A.C. EDWARDS

WHITE
TIGER
PRESS

ISBN: 9780-6458-6736-7
A PDS record for this book is available at the National Library of Australia

The Mandalay Protocol: Bishop & Carter series, Book One
Cover Design by Red Tally
This novel's story and characters are fictitious. Certain real locations, products,
institutions, agencies, and public offices are mentioned, but the characters involved
and events described are wholly creations of the author's imagination.

For Liz, Shannon and Duncan

For the real Swe and Zaw

The bigger the tiger, the bigger the tracks.
Burmese proverb

PROLOGUE

KAISERSLAUTERN, Rhineland-Palatinate, Germany, 2010

'Corporal?' the voice was soft, feminine, accented. He sighed, luxuriating in the caress of the gentle tone. 'Corporal Bishop?' More insistent, but still gentle.

He opened his eyes and blinked against the glare of the bright lights in the room. Glancing around, he took it in. It was spotlessly clean, and it smelled good. Crisp, white sheets were folded down neatly to his chest. Turning his head to the left, he saw the cannula in his arm that snaked away to two bags of clear fluid suspended from an IV Pole.

Beside the pole stood a patient monitor and he watched for a moment as the screen's data display scribbled out his vitals – heart rate, blood oxygen, temperature, blood pressure. His right shoulder was secured in a cast, and the arm was slung above the bed. He turned his head again and looked up at the woman standing at the end of the bed. She was blonde, short and shapely, and wore immaculate blue scrubs that looked as if they had just come from the drycleaners. Her name tag said, "Fr. Dr. Müller". He unstuck his tongue from the roof of his mouth.

'Where am I?' he croaked, his tongue thick.

'Landstuhl. Germany. You are in hospital. You were evacuated here after you were stabilised at KAF.'

'How long...?'

'Drei tage... Sorry, you have been here three days now.'

'My men... How are they?'

She shrugged. 'I don't know. We just deal with the mess.' She glanced down at the chart in her hands. 'Australian. Special Operations Task Group,' she said. 'Operation Hamkari, Shah Wali Kot. I can call Kandahar, but I do not think they will tell me anything about the operation and your men.'

Bishop shook his head. 'You're right. They'll tell you bugger all...'

'Bitte? I'm sorry...?'

'Bugger all... Nothing. They will tell you nothing.' He smacked his dry lips and cleared his throat. 'May I have a drink, please?'

The doctor moved around the bed and poured a small cup that she held to his mouth. He gulped thankfully at the cool, clean water, then lay back in the soft pillows and studied the ceiling.

'What happened to me?'

'Are you in pain?'

'On a scale of one to ten, I'd say a one...'

The doctor inclined her head toward the IV.

'Fentanyl. You will feel no pain for a while, but you will as we turn down the dose. Then it will be quite acute. Pain management will be an ongoing issue for a while. Anyway, you asked what happened. So, you were very seriously injured. The headwound cracked your skull, and you had a brain bleed...'

Bishop's memories were of the assault on the mud-hut village, the RPG detonating at his feet, and the hammer blow into his shoulder. Then, nothing more. He reached up to his head and felt the bandage wrapping. 'I suppose I have a shit haircut now?'

'Yes,' the doctor said, her face serious. 'I'm afraid it is not attractive. So, brain bleed and we are unsure what neurological effects this will have. We will do an electroencephalogram, an EEG, in the coming days to test and measure the electrical activity in your brain.'

She flicked through the pages of the chart. 'The right shoulder is a mess. The impact of the round shattered the clavicle and scapula, and you were extremely lucky fragmentation did not sever your brachial artery. Your rotator cuff was very badly damaged, and some of it had to be debrided during surgery. Do you know what...'

'I know what that means. You cut it away.'

'Ja, some. So, the scapula has been pinned and plated, and we are running a course of strong antibiotics into you – possible infection at the prosthesis site is a concern.'

Bishop closed his eyes. 'Well, that isn't good. Will I regain use of the shoulder?'

She shrugged. 'I do not know. I don't think so. I think it will always suffer reduced movement. But with good rehab... who knows?' The doctor reached out and gently patted Bishop's left hand. She had seen it before. All of these men reacted the same. At least this one still had all of his limbs. 'I'm sorry.'

Bishop closed his eyes and turned his head away. He knew what this meant. He was out of the Regiment. It didn't matter how hard he worked; they would never take him back unless he was one hundred percent. And the odds of *that*, with a buggered shoulder, were slim to none. Special operators didn't get second chances with injuries like his. He clenched his teeth and groaned. That would make it two families he had lost.

His eyes still closed, he heard the doctor leave the room and the door click softly shut behind her.

1

SINGAPORE, present day

At 3:00 a.m. the Tampines Expressway is empty. It is a late-night favourite of the city state's boy racers, a broad, smooth road stretching east-west across Singapore, well-lit and just begging for its long, sinuous curves to be ridden.

Flicking his eyes to the speedometer, Bishop opened the throttle as he leaned the Yamaha YZF-R7 into a right-hand sweeper, hugging the inside lane marking in a tight counter-steer. Another quick glance down. 140...150...165. Even crouched low behind the fairing, the wind buffeted at him and screamed through the full-face helmet. The noise of the wind, the road, and the engine roared in his ears as he made minute adjustments to the bike's line, his right knee only millimetres from the bitumen. Streetlights snapped by, too fast to count, and the centre-line markings blurred into a single, unbroken white smear against the black road.

The curve swung away to the left, and Bishop, shifting his weight smoothly, caressed the bike over and toed down a gear before leaning back over to the right as the road snaked east. The exit sign to Loyang Avenue flicked by. Bishop fingered the front brake lightly, drew in on the clutch, and tapped down again with his left toe – once, twice. Rear brake.

The bike's 700 cc engine roared as it decelerated into the exit and turned left onto Loyang Avenue. Then, its leather-clad rider threw open the throttle, and the bike leapt forward again with an angry snarl. The bike swayed like a dancer. Left, right, and then left again as Bishop led it lovingly and seductively through the curves past a sleeping Changi toward the sea.

As he exited onto Nicoll Drive, Bishop eased the bike to a crawl and into the deserted Changi Beach carpark. Nosing the bike to the far edge of the carpark, he switched off the ignition and flicked the kill switch before kicking down the stand. He raised the visor of his helmet and breathed deeply at the air that tanged with salt and mangrove. His left hand trembled slightly as he fumbled at the helmet strap, and he cursed quietly.

His shoulder ached the familiar throb that he had lived with for years, and he shut his eyes tight against the fog that was beginning to settle in his head as the clamping sensation against his skull began again. Removing the helmet and propping it onto the right-hand wing mirror, Bishop drew in a deep breath and exhaled slowly, his eyes still shut. He counted to ten then, opening his eyes, unzipped the jacket of his leathers, reached in and drew out a small, white bottle.

In the channel, the lights on the anchored barges twinkled in the dark and reflected off the black water like cats' eyes. Above, a fat tropical moon lit the cloudless sky and shone brightly down on the man and his motorcycle. It was quiet. The only sounds were the gentle lapping of the waves on the beach and the ticking of the bike engine as it slowly cooled in the humid night.

Bishop sighed and popped the lid from the small bottle with his thumb. He shook out two white tablets. Staring into the dark, he could hear the gunfire and shouting and taste the dust in his mouth. A runnel of sweat trickled into his right eye, and he cuffed at it, expecting to feel the forehead strap of a Light Patrol Headset. It wasn't there. The noise in his head stopped. He rubbed his eyes and, in a single motion, threw the tablets into his mouth and swallowed. Relief was quick and Bishop relaxed into its warmth as he settled back on the bike to await the sun's rise over Tekong Island.

2

THE RED LIGHT blinked on the phone, and Bishop sat up in the chair, suddenly alert. It had been a long wait – longer than usual – but the call had finally come through. Glancing up at the glass walls of the small room, he checked the office across the corridor. Satisfied the man he was looking for was sitting at his desk, he reached across and punched a button. The man in the other office picked up. Bishop slipped on a headset and answered the call.

He could hear the familiar hissing that had characterised the calls over the past six long weeks of negotiations, and he waited in silence for the other man to speak. The phone crackled, and he waited. Finally, a male voice. Soft, low timbre with a slight gravelly edge.

'Hello? Bishop? I know you are there. Do not play games, my friend.'

'Nasir, I'm here. You know I always wait politely for you to speak first.'

'So you can record our call...'

'Of course I record our calls. You wouldn't want me to get your instructions wrong.'

'No. That would be... unfortunate.'

'Nasir, I always enjoy talking to you but may we get down to business?' Bishop leaned across and tapped at the laptop screen. An image of a man and a woman, their eyes haunted, figures gaunt and frail, stared back at him. The man held that day's *Manila Times* up before the camera. 'Your latest Proof of Life is accepted. Thank you.'

'It is my pleasure. As you can see: both alive and well.'

'I would expect nothing less. You wouldn't want to jeopardise the payment, would you.'

'Indeed. And speaking of which...?'

Bishop tapped again at the screen. An email from the Zurich bank confirmed that the money had been wired to the firm's Singapore account. 'We will have the funds in six hours, and they will be delivered, as you request, on Basilan nine hours later.'

'Good. It must be you, Bishop. Do not send a team. I want to meet you in person. That's the deal...'

Bishop flicked his eyes across the corridor. The other man was shaking his head. 'Nasir, that's *not* the deal, and you know it. It has to be a team – that's how we work.'

'I have changed my mind, my friend. You deliver the ransom, or the deal is off, and the hostages die.' Nasir chuckled. It was a menacing sound. 'I have grown to like you these past weeks, and I feel we must eat and talk... celebrate a successful conclusion to our business. You will be here, and you will just have to trust me.'

'Yes,' Bishop said quietly. 'Trust is important. You need to trust that I will hand over five million US, and I need to trust you won't kill me and the hostages...'

'That seems fair to me. You have 12 hours.'

The call ended abruptly, and Bishop slowly removed the headset. He drew a deep breath. He was a negotiator, not a field operator – at least not any longer – and he knew what would happen to the two Swedish hostages if he ghosted Nasir. But something bothered him more than the thought of walking into Nasir's lair.

From the start of the job, Bishop had been plagued with doubt. There was something about Nasir that didn't add up. The region's security agencies kept close tabs on these groups and their leaders. Every other hostage negotiation Bishop had done had been well informed by voluminous intelligence on the target. But Nasir was a different picture altogether. There *was* no picture, and that was the problem. Where was all the intel on him, his movements, his suspected location, his group's structure and tactics? There just wasn't any, and that was unusual.

He sat back in the chair as the door swung open, and the other man stepped in. Major (Rtd) Brian Nesbitt ran a hand through his long, greying hair and, crossing his arms, leaned against the door-frame of the small room. Bishop looked up.

Nesbitt headed the firm's operations in Southeast Asia. Bishop figured he was somewhere around sixty, but no one knew. He was urbane and Savile Row from head to toe, and had been in the same battalion of the Scots Guards as the firm's Chairman. To Bishop's Australian ears, Nesbitt was about as old Etonian and pukka as they could get. But he wasn't fooled by the slightly bewildered and eccentric persona Nesbitt liked to portray. The man was ruthless, a veteran of many military actions and secret wars, and was always two steps ahead of everyone else. He also loved the firm and every man and woman who worked for it, looking on them as his children.

'What do you think?' Bishop asked, leaning back with his hands behind his head.

'What do I fucking think, old boy? What do *you* think I think?

'*I* think you think I'm not doing the drop, and *you* think you'll be sending a team to do it. But you'd be wrong. I'm going. We have no choice.'

Nesbitt pinched the bridge of his nose and shut his eyes for a moment. He liked Bishop. The rough-edged Aussie reminded him of his son, who had been killed at Sangin years before. He also had a brilliant mind and was the best negotiator Nesbitt had ever seen. But he was guarded, and no one ever got in close.

The lad was a walking defence system that no one could hope to penetrate. He did not attend staff parties and had few, if any, friends in the firm. Nesbitt had made inquiries into the lad's past but, apart from a service record and some medical docs from Germany, he had come away empty-handed. Nesbit often wondered what had happened – or *was* happening – to make the young man the way he was.

With a sigh, he scratched under his chin and eyed Bishop. 'You fucking convicts are a rude bunch. Insubordinate. But, yes, as you mention it, I know that. We have no choice.' He regarded Bishop for a long minute. 'You do realise there is every chance this bastard will take the money and kill you and those two Swedes. Abu Sayyaf do not fuck about.'

Bishop shrugged. 'Yeah, but what options do we have? None. Nasir has planned this all along and left it to the last minute to throw a spanner in the works. He's fucking with us. It's no skin off his nose either way: either I turn up, and he gets the cash, or I don't, and he gets an execution video. Win-win.'

'Note, also, he's now shaved a few hours off your carefully planned timeline...'

'No, he hasn't. We already have the funds – they are bagged and waiting for us at the bank – and it will take me seven hours to get there. So, by my careful calculations, I've got four hours up my sleeve.'

Nesbitt smiled. 'Clever bastard. I always knew you were, from the moment you came skulking around here with your shabby cap in hand.' The older man took a deep breath and huffed out through his nose. 'But I'm still sending a team.' He held up his hand as Bishop started to object. 'None of my flock are *ever* going into something like this alone. *But* the team will stand off. Far enough away to be inconspicuous but close enough to move if things go pear-shaped. That's final.'

Bishop stood and grabbed up his jacket from the back of the chair. 'Okay, you're the boss. I better get going. The jet is on standby out at Seletar. I have to get to the bank and grab the cash. We leave in seventy-five minutes. Make sure the team aren't late, or I'll leave without them.'

Bishop picked up his black mission bag from under the desk and moved past his boss. As he did, Nesbitt reached out and took him by the elbow. 'Do *not* fuck this up, young man. Oh, and try not to get killed.'

Bishop nodded. 'Your concern is touching, sir. See you tomorrow.'

3

MANDALAY, Central Burma

Bill Reilly stood at the window of the suite and looked west across the wide, brown band of the Irrawaddy River. The sunset was a giant red orb that shimmered in the heat of the early evening, and the sky, clear and wide, was changing through hues of pink, red and purple.

He rubbed the bristles of his crewcut and sucked at his teeth, unmoved by the scene. After a thirty-year career, much of it in Southeast Asia, he was tired of the place. Tired of the smell, the noise, the chaos and the damn food. Tired of the people, their impenetrable cultures and their incessant chattering.

He shook his head. Only months to go now, and he would retire. He would go home and settle down with his wife and dogs in the house they would build in the hills. Peace. At last. But first, this goddamned job had to be seen through to a successful conclusion. He wanted to get the hell out, it was time after all, but he had worked too hard, for too long, on this job. He'd be damned if he would cut and run before it was done.

There was a polite cough behind him, and he turned to face the room. From the corner of his eye, he glimpsed his phone, face down on a bookshelf and recording. The other man in the room, a middle-aged Burmese general in a crisp, dark green uniform, sat on the sofa, one arm draped across the back. The general was smoking, and Reilly watched as he leaned forward and poured another shot of whisky.

'He is late,' the general observed as he sipped the whisky and ashed the cigarette with a flick.

'He'll be here,' Reilly growled. 'Have some patience.'

'I'm nothing if not a patient man. After all, I am here am I not? This meeting has taken a very long time to come around. I have been extremely patient with you.'

'These things take time.'

'I do not doubt that.' The general leaned forward and stubbed out the cigarette in a heavy glass ashtray. 'I have waited this long because, as unpleasant as it may be to meet this person, the payoff will be worth it. For me. But I am unsure, still, of what is truly in it for *you*.'

If only you knew, you asshole, Reilly thought. 'We want only a stabilised security situation. Better for business.'

The general smiled. Did this taung kyi, *foreigner,* think him a fool? 'Which, of course, will occur once I make my call to the United Nations. Meanwhile, the river of gold continues to flow...'

Reilly didn't react but took a seat, flicking a piece of lint from his trouser leg. They wouldn't know all there was to it – they weren't that smart. They could *suspect* – probably did – but they wouldn't know. Even if they did, it meant nothing – as the presence of the uniformed man in the room attested. The general's lust for power was too strong.

The two sat in strained silence for a minute or two, and then the doorbell rang. Crossing the room, Reilly opened the door and waved the visitor in. The general chose that moment to study his fingernails.

The visitor stepped in. He was short and wiry, and Reilly knew he was aged in his mid-thirties. He knew a lot about this man. Most of all, he knew what the visitor wanted, what he wanted most in the world, and Reilly was in the business of making dreams come true. The visitor was dressed in a pair of baggy khaki pants and a white shirt, over which he wore a loose-fitting khaki jacket. His shoes were black canvas, dusty and scuffed. Without speaking, he moved to stand in front of the general, a low coffee table between them. Slowly, the visitor removed his sunglasses and folded them into his jacket pocket. He nodded at the general and bowed slightly.

'Bogyoke Min Ko,' he said, using the Burmese honorific for a military officer. 'Mingalaba, *may you be blessed.*'

Major General Min Kyaw Ko, commander of the Myanmar Army's Eastern Command, looked up at the man standing before him and nodded. Politeness demanded it, so he stood. 'Khun Sai Maung,' he said crisply before sitting and lighting another cigarette.

Reilly waved the visitor to a chair and poured them both a whisky from the bottle on the coffee table. He passed one to the visitor, who sat, silently watching the general like someone who had found a cobra coiled on their bicycle seat. The general stared back, his eyes hooded and a look of loathing darkening his smooth features.

Reilly sighed and took a big pull at the whisky. This wasn't going to be easy, but at least he had these two assholes in the same room. He wasn't letting them go until they had hammered out an agreement.

'Gentlemen,' he said, lowering his glass to the coffee table. 'Shall we get down to business?'

4

At the same time the three men sat hunched around a coffee table in a Mandalay hotel room slowly filling with cigarette smoke, Thai Airways flight TG303 touched down in Yangon. The modern, spacious arrivals hall was busy, but the crowds of disembarking passengers, milling in the air-conditioning around the luggage carousels, were a shadow of the numbers arriving in the Burmese city pre-2020. Announcements in Burmese and English echoed through the hall as the young woman checked the carousel display board for her flight. She eased the weight of the backpack on her shoulders and mumbled the carousel number to herself as she turned and weaved her way through the crowd.

It had been a long trip, and Sophie Bouchard was tired. Forty-six hours from Montréal-Pierre Elliott Trudeau International. First to Incheon, then on to Bangkok, and, finally, the one-hour flight to Yangon. Standing by the luggage carousel, she wrinkled her nose in distaste as she sniffed at her own unwashed scent. She shrugged. It would be a whole lot worse once she started the new job. She doubted there would be a beauty spa where she was going.

Her large black and red rucksack moved into view. She transferred her backpack to her chest as she politely elbowed her way to the edge of the carousel. Grabbing a shoulder strap, she swung the heavy rucksack clumsily onto her back, bouncing once as she tugged down on the adjustment straps. Moments later she was queued in front of one of a line of desks at Immigration.

She was finally here and still found it hard to believe that, after all this time, all the arguments over sullen dinners, she had made the decision to leave her native Montréal. She was here and, soon, she would be bringing care and aid to the poor and the vulnerable in this war-torn nation.

Her mother had cried when she had first announced her intentions, but it was her father with whom she had had the biggest fights. Nom de Dieu, why would a daughter of his want to leave all that she had, all that she could *be*, to grub around in a pile of shit country handing out rice to people who did not give a damn about her? It was there, in Montréal, that she was loved and needed, where she belonged! *No*, it would not happen. He forbid it!

Sophie Bouchard sighed as she shuffled forward. She loved her father dearly, but he was suffocating her – the family's money and privilege were smothering the life out of her. Here, at least, she had a purpose. She had not, however, made a complete break – that would be silly. She had kept her platinum credit card and knew the bills would, as ever, be paid in full and on time when they arrived at the corporation's offices on Boulevard René-Lévesque in Ville de Montréal, the city's central business district. No point in living poor if she did not have to, she mused. Finally, she stood before an Immigration Officer.

Dressed in a crisp, white shirt with black epaulettes, the officer held out his hand, and she passed over her passport and arrival documentation. The officer inserted the passport into the scanner, then removed it to thumb through its pages. He leafed through her arrival documents, that included a letter from her new employer attached to the approved visa application. He looked up at the woman standing before him.

'You are to be working for Global Horizons?' he said in flawless English. 'To where will you be assigned?'

Sophie shrugged. 'I don't know. I guess I will be allocated to a field office when I have completed induction training...'

'The duration of your intended stay?'

'I will be here for the period of the visa. Seventy days, then will apply for re-entry.'

'And your accommodation while in Yangon?'

'I have a reservation at the Lotte Hotel...'

The officer's eyebrows shot up at the mention of the five-star hotel on Pyay Road. Aid work was paying well, it seemed. From the look of her, the woman had money. Just another rich Westerner coming to his country to polish her virtue. He supposed they did some good, but it did not stop his dislike for them.

Satisfied, the Immigration Officer took one last look at the paper-work and passport before stamping them and handing them back. 'Welcome to the Republic of the Union of Myanmar, Miss Bouchard. Enjoy your stay... Next!'

5

BASILAN ISLAND, *Philippines*

Bishop arrived early at the designated rendezvous at the small food stall on the water in Isabela, looking across the water to Malamavi and, further still, to the Zamboanga Peninsula. It was Abu Sayyaf hunting ground, and the atmosphere was thick with tension and threat.

The terror group had taken a battering from Philippines security forces in recent years and was much less a problem than it had previously been, but it was still active and still killing people. In particular, its kidnapping campaign targeting unwary Westerners had ramped up in the last twelve months, and that nagged at Bishop.

His support team was in place. They were all former Malaysian and Philippines special forces, selected by the firm specifically for their ability to blend easily into the scene around the southern Philippines and Malaysia's Sabah state. Bishop felt comforted by their watchful presence. One was hidden in the jungle fringe off the small market square, his eyes glued to the sniper scope of his rifle; another sat behind the wheel of a battered pickup, cradling a Heckler & Koch MP5. Two more sat drinking tea only metres from him. He couldn't make out their concealed weapons but knew they would be brought into action in a split second.

Nasir arrived precisely on time. Bishop sat with his back to the food stall and watched his approach across the square. He was accompanied by four men, all skinny and dressed in a ragged mix of uniforms and civilian clothing. Nasir's crew were threatening and looked out at the world with the dead eyes of killers. The men spread around the small market square and faced out against any incoming threat. Thanks to successful ambushes against local police, they carried well-oiled, modern weapons and made no effort to conceal them.

Nasir stopped a metre from Bishop, and Bishop stood. He examined the terrorist. Bishop had spoken with him numerous times over the past weeks but had seen him, briefly, only twice on video and, even then, he had been masked up.

Nasir Abdulmari, known by his nom de guerre as Jaafar, looked like a university student – which he had been only two years before when he completed his Masters in Biochemistry at the University of Malaysia. His skin was smooth and glowed with health, and his dark eyes were clear and bright. His hair was cut short and looked to have been done professionally – no jungle-camp razor trims for him, Bishop mused – and his chin beard, in the Malay style, while long, was well groomed and oiled. The terrorist leader openly wore a dark green camouflage uniform that was still creased from the packaging, and his boots were near new 5.11 tactical lace-ups. There was no doubt about it, Bishop thought: Nasir was dressed to impress.

Abdulmari nodded his head in greeting, his face a mask of calm. 'Masaa al-khayr, Bishop,' he said. *Good afternoon.* 'As-salaam alaykum,' he added, briefly touching his heart with his right hand.

Bishop nodded his head in return; thankful Abdulmari had not put out his hand in greeting. 'Wa alaykum as-salaam.' He waved at the plastic table and two chairs. 'Shall we?'

They both sat, and Abdulmari immediately looked at the owner of the food stall, who shifted nervously from foot to foot, a muscle twitching in his cheek. Seconds later, two plates and two spoons, two plastic cups, and two cold Cokes landed on the table. Bishop poured a Coke and took a long drink, using the moment to gather his thoughts. It was hot and humid, and he was annoyed to feel a trickle of sweat break free from his hairline, run past the corner of his eye, and down his cheek. Abdulmari watched the glistening little bead with interest.

'Are you scared, Bishop?' he asked quietly, sipping from his Coke.

'Should I be?'

'Whether you should or should not really has no bearing on whether you are.'

'I'm not. We are here to transact business, and I want to see that that is done swiftly and smoothly with no one getting hurt.' As he spoke, Bishop looped his right foot through the handles of the large grey canvas bag at his feet. He was about to speak again when two plates, piled high with food, hit the table. Abdulmari smiled.

'Did I not say we should eat, talk, and celebrate a successful conclusion?' He waved at the food. 'Please. You are my guest.'

Bishop leaned back in the plastic chair. He kept his voice even and quiet. 'Nasir, I have nothing to celebrate here. I am doing a job. Yes, I will be pleased to get the hostages home, but I don't feel the urge to *celebrate* anything about this with you. I hope you understand.'

Abdulmari did not reply. Instead, using his right hand, he scooped up a serving from the dish closest to him, along with a pinch of rice between his thumb and forefinger. He stuffed it into his mouth and licked his fingers.

'Pyanggang Manok. Magnificent! It is chicken marinated...'

'...with turmeric then grilled in a rich coconut milk sauce. I know. It's a Tausug specialty.'

Abdulmari smiled. 'I should have known you would be familiar with the food of my country.'

'Except it isn't, is it Nasir? Your country, I mean.'

'You make a good point. Indeed, this is *not* the country we want.

An independent Islamic state, across the Muslim provinces of the southern Philippines. *That* will be my country.'

Bishop finally gave in to the hunger cramping his belly and spooned a mouthful of rice and chicken into his mouth. He washed it down with a gulp of Coke and belched. Leaning slightly across the table and keeping his hands in view, he pointed a relaxed finger at the terrorist.

'You and I both know,' he said, 'this isn't about the good of the Ummah. How are you advancing the interests of the collective Islamic world? How is murdering and stealing helping to improve anything for your people?'

Abdulmari cocked his head and seemed to consider that for a moment. 'A means to an end. Sometimes violent revolution is necessary...'

Bishop wanted to laugh. But he didn't. 'You're no Robespierre, Nasir, and I can't imagine anything being further from Liberté, Egalité, and what not, than this. You're a bandit, that's all.'

That finally seemed to get under Nasir's skin, although that wasn't strictly Bishop's intention. He realised he might have gone too far. It was not as if he held all the cards in this game. He wasn't even sure he had a playable hand. All Nasir had to do was shoot him in the face and walk away with the money. He sat perfectly still, waiting for the next move. Abdulmari scowled briefly, then quickly re-arranged his features as he leant forward.

'Do you have a death wish, Bishop? Do you want to die here?'

Slowly, the terrorist reached behind him and withdrew a large, chrome revolver and placed it on the table between them. From the corner of his eye, Bishop saw his two men lower their teas and slowly slip their right hands inside their shirts. Bishop looked down. Smith & Wesson .357, six-inch barrel, with a well-used grip. It was a cannon, and he was not happy to see it. With a conscious effort, he took a sip of the Coke and looked up into Abdulmari's eyes.

'No,' he said, lowering the cup to the table beside the revolver. 'I don't especially. At least not today.'

Abdulmari eyed him long and hard, his elbows on the table and chin propped on his clenched hands. Bishop was interesting. For a kāfir. For all his pretence of calm and a very casual Western attitude, Bishop was dangerous. Abdulmari knew that. The man sitting across from him had a streak of darkness running through him, and it would be unwise to underestimate him.

Abdulmari sensed Bishop was an implacable enemy, and he resolved to think further on it. Perhaps he should just kill him now and be done with it. But then there was the matter of the two men that sat only metres from them with a clear line of sight to the table. Finally, he sat back and nodded at the revolver.

'You are an interesting man, Bishop,' he said mildly. 'You annoy me, but I do not think there is need for violence today.' He glanced up. 'So, you can tell your men to sit very still and relax.'

Without taking his eyes from the man across the table, Bishop lowered his left hand to his side and patted down twice. Stand down.

'Did you think I would not see them?' Abdulmari asked.

'I didn't really care, Nasir. But I'm happy for you to know that you die where you sit if you do anything foolish.' He gestured with his head to the square. 'Your men? They'll be dead in a heartbeat. I came prepared.' He inclined his head to the bag at his feet. 'Let's just do this.'

Abdulmari sucked at his teeth. So be it. He looked across at the nearest of his men, and nodded once. The terrorist nodded back and spoke briefly into a radio clipped to the front of his tattered chest rig. Seconds later, a white commercial van roared into view and braked hard in the middle of the square. The driver climbed down from the cab, walked to the rear of the van, and swung open the doors. Abdulmari looked back at Bishop.

'The money. Now, if you please?'

Bishop shook his head. 'Not until I see the hostages. Get them out and move them forward five metres. The driver gets back into the van. Move the rest of your men to the van. When that is done, you get the cash.'

'You are not in any position to be making demands, Bishop...'

'For fuck's sake, Nasir!' Bishop said, his teeth clenched. 'Read the room. Just do as I say. That way, we all get out of this alive.'

Abdulmari scowled but shouted to his men and they began to move. Bishop watched as the hostages were pulled roughly from the van and hustled forward. Their hands were bound, and both were blindfolded. The woman was sobbing. When Bishop was satisfied, he stood and hefted the large canvas bag. Thumping it onto the table, he unzipped it and pulled back the edges. Abdulmari peered in.

'Five million? You would not cheat me, Bishop?'

'A deal's a deal, Nasir. It's all there. Now take it and go.'

With a final, long look at Bishop, the terrorist leader zipped the bag, shouldered it, and walked to the van. As he passed the two hostages, he turned back.

'It has been a pleasure, Bishop,' he called. 'I do not doubt we will meet again.'

Abdulmari climbed into the front of the van, and it sped off with a screech of tyres. The team emerged and rushed toward the two frail figures who stood shaking in the centre of the square. Bishop rose and watched as their bindings were cut and blindfolds removed. The woman collapsed into the arms of one of the team, and the man sank to his knees, his head hung and shoulders heaving. Bishop let out a long breath. The deal was done. The hostages were safe. He looked at the plates of food on the table and choked down on the vomit that had risen in his throat.

It had been a long thirty hours, and Bishop was tired and moody. Boat Quay was busy in the early evening, as the office crowd mingled with tourists, the former in search of a cold beer, the latter eyeing off tasty but overpriced meals in the restaurants that bordered the Singapore River.

The humidity had barely eased as the sun began to set, and Bishop pulled at his T-shirt, peeling it from the sweat that stuck it to his chest. He reached out for the cold bottle of Tiger beer on the table and grunted as he noticed the tremor in his left hand. Gripping his hand in his right, he shut his eyes for a slow count of ten, then lifted the beer and drained the last of its contents.

Sitting back with a sigh, Bishop was conscious of the press of the small, white bottle in the pocket of his jeans, and he reached for it before stopping himself with an effort. Looking around, he signalled the barman for another beer.

A fresh Tiger arrived, and Bishop swigged at it. The press of the crowd on Boat Quay was thicker now, and a thousand voices chattered and laughed and shouted around him. Yes, all things considered, the job had gone off smoothly. London would be happy, and so would Nesbitt.

With the hostages under care in Singapore General and their relatives inbound from Stockholm, it was "Task Complete". Things were quiet for now, but Bishop knew it would be all over the media within hours as journalists and their on-call "Talking Heads" tried to piece together what had happened. They never would and, as usual, they would fill the gaps with a raft of outlandish theories. Let them. The role Bishop and the firm had played would never out, which was all to the good. So, yes, another job well done. Why then, Bishop wondered, did he feel so bloody terrible?

He was a negotiator, employed by the firm to bargain the best price for the release of hostages – most of whom, in this region, were taken across the Sulu Archipelago. He was good at what he did. The best. But, deep down, Bishop felt complicit. He was part of an industry that rewarded terror groups for snatching and abusing innocent people, leaving them with life-long and debilitating mental scars. Those they did not kill.

Separatist Islamist ideology had fuck all to do with it, Bishop knew. It was all about the money, and it was grubby. But what else could you do? It was a simple choice of do the deal or wait for staked heads to appear on the side of a dusty jungle track. It was a vexing question, and he *was* saving lives, but it had not stopped Bishop from feeling dirty with every ransom payment he had negotiated in the past five years.

He finished the beer and fished thirty dollars out of his wallet. Dropping the cash on the table, he stood and walked out of Boat Quay, across Circular Road and headed west along North Canal Road. It was a half-hour walk home, but he needed it and he longed for the hot shower that awaited him.

6

THE OLD MAN is drunk again. Blind, roaring, brutally drunk. The boy knows what that means as he drops his bicycle in the overgrown front yard. He stands listening to the shouting coming from inside. It's been going on like this for years – in fact, the boy cannot remember a time when it hadn't. There is no escape. The old man has always been a drunk, but it got worse when he was laid off from the cotton gin. He had only been sweeping the floors, but it was the first real job the boy can remember him having. The boy knows he is in for a beating if the old man sees him – it happens every time, sure as eggs – and he begins to reach for the handlebars of the bike. He is tall for fourteen but knows he can't take the bastard on. Bugger it. He'll shoot through to Tim's place. Tim's old man is a good bloke, and Tim's fat, red-faced mum can cook even better than they do at the pub. She feeds him more often than not, and the boy's stomach grumbles at the thought. The shouting gets louder and the banging of cupboards can be heard as the boy scuffs his bare feet in the dust and stares at the front door. The house is run-down. A low-set timber cottage on James street, a short walk from the rail line that parallels the Warrego Highway and cuts across the Western Downs like a shimmering sword in the sun. The front porch is littered with toys and a yellowed baby bouncer sits next to an over-stuffed, old sofa covered in dog hair. The flyscreen is rusted, and the front door is open. A roar from inside is followed by a scream and a fleshy thud. Then another. He can hear his baby sister crying in the back room. The boy stands straighter, his jaw clenched. The bastard is belting mum. Dropping the bike again, he turns and runs around the house to the shed. The wooden door is hanging off its hinges, and he barges in, his eyes scanning left and right. There! He grips the long handle of the shovel and swears as a splinter spears the palm of his hand. His bare feet slap on the back steps, and he surges into the kitchen. His sister is sitting huddled in the corner near the fridge. There is food everywhere, and fragments of a shattered plate lie like shards of bone on the lino. Another scream from the loungeroom, and he rushes in. The old man stops, his right arm cocked ready to deliver another blow. The boy's mother crouches on the floor at the old man's feet. Her lip is split, and her left eye is puffed shut. You, you little cunt, the old man says. Fuck off out of it. Leave her alone, the boy screams and thrusts the shovel forward. The tip catches the old man in the guts, and the boy shoves down on the handle. The shovel blade flicks up and catches the old man under the chin, and he staggers back. The boy steps around his mother. The old man is bent over, holding his chin and mouth in his hands. There is blood on his boots. Look at me, you bastard, the boy says quietly, then raises the shovel high and slams it down onto the old man's head.

Bishop woke with a start. The apartment was dark, and he could hear rain pattering on the roof above. The dream still coursed through him like an electric shock and he lay still for a moment, willing his heart rate down. With a deep breath, he rolled his feet to the timber floor and sat on the edge of the bed, his head in his hands. His eyes slowly adjusted to the dark, but the fog was lowering as the familiar feeling of thickness descended over him.

He checked his watch. 0510. His left hand trembled, and he clenched it into a tight fist. Reaching across to the bedside table, he grabbed the small, white bottle and flipped off the lid. He shook two of the tablets into the palm of his hand and threw them into his mouth, swallowing them down dry.

With a groan, Bishop stood, rolled back the glass door to the small verandah and stepped out. The wind was gusting, and rain blew in on the hot air, warm and fat as it struck his face. Below him on Eng Watt Street, it was quiet. A young couple hurried by, sheltering under a large, black umbrella, and he could hear frogs croaking merrily in the wet gardens. He shut his eyes, feeling the rain on his face and the cool water under his feet as the drugs began their work. He was still standing there an hour later as the hesitant first light of dawn began to crack over the Singapore Strait.

7

Narhkan Township, Shan State, Burma

Sophie Bouchard hugged the little boy and, with a pat on his back, sent him scurrying away with his friends. The children's laughter slowly faded as she stood in the dust of the little street leading from the township's centre to the old sports field where the team had set up camp. Beyond that sat Highway 45.

She pushed back the blue, wide-brimmed hat and cuffed the sweat from her eyes with the sleeve of her shirt. That done, she hitched the cargo shorts a little further up her waist and cinched the belt tighter. The Global Horizons uniform was not what she would call *haute couture,* but it was practical – loose-fitting and light in the stifling Burmese climate. The best thing about it was that it did not hold body odour – which was a very good thing, seeing as she had not showered properly for nine days.

It had been nine days since she had left Yangon for the long journey into Shan State, following her induction training. First to the Field Office in Taunggyi, the state capital, then the short journey to the township and project site. Her welcome to the NGO had been friendly enough but the General Manager had been abrupt when she had greeted Sophie and given her the initial briefings. Sophie had quickly been introduced to the team in the office and had felt relieved they had, mostly, been about her age and had all been warm and welcoming. The nagging doubts, and mild homesickness, she had experienced in the days before soon disappeared as she settled into her routine and into the one-week training course.

Now, she stood in the dust of the township street, the afternoon sun searing down in a bright blue sky. Her shirt was wet with today's sweat and marked with the salt lines of yesterday's. The project to provide fresh drinking water had been in progress for months but had only recently accelerated toward completion, and she was assisting the young engineer with rations distribution and running a makeshift first aid clinic in the township.

She had barely heard of Burma – they called it Myanmar in the office. Before applying for the job and leaving Canada, she had spent some time at the Bibliothèque Père-Ambroise with her nose buried in dusty old books, and even more time on Google in the comfort of her bedroom. She had learned that the country had been a war zone for much of the time since independence from Britain, and that Ethnic Armed Groups, or EAGs as the initiated called them, abounded across the country, each fighting their own wars, many for decades, in the pursuit of ethnic autonomy in their states.

There were dozens of EAGs in Myanmar. Some were allied, some were warring, and all alliances and conflicts were fluid and influenced by rapidly shifting political, territorial, and economic interests. Most of the analyses Sophie had seen agreed that Myanmar was on a path to fracturing into self-governing statelets in the borderlands while the military junta held on grimly in the centre.

The Shan State Army was no exception, and it held sway in the state along with its political wing, the Restoration Council of Shan State. She had seen them, in numbers, in Kyethi during her short visit to the small Field Office, and they were known to be using the town as a base from which to launch operations against rival EAG, the Ta'ang National Liberation Army.

Alongside its ongoing conflict with the central government – that peculiarly, she had been told, seemed to have dropped away in recent months – the SSA was consolidating control of its ethnic homeland by expanding its governance and administrative systems, all toward the end goal of an autonomous Shan ethnic state.

Violent men with guns, she thought. As always, the people who suffered the most in this conflict were the poor and the vulnerable. The villagers and farmers who populated the vast swathes of the state – the whole damn country, for that matter – struggled daily for a safe and secure life for themselves and their families. Sophie squared her shoulders. Her job was to bring some level of safety, shelter, and aid to the people as best she could. She admired Global Horizons' work, and she was proud to be doing her bit.

She shielded her eyes as she looked down the street and watched a Land Cruiser approach through a cloud of dust. The vehicle pulled up, and the young engineer climbed down from the cab. He walked toward her with a broad grin, his battered blue baseball cap pushed back on his head.

David Sutton was in his mid-twenties and American. Chicago, he had told her. He was rake thin, blonde, and tanned, with a spray of freckles across his nose and cheeks. He was also beyond bashful. In fact, the young man was crushingly shy, but he and Sophie had struck up a friendship of sorts. Sophie treated him carefully, like a stray kitten, and he seemed to respond. But the young American remained embarrassingly awkward nonetheless.

'Hey, Soph,' David called as he walked up. 'Are you on school crossing duty?'

Sophie looked around at the deserted street and the ramshackle tin and timber huts that bordered it. There was no one around at that time of day – it was too damn hot.

'Funny. No, just taking it all in. You know, newbie and all...'

David chuckled. 'Yeah, I was like that. It's all kinda the same now.' He paused and pointed back down from where he had come. 'Your stores have arrived. The truck pulled in about ten minutes ago, but the driver wanted you to check it over before he unloaded.' He gestured at the Land Cruiser with his head. 'C'mon. I'll give you a ride back to camp.'

Ten minutes later, Sophie jumped down from the back of the large truck, a clipboard tucked under her arm. It was all there. Two tonnes of non-perishables, all in tins, and a tonne of rice in fifty-kilogram sacks, three dozen 25-litre plastic drums of fresh water, tarpaulins, boxes of tools and nails, sheets of tin, medical stores, supplies for the small school, and fuel for the team's generator. There was one more thing. She turned to the team's interpreter.

'Tin, would you please ask the driver if he was given a small package for me?'

The "terp" spoke to the driver, both grinning hugely. The driver reached into his cab to pull out a package wrapped in newspaper. He handed it to the pretty Western woman, who smiled at him. Sophie unwrapped it and held it up for David to see.

'*Ta-da!*' she cried. 'Look what I got us...' It was a bottle of Orphan Barrel Rhetoric 23-year Bourbon. Very smooth and very expensive.

David Sutton's eyes widened. 'Damn, Sophie! I don't know about that... Yangon will freak if they find out. But, I'm not a drinker, so I'll leave it to you.'

Sophie shrugged. 'Okay, suit yourself. I'll manage on my own, I'm sure.'

David shook his head and climbed back into the Land Cruiser's cab. 'I have to go visit someplace else, and I'll be back tomorrow. Tin will organise some men to unload for you. Enjoy the whisky.'

Sophie watched as the skinny American fired up the Land Cruiser's diesel engine and spun the wheel around to fishtail the vehicle away from the sports ground and onto Highway 45. She wondered where he was going. Shrugging, she turned back to the driver and the terp.

'Okay,' she said, rolling her sleeves up. 'Let's get to work.'

8

SHAN STATE, 20°25′24.1″N 98°38′50.2″E, Burma

The sentry south of the camp stood and squinted down the hill. He pushed his red baseball cap back and, shielding his eyes, angled his head slightly until he picked up the movement again. It was hot, even under the canopy, and the air buzzed with cicada song as it shimmered in the heat. On the track below, winding its way through the clearer vegetation on the edge of the forest, a train of mules and men plodded slowly toward him. He checked his watch before speaking briefly into the radio in his hand. They had arrived on time.

He raised a small set of binoculars and studied the slow-moving convoy. The mules were laden with large, conical baskets strapped securely to wooden pack saddles, and each basket was full to the brim with small, square parcels wrapped in brown, waxed paper. The sentry quickly counted the baskets as each mule moved out of sight into the forest. He nodded. A good load this time. The farmers had done well and suuhtayy, *boss*, would be happy.

The sentry caught a waft of the familiar acrid smell on the wind and wrinkled his nose. His older brothers had told him he would get used to it, but he doubted that – it was a stink like no other, and it seemed to burn his nose and throat every time he inhaled it. It explained, he thought, why there were no birds for hundreds of metres around.

Pocketing the binoculars, he moved back to his small pack at the foot of a large, vine-wrapped teak tree and rummaged about inside. With a smile, he drew out a small newspaper packet and unwrapped it. He popped a tofu fritter into his mouth and sat back against the tree, munching contentedly. Yes, suuhtayy would be happy, and that was a very good thing.

Forty minutes later, the mule train entered the camp, and the farmers led their animals to a makeshift shed and began to unload. It had been a long trek, and they were tired, but the farmers knew they would return to their villages and fields with pockets stuffed with US Dollars. As they worked, the camp's routine continued around them, a bustle of noise and industry in the quiet of the forest under the watchful gaze of armed guards.

On his hill, the young sentry scanned the large camp through his binoculars. It was located in a remote gorge deep in the hills, with an ample water supply, just north of the Thai border and east of the border with China. He had been told that it was ideally located to manufacture and transport the final product destined for those two nations and further around the world via the Port of Hong Kong.

He could see makeshift shelters, constructed from bamboo poles, sheets of tin and green tarpaulin, that dotted the clearing hacked into the forest. Camouflage netting, strung from trees and propped on poles, covered everything. He had asked about that and been told the dense forest and netting provided cover from aerial observation. The temporary nature of the structures meant the entire operation could be dismantled and moved to the alternate site at a moment's notice. He hoped that would not happen.

The centre of the camp housed a tarpaulin-covered shed that held large plastic drums of the chemicals that would be added to the blocks of raw sap brought in by the farmers. He did not know what the chemicals were called, but knew the poisonous stink in the air was because of them. A long, open-sided hut sat beside the chemical store. The lab was the centre of the camp's activity and groups of men, gloved and masked, moved purposefully about as they worked their part of the production line.

The young sentry did not fully understand the process – although one of his brothers had tried to explain it. But he did know it involved boiling and filtering, the addition of chemicals, then more filtering and drying. More chemicals and more heating and filtering. It was all very complicated but, when it was all done, it would birth the final product that could be further refined, dried then packaged for distribution. Heroin.

Heroin that flooded out of his country, now the world's largest producer. His brother had told him that, each year, nearly two hundred tonnes of the stuff poured across Burma's borders with Thailand, China and Laos to be sold on by organised crime groups and into the arms of addicts around the world. It was worth billions, and he wanted his cut.

On the hill above the camp, the young sentry pocketed the binoculars and, sitting against a tree, lowered the bright red baseball cap over his eyes. He lit a cigarette, stretched out his legs, and reached into his shirt to pull out a small brass locket that hung around his neck on a thin metal chain. He rubbed the lotus etched into the weathered patina of the locket's surface before turning it around. With a thumbnail, he clicked a small, hinged lid and gazed wistfully at the small photo of a young woman before closing the locket and tucking it away.

He closed his eyes and allowed a slow smile to crinkle his face. He would be given a week's vacation soon and would return to his town on Highway 45, where she waited for him. He would have some money with him, and she might, finally, say yes to the marriage proposal. Then, if he worked hard, he could buy a small parcel of land and plant a crop of the pretty, and profitable, flowers. A wife, children and money. He smiled again and scratched his chest. Life was good.

9

It had been four weeks since Bishop's encounter with Nasir Abdulmari. In that time, he had thrown himself back into work, focusing on producing geo-strategic analyses, his day job when there was no Kidnap and Ransom task on the board. It had been a stress-free time, and Bishop had felt himself finally unwinding after the tense negotiations for the Swedish hostages.

He had committed himself to more time in the gym, and his weights were heavier and reps more numerous than they had been in a long while. But his rotator cuff was still weak, the pain of it more often than not masked by the constant dull ache from his shattered and patched shoulder. He supposed it would never be right, and that upset him. Add to that, the little white tablets still called to him day and night but, fuck it, he had it under control. Didn't he?

It was Saturday afternoon and he was reclining on a lounge under a palm tree on the southern end of Tanjong Beach, a copy of Xenophon's *Anabasis* in his hands. He had read it a number of times, but Bishop was always struck by the epic tale of ancient warfare, endurance and hardship, with each new reading revealing fresh detail. He did not look on it as a self-help book – he loathed those –

but Bishop had always found solace, and a measure of validation, in the story of the famed Ten Thousand. He was on Book IV, and the Hellenes were progressing slowly through the land of the Carduchii, fighting for control of the hilltops along their route and ...

'And a good afternoon to you, Your Eminence,' a lilting male voice said happily. 'Didn't expect to see you here, Bish.'

Bishop smiled and lowered the book. He knew the voice, with its soft brogue, and only his former comrades from the Regiment called him 'Your Eminence' – a play on his surname. He turned his head and looked up at the large, bearded and tattooed man standing beside him in the sand.

'G'day Terry,' he said. 'It's been a while, mate. What brings you here?'

Terry Dougherty had migrated from Ireland at the turn of the century, and had been in Bishop's section on their second tour of Afghan until the big Irishman had taken a blast of fragmentation to the right knee. He had been repatriated to Australia soon after, and the Army had, with indecent haste and little thought for his future, discharged him. The last Bishop had heard, Dougherty had left the country, married and was running some sort of tour business in Thailand's Chiang Mai.

'Ah, sure, and it's been too fucking long, mate,' Dougherty beamed. 'What is it now? Nearly eight years or more? Jaysus.' Suddenly remembering the petite woman standing beside him, Dougherty spread his hands toward her. 'This is Fah, the missus.'

Bishop stood and pressed his palms together in a slight bow as Dougherty bent and kissed his wife.

'Sawatdee tohn bai, Fah,' he said.

The woman smiled and returned Bishop's wai. 'Sawadee ka. You know how to say, "good afternoon". You speak Thai?' Her voice was clear and tinkled like crystal.

Bishop smiled. 'No. Basic only. It is very nice to meet you. And I am pleased to see Terry doing so well for himself...'

Fah laughed. 'He is a big white elephant but, of course, in my culture white elephants bring success in business and life. I am very lucky to have him.' She wrinkled her nose. 'But his tastes in food are something I cannot believe.'

Dougherty laughed. 'Meat and three veg, me!' He looked behind him. 'Speaking of which, Your Grace, how about joining Fah and me for a spot of lunch and a cold one?'

Bishop nodded, grabbed up his towel and book and slipped on his flip-flops. 'Sure,' he said. 'The Beach Club is just at the end of the beach. It'll be busy but I know the manager so we should be right.'

Fifteen minutes later, the three sat at a high bar, under an awning on the Beach Club's terrace, with a view over the pool area and the beach. Bishop and Dougherty each nursed a cold Tiger beer, and Fah sipped languidly at a tall Gin and Soda. They drank in companionable silence for a minute or two before Fah excused herself and walked off in search of the bathroom. Dougherty watched her go, then took a big swig of his beer and threw some peanuts into his mouth. He turned to Bishop.

'So, Bish. You married?'

'No.'

'Girlfriend...?'

Bishop swigged at his beer. 'Nope. I just haven't found anyone really. My work is my life. Too busy for much else.'

Dougherty nodded wisely. 'Ah sure, still the warrior monk then.' He paused for a moment. 'How's the pain?' he asked quietly. 'Any better since I last saw you?'

Bishop looked up and rubbed his chin. 'Not great,' he finally admitted. 'The shoulder is buggered and hurts all the time, but it's the head that worries me...'

'That's not a surprise after what happened. That RPG nearly took the top off your skull. What's happening?'

Bishop drew a deep breath and exhaled slowly. 'I don't know. Sometimes, I feel like I have a blanket wrapped tight around my head, and my mouth is stuffed with cotton wool. It's... thick. When that happens, I have problems focusing, problems even stringing a lucid thought together. I can't do anything when it comes on me: I just have to sit still and ride it out.'

'Does it happen often?'

'More than I would like...'

Dougherty paused again. 'And what about those fuckin' pills? Are you off them? Christ knows it took me long enough.' He shrugged. 'But the whisky just took over where they left off.'

Bishop looked his friend in the eye. 'I've been off them a while now. All good in that department.' There it was, he thought. The addicts lie.

Dougherty raised his beer bottle. 'Well, cheers to that. Fucking Oxycodone... Sure and what the fuck were they thinking giving us that shit by the truckload?'

Bishop didn't answer. He hoped his face gave nothing away. He hated lying to his friend, and he hated what the opiates were doing to him. An uncomfortable silence stretched out before them until Dougherty spoke.

'You still working for the firm?'

Bishop smiled. 'Did we meet by accident, Terry, or have you hunted me out?'

'I swear to Christ, pure happenstance, mate,' Dougherty protested, raising his hands. 'Sure, and I'm just asking?'

'Well, as you ask, yes I am. It's been a little over five years now.'

Dougherty nodded and gazed out over the pool. 'Word is you're a negotiator. That right?'

Bishop eyed his friend. 'Terry,' he said. 'I'd have to kill you if I told you.'

'Mate, *everyone* knows it. It's a small world in which blokes like me and you move...'

'Well, strictly speaking, I'm an analyst, but I developed a knack for K and R, so when the firm has one on, I get called up.'

Dougherty seemed to think about that for a moment. 'Does the firm employ fellas with *my* particular skill set?'

'Aren't you running a tour business?'

'I am, but... you know... a man misses it sometimes.' Dougherty shook his head. '*All* the bloody time.'

Bishop sighed. He had heard it all before, but that didn't make it any less real. Once a man had been there it was bloody hard to go back. 'Sorry, Terry. All our shooters are LNs. We recruit local nationals for solid operational reasons. They blend in, and we need them to.'

Dougherty shrugged and spied Fah heading toward the table. She seemed to him to glide through the crowd and the maze of tables on the terrace. She really was beautiful 'Fair enough,' he said. 'But promise you'll think of me if your man has a need, yeah?'

Bishop nodded non-committedly and sipped his beer as Fah sat back down. He couldn't promise his friend anything, but he would keep him in mind. Bullshit story or not about bumping into him, there was no doubt: Terry Dougherty had skills.

'Talking war stories, boys?' Fah asked, reaching for her drink. 'Bishop, please do not listen to my husband if he asks you for a job...'

Both men laughed, and Dougherty hugged his wife. 'Never, my love,' he said softly. 'What more could I want than what I already have?'

10

The woman looked up sharply at the man standing in her office. He was infuriating. He was leaning against the wall, his arms crossed, gazing placidly out of the window over the view above Hanthawaddy Road and toward the Yangon River. He didn't seem to have heard a word she had just said or, worse, he *had* but didn't give a damn.

'Did you hear what I said?' she asked, her face flushing in temper.

Slowly, Bill Reilly adjusted his gaze to look at her. 'I did,' he said in a low drawl. 'It's just that I'm ignoring you.'

'I'm telling you, it can't go on! It is only a matter of time before the penny drops and it's all discovered.'

Reilly uncrossed his arms and leaned forward, the palms of his hands on her desk. 'Let me clue you to a few facts, *Melissa*.' His voice was calm but, to the woman, it dripped with menace.

'First, and probably most important as far as you are concerned, all of this...' he waved his arms to take in the office and busy cubicles through the closed door. 'All of this is mine. I created it, it's bought and paid for by me, and if you want to be a part of it, want to continue to pursue your noble cause, you do as you're damn well told.' He stabbed a finger at her. 'You did a deal with the devil, Melissa, and you're in this as deep as I am. If it comes out, don't think your sorry reputation will save you. I'll get out, but you'll be jailed or shot. You can bet your big ass on that.'

The woman shuddered.

'Second,' Reilly went on. 'The very reason you are here, the reason that this office exists and those busy beavers are out there with their fucking chai lattes and quinoa salads, is to allow me to do what I need to do. And that means *you* doing *exactly* what I say, when I say it. Have you got that?'

The woman swallowed and nodded. What on earth had she done? She felt faint. Reilly leaned back against the wall and continued.

'And don't worry your head about it being "discovered". That's all in hand. There are measures in place to ensure it won't be. In the unlikely event it is, it will be swept under the rug most ricky-tick.' He turned his head to look out the window. '*Damn*, but it's a nice view from here...'

The woman found her voice but heard it tremble as she spoke. 'When is the next run?' she asked.

Reilly pulled at his ear. 'There is one coming out today. A big one. One going in the day after tomorrow.' He paused and looked back out of the window. 'Need I remind you, keep your Gen Z asswipes away from my trucks. My man will be there to make sure that happens.' He pushed himself away from the wall. 'I think we're done here,' he said as he moved to the door. 'It's been a pleasure.'

Grasping the door handle, Reilly turned back to the woman sitting frozen at her desk.

'Melissa, make sure your people don't meddle. If any of them stumble on it, on what we're doing, I'll be forced to take... measures. And that won't be nice.'

Out on Hanthawaddy Road, Reilly quickly hailed a taxi and, fifteen minutes later, pulled up outside a low-rise building on Sule Pagoda

Road, diagonally across from the grand colonial edifice of Yangon City Hall. He paid the driver and took the staircase to the second floor of the building. The hallway was dim and smelled of fish and curry. Somewhere at the back of the building, a small child cried. He unlocked the door to the safe house and stepped in, sighing as the air-conditioning swept over him.

Moving to a teak console against the wall, he poured a long shot of bourbon and lowered himself into a chair. The window shutters were partially closed, but enough light creaked through to raise the darkness. He liked the apartment. It wasn't where he lived, but it was comfortable and out of the way. It was under the radar and perfect for his needs. He liked that.

He watched as sunlight drew bright horizontal lines in the gloom. Goddamn, that woman. She was a royal pain in the ass. He would never have gone with her, preferring to staff it all with his own people, but they had needed legitimate professionals working in it to shield it from curious eyes. It was the operation's greatest weakness and the one that kept him awake at night. His boss had certainly hated the idea, and it had taken a lot of arguing to get him to agree. The hell with it. It was done now, and there was no going back. Besides, it only had to hold together for another month – two, tops – before he brought the curtain down on the whole thing.

He leaned across to a small coffee table and took up a packet of cigarettes, tapping one out and lighting it. Drawing deeply on the smoke, he leaned back to exhale and watched the blue cloud as it swirled away in the blades of a ceiling fan. He sipped meditatively on the bourbon.

The pieces were all on the board, and he was moving them like a fucking chess master. No one but him and the inner sanctum of the planning team knew what the end game was, and this was a chess board with double the usual number of pawns. They all thought they were moving in one direction, toward a shared attack on the Queen, when, in reality, he was playing a Siberian Trap. It was a daring and exhilarating move, loaded with unpredictability and complexity. And danger.

He checked his watch, peering at it in the dim light of the room. It was time for the progress report. Shifting his weight, he pulled a cell phone from his hip pocket and opened the secure messaging app. He scrolled through the contact list and then stabbed at the screen. It was a cut-out number, and he knew the call would be securely routed. A woman's voice answered.

'Yes?'

'Everything is fine here. The weather is great, and we're having a fun time. Our hosts are marvellous. The countryside is really pretty.' *All according to plan. On schedule and no issues. The players were moving as planned. Shipments were all in order.* He ended the call and dropped the phone on the arm of the chair. With a roll of the eyes, he swallowed down the last of the bourbon. Jesus H. Christ, who made up these code phrases?

With a sigh, he cleared his throat and rubbed his eyes. He was tired and decided that would be the end of the day. He would head home, grab a shower, cook a steak, and then hit the sack. He wondered what his wife was doing back home where none of this shit was happening. Inexplicably, his mind turned to the Philippines. He dismissed the thought, crossed the room, and dropped the glass in the kitchen sink before turning to the door.

He was reaching for the handle when his phone rang. It was the secure app again, and he felt a shiver of anxiety course through him as he saw the name of the contact. He answered the call and placed the phone to his ear.

'It's me,' a male voice said. 'We've got a problem.'

11

SINGAPORE

Bishop studied the laptop screen for a moment and began to type.

On January 13 this year, Taiwan elected Lai Ching-te to be its next president. His election, unsurprisingly, marks the continuation of a government that promotes an independent Taiwan. Two days later, the Micronesian nation of Nauru severed ties with Taiwan and shifted its diplomatic allegiance to Beijing.

The South Pacific is a region over which the world's major powers are competing for influence, and China's influence in the region is growing, as a not-too-subtle shift by South Pacific nations toward Beijing shows. But what are the reasons for the significance of the region? And how does

The phone on Bishop's desk buzzed, and he picked it up. It was Nesbitt.

'What are you doing?'

Bishop frowned. 'That South Pacific analysis piece you wanted for the Australian client. Why?'

'Drop it and come in. I want to have a chat.'

Nesbitt hung up and Bishop slowly replaced the receiver of his phone. A "chat"? The Old Man never had a *chat* with anyone. Unless a big fan was running, and the shit was incoming. Unconsciously,

Bishop ran through his last submitted analysis pieces. No issues there – it was all good stuff. He had been functioning well the past weeks, keeping his head down, and hadn't crossed swords with HR lately. Puzzled, he stood, picked up his notebook, and left his desk, walking the carpeted corridor to Nesbitt's office. He knocked once and opened the door.

'You want to see me, boss?'

Nesbitt looked up from a sheaf of papers on his desk and waved to a chair. 'Have a seat.'

Nesbitt returned to the papers on his desk and flicked slowly through them, now and then making a pen annotation in the margins. Bishop sat, pulled out his notebook and watched his boss silently. Finally, Nesbitt looked up and placed his elbows on the desk, steepling his fingers. He seemed to be wrestling with a decision, and Bishop let him run.

'We have a job,' Nesbitt finally said, leaning back in his chair. 'As of now. I've just decided we will take it on.'

'Right,' Bishop said, nodding. 'And that has to do with me how...?'

'It's not something we would usually tackle. But I've given it a lot of thought, and you are the only one who can do it. You showed that after your little jaunt to Basilan and lunch with Jaafar... *And* you have in-country experience with this place.'

'Kidnap and Ransom? Where?'

'It could be K and R. Myanmar... I should say, Burma. What do you think? Initial reaction...'

Bishop shrugged. 'Burma is a hotbed of human trafficking, but it's always citizens from neighbouring countries kidnapped into forced labour. If you are talking about a Westerner – I assume you are – I can't recall a single case of one being taken. At least not for a very long time. My gut tells me you're about to tell me something that isn't a kidnap.'

'Maybe. More a "recovery".' *Maybe a lot more than that*, Nesbitt thought.

'Can I ask what that means?'

'Of course, dear boy, that's why you are here. Naturally, I'll give you orders and there will be more detail in them...'

'Naturally...'

'But, in outline, the situation is this.' He turned his laptop around to face Bishop and clicked a presenter remote on his desk. The image of a man came up on the screen. It was a corporate PR head-and-shoulders shot. Middle-aged, smartly dressed in a dark suit, white shirt and red tie, well-groomed greying beard. Piercing blue eyes.

'This is Alex Bouchard. He's a Canadian billionaire – made his money primarily in oil sands mining. He is a *very* big mover in Canada. Quebecois, born and raised in Montréal. He's a bit of a sovereigntist and a big donor to Bloc Québécois. He is the client.'

Bishop nodded, his pencil skipping over the pages of the notebook. Nesbitt continued, clicking the presenter again. The photo of a young woman appeared on screen. Slim, dark hair, medium height, round face with wide-set dark eyes and a narrow nose. She was in a crowd, wearing a keffiyeh around her neck, and her mouth was open in a shout, her face twisted in anger. She was holding a placard on which Bishop could just make out the words "crise climatique". Climate crisis.

'Mademoiselle Sophie Bouchard. Daughter, and only child, of Alex Bouchard.'

'Activist,' Bishop said. 'Bit ironic, isn't it? Her screaming about a world on fire while daddy's money is tied up in oil sands.'

Nesbitt nodded. '*Monsieur* Bouchard has told me his daughter is very "independent" in her thinking, if not in her wherewithal. She manages to neatly compartmentalise that aspect of her life. All her bills are paid by the family corporation, and she has limited access to a significant Trust Fund – that opens fully for her when she turns twenty-five.'

'Well, that's handy. Well-heeled slacktivism is all the rage these days.'

Nesbitt wagged a finger. 'Steady old boy, your slip is showing.' Bishop shrugged. 'Anyway,' Nesbitt said, 'Bouchard and his wife love their rebellious daughter very much, and they want her back.'

'She's disappeared? In Burma?'

'She *has* disappeared, and yes.' The clicker again. A scan of a Thai Airways passenger manifest appeared on the screen. 'Miss Bouchard arrived in Yangon five weeks ago, just before your trip to Basilan. She spent a little over a week in Yangon being inducted by her new employer before heading into Shan State to a project site. She stayed here...' A photo of one of Yangon's premium five-star hotels flashed up.

'I know it,' Bishop said. 'The Lotte.'

'Good. So, before you ask, Miss Bouchard is a contract project employee of Global Horizons, an NGO operating in Burma. This is her first assignment.'

'I've never heard of them,' Bishop said. 'Mind you, that doesn't mean anything. These organisations pop up all over the place. Where else are they operating?'

'You're right not to know them. They are quite new in the space and seem to operate exclusively in Burma. They are registered with the US Government and based in Seattle, Washington State. They're on the United Nations Development Programme's list of approved providers. They perform the usual food aid and humanitarian assistance but mostly focus on civil engineering. Fresh water, sanitation and hygiene, that sort of thing.'

Bishop made a note. 'Okay. Sounds legit, but I'll look into them.'

Nesbitt clicked the presenter again, and the laptop screen went blank. He turned it back toward him and closed the top. 'Miss Bouchard arrived at her project site, in a town called Narhkan, a little over three weeks ago. She was active there, and communicating frequently with her parents via social media and a messaging app. That is, she *was* up until five days ago when her messages abruptly ceased. She was last seen by a colleague at the project site. There has been no contact since.'

'Her employer have anything to say about this?'

'They think she gave up and walked off to a Buddhist meditation retreat to find herself.'

'Maybe she did. I get the feeling she could be the type.'

Nesbitt scratched his cheek. 'Perhaps.'

Bishop thought for a moment. 'How do we know all this? Is the information solid?'

Nesbitt nodded. 'It is all from Alex Bouchard. He obtained the passenger manifest, and has been in regular contact with Global Horizons office in Yangon.'

'And I suppose there have been no developments?'

'Correct.'

'And Bouchard wants us to find her.'

'Again, correct. You *are* a smart lad. So... kidnap?'

Bishop shook his head. 'You mentioned Shan State, so my first thought is maybe Shan State Army. But, no. Kidnap – particularly of Westerners – isn't their style. They're too busy with their main game. On top of which, they've been working hard recently to raise awareness of, and sympathy for, their cause in the West.'

Nesbitt paused, thinking. 'Still, it could be, so let's not discount it. The fact is, Miss Bouchard had disappeared, and we need to find out how and why, and get her back.'

'So why us? What about the Canadian Government? Has Bouchard contacted the RSO at the embassy in Yangon?'

Nesbitt shook his head. 'He tried, but he came up empty. The Canadians don't run a diplomatic security service. Global Affairs Canada does have what they call the "Security and Emergency Management Bureau", which is responsible for ensuring the safety and security of Canadian embassies, but there isn't a Regional Security Officer post as we would know it. Bouchard told me the Yangon embassy has a security liaison officer inside the Office of Protocol. He spoke to someone in that office and, to quote him: "fucking useless." To be fair, she hadn't been reported missing to the police, so there's not a lot the embassy can do.'

'Canadian Security Intelligence Service?'

'A runaway kid? Not their brief, really.'

'What about Bouchard reporting her missing to the Burmese Police Force?'

Nesbitt shrugged. 'Would they care? Let's be honest: they have bigger fish to fry.'

Bishop took a deep breath and closed his notebook. 'So, if I may sum up. We have the daughter of a Canadian billionaire, working with an NGO in Burma, who has disappeared without a trace. We have nothing to go on except a last sighting, the Canadian embassy doesn't seem to be offering much help, Burmese Police are probably worse than useless, and her father wants us to go in, find her and bring her out.' He shook his head. 'That's a pretty big ask. Burma isn't exactly the easiest place in which to operate.'

'Can you name one place we operate that *is*?'

'Fair point. But any team we put in will be dropping into the middle of a civil war. They'll be caught between the military, the armed wing of the National Unity Government – the People's Defence Force – and Christ knows how many Ethnic Armed Groups. Given the location of her disappearance, the Shan State Army looms large in my mind as a risk. That's just for starters...'

Nesbitt shifted in his chair. Shan State Army *did* loom large, but not for the reason Bishop thought. 'Complex, but not impossible,' he said. 'I should tell you that Bouchard is funding the entire operation. Op costs are no impediment. In addition, the huge sum he has offered for us to undertake this is too good for the firm to pass up. London simply won't let this one go. Not to mention the significant bonus should we successfully return his daughter to him.'

Bishop pulled at his earlobe. 'Sure, but, I mean, this isn't something we do. And *Burma?* Jesus.'

Nesbitt tilted his head to the side and looked hard at Bishop. 'You're not planning on saying "no" to me, are you old cock?'

'Of course not. I'm just pointing out two pretty obvious conclusions thus far: one, we have very little to go on and, two, it will be, largely, a blind operation in a very difficult environment, *and* my experience in the country is dated. We'll have to be covert; there will be a lot of planning gaps, and even more fuck-around-and-find-out. That worries me.' Nesbitt began to speak, but Bishop held up a finger.

'One more thing, sir. *If* I'm to run this, I want to do it my way. Minimal interference from "interested parties".'

'Do you include me in that esteemed group?'

'Yes, sir, I do. I'll brief you fully on the plan, of course, and I'll keep you updated as regularly as I can. But I just need the resources and for you to fly top cover. Keep daddy away and keep London off my back. No reaching down into the field. Please.'

Nesbitt's face was impassive. London. There was a lot in that city tied up in this. Nesbitt held Bishop's gaze and smiled. 'Ah, you have me! It's true, I do miss being in the field, but I know those days are behind me.' He sighed. 'It's a young man's game. Anyway, what you have just said is nothing less than I would have expected – cheeky bastard that you are – and it's just one of the many reasons I selected you.'

'*And* I want a bonus,' Bishop said. 'Regardless of the result. A *big* one.'

'Agreed and already factored in.' Nesbitt stood and faced the young man in his office. He slapped Bishop on the shoulder.

'Well, you better get started. Clear your desk. Hand that South Pacific piece to Jenkins – he can finish it off. Formal Orders here tomorrow then I want a brief-back on your plan the following day.' He paused, his face serious. 'Good luck, Bishop. You'll bloody well need it.'

Nesbit watched as Bishop walked off along the corridor. This job was new ground, and he could not remember the firm taking on such a risky operation. Ever. True, many had been dangerous, but all had some level of certainty, some clearly balanced risk. Bishop was right. He and his team would be able to plan very little on this op and would have to feel their way for much of it. That was troubling.

What interested Nesbitt was the team Bishop would choose. He was sure he knew who the Australian would call, and that was what they *all* needed to happen. Nesbitt just hoped his faith in Bishop was not misplaced.

The banks were circling after a recent audit had revealed "irregu-larities" in the nature and location of some of the firm's payments.

Nesbitt had only heard the day before that the bank was considering freezing the firm's accounts for "compliance verification," which deeply concerned the corporate office in London. More worrying to Nesbitt was the sizable sum of his personal savings that he had poured into the firm to keep it afloat during the pandemic—a sum now at risk.

He rolled his shoulders and closed his eyes briefly before returning to his office. The view from the large window, facing east over the Singapore River, barely registered as Nesbitt stared off into the distance. He needed the secretive young Australian to adapt, react, and, most of all, succeed. A possible forty-five million US payday was a lot of money that the firm needed. And then, there was the other matter.

12

THE SUN HAD SET, and the apartment estate was busy as the residents – mostly young professionals – moved around the street hawker stalls, eating stir-fried prawn noodles or barbecue pork and rice, washed down with a cold lemonade or beer.

Singleted old men, *Ah Peks*, took tea by the bird aviaries, relaxing to the melodious trills and chirps of robin, shrike and prinia, while their wives chattered and drank their Kopi C. Red lanterns and strings of festoon lights threw a happy radiance over the scene, as young couples walked hand in hand, and children ran about in a raucous declaration of their freedom while their parents sat and talked or played Mahjong.

The apartment estate was a classic. Built in the 1930s with a blend of art deco and Straits Settlement shop-house architecture, Tiong Bahru retained a timeless charm. It was part up-market hangout, part close-knit kampung, and it was a very typical Singapore evening. But, in an apartment upstairs, one man saw and heard nothing of it.

The room was well-lit as Bishop stuck another photo to the wall and sat down. The low table before him was scattered with documents. To Bishop, the wall looked like a crazy conspiracy board of Post-its, maps, photos and newspaper photocopies. He stared hard at it. He did not expect it to shout out an answer, but he did expect it to order his thoughts. Thoughts of the ground, own and enemy forces, and courses of action. The Military Appreciation was a tried and true process, learned during his promotion course with the Regiment, and Bishop had never stopped using it.

He sipped slowly from the crystal tumbler in his hand, savouring the whisky's warm rush as he sifted through the items on the table, glancing now and then back to the wall. Nesbitt had delivered his Formal Orders for the operation earlier that morning, and, as Bishop had expected, there had not been much to go on, and the orders had been brief. The situation was clear but lacked detail: Sophie Bouchard had disappeared, last seen at the Global Horizons project site in Narhkan Township, in Shan State. She had been missing for ... Bishop checked the date on his watch... six days now. There were no leads.

Mission: Locate Sophie Bouchard in order to return her safely to her family.

Nesbitt had agreed that the execution of the mission was largely up to Bishop but that, critically, it was to remain covert. The operation was, and would always be, deniable. Bishop knew that meant one thing: if it all went to hell, he was on his own. If it *did* go wrong, there would be no official acknowledgement of him or his team, nor would any efforts be made to recover him from whatever situation he found himself in. That cheery thought brought him back to the team.

As he had worked his way through his assessment, it had become increasingly clear to Bishop that smaller was better – at least for the on-ground team. That probably meant just him and one other. A two-man team would blend easier, move quicker, and attract as little attention as possible. He knew who he wanted to call and made a scribbled note. The support team was another matter, the require-ments of which would fall out of his Courses of Action analysis. Terry Dougherty's name kept coming to mind as he studied the photos on the wall.

Bishop sipped at the whisky and picked up his notebook. What *had* been welcome news had come under the later orders sections of

Administration & Logistics, and Command & Signals. While the op was to remain covert, he was approved to use the firm's front organisation – an engineering consultancy based in Singapore that ran irrigation and water reticulation projects for various governments and NGOs across Southeast Asia. It was a profitable business and provided the firm's operators with a nearly impenetrable cover when needed – just as it made it easy for the firm to distance itself from anyone posing as one of their consultants should the wheels fall off an operation.

Nesbitt had reiterated the funding arrangements for the operation and money was no object. That had also eased Bishop's mind. He knew that he would have to reach out to a range of people, most of whom were on the periphery of the international security circuit, and all of whom played fast and loose with the law. None of them came cheap.

Crucially, Nesbitt had, apparently, pulled some strings with senior contacts within the UK Ministry of Defence and GCHQ and had obtained imagery of a reconnaissance satellite pass over much of central and southern Shan State. The photos were now twenty-two hours old. They were scattered on the table and stuck to the wall.

Bishop finished the last of the whisky in the glass and poured another. A bigger one. He moved to a floor lamp in the corner of the room and switched it on before dimming the downlights. Sitting in a darkened room had always helped him concentrate, and he needed to do that now. His eyes flicked across zoomed images of forest and small towns, settling on the photo of Narhkan Township. There wasn't much to it. It was a typical township for much of rural Burma, except for the white Landcruisers and trucks parked neatly on the disused playing field. Global Horizons. He was going to have to start there. But how? He made a note.

He turned to a photo of Sophie Bouchard. This one of a happier woman, smiling at the camera with her arms around her parents. They were in a city park. The sun was shining, and people and dogs wandered everywhere behind them. She looked a different woman to the angry climate activist of the other photo – and a lot more like the snaps of her as a child and young teenager. Kids grew up, Bishop supposed. You did everything you could to prepare them, but you couldn't protect them forever. One day, they were unwrapping presents under the Christmas Tree and then, the next, they were throwing paint at a violent demonstration and disappearing in a foreign country.

'Where have you gone, Sophie?' Bishop muttered, swirling the whisky around in the tumbler.

He sipped at the glass and then gently placed it on the table. He had a plan to write in preparation for his brief to Nesbitt the following day. But first, there were two flights to organise, and then he had a call to make. Fifteen minutes later, with the flights sorted, Bishop picked up his phone and flicked through the contacts. Finding what he was looking for, he took a deep breath and tapped the number on the screen.

13

The Ferretti 580 bobbed at anchor in the cobalt waters off Capri. Crisp and white, with varnished timber decking, its swept-back lines shone brightly in the sun against the blue of the water. With an exhalation of breath, a woman emerged to the surface and flicked her head back to shake the long blonde hair from her eyes. Pulling off her fins, she tossed them to the deck and pulled herself up the ladder onto the aft swim platform.

Sky and sea were one, a sweep of cerulean. It was a curious optical illusion that made her a little dizzy as she stood in the sun, looking back to the island. She stood tall, her athletic frame strong and graceful, without an ounce of softness to spare. Her brown skin shimmered in the sunlight, diamond beads clinging to her from the dive, catching the light as she breathed. The sun played over her and painted a fresh sheen across the tattoo of a Viking shield maiden on her left upper arm. The broadsword brandished by the female warrior seemed to move and weave, the woman's arm muscles flexing as she breathed slow and deep to recover from the free dive.

She checked the G-Shock Frogman on her left wrist. One hundred feet with no weight belt. Not bad.

Behind her, the party kicked on. Tanned men in shorts and women in revealing microkinis laughed, chatted and drank chilled champagne. The sounds of an Italian dance compilation blared out over the sparkling blue sea. She felt a tap on the shoulder and turned.

The man, his burnished olive skin tanned a deep brown by the sun, smiled and offered the woman a champagne flute, its contents golden and effervescent. He leaned in and kissed her lightly on the cheek.

'Champagne, mia cara,' he said, his voice deep and soft. 'To celebrate another successful dive. Oh, and buon compleanno.'

The woman smiled back, and sipped gratefully at the glass, then raised it in salute. 'Grazie, Matteo. Another birthday. Another year gone, no? Where *do* they go?' Her accent was English, posh, a marker of her upbringing.

She eyed the man in front of her. Christ, he was handsome! Matteo was a darling, and she loved him, but she knew he wanted to settle down and marry. His mother in Napoli certainly wanted that of her son. She smiled at him again. She wasn't ready for that – not by a long shot. There was simply too much to do before she was ready to take up life in the stables, pushing out little Italian foals for a grateful Italian nonna. She swallowed the rest of the champagne and passed him the empty glass. That was a worry for another time and, for now, it was party time.

'Another glass, please, my love. While I change.' She kissed him lightly on the cheek and weaved her way through the crowd, her bare feet soft on the warmth of the heated timber. Taking the stairs beneath the main deck salon, she moved amidships into the large cabin and closed the door.

Five minutes later, and showered, she emerged into the room wrapped in a thick, white towel. She was reaching for a singlet top and a pair of denim shorts when her phone rang. She dropped the towel, pulled on the shorts, and picked the phone up from the bed. It was the secure message app, and she frowned as she looked at the contact on the screen. What the hell? She checked the cabin door was locked, then answered the call.

'Bishop,' she said, her voice cool. 'This *is* a surprise.'

'Hi, Maddy,' Bishop said. 'Am I disturbing you? I can hear music...'

'No, not really. I'm on a boat. A bit of a bash happening. My birthday, as it happens... I imagine your card is in the mail.' Madeleine Carter paused, a grin curling her lips. She could almost hear his discomfort.

'Oh, shit,' Bishop said finally. 'I'm sorry, Maddy. Completely forgot.'

'That's okay, Bishop. I really didn't expect you to remember. I'm just teasing.'

'It's been a while...'

'It has.'

'Look, about what happened... You know, between us.'

'Forget it. It was fun, and we both needed it at the time. No harm done, you big pillock.' Madeleine checked her watch. 'Look, Bishop, it's 1330 here, and I have a party to go to. I don't mean to be rude, but why are you calling?'

'I've got a job, Maddy. I need you. No one I know has your skills.'

'I'm not interested, Bishop. I don't need the work, and life is good. I'm actually thinking of getting married...'

'You *are*? Really? That's not the Maddy Carter I know.'

'Okay. I'm not, but I might. Why not?'

'Look, it's none of my business,' Bishop said mildly. 'The job Maddy. I need you. It's a missing girl.'

Madeleine paused and took a deep breath. The bastard. He knew exactly what buttons to push with her. He always had. Above her, the party went on, getting louder as the champagne flowed and the music pulsed. She exhaled and sat on the bed.

'Okay. I'll give you five minutes. Tell me about it... and Bishop, don't bullshit me.'

So Bishop told her everything he knew, or at least what little he knew. He told her about Sophie Bouchard and her father Alex, Global Horizons, and Sophie's last known location. He then quickly ran her through his assessment and gave her the headlines of the Outline Plan.

Bishop paused briefly. 'Before you say it, I know it's all pretty slim...'

'Slim? It's positively twig-thin! You can't be serious.'

'Maddy, I am. I'm going in with or without you... but I'd prefer it to be *with* you. I know you, and I *know* you're already considering options. The more I think about it, the more I think she hasn't just shot through. My gut tells me something's up here, and we need to find out what that is. That's where you come in.'

Bishop knew he was right. He needed her and her skills. The job couldn't go ahead without her. No one was as good at what she did as Madeleine Carter. Among tough men who knew their business, it was acknowledged worldwide that Maddy Carter was simply the best surveillance and tracking operator around.

'How, exactly?' Maddy asked. 'Why do you need me?'

'You want me to run through your CV?'

'No, but there must be a dozen men you can reach out to for this...'

'None of them with your pedigree, Maddy. Wild child, raised by your father's gamekeeper. Taught to track and hunt at a young age. RMA Sandhurst, Intelligence Corps, Special Reconnaissance Regiment, languages, operations in Somalia. Not to mention, you're some sort of tech savant... Need I go on?'

'Chi ti lusinga più di quanto desideri...' Madeleine replied.

'I have no idea what you just said.'

'Italian. It means "He that flatters you more than you desire." It's an Italian proverb. It ends with "either has deceived you or wishes to deceive." Are you deceiving me, Bishop?'

Madeleine heard Bishop sigh. 'No, Maddy, I'm not,' he said. 'I wouldn't do that. But I do need you.'

Madeleine turned on the bed and looked out the window. The sea sparkled, and she squinted against its glare, her mind a world away. She remembered Bowdyn, her father's gamekeeper, with an ache that had not healed in the fifteen years since his death. The craggy old northerner had been a poacher in his youth, and a magistrate had given him a choice early on: twelve months in HM Prison Risley or enlistment in the British Army. As it turned out, he had done his time in both. Bowdyn had taught her everything she knew.

She remembered him, a wreath of pipe smoke curling about his head, watching her from the doorway of the gamekeeper's cottage when, as a young teenager, she would walk off into the woods, sometimes for days. She remembered his deep belly laugh when she would return, muddied and covered in leaves, carrying a deer haunch and dead hares at her belt that she offered up to the horrified cook.

She thought of the selection course for the Special Reconnaissance Regiment. The eight weeks in the wilds of Scotland and Wales had been gruelling, but Bowdyn's lessons had stayed with her on the wet and lonely nights as she pack-marched from one checkpoint to the next across the mist-shrouded heather of Ben Nevis and grassy moorland of Pen y Fan.

Madeleine blinked and shook her head. The party went on above her, and she could hear champagne corks pop and people talking and laughing. Bishop's call had come out of the blue. She was certainly thrown by it. But, it all seemed straightforward: Find a girl and get her out. How hard could it be? What would Bowdyn say if he were there now? She stood and silently paced the small cabin.

In Singapore, Bishop waited patiently, the phone to his ear, as he opened the terrace door and looked out at the lights of Tiong Bahru. He forced himself to remain quiet and let Maddy think it through. He knew if he pushed her, she would tell him to fuck off and hang up. Minutes seemed to tick by, and Bishop realised he was drifting off, distracted by the sights and sounds of the crowd below him. He shook his head and crossed the room to pick up the whisky glass. He had taken a sip and was swirling the drink around in his mouth when Madeleine spoke.

'Okay, Bishop. I'm in,' she said. 'But, it's going to cost you. A lot. Email me the imagery and your plan; then we'll have a call to discuss the next steps.'

Bishop sighed in relief. 'No need for a call, Maddy. We can talk in

Bangkok. Pack your kit – make it a ruck; I have a feeling we'll be spending a lot of time in the bush. There's a flight booked for you, Emirates First Class, leaving Rome Fiumicino tomorrow at 1540. A driver will meet you on arrival and bring you to the hotel in Sukhumvit.'

'Jesus, Bishop,' Madeleine breathed. 'Nothing's changed, has it. You really are a pushy bastard – and you bloody well know my kit is *always* packed. Now, if you'll excuse me, I have cold champagne and a hot man to attend to. I'll see you in Bangkok.'

Madeleine ended the call. The boat rocked slightly beneath her, and she paused for a moment, a frown knitting her forehead. They would want to know. She had another call to make before she rejoined the party.

14

Sophie Bouchard sat on the hard dirt floor, hugging her knees. She could feel herself losing control.

The air was thick in the tin shack, and the heat was oppressive. She struggled to breathe, each breath a shuddering intake of filth, as fat blowflies buzzed lazily around her and the rancid bucket in the corner. She hunched on the floor shirtless, her bra grimy and sweat-stained; the torn remnants of her shirt lay scattered by the bucket so she could wipe herself. Her shorts were torn, and her left knee was bloodied. They had taken her shoes. Her face was smudged with dirt, and it throbbed as she reached up gingerly to feel the swollen lump on her right cheek. There was a cut above her right eye that had dried in a streak of caked blood.

When they grabbed her, they had taken her watch, and her phone had dropped. Time flowed like molasses, the minutes and hours crawling forward sluggishly, imperceptibly. She had marked the passing days – the rising and setting of the sun – by scratching marks on the tin wall with a piece of broken glass.

She turned her head and counted the scratches. Six days now. Six days of not knowing who had her, where she was or what would happen. What she did know was "why", and it had all started with the truck's arrival.

She was preparing the latest arrival of food aid with her small team of locals when the truck arrived. She was alone in the township. The rest of the project team was at the reservoir site as David Sutton supervised the final concrete pour. Sophie and her team were busy slitting the large bags of rice and portioning their contents into smaller bags, one for each family on the register. They also shared out the tinned goods and allotted the building supplies to those most in need. She was counting the bags and marking off the list on a clipboard when an old woman, her brown face weathered like a walnut, entered the lean-to shed. Sophie looked up.

'What is it, Mya?'

'Ma, *Miss*, Sopee,' the woman said, pointing back the way she has come. 'Truck here. Come now.'

Sophie frowned slightly but followed the woman outside into the sun. Parked on the dusty street was a medium-sized truck, the Global Horizons logo and colour scheme clear on the cabin and the tall canvas cover of the cargo bed. Sophie's frown deepened as she checked her clipboard. No deliveries were scheduled, she noted. Not for another two days and not just a single vehicle.

She walked to the front of the cabin and peered in through the windscreen. It was empty. The driver's door was open. She looked about and could see no sign of the driver but noticed a large pool of black oil seeping from under the truck and running into the dust of the road. She moved to the rear of the truck and, passing the clipboard to the old woman at her shoulder, unclipped the canvas cover and flipped it back. She could not see over the tailgate, so she reached up and unhooked the locking levers. The tailgate dropped with a loud bang, and Sophie peered inside.

It was dark in the rear of the truck, but she could just make out wooden pallets on which were stacked symmetrical, square piles, each covered with a green canvas tarpaulin. She reached up and, placing her hands on the tailgate, heaved herself into the truck.

As she moved toward the first pallet, she noticed a faint odour of vinegar that seemed to get stronger the closer she got. She gripped the first tarpaulin by a corner and lifted it up, folding it across the top of the waist-high stack. She crouched down and squinted in the dim light at the contents of the pallet. With a gasp, she stood and stepped back. *Mon Dieu! It can't be.* She reached behind her and pulled her phone from the back pocket of her shorts. Holding the phone steady, she snapped off half a dozen shots, then moved to another pallet and repeated the process. That done, she pocketed the phone and dropped the tarpaulin back over the pile.

'Holy shit,' she murmured as she stepped onto the tailgate and jumped down into the street.

'Soph. What's this?' David Sutton stood to the side of the truck, shading his eyes with one hand and holding his phone in the other.

'*David!*' Sophie shouted, startled by his sudden appearance. 'What are you doing here?'

'I came back to pick up some cable. What's going on? You look like you've seen a ghost.'

Sophie waved an arm at the rear of the truck. 'David, you have to see this. Inside... It's incredible. I can't believe it...'

David held up a hand. 'Slow down, Soph. Easy.' He moved to the tailgate. 'I'll check it out,' he said as he vaulted lightly into the truck and disappeared into the gloom. Seconds later, he reappeared and jumped down. His face was pale, and his hands were fidgeting anxiously.

'Jesus Christ,' he breathed. 'I have to call this in. I have to tell Yangon. We need to get the cops.' He raised his phone to his ear.

Angry shouts suddenly sounded loud in the still afternoon as a group of men moved up both sides of the truck and surrounded Sophie and David. They were armed, and they pointed their weapons threateningly at the two aid workers. One of the men shoved Mya, who stumbled back to stand on the side of the road, her head lowered. Sophie stared in shock, and David slowly raised his hands.

The men continued to shout, becoming more agitated, until one of them, shorter than the others, raised his hand for silence and then unholstered a pistol as he stepped forward. He pointed the pistol at David.

'You! Why you here?' he demanded.

'We... we're aid workers,' David stammered. 'We have been here for weeks. We're doing the water supply...'

The short man rolled his eyes. 'This I know! What you doing *here*, at truck?'

David thought fast. 'Nothing, we just saw it arrive...'

'You have been inside!' the short man yelled. 'You have seen!'

'No! No, we haven't... Please, just let us go.'

The man shouted an order and waved his arms forward. His men surged in. Two grabbed Sophie roughly and pinned her arms behind her, while a third punched her twice in the face. A man leapt at David and delivered a savage butt stroke to his midriff that doubled him over, gasping for breath. In the confusion of the melee, Mya darted forward. A bag slipped over Sophie's head, and she screamed against it as she struggled. Another punch silenced her as her head spun and her senses whirled. The last thing she heard before she was bundled away was David Sutton shouting *'No!'* and a single gunshot.

The heat in the shed beat down on her, and her breathing became faster, accelerating through panic. She felt her bladder give way. Sophie Bouchard sobbed once, then tilted her head back and howled. It was a guttural, animal sound that spoke of the rising terror that threatened to choke her.

15

BANGKOK, Thailand

'How was the flight?' Bishop asked. He sipped the strong espresso and turned from the large window. The opulent corner suite was on the Rosewood's twenty-third floor, with a commanding view over Bangkok's skyline to the west. It was breathtaking but Bishop wasn't in Bangkok for the view.

Madeleine Carter shrugged and leaned back on the sofa, tucking her feet beneath her. 'You know, long. But Emirates First makes it all bearable.' She looked past Bishop to the timber-panelled wall, on which were stuck a series of photographs and maps. The coffee table in front of her was scattered with documents.

Bishop ignored the glance. 'You check-in okay?'

'Fine, thanks. The room is beautiful.' She pointed at the wall. 'But I guess I won't spend much time in it.'

Bishop nodded. 'You guess right. We've got a lot to do and not much time to do it. We may need to take another quick trip, but I'll get to that.'

Madeleine nodded. He had been all business since they had met in the lobby. No small talk, no fond embrace. Fuck all, really. She studied the man across from her. He still looked good. Tall and muscular. Narrow, well-shaped nose set neatly between two round, brown eyes. His lips were full – she already knew they were kissable – and the small scar in the bottom left corner only served to enhance them. He wore his brown hair long to hide the thick scar that ran from his forehead to his left ear, and it was swept back and neatly groomed. The stubble on his face was edged and neat. His shoulders were wide, and she remembered with a thrill the feeling of those strong arms wrapped around her, his hips pressed against her.

But Bishop looked tired. He had small bags under his eyes, and the eyes themselves had a haunted look. Her gaze drifted to his left hand, and she noticed the slight tremble and tightening of his tendons as he fought to control it. Bishop was a powerful man in many ways, but he was suffering, and she knew why.

'Does it still hurt?' she asked quietly.

Bishop shook his head. 'Why is everyone asking me that? There's no pain.' He caught her eyes slip to his hand. He looked down. 'It's just nerve activity. Perfectly normal.'

'And the drugs you were swallowing like sweeties the last time I saw you?'

Bishop paused. 'I still have a prescription, but I use them only rarely – when the pain gets too bad. Hardly ever.'

'One of the last two statements is a lie, Bishop. Either you have pain, or you don't.'

Bishop sighed and moved to put the coffee cup in the kitchen. His back turned, he used the pause to compose himself. Rinsing the cup, his back still turned, he said, 'Okay. The shoulder hurts now and then but not much, and it's rarely severe enough for me to reach for the pill bottle.' He turned back to Madeleine and smiled. 'It's all good. Really. You happy?'

'What about your head? I always thought it was worse than the shoulder. It certainly was the last time I saw you...'

Bishop looked her in the eye. 'Maddy, it's fine. I haven't had an episode in weeks.'

Madeleine tilted her head and looked hard at him. Bishop stood perfectly still.

'Okay,' she said finally. 'I'll accept that. But if we are to do what you're planning, you better not lie to me, Bishop. I'll fucking walk away... after I've killed you and hidden the body.'

Bishop smiled again and clapped his hands. 'Deal,' he said. 'So, shall we get to work?'

Madeleine nodded, lowered her legs, and leaned over the coffee table. 'So what have we got?'

Bishop sat in a chair opposite her. 'Well, it's as I initially briefed you. There's not a lot to go on. The girl has gone missing in Burma, and her father wants her back. She hasn't been reported missing – her employer thinks she has done a runner – and neither the police nor the Canadian Embassy are involved. All we have is where she stayed in Yangon, an office address in Taunggyi – the Shan State capital – and a last known location – Narhkan Township, also in Shan State. We don't know exactly *when* she disappeared or from where. Just a date and time of her last message to her parents – and that was nothing out of the ordinary. Just chat.'

He ran a hand through his hair. 'So, not much really. We're going to have to go in and start looking around. Build the picture – if we can. We'll start with where she stayed in Yangon and with her employer, then go from there. Nesbitt said he might be able to hook us up with Canadian SIS and their spook in Yangon. It could be useful, but no word on that yet.'

Madeleine remained silent. She doubted it would happen, but if CSIS got involved, it would make things... complicated. She would make a call and have the kibosh put on that. In the meantime, they had sod all to go on. She thought she could hear Bowdyn in her ear. *You've got nowt, lass. It's a fucking mess, so you be extra careful.* She also heard her handler's voice as she looked up at the photos on the wall. *Something's going on there, and we want to know what.* Bishop waited while she processed. Finally, she nodded slowly.

'Okay, I've worked with less,' she said. 'I agree. We'll need some kit. Comms and surveillance. The problem is the sort of stuff I'm thinking won't be easy to bring in through Yangon International.'

'Satphones are illegal, but I think we can chance it with a couple.

The firm has teed up a fake permit for them. It's on the table. The legend is a good one and, given it is in the aid sector, it will give us a little more freedom than the average punter.'

Madeleine nodded. 'Satphones will work up to a point, but I think we need a greater capability.' She paused. 'What about passports?'

'We will be going in on our own. There's no way around it – counterfeit passports are out of even the firm's league...'

Madeleine thought she might use her second, covert, identity but quickly ruled it out. She didn't want it blown and, besides, to use it she would have to tell Bishop. She realised he was talking.

'The rest of the legend will be solid,' he was saying, 'and we'll carry all the usual pocket litter. I'm not expecting us to draw any particular attention – at least not initially, but that will probably change once we start digging.'

'Weapons?'

'No. The risk and mission profile don't call for them, and if we're caught in Burma with weapons, they'll put us up against a wall.' Bishop shook his head. 'Besides, I haven't touched a firearm since 2010, and I don't intend to again. Ever. If we carried, I'd be more of a risk to both of *us* than anyone else.'

'That brings us back to the kit,' Madeleine said. 'If I try to carry military-grade comms and surveillance gear into the country, that *will* attract attention. We wouldn't make it out of the airport.'

Bishop scratched his ear and thought for a moment. 'That's why I'm planning on us taking that quick trip tomorrow. I've got an idea where I think we can pick up what we need, along with a way of getting it in.'

'You going to share this genius idea with me?'

Bishop shook his head. 'Not just yet. I need to work a few things through first. I'm going to make a call to suss it out after we're done here. Then I'll brief you – if we're going.'

Madeleine shrugged. 'Roger that.' She stood and walked to the wall. 'Take me through these,' she said.

Bishop joined her and pointed at the first series of photographs.

'Sophie Bouchard. The girl we're looking for. Twenty-three. One hundred and fifty centimetres, about fifty-one kilograms. Takes a small in tops and is size six for the rest. Foot size women's six. Activist, so she's political. Catholic but not religious. Wannabe aid worker and saviour of the world. Spoiled rich girl trying to find her way - trust fund and all her bills are paid by her father's company. She's carrying an Amex Platinum credit card, so she has access to cash – a lot of it. No criminal record, not even a parking fine. No known illnesses or disabilities. Uses an iPhone and a Mac. Wears an Apple Watch. Twitter account – *very* active – Instagram and Facebook. Facebook was last used seven days ago, but no location pin. Sexual preferences are unknown, but Mum and Dad assume she's straight. A bit of weed now and then but, other than that, no known drug use. That's about it.'

Madeleine stared hard at the largest photo of the girl. 'So not a kidnap?'

Bishop shook his head. 'It doesn't fit the profile. She could have been taken but not, I think, for the run-of-the-mill K and R.'

'Could she have sided with the SSA? I mean, activist and all... maybe *that's* her cause.'

Bishop raised his eyebrows. 'Good point. But I don't think so. She doesn't speak Burmese, let alone Shan, and the SSA is nothing if not all in on the autonomy of their own people. Mind you, she *would* be useful to them with propaganda messaging into the West, so let's not discount it.'

Bishop stepped to the side and tapped the first high-resolution satellite photo. 'This is Narhkan Township. Small, rural, poor. It's the site of the Global Horizons aid project. They're doing water supply, which dovetails nicely with our cover as irrigation consultants. The playing field, here,' he tapped the photograph, 'is the base of operations for the project – you can see the Global Horizons trucks and Landcruisers parked there beside the army surplus tents they are using for accommodation, offices and storage. The project is here.' Another tap. 'It's a little to the north-east of the town on the small river.'

Madeleine frowned and moved to the coffee table, sifting through the documents until she found what she was looking for. She held up the two sheets stapled in the corner.

'Global Horizons. What do we know?'

Bishop shrugged. 'Nothing other than what I've already told you. There's not much out there about them, but I plan on taking a deeper dive into them. Given that's where she worked and where she disappeared from, it's worth knowing what we can about them. The plan is to get in front of them once we hit Yangon – ask about Narhkan, that sort of thing. That's where the cover comes in.'

He bent to the table and picked up a single sheet of paper on Singapore Government letterhead. He passed it over. 'Our official introduction as irrigation consultants, assessing project viability on behalf of the Singapore and Myanmar governments.'

Madeleine eyed the document. 'This is good work,' she said, turning the sheet over. 'I have never worked for them, but I hear whispers the firm's capabilities are... shall we say "extensive".'

'We do okay.'

The two moved back to the wall, and Madeleine studied the rest of the satellite photographs. She suddenly stood back, reached for her phone, switched on a magnifier app, and leaned in close to one of the photographs in the series. She looked at it for a moment, then stepped back.

'So the bird's pass was roughly east-west. Low Earth Orbit,' she pointed to the photograph. 'This one is from about five hundred kilometres altitude. The high resolution means the swathe width was probably about twenty kilometres.' She paused and then tapped the photo. 'What's this here? The small irregularity in the canopy of the forest?'

Bishop stepped forward and peered at the photograph. Madeleine passed her phone over, and Bishop leaned in, studying the image closely.

'Jesus,' he murmured. 'I hadn't seen that – not surprising, really. It's so slight I'm still not sure I'm even seeing it.'

'You are. It's there. I bet that the irregularity is camouflage netting. And check the scale on the photo – whatever it is, it's big.'

Bishop looked again at the photograph and studied a map on the wall. He stabbed a finger into the map. 'That would be about here... Tatmadaw camp?'

Madeleine shrugged. 'Could be, but it's a bit far from the MSR for that, don't you think? It's pretty out of the way... and bloody close to the Chinese border.'

Bishop looked at her. 'You're right. If it were army, it would be on, or close to, the Main Supply Route which would be this...' he tapped the photograph, 'Highway 45.'

'So what is it?'

'Shan State Army? It's right in the heart of their AO, and it's not that far from their headquarters in Loi Tai Leng to the south.' He pointed at another satellite photo. 'This is Loi Tai Leng – I checked the lat-long. I have no idea why that was included in the photo run. It's well outside our Area of Operations. As far as I can see, it's irrelevant.'

Madeleine studied the photo closely. 'Put it on the list,' she said. 'I've got a feeling we need to find out what's happening there.'

An hour later, the two were satisfied they had a better appreciation of what was in front of them and how, at least initially, they would proceed. Bishop had made the call he intended and was happy to hear what he wanted. He told Maddy they were taking the short flight to Chiang Mai the next day. They would return to Bangkok early the day after and then fly out to Burma that afternoon.

They walked around the block to a narrow street, where they sat on rickety metal stools at a street food stall. There, they ate a mouth-burning fish curry washed down with cold Chang Beer while continuing to discuss the operation.

Madeleine watched Bishop closely but could see no signs of his neurological disorder. That did not mean she wasn't worried – she was. Where they were going, and what they were planning to do, meant she needed a partner at her side who could be relied on. Without hesitation, every time. She liked Bishop a lot – maybe even more than that – but she was worried he wasn't up to it.

Bishop finished the beer and dropped some notes on the table as he stood. 'I know it seems like we're messing about,' he said. 'But we have to prepare. If we don't, we'll be doomed from the start.' He watched as Madeleine slipped in beside him before walking toward the hotel. 'Wherever she is,' he said, 'I just hope Sophie Bouchard can hang on.'

16

Sai Wint Maung watched from the sharp ridgeline above Loi Tai Leng as the rifle company surged across the stream and up the hill toward the "enemy" defensive position. He nodded in satisfaction. The troops were responding well to the training, and their assault was orderly and rapid. Ranks of dark green tiger-stripe camouflage rose up and ran forward, firing as they went, their bright orange neckerchiefs clear from where he stood. The "enemy" were retreating in disarray.

With a grunt of irritation, he noted a fire support element on one of the flanks had lagged behind. Their supporting fire from that position would be useless. He called a subordinate to him and rattled off an order. The junior officer made a note in his notebook, saluted, and sprinted off to correct the error. Still, Sai was pleased. The exercise was going well.

He glanced over at the taung kyi, *foreigner*, standing slightly away from Sai's command group, and his enjoyment soured. The taung kyi watched the exercise with interest, pausing now and then to mop his brow with a damp cloth. His white skin was flushed pink like a boiled nga-phaa, *prawn*. Sai disliked them and their ways. They lacked a sense of pride in their own cultural and moral values, and Sai's own rich and ancient culture was under threat from foreign influence.

Sai particularly did not like this skinny foreigner, this American. He did not trust him – nor did he really trust their mutual friend – but they were a necessary evil. They had, after all, brought the agreement to life, and it was the agreement that had tilled the soil in which he would sow the seeds of the greatest victory in SSA history. The taung kyi wiped his face again and sucked greedily at a water bottle. Sai snorted in derision. Weak. Foreigners were all weak in body and dark in heart.

Sai stepped out of the burning sun and into the shade of a tent, where he paused before a trestle table laden with maps. He was alone, and he ran a finger, almost tenderly, across the battle map. Studying the pencilled unit symbols, boundaries and lines of advance that depicted the plan, he nodded in satisfaction. He dropped the indirect fire trace over the top of the map and ran his eyes over it. It was all in place, and the plan was good. They had the element of surprise. They had the force they needed to both seize and hold the ground, and they had the weaponry. It was daring, and it was dangerous, but it would work. He sat down in a canvas chair and removed his cloth cap.

The Shan State Army now had better weapons than it had in decades, more of it than ever before, and Sai was happy. They had thousands of assault rifles and grenades, hundreds of anti-armour weapons, and millions of rounds of ammunition. Their arsenal also included nine 88 mm M29 mortars and an entire battery of Yugoslav 76 mm mountain guns, all thanks to a mysteriously unmanned gate and unlocked Tatmadaw compound in the west of the state.

Sai poured a glass of cool water, then peeled and bit into a rambutan, savouring the pale pink flesh and sweet, mildly acidic flavour. His mind turned to the girl. He snorted back in his sinuses and spat onto the dirt floor of the tent.

One broken-down truck from the convoy, and the girl had stumbled onto it and seen everything. It was more than unfortunate, it was a risk. *She* was a risk. It was true; they had her under lock and key, and the risk was contained. For now. Sai scratched under his armpit and sucked his teeth. He resolved to speak to the taung kyi outside about the matter. "For now" was not good enough. The risk needed to be eliminated.

17

CHIANG MAI, *Thailand*

'What the fuck is this?' Bishop asked, a look of shock on his face.

'It's the chopper,' Terry Dougherty said. 'Sure, what does it look like?'

Bishop pulled out his phone and opened the browser. He tapped twice and held the phone up to Dougherty. 'This is your website, Terry, and *this* is the chopper you're telling the world you have. Take a look, mate.' Dougherty leaned in and studied the small screen. He shuffled his feet and pulled at an ear lobe.

'Ah, well,' he said. 'It's an old photo...'

Bishop gritted his teeth. 'Terry, mate,' he pointed to the phone. 'This photo is of a Bell 412. Composite four-blade main rotor. Twin engine.' He pointed at the battered, dark green helicopter squatting on the pad cut from the jungle. '*That* is a Bell UH-1 Iroquois. Single engine, twin blades. They're different aircraft, Terry.' He shook his head. 'I mean, look at it! It looks like a Vietnam-era Huey... *Is* it a Vietnam-era Huey, Terry?'

Dougherty grinned. 'Close, but no. Thai Army. We picked it up for a song.'

'I'm not fucking surprised. Does it fly? It doesn't look like it flies.'

Dougherty turned to the man standing at his side. 'Tell him, Tak.'

Tak was Thai, of average height and slim. His black hair was cropped short, and his dark brown eyes twinkled as he smiled and nodded.

'It flies.'

Dougherty grinned broadly. 'There. See? It flies. Tak's the pilot and engineer. Like that magnificent machine over there, he's also ex-Thai Army.'

Bishop gaped. Tak wore floral boardshorts, flip-flops, and a stained blue T-shirt with sleeves rolled up to the shoulders. A packet of Marlboro and a box of matches were jammed in under the last roll of the left sleeve. Bishop shook his head and turned to Madeleine.

'This just keeps getting better...'

Madeleine shrugged. 'There's not much we can do about it now. Maybe we should get out of the sun and discuss all of this.' She smiled, her face radiant. 'Terry, darling, be a dear and lead on.'

Dougherty smiled warmly, his eyes alight. 'Maddy, you're as polite as you are beautiful.' He gestured to Bishop with his head. 'Not like this grumpy little bastard.'

Five minutes later, Tak, Bishop and Madeleine were seated around a battered teak table under the thatched roof of an open-sided bamboo hut. Dougherty rummaged in a large ice box, finally drawing out four bottles of Singha beer and tearing the caps off with a bottle opener hanging from a post. He passed around the bottles and held his up to the group.

'So you'll be after staying the night, right?'

Bishop and Madeleine nodded, raising their cold beer bottles.

'Plenty of room, so no worries... Well then. Cheers, all,' Dougherty said, drinking deeply from the bottle. The others replied in kind. Dougherty placed his beer on the table and lit a cigarette. He turned to Bishop.

'So, Bish,' he said, drawing on the smoke. 'You were a bit cagey on the phone. That's understandable. Care to fill me in?'

Bishop glanced at Tak.

'Tak's solid,' Dougherty said quickly. 'I vouch for him. Fully.'

Bishop nodded. 'That's good enough for me, Terry.' He sipped his beer while he gathered his thoughts, then slowly and quietly laid out his and Madeleine's mission and plan. Madeleine occasionally took up the narrative, injecting her take or underlining a point. Dougherty sat silently throughout, occasionally sipping his beer or flicking a glance to Tak, who slowly spun his box of matches on the table.

When Bishop had finished, he sat back and waited as Dougherty mulled over what he had heard. The Irishman was usually garrulous, quick with an amusing anecdote or cutting comment, but Bishop knew Dougherty was a thinker – that was part of the reason he trusted him so much. Dougherty drained his beer and belched quietly.

'That's all clear, so far.' he said. 'Tell me more about what you need from me.'

'We need the gear you have – or can get your hands on,' Bishop said. 'Maddy will fill you in on that. And we need that chopper.'

'To get the kit in?'

'That, and for an extraction if we need it.'

'What makes you think you will?'

Bishop shrugged. 'The more I look at this, the more I'm convinced it's not as simple as it looks. I don't think the girl has just taken off. I think she's involved in something, and involvement in anything in Burma can get ugly very quickly. I don't think we can just walk into Yangon International with the girl and onto a flight. So that means we need another option to get her out.'

Dougherty nodded. 'Makes sense.' He turned to Tak, who had stopped spinning the matchbox and was leaning forward, his hands clasped on the table. 'What do you think?'

Tak rubbed his chin. 'We're a little over two hundred kilometres from the border, so, if we don't need to go too deep and can get in and out without having to loiter, the Huey has the range.'

He sipped his beer and lit a cigarette, puffing out the blue smoke through his nostrils. 'But there are the Tatmadaw air defence systems along the border. I have snuck in before – anti-drug ops – but it is well covered. They have radar early warning and surface-to-air missile batteries. They got everything from man-portable units all the way up to surface-launched medium-range air-to-air missiles. Very serious.'

'So, can we get in and out undetected?' Madeleine asked. 'Is it possible?'

'It's possible, Khun Maddy,' Tak said. 'But flying low, below the radar in a Nap-of-the-Earth profile, which we would have to do, will reduce our range. Depending on where we need to go, it will be close.' He tilted his head. 'I may be able to fit external auxiliary tanks, and we can strip out the interior to lighten the load. That will boost our range.'

'Okay,' Bishop said. 'Can you look into that? We need to have some confidence we're not on limits getting the gear in or us out.'

Tak nodded solemnly. 'Khrạb thān, *yes sir.*'

Bishop turned to the Irishman. 'Let's take a look at the kit, Terry.'

Dougherty nodded, stood and left the hut, the others trailing in his wake. He turned left and walked between the hut and his house – a traditional structure in bamboo and wood, raised on stilts and topped with a steep gabled roof – then entered another smaller wooden shed. Bishop and Madeleine followed him in while Tak stood outside.

Dougherty moved two wooden crates to the side, rolled back a rattan floor mat, and lifted away a wooden panel set into the ground. Reaching in, he flicked a switch and stepped into the hole. Bishop looked at Madeleine, his eyebrows raised, and the two followed Dougherty down.

The flight of six steel stairs stopped at a concrete floor, and the three of them were standing in a bunker, lit blue-white by powerful neons. A wide wooden workbench with vices and clamps stood on one side of the room. Armoury tools were hung neatly on a pegboard above the bench. A fully stocked gun rack and four long, steel shelves stood on the opposite wall. The gun rack held three M4 carbines, each with an optical sight, two Remington Model 870 pump-action shotguns, and three SIG Sauer P226. The bottom two shelves were lined with boxes of ammunition, trip flares, and smoke grenades.

Above these, two shelves were laid out with an array of surveillance, satellite communications, and radio equipment.

'Christ, Terry,' Bishop breathed as Madeleine moved to the shelves. 'Are you expecting the apocalypse? Where did you *get* all of this?'

'Good, huh? I've been collecting for a while.'

'Yeah, but *why*?'

Dougherty shrugged. 'Thought it might come in handy.'

'What about the police? If they catch you with this lot...'

'Tak's brother-in-law is the deputy police commander for the district.'

'Should I ask other questions about that?'

'Best not to.'

Madeleine was standing at the shelves. She whistled lowly as she reached out and picked up a tan-coloured device. 'HISS-XLR thermal weapon sight. Detects and recognises man-size targets in excess of two thousand metres. Wow!' She put the sight down and picked up a set of binoculars.

'M25A1 stabilised binos. Fourteen-by optics, with a four point three degree field of view. Maximum effective range of four thousand metres.' She pouted, and Bishop thought she looked like a young girl in a toy store. 'They're direct-view optical devices, for day use only. Bloody lovely, 'though. We'll take both.'

'I'm glad you approve, Maddy,' Dougherty smiled. 'Take a look around. I think it will be to your liking. Give me a list of anything you need that I don't have. He turned to Bishop. 'Will this lot do?'

Bishop clapped his friend on the shoulder. 'It will do. So, Terry, are you in?'

Dougherty nodded. 'When I tapped you in Singapore,' he said, 'I didn't expect to hear from you so soon, nor, honestly, did I expect to be invited to a gig like this. I'm in.'

Dougherty shook Maddy's hand and stole a quick kiss on the cheek, then, the three of them left the bunker. By the time they returned to the hut, Dougherty's wife had emerged from their house and had placed dishes of curry, vegetables and rice, and a long plate holding a large, fried fish garnished with red chillies, on the table. Tak was seated, spooning curry into a bowl, and Fah was standing with her hands on her hips, her head tilted to the side, a stern look on her face.

'What are you doing, my big white elephant?' she asked softly. She looked at Bishop with pain in her eyes. 'What have you done?'

Dougherty gently took his wife by the shoulders and looked down into her deep, brown eyes. 'Don't blame him, my love,' he said. 'Ah, sure, it was my idea. They're after finding a girl and bringing her back to her family. They need me.' He kissed her lightly on the forehead. 'It's good to be needed again.'

Fah looked up at her husband and gently rubbed his beard with the palm of her hand. 'You are *always* needed, and always loved, sùt têe rák, *darling*. When you go, I will be here waiting for you to return to me.'

Dougherty wrapped her in his arms then and kissed her. Fah broke away and dashed the tears from her eyes. She waved her arms over the table. 'Now, all. Eat!'

In no time, the conversation was loud and getting louder as the beer flowed and the food was devoured. It was shaping into a long night as Bishop and Dougherty pushed their plates aside and started into their war stories.

Madeleine glanced at Bishop and saw he was smiling. Was that happiness? She doubted it. She had never known Bishop to be what ordinary people called "happy". She also noticed the set of his shoulders and the brightness in his eyes. He looked less tired than yesterday. Fresh and ready to go. *He better be*, she thought as she opened another beer.

18

THE BLISTERING *Afghan sun is high in a dust-laden sky, burning a bright orange through the haze. The Corporal checks his watch before glancing around at his section. They are good lads, he thinks. Solid. Reliable. He wants no one else around him but the band of men who lie silent in the dust and rocks outside the village in Shah Wali Kot. They are ready to go. Women and children stream out of the rear of the village and away. The silence of the morning shatters as mortars crump in. FN MAG58 and Browning .50 calibre machine guns open up from the fire support position. Immediately, withering small-arms fire cuts across the fields from the village, cracking through the air and kicking up dirt as the Commandos rise and begin their assault. He waves his men on, and the Section leap-frogs forward, firing and moving, each group covering the other as they run ahead, zig-zagging, diving, and crawling. He slithers in behind a boulder and raises the M4 to his shoulder, snapping off four rapid rounds as the man beside him stands and runs forward into the fusillade from the village. The Section's FN Minimi hammers out short bursts as the gunner seeks out and targets the enemy. Behind and above them, snipers work the bolts of their rifles. With each rapid sighting and shot, an insurgent drops. He hears dull thuds in the distance and looks up as two RPG rounds scream in, followed by more. Too many to count. He rises to his feet and runs. No time to shout a warning. His breath rasps in his throat, and his heart pounds. The sound of battle recedes, and all he can hear is the thud of his boots on the ground and his desperate, agonised pants as he drives forward. He takes three steps when an RPG detonates in the dirt at his feet, and he is thrown up and back. The sky is suddenly clear and blue, and everything is quiet as he soars gently above the ground. He watches, fascinated, as his hands wave slowly above him. It is soft and peaceful, and he relaxes. With a thud, he hits the rocky ground, spread-eagled, and blinks rapidly as the light and fury of the battle roar back into his consciousness. He runs a quick mental check as he lies coughing in the dust. No pain. He can move his hands and feet, but he is blinded by a flood of blood into his left eye. The vision in his right eye is blurred. He feels his head and his hand comes away sticky with blood. Where the fuck is his helmet? Rolling over, he sees his men well ahead of him, entering the village. He wipes the dust and grit from his right eye and watches as his men move in deadly pairs through the narrow alleys between the mud and stone houses. His rifle lies only centimetres away, and he reaches for it, rolling onto his right side as he grabs the stock and drags it toward him. He fingers the press-to-talk on the radio at his chest. Nothing. Looking down, he sees the pouch is shredded and the radio is shattered. With the weapon in his hands, he rises to his feet as rounds crack around him. He jogs slowly toward the village and the firefight, then the 7.62 mm AK round slams into his right shoulder, and everything goes black.*

Bishop lay on the camp stretcher beneath a mosquito net, the rough canvas slick against his sweat-dampened back. His chest rose and fell with steady breaths, but his mind was still in the dream – dusty roads, gunfire, and the heavy weight of his gear. Most of all, the blood. Across the room, Maddy's gentle breathing steadied him, a quiet rhythm that reminded him he was no longer in the war. In the next room, Terry Dougherty snored loudly. Bishop exhaled, long and slow, forcing himself to focus on the present.

The night outside was alive. Crickets chirped in an endless, hypnotic cadence, their song ebbing and flowing like a tide. From somewhere in the roof beams above, a gecko announced itself with a sharp, ticking call, its presence as ordinary as the worn wood of the house. A pair of bats swooped nearby, their wings whispering through the still air.

Through the open window, the tall bamboo grove behind the house swayed gently, the stalks knocking together like hollow chimes. Every so often, the breeze gave a stronger gust, and the bamboo creaked, an eerie groaning sound that felt ancient and alive, as if the forest itself was speaking.

Bishop shifted on the stretcher, staring through the dark at the wooden ceiling. A motor scooter putted by on the dusty road at the front of the house. He closed his eyes, willing the sounds to anchor him there, now, where the night was alive but safe. A deep breath. Another. The crickets carried him back to sleep.

19

TAUNGGYI, Shan State, Burma

Bill Reilly had always thought it was better to be aggressive. Aggression put his opponents – his enemies – on the back foot, and, in this business, it paid to have his enemies off balance. He shifted in the chair and reached for the packet of cigarettes.

Pulling one from the packet, he toyed with it, rolling it through and over his fingers. The thing about aggression was that it was much more enjoyable than meek acceptance. Fuck the meek – they were goats, and he was a tiger. The meek were meat, put on this earth to be dominated and consumed, and he had never shied from physical violence.

After all, during the Civil War's Shenandoah Valley Campaign, General Sheridan had said, "The only good place for the enemy is six feet under." He believed in that. It had served him well over the years.

He lit the cigarette and drew back deeply, his eyes closed. There was no going back now. The plan was in motion and had developed a momentum of its own. He couldn't stop it now if he wanted to, which he didn't. He had played chess since he was a child, and he had opened this game, his very last, with the Sicilian Defence. He had quickly developed his Knights to set the trap, and White would lose its Queen, or, if not, it was checkmate. Either way, he knew that, with one or two more moves of his Knights, he would have the game. Siberian Trap. And the beautiful part of it was no one – not Washington, not Beijing, and certainly not the fucking UN – would see it coming.

Everything was in play, and things were going well. Up to a point, that is. There *was* one snag. A fucking white pawn had bumbled into the path. He ashed the cigarette. That goddamned girl.

What were the odds that a single truck in the convoy would break down and then limp into the very township where she was working? They were fucking astronomical, but it had happened, nonetheless. She had seen everything and, in that instant, had come close to derailing the entire operation. He shook his head. Thankfully, they had discovered her. That troublesome pawn was now safely off the board, and they had dealt with the fact that Sutton had been there too – it was probably just as well he had been. But what now?

Reilly closed his eyes again and willed his mind to settle. Think it through. As long as she lived, she was a risk, but would it matter when the final act had played out? Probably not. She had no evidence, and who was going to believe her anyway? Who would believe a demented activist who had written the sort of shit she had on Twitter for the last three years? He chuckled lowly in the dark of the hotel room. Those tweets about burning down the old order, blood in the streets, and freedom for the oppressed would resurface to bite her on the ass. Her own stupidity would shut her up.

However, she *was* a risk, and if he had learned anything over the years, the most effective way to deal with risk was to eliminate it. His partners in the venture certainly wanted her dead.

No. Not yet. He stubbed out the cigarette and poured another shot of bourbon. He would hold on to her for a while. Teach the bitch a lesson first. Then, if it became necessary, he would have her killed. Hell, he'd do it himself if he had to. He swallowed the shot and sighed. Tomorrow, he would return to Yangon.

20

YANGON, *Burma*

Departure from Bangkok Suvarnabhumi had gone smoothly, and, once in the air, Bishop mentally checked off his plan and their next few moves. They needed to know more, much more, before they could have a clearer picture of their direction, but he was clear on the start point. It had to be with Global Horizons, but he was conscious of the need to proceed with caution. After all, they were supposed to be in Burma to scope a potential irrigation project, not hunt for a missing woman.

The day before, he had changed the SIM card in his phone and called Global Horizons in Yangon to set up a meeting with their General Manager. The GM's secretary had been polite, and the meeting was scheduled for 0900 the following day. So far, so good.

Bishop was nervous about the two satellite phones in their luggage but confident that they would overcome any difficulties with the phoney permit he carried in his passport wallet. It was just one of a growing list of risks, but they were committed now, so there was no point in worrying about it.

He glanced across at Madeleine, who sat silently, her eyes closed. He knew what was running through her mind. There was so much that could go wrong with this, and it was just too loose for her – nowhere near the level of intricate planning she would require before an operation. To cap it off, before boarding, he had noticed her watching as he clenched and unclenched his left fist. Bishop knew she was uneasy and that he would have to deal with that.

A little over an hour later, the Thai Airways flight landed with a slight thud on Runway 03 at Yangon International. Minutes later, it slowed to a halt at the arrival gate. The cabin was suddenly noisy with the sound of seatbelts unbuckling and passengers standing to open the overhead lockers. Bishop dropped his seatbelt away and turned to Madeleine.

'Well, this is it,' he said. 'We'll be fine,' he added with a reassuring smile. Madeleine nodded back, unsmiling.

Exactly thirty-two minutes later they exited the Arrivals Hall. Their arrival had gone without a hitch. Neither the immigration, nor customs, officers had given them so much as a glance as they had breezed through arrival formalities, and both had slowly relaxed as they had stepped into the crowds milling around the money changers and hotel greeting points.

The hotel's uniformed limousine driver had met them with a smile, a sign with their name held to his chest, and now walked in front of them, pushing Madeleine's rucksack in a trolley. Bishop, too, carried a large ruck over his shoulder as they walked out into the late afternoon heat.

The black Mercedes glided smoothly out of Yangon International Airport, the engine's hum a soothing constant as the city unfolded around Bishop and Madeleine. The afternoon sunlight cast a sharp clarity over the streets, an Impressionist painting giving prominence to light and colour. The scene rushed by, fragmented touches of bright colour and complements of shadow and shade; the limo's tinted windows offering a cool, darkened reprieve from the sweltering heat outside.

As they merged onto Pyay Road, the urban landscape twisted in a kaleidoscope of movement and colour. Rickshaws weaved through the traffic, their drivers adeptly dodging the potholes and each other, and Bishop noticed the absence of motorcycles. Shop stalls lined the road, laden with vibrant-coloured fruits and sizzling street food, their vendors calling out invitingly to passersby. The scent of grilling meat and ripe mangoes occasionally wafted through the car's air-conditioned bubble, a tantalising reminder of the world outside.

Golden spires of pagodas pierced the skyline, their ancient grandeur contrasting with the modernity of glass-fronted office buildings. Monks in saffron robes moved serenely among the chaos, their presence a calming counterpoint to the city's frenetic energy. Military uniforms were everywhere. On every corner and at every intersection, groups of hard-eyed young men cradling assault rifles eyed passersby suspiciously, now and then pulling one or two aside to examine their documents.

As the limo approached the city centre, the Lotte Hotel loomed into view, a sleek luxury tower stark against the backdrop of Yangon's older, colonial-era architecture. The street markets gave way to upscale boutiques and cafés, signalling their arrival into one of the city's most affluent districts. But the footpaths were nearly deserted. The few pedestrians, heads down and moving fast, were eyed balefully by soldiers with closed faces. No one, hunter or hunted, was aware of the two people in the car nor their purpose in the city.

The Mercedes rolled to a stop at the hotel's entrance, the doorman already stepping forward to open the car's door. Bishop took a deep breath, and stepped out onto the driveway.

'Mingalaba, and welcome to the Lotte Hotel, U Bishop, Daw M'lane,' the young woman at reception said as she returned their passports.

She wore an intricately patterned *htamein*, a traditional Burmese skirt, wrapped around her waist and falling to the floor, secured at the waist with a simple tie. Above the htamein, she wore a fitted blouse with elbow-length sleeves and mandarin collar. Her long, black hair cascaded over her shoulders, and her dark brown eyes held Bishop's as she spoke.

'We have you each in a Junior Suite with views over Inya Lake, ' she said. 'I am sure you will be very happy. Your luggage will be in your room when you go up. Now, if I may point out some wonderful local attractions. First, there is Shwedagon Pagoda...'

Bishop interrupted with a smile. 'Thank you, but we will be very busy with meetings. Perhaps we can take a look at that at another time.' He pulled a small photo from his backpack and handed it to the young woman. 'I'm hoping we can find a friend of ours while we are here... I believe she is staying here, or at least she was recently. Might you be able to help?'

The young woman studied the photograph and then handed it back with a polite smile of regret. 'I am sorry, U. I do not recognise this young lady. I do not think she is with us. But perhaps our head of security may know her. May I call him for you?'

'No, that's fine. No need, thank you.' Bishop made to pick up his backpack then paused, an idea seeming to come suddenly to him. He smiled warmly at the young woman and leaned forward a little over the counter. 'Perhaps you might check your records for me? Her name is Sophie Bouchard. It would help me to know when she stayed here so I can guess when she will return – she may be away at work...'

The young woman eyed Bishop, then Madeleine, and threw a furtive glance to her left and the door to the Duty Manager's office.

'Yes, U, I will be pleased to help you and Daw.' She quickly tapped at the keyboard in front of her and looked up. 'Yes, here we are. Ma Sophie stayed with us for a little over a week. She checked out almost three weeks ago, on Saturday.'

Bishop smiled again and picked up his pack. 'Thank you. You have been a big help. I am sure we will meet her at work.'

He nodded at Madeleine, and together, they left the ornate glass and marble lobby, taking the elevator up to the ninth floor and their suites. Once in the lift, Madeleine turned to Bishop.

'You're a smooth bastard,' she said with a wry grin. 'That poor girl didn't stand a chance once you turned on the charm.'

Bishop watched the floor lights flicking upward on the display. 'I have no idea what you mean,' he said.

When they reached their floor, the lift doors swished open. Madeleine followed Bishop as they padded silently along the dimly lit, carpeted corridor. Small pottery and sculpture pieces sat in wall alcoves, highlighted by delicate pin-downlights. The air was fresh with the scent of lemongrass.

Stopping, Bishop pointed at a door. 'This is you,' he said. 'I think I'm two down. Meet later for a drink and early dinner? I'd like to go over the plan for the meeting tomorrow. Get your take.'

'Sure,' Madeleine said over her shoulder as she swiped the key pass and pushed the door open. 'I'm going to have a rest – I'm pretty weary. See you at six?'

Bishop waved a hand in acknowledgement as he walked off to his room.

Madeleine closed the door, double-locked it, and slipped the privacy chain. She moved to the large window in the bedroom, its curtains pulled back. Below her, Inya Lake glistened in the mid-afternoon sun, its dark green waters ringed by spreading trees and grasslands dotted with gardens of large, tropical broadleaf plants. Along the lake's foreshore sat cafes and restaurants but, peering down, she could see they were empty. Not many people took relaxing strolls around Yangon these days.

She pulled her phone from the back pocket of her jeans and opened a secure messaging app. She had called in Bishop's first approach a few days before – it was procedure – and her handler had sounded interested, telling her he would make some inquiries and get back to her. He had done so late the following night, with a secure text message pinging in while she had been on the flight from Rome. The Masters had been looking for a way in there for a while, and this opportunity was perfect. Ask no questions, Madeleine; it was "need to know", and, at this stage, she didn't. The message had ended with a reminder to Madeleine of who she worked for.

She sighed and tapped a contact called 'Gardening Service' and waited while the call connected. It was answered almost immediately. A male voice.

'Yes?'

'We're in,' Madeleine said quietly. 'No issues.'

'Good. He still doesn't know?'

'No, not a clue. I feel shit about this...'

'Don't. It's a luxury none of us can afford. Just do your job. Madeleine, this is a serious game you're playing. Keep your head screwed on.'

'Do you mind telling me what I'm looking for?'

'I do, as it happens. Principally, because we don't really know – that's why you're there. Having an asset like you in Shan is a heaven-sent opportunity. We have heard whispers – very vague but also very disturbing. If there is anything to them, we think your investigation into the missing girl will cross over with our interests.'

'Which are what, exactly...?'

'World peace, Madeleine. Nothing too ambitious. Just world peace.'

Madeleine thought back to the satellite photo of Loi Tai Leng, far to the south of their proposed Area of Operations. Why had that been included in the imagery packet? 'How will I know I have found what I'm looking for?'

'Oh, ye of little faith! You'll know, and when you do, so will we.'

Madeleine ended the call and tossed the phone on the bed. Peeling off her jeans and pulling the T-shirt over her head, she entered the bathroom and turned on the bath taps. As the bath ran, its hot water dissolving a packet of fragrant bergamot salts, she sat on the cool marble floor, alone with her thoughts.

21

The two men sat close together on the low granite bench. Mid-morning joggers crowded the foreshore track around the Tidal Basin, and the trees above them were bare, awaiting the first burst of early spring blossom. It was cold, and one of the men pulled his overcoat tighter around him and flicked up the collar.

Across the chilly water of the Basin, the obelisk of the Washington Monument rose tall and proud into a cloudless blue sky. To their right, the rotunda of the Thomas Jefferson Memorial, an American Exceptionalist pantheon, shone brightly in the sun. The man in the overcoat was unmoved and wiped his nose with the back of a gloved hand.

'I don't mind telling you, this whole thing gives me hives.'

The man next to him, the younger of the two, was wearing only a light windbreaker over his dark suit. He watched a jogger trot by and then turned his head.

'You should get some cream for that.'

'I'm serious,' the older man said. 'I've been in this game for over thirty years, and I've never played it this close to the line.'

The younger man shrugged. 'There *are* no lines in this. At least there are none we won't cross to achieve the goal.'

'Yeah, I'm sure Howard Hunt said something like that before he, Liddy and those Cuban clowns picked the locks at the Watergate.' He paused for a moment. 'Maybe Ollie North is a better example... you know, given what we're doing.'

'This is different. *Times* are different. We're not talking about bugging a bunch of political nerds here, nor even about supporting some raggy-assed guerilla group. We're talking about derailing the ambitions of this country's greatest enemy, about building the defensive line.' The younger man sighed. 'Jesus, just relax, will you?'

'*Relax*? Christ, so much can go wrong with this. There are so many variables in play we can't *possibly* know how they'll respond...'

'Oh, they'll take the bait. They can't not. It's not like poking a bear in the ass won't cause a reaction. They'll come out swinging, and that's exactly what we need. Then with our man in place, and with the Congressmen we have, the President will get the congressional authorisation and the funding.' He paused and sucked at his teeth. 'Need I remind you, the President wants this, and what he wants, he gets.'

'The goddamn Joint Chiefs don't even know about this. They're going to be pissed when they work out they've been blindsided.'

The young man shrugged. 'Let them be.'

'I don't know. This whole thing is a Hail Mary; it's so high-risk.'

'You like football, I like football, so here's the deal: We're in the red zone, inches from a touchdown. It's fourth down, high stakes – but we're going for it. And when we score? We're not fucking around. We're going for two.'

The older man nodded. 'Yeah, I guess. So long as the Quarterback doesn't fumble.' He turned and faced the man beside him. 'This is still in the vault, right? The Director doesn't know?'

'She doesn't know shit, and she won't.'

The older man eyed his colleague. The little prick was playing a side game here, and he knew it. 'Well, just remember me when you're in the chair. Maybe a posting to Paris...'

Ascendancy to the Directorship was, indeed, a part of the younger man's plan. If anything, that was even more secret than the main game. He had had a genial chat with the President's Chief of Staff only days before, and the reward for pulling this off would come his way. He smiled, a feeling of warmth coursing through his chilled body.

'I'm flattered but don't be ridiculous,' he said. 'I exist to serve. That's all.'

'Of course.'

The younger man stood and looked around the Basin and the heart of American democracy: the National Mall with its memorials, the White House a little further up Pennsylvania Avenue, and the Capitol, just across town. Iconography spoke to him, calling to him with every waking moment. It was the reason, the *only* reason, he was journeying down this dangerous path. He looked down at the man on the granite bench, huddled deep in his overcoat.

'Get some cream for those hives,' he said as he turned and walked away.

22

Bishop and Madeleine had been ushered into a conference room and left alone to wait. The room was spacious and light. Its wall-to-wall windows provided a view east over the red tile and rusted tin rooftops, the Okala Golf Course and, further on, Pazundaung Creek that flowed lazily north-south through the city to empty into the Yangon River. The room was air-conditioned and quiet. Bishop poured a glass of water and glanced at Maddy.

She looked preoccupied as she stared out of the window. She had seemed that way over dinner the night before, barely engaging with Bishop. She had been distracted but had dismissed it as travel fatigue when he had raised it with her. Perhaps it *was* jet lag, he thought, but he knew Maddy well, and he wasn't so sure. Something was troubling her, and he needed to get to the bottom of it. There was too much at stake for her not to be on her game.

'Are you okay?' he asked.

She looked at him and smiled. 'Sure. I'm fine. Just a little tired, that's all.' She poured a glass of water. 'This should be interesting,' she said, indicating the offices behind her through the privacy glass.

Bishop nodded and was about to answer when the conference

room door opened. A woman entered. She was middle-aged, short, and slightly overweight. Her greying hair was long and pulled back in a neat ponytail. She was dressed casually in jeans and a blue polo shirt with a white Global Horizons logo over the left breast. She looked like she had not slept in days, and her smile was hesitant as she entered the room.

'Mr Bishop, Ms Carter.' American accent. 'I'm Melissa Downs, the GM of Global Horizons,' she said as she sat across from them, her back to the window. She looked at her watch. 'Unfortunately, I am quite pressed for time this morning, so how may I help you?'

Bishop nodded. 'Of course, and thank you for giving us your time. I will get straight to it.' He slid their business cards and the Letter of Introduction across. Downs picked up the letter and quickly read it before placing it back on the table in front of her.

Bishop spoke. 'As you can see from the LOI, we have been engaged by the Singapore Government to assist in a proposed irrigation project to be conducted on behalf of the Myanmar Government...'

'The "junta", you mean.'

Bishop cleared his throat. That was an unusually overt political statement from the head of an NGO. 'Ms Downs, I'm not here to comment on that. We are here merely to assess the viability of the proposed project and report back.' Downs nodded curtly, and Bishop went on.

'It's our understanding Global Horizons has a water reticulation project in the vicinity of the area we plan to assess, so we thought there may be some synergy in us working together.'

Downs eyed the two people across the table from her, the skin on the back of her neck starting to prickle. The woman across from her was studying her openly, and she could feel her reaching into her head. That one was dangerous, she decided. The man, Bishop, was too smooth, too collected to be from her industry. In her experience, NGO staffers and aid-sector consultants had a certain look about them, sort of hippy chic, and they tended to talk that way. This one was buttoned up and alarmingly professional. Still, the credentials looked legitimate, and, God knows, the country was awash with aid projects, despite, or perhaps *because*, of everything that had been going on. She drew a breath and sighed.

'And the location of this proposed project, Mr Bishop?'

Bishop affected to flick through his notes as if unsure, then looked up. 'Narhkan Township, Shan State.' He eyed Downs steadily, taking in her reaction. She was good but not good enough. Her eyes widened momentarily, and a slight flush rose to her cheeks. Bingo! *Best not to push it*, he thought. He and Maddy had decided the night before not to raise the question of a missing staff member at Narhkan. It was too obvious and, if there *was* anything untoward happening here, would only serve to ring alarm bells. Steady as she goes.

Downs spoke, her voice light, casual. 'Yes, we have a project in Narhkan. As you say, water reticulation, so an irrigation follow-on would make sense. However, there are two other projects you might wish to see first that might better suit your purposes...'

'Thank you,' Madeleine interrupted. 'But Narhkan was very specifically raised by our clients. Given the recent treaty between the government and Shan State Army, the feeling is that a community project there would be an important sign of goodwill.'

Downs nodded. 'Indeed.' *Bitch*. 'Can I offer our assistance with the travel into Shan?'

'No, thank you,' Madeleine replied. 'We will hire a car once we get to the capital, and make our own way...'

'It can be a dangerous trip, Ms Carter. You will be encountering roadblocks from both the Tatmadaw – the Myanmar military – *and* two, possibly three, Ethnic Armed Groups. Perhaps it would be better if...'

'We understand that. We are carrying full authorisation from both governments and are quite used to such environments. I'm sure we will be fine. However, we would be grateful if we might meet your project lead in Narhkan.'

'Of course,' Downs said unenthusiastically. 'I will have him meet you at our Field Office in Taunggyi and guide you up. You can get the office address from my receptionist.' She pointedly looked at her watch. 'Now, if there is nothing more, I really need to get away to another meeting.'

'Thank you again, Ms Downs,' Bishop said as he and Madeleine stood. 'We're grateful for your time, and I look forward to working together. I'll see that you receive a copy of our report once it has been approved.'

Downs nodded and guided them out of the room, feeling the woman flinch when she lightly touched her back as they edged through the door. At reception, the address of the Taunggyi Field Office was handed over, and Downs watched as Bishop and Carter exited the office and stepped into the elevator. Once its doors shut, she pulled her phone from her pocket and strode into her office, locking the door behind her. Her hand shook as she dialled the number. It answered after three rings.

'Someone was just here inquiring about Narhkan,' she said quietly.

There was a pause on the other end, then Reilly's voice. 'How many? What did they want?'

'A man and a woman. Irrigation Consultants looking at a possible project in Shan. They mentioned Narhkan specifically and plan on visiting...'

'Credentials?'

'An LOI from Singapore, countersigned by the department in Naypyidaw. It looks legitimate. And two business cards.'

Another pause. 'Photograph and text them to me. I'll look into it. Did they mention the girl?'

'No, thank God. I'm sure they don't know.'

'I'm not. Someone was asking after her at the hotel yesterday, and I don't believe in coincidences. Where are they now?'

'They left, and they're travelling to Taunggyi tomorrow. They will be moving to Narhkan the day after.'

'Are they travelling alone?'

'Yes. I think so... Driving themselves.'

'Okay. I'll deal with it.' Reilly paused again then his voice hardened. 'Melissa, just hold your nerve. And keep your damned mouth shut. Remember what I said. There's a firing squad waiting for you if you fuck this up.'

The call ended, and Melissa Downs collapsed, shaking, into her office chair. It had all started well enough. She had thought she was doing her bit, serving her country. But as she had learnt more, and sunk deeper into the conspiracy, she had known she was teetering on a precipice, with the wind howling at her back and no way of retreating. She suddenly leaned over and vomited into the waste basket under her desk. Wiping her mouth with the back of her hand, she lowered her head onto the desk and sobbed.

23

'SHE KNOWS SOMETHING,' Madeleine said as they stepped onto Maha Bandula Road.

Bishop nodded, casting about for a taxi. 'The question is: what? She was on edge the whole time, and she nearly fell over when I mentioned Narhkan.' He shrugged. 'Maybe it's nothing. Maybe she's just highly strung, but I don't think so.'

'She didn't like the idea of us sniffing around the Field Office either, but she couldn't very well refuse. She's the one who told Bouchard his daughter had legged it?'

'Yep. According to Nesbitt, Bouchard was clear she was emphatic that Sophie had just given up and walked off.'

'If Sophie did that, why was that hard-faced bitch so itchy?'

Bishop didn't answer. It was a good question. Was it the girl, or something else? Was it both? A black and yellow taxi pulled into the curb in response to his hail. He opened the doors, and they climbed in. After giving the driver the hotel address and negotiating the flat fare, Bishop turned to Madeleine as the car pulled into traffic.

'The more I think about Global Horizons, the more I'm sure something's up. My instinct tells me it's central to Sophie's disappearance somehow. I just don't know how. But I'm going to find out.'

Madeleine nodded silently and looked out of the window as the city sped past them. Her handler had not been able to give her much – they didn't have much. Or they did but weren't telling her. There was always *that* chance. Her job was to sniff around and report anything noteworthy. She had asked what constituted "noteworthy" and her handler had replied that he was trusting her to know that when she saw it.

Madeleine could not shake the feeling that they knew much more than they were telling her. But that was the nature of the job: keep things tight, compartmentalise everything. She understood that, but that didn't mean she had to like it.

24

IN THE SOFT light of his hotel suite, Bishop opened the burner laptop and placed a notebook and pencil beside it. He stared at the dark screen momentarily before powering it up, inserting a new pre-paid SIM into his portable Wi-Fi modem, and connecting to it.

He began to write in the notebook, scribbling down a series of steps he would take in the coming hours, circling some and linking others with arrowed lines. It was his Open Source Intelligence, OSINT, investigation plan.

Bishop planned to systematically gather publicly available information on Global Horizons, some of it buried deep, to build a clear picture of the organization. He knew that picture would be useful in the days to come, but he was looking for indicators that Global Horizons was not what it appeared to be on the surface. If they were there – and he was almost sure they would be – he'd find them. Cracking his knuckles, he double-checked his VPN and began to work.

He started with the basics by navigating to Global Horizons' official website, which, at first glance, looked professional and polished. The homepage boasted numerous successful humanitarian projects, with glossy photos of smiling children and villages transformed by clean water initiatives. Everything looked legit. He opened a blank document on his laptop, his investigation record, and noted the details, saving screenshots of key sections for later reference.

Bishop scrolled through the Global Horizons website, his unease growing with every click. Something about the organisation's flawless presentation felt manufactured, as if it were papering over cracks beneath the surface. He downloaded their latest annual report, a glossy PDF boasting impressive metrics and feel-good stories about rural clinics and water projects in Burma.

He opened ExifTool, a no-frills program favoured by investigators for uncovering hidden metadata. The details of the PDF spilled out like the innards of a gutted fish: creator, timestamps, software. His eyes zeroed in on the document author field.

'Well, that's interesting.' The author wasn't some communications officer or marketing hack at Global Horizons. It was someone with a name he didn't recognise – but the domain attached to their email address was far more revealing: @doa.contracting.gov. Bishop sat back. The US Department of the Army?

A quick search on the name turned up more. The document author was listed as a project manager for Longbow Defence Solutions, a defence contractor specialising in "civil-military stabilisation initiatives." Five minutes later, the Pentagon's contracting database confirmed it. The company had its fingers in everything from water systems to mobile field hospitals – and narcotics interdiction.

The mix of humanitarian and military work wasn't unusual, but something about Longbow's portfolio didn't sit right. Most of their contracts were in the Middle East and Africa. Nothing in Burma – nothing anywhere in Southeast Asia. Why would a defence contractor – one with no public record of development work in Southeast Asia – be writing reports for a grassroots aid organisation?

If Longbow Defence Solutions was writing their reports, what else about Global Horizons was fabricated? He decided to dig deeper.

He moved on to the "About Us" page, where the profiles of the board members were prominently displayed. The names were unfamiliar,

which wasn't surprising, but the credentials listed were impressive –
MBAs from top American universities, years of experience with
renowned international organisations, a clear commitment to
humanitarian work. Runs on the board. Bishop clicked on each
photo, downloading them to his desktop. They were going to need a
closer look.

Switching tabs, Bishop opened TinEye, his favoured reverse
image search tool. He uploaded the first of the board members'
photos. It didn't take long for the results to load. His heart skipped a
beat as he scrolled through the matches. The photo was a stock
image, available on multiple websites, completely unrelated to the
person it was supposed to represent. He quickly ran the other images
through the tool. Same result. All the images were either stock photos
or lifted from unrelated online profiles. The board members were a
façade. Bishop's fingers flew across the keyboard as he made notes.
This was his second red flag, but he needed more. He had to be sure.

Next, he turned his attention to the financials. He navigated to
GuideStar, a website that provided detailed information on US-based
non-profits, including their financial reports and IRS Form 990
submissions. He typed in "Global Horizons Aid Network" and waited
as the results populated.

There it was – a listing for Global Horizons. But as Bishop
scrolled down, his brow furrowed. The Form 990, required by the US
Internal Revenue Service, had not been submitted for two consecu-
tive years, despite the organisation claiming in its Annual Report to
have gross receipts of $375,000 and total assets of $625,000. This was
not a minor oversight; it was a serious omission that could jeopardise
the organisation's tax-exempt status. Moreover, the available financial
information was suspiciously sparse. There were no detailed break-
downs of expenses and no information on how funds were being
allocated. The numbers felt inflated, with little to no supporting
documentation. Flag three.

Bishop shifted his focus to Global Horizons' social media presence. A quick search revealed accounts on all the major platforms –
Facebook, Twitter, LinkedIn. But something was off. The Facebook

page had not been updated in over three months, with the last post being a generic "Happy Holidays" message. The post before that was eight months old. The Twitter feed was similarly inactive, with only a handful of tweets in the past year, most of which were reposts from other accounts, and none of which provided any meaningful insight into the organisation's activities. LinkedIn was worse; there was no information on company structure, employee numbers, or even the board members who were supposedly leading this NGO – although, by this stage, Bishop had evidence the board members did not actually exist.

Bishop drummed his fingers impatiently on the desk. This was too sterile. Too empty. An NGO with the reach that Global Horizons claimed would have a vibrant online presence, especially if it sought to engage the all-important donors and volunteers. The lack of activity was another glaring red flag.

Turning his attention to the registered address of Global Horizons in Seattle, Bishop opened Google Earth. He typed in the address listed on the website and waited as the program zoomed in on the location. What appeared on the screen sent a chill down his spine. The address was not a glass-fronted office tower, nor even a small shopfront. It was a disused factory site, long abandoned, covered in graffiti, and now overgrown with weeds.

Bishop sat back in his chair, running a hand through his hair. He had expected some irregularities, but this was a different level altogether. This wasn't just an NGO cutting corners; it was something far more sinister.

He took a deep breath and leaned forward again, this time venturing into the internet's darker corners. Using the covert login he employed during K & R investigations, he accessed the Tor browser and navigated through a maze of links until he reached a forum he had visited before – an underground site frequented by hackers and whistleblowers. It was a place where information could be bought, traded, or simply shared, depending on who you were and what you had to offer.

Pausing momentarily in thought, he posted a vaguely worded

query about Global Horizons. He sat back and watched the screen, not expecting much. To his surprise, a user with the handle "CryptoKnıght" responded almost immediately. The conversation was brief, filled with the usual evasive and veiled language, but CryptoKnıght hinted at something big – deeply hidden links between Global Horizons and the US Government.

Bishop's pulse quickened. He pressed for more details, but the hacker was cagey. CryptoKnıght suggested the existence of a document, but refused to give any details. There was a minute's pause in traffic, and then a message appeared in the chat:

I need to think about this. It's some serious shit, my man. Check in with me in 24 hrs. CryptoKnıght logged off, leaving Bishop staring at a blinking cursor.

The faint hum of the air conditioner was the only sound breaking the silence of the dimly lit hotel room. Bishop sat hunched over his laptop at the small wooden desk. A single lamp cast a warm, yellow light over the keyboard, leaving the rest of the room in shadow. It was late, and his eyes were weary as he scanned the lines of text and images that flickered on the laptop display. His mind raced, and he felt the fog lowering around him. His focus was slipping, but now was the time to concentrate. He leaned back, shut his eyes tight and breathed steadily for a count of ten.

The pieces tumbling into place formed a disturbing picture. Global Horizons wasn't just a spurious NGO; it was beginning to look like a front for something much darker. He opened his eyes, sat upright, and quickly copied all the files and screenshots to an encrypted flash drive.

Closing his laptop, Bishop sat back again in his chair, his discovery weighing on him. The dim light of the hotel room seemed to close in around him as he realised just how deep this rabbit hole might go. Sophie Bouchard had worked for a fake NGO with possible ties to the US Government, and she had disappeared. What the hell was going on?

The hacker was right; this *was* some serious shit, and he needed to move carefully. He checked his watch. It was late – the curfew was in force outside – and Maddy would be asleep. He decided to let her rest. He would brief her on the flight in a few hours.

Feeling the tremor in his left hand, Bishop looked down. He moved slowly as the thick blanket began to wrap and bind him. Swearing, he stumbled to his feet and into the bathroom. He grabbed at his toiletries bag and fumbled with the zipper. His eyes were blurred, and he felt about inside, his razor nicking the tip of a finger. Grasping the small, white bottle, he flipped off the lid, shook out two tablets and threw them into his mouth.

Sinking to the tiled floor of the bathroom, he leaned back against the wall and watched his G-Shock tick away the seconds as he gave himself over to the drug.

25

TAUNGGYI, Shan State, Burma

The twin-engine Pratt & Whitney turboprop engines roared as Mingalar flight K7-846 pulled from the runway and surged skyward. The ATR 72-600 climbed steeply, quickly penetrating the thick, grey cloud that had settled over Yangon. Then, suddenly, it burst into a clear, bright sky. Sunlight blazed through the plexiglass window, and Madeleine, in the window seat, lowered sunglasses over her eyes as she turned to Bishop.

'So, you're sure? I mean, that's a hell of a thing if true.'

Bishop leaned in closer and spoke quietly. 'I'm sure. Nothing about Global Horizons stacks up. Every photo it has used – except the one of Downs – is either a stock shot, stolen from someone else's innocent profile or has been digitally altered. The board are all ghosts, and the financials are fake. Worse, there's a powerful defence contractor embedded somewhere in its setup. Why? Whoever built this thought of most angles but didn't go deep enough – it's sloppy work, and any kid with a laptop and two hours on their hands could blow it open. My only guess is they just didn't expect anyone to really dig.'

'But they're on the United Nations Development Programme's list of approved providers!'

'Since when was that a ringing endorsement of anything?'

'Good point. So, who's your chum on the dark web?' Madeleine asked. 'Can he be trusted?'

Bishop shrugged. 'I have no idea, and who can you trust once you go down that hole? It's a dark and nasty place. But he... she, I don't know... seemed genuinely concerned and wasn't keen to push it. I'll find out more tonight if I'm lucky.'

Madeleine sat in silence, turning her face to the window. Was this what her handlers were looking for? A US Government front in Burma? *It's need to know, Maddy, and, at this stage, you don't,* her handler's voice echoed. It wasn't as if governments were shy about setting up front organisations to carry out covert activities. But what were the Yanks up to – and why Burma? Her thoughts were interrupted as Bishop spoke again.

'Anyway,' he said, 'while it's all very interesting, it's a sideline to our mission. Our job is to find the girl and get her out. I don't care about much else.'

'And if her disappearance is connected to Global Horizons and some US op?'

'It's only important insofar as it might be relevant to what has happened to her and where she is. If it helps us find her, then good. Otherwise, I don't give a shit.'

Madeleine nodded. She knew she couldn't push Bishop on this without raising his suspicions. They were here to find and extract the girl. But if what Bishop had discovered *was* true, it was too improbable that a U.S. Government operation and the girl's disappearance weren't linked. If they were, she and Bishop would find out, and they might also find the girl. But would she have what her masters wanted?

'You're right,' she said. 'The girl is priority one – but, in finding her, we need to get to the bottom of her disappearance. Agreed?'

'Agreed,' Bishop said as they felt the aircraft tilt and begin its descent into Heho Airport, an hour west of Taunggyi.

The countryside between the airport and the city was open and cropped with potatoes, tomatoes, and beans. The ridgelines above the road were terraced and planted with rice paddies and tea shrubs. Driving on the right side of the road, in a right-hand drive vehicle was a Burmese peculiarity and an interesting challenge. Bishop took it easy. He drove the rented Toyota Hilux sedately on the narrow, pitted road, using the shoulder to avoid oncoming trucks and the slow, plodding ox-drawn carts piled high with produce.

Besides the vehicles, people were everywhere, many wearing brightly coloured turbans, walking the side of the narrow rural road, and carrying loads on their backs.

'Who are they?' Madeleine asked, taking a photo of one group as they passed.

'Pa'O,' Bishop said. 'They're a minority ethnic group that live mostly in Southern Shan. They stick pretty much to themselves. Very traditional agrarian lifestyle. I met a few when I was last here – years ago – and they're a dignified and reserved people. I like them.'

Bishop had thought about it for days, wondering how it would feel to be back in Shan. His time there had been a seminal moment in his life, one that had left its memories – and its mark. But those days were gone, and this was a new job. It was... bittersweet. He steered the Hilux around a cart, the foliage of the stacked tomato plants brushing the side of the utility, then geared down to pass a clanking, rusted truck piled high with bamboo poles.

'Here's a fun fact,' he said. 'The traditional loose clothing of the Pa'O is both practical *and* symbolic. The dark colours represent the earth, and the bright headgear symbolises the sun.'

Madeleine smiled. 'It's one of the things I love about you, Bishop: your seemingly bottomless well of arcane and obscure general knowledge.'

'As I said, I've been here before – a while ago. But that's another story.'

Madeleine looked sideways at Bishop. She had not known that, but, then, there was a lot about this man she still didn't know.

They settled into a comfortable silence. As the Hilux rolled into Taunggyi from the north, the road began to climb, winding through lush, green hills that gradually gave way to the bustling outskirts of the city. The air was cooler there, a welcome respite from the heat of the lowlands. On either side of the road sat small roadside stalls, selling everything from fresh fruits and vegetables to handmade crafts and steaming bowls of *mohinga* – fish soup with noodles. The sweet scent of jasmine, mingled with the earthy aromas of cooking fires, and rich, fertile soil, wafted through the car's air-conditioning.

They were minutes from their destination, and passing Basic Education High School 7, when Bishop pointed left to a large, securely fenced compound, the road lined with concrete barriers.

'Tatmadaw Eastern Command,' he said. 'A Light Infantry Division – maybe the 99th – infantry and light infantry battalions, artillery regiments and engineering battalions. The current Commanding General is Min Kyaw Ko. That's about all we know. Other than the fact that there will be troops everywhere we plan to go.'

'Good to know...'

Bishop nodded grimly. 'With them and the SSA, we'll need to stay low and move fast.'

Entering the city, the streets narrowed, lined with a mixture of colonial-era buildings and newer, more modern structures. The footpaths were crowded with vendors hawking their wares, and the streets hummed with chaotic energy as motorbikes, rickshaws, and pedestrians all vied for space. Here and there, the occasional bell-shaped stupa peeked through the urban landscape, a reminder of the city's deep-rooted Buddhist spirituality.

As they drove further into the heart of Taunggyi, the road began to level out. The city sprawled before them, a patchwork of red-tiled roofs, golden pagodas, and green treetops. The distant Shan Hills framed the view to the west, their peaks fading into the mist. They reached the Mya Kan Thar Roundabout, and the Mountain Star

Hotel, a little over an hour after leaving the airport. The hotel was modest and nondescript. Out of the way. It was just what Bishop had wanted, but he still felt like he was stringing his hutchie in enemy heartland.

26

MADELEINE BELCHED SOFTLY as she placed the beer bottle back on the wooden table. She scratched the back of her head and looked around.

A short walk south from the hotel, and nestled along a side street off E Circular Road, the Pa-Oh Kitchen was a cosy local restaurant frequented by both locals and travellers, and known for its authentic Shan and Pa'O dishes. Bishop had suggested it – 'If it's still there' – and Madeleine was beginning to think the phlegmatic Aussie knew much more about this town than he was letting on.

The restaurant was modest, with simple wooden tables and chairs set under a corrugated tin roof that provided shelter from the sun and rain. Soft lighting threw a welcome glow over the place, and the walls were adorned with colourful posters of bucolic scenes in the surrounding villages. A small counter near the entrance displayed a variety of fresh ingredients – baskets of herbs, bowls of chilli, garlic, and ginger, and piles of fresh vegetables.

'Will you order?' Madeleine asked. 'I have no idea what any of this is.'

Bishop took a swig of his beer and picked up a menu. 'Sure,' he said as he ran his eyes over the food list. His decision made, he signalled to the waiter, a young boy in grey shorts and a vintage AC/DC T-shirt. The kid slipped up to the table and smiled.

'English?' Bishop asked.

The boy shook his head, still smiling.

'Okay,' Bishop murmured. 'Fair enough, why would you hey?' He paused. 'Man nee ka, *these please*,' he said in Shan, pointing out several items and watching as the boy nodded with each one. Shan noodles – rice noodles served with a savoury broth, minced pork, and a sprinkling of fried garlic and peanuts; *lahpet thoke* – a tea leaf salad mixed with tomatoes, peanuts, and crispy fried beans; and, finally, *nga htamin*, fish rice.

The kid nodded one last time, picked up the two empty beers and darted back to the open kitchen, shouting out the order while he dived into a large fridge and pulled out two fresh beers that he brought to the table. With an expert flick of his wrist and a table knife, he opened the bottles.

Madeleine sipped her beer and then said quietly: 'Do you get the feeling we're being watched?'

Bishop nodded. 'Yep. Since we got off the plane. There was a man on a scooter behind us all the way into the city.' He pulled his earlobe and pretended to look at his phone. 'He's sitting across the road outside that small clothing store.'

Madeleine flicked her eyes over Bishop's shoulder. 'Shit. I completely missed that. Who do you think he is?'

Bishop shrugged. 'Police, intelligence, military, SSA? Who knows, but whoever he is he is very interested in us and, doubtless, is reporting back on our movements.' He swigged his beer again. 'But fuck him. We know he's there, and we'll lose him when we need to.'

Madeleine glanced at the man. 'He's not making much of an effort, is he? He doesn't seem to care we know he's following us.'

'Why would he? He's on home ground, and we're out here alone... He doesn't have to bother with cool tradecraft.'

'Maybe he's not bothered because he thinks we won't leave here alive.'

Bishop nodded and picked up his beer. 'Maybe.'

The food, piled up on blue, hard-plastic plates, arrived and the boy carefully placed four spoons on the table, along with a steaming jug of green tea and two cups. Madeleine and Bishop smiled at him, and he pointed at his T-shirt.

'AC/DC,' he said, grinning. 'Much good! Angus!' he said before duckwalking back to the kitchen, nodding manically and furiously playing an air guitar.

Madeleine chuckled, and they began spooning food onto their plates. They were both ravenous after a long day of travel, and their conversation petered out as they ate. Across the road, the man sitting outside the clothing store lit a cigarette and watched them.

Bishop was spooning some fish rice into his mouth when his phone buzzed on the table. He wiped his mouth with the back of his hand and picked the phone up. It was a text from Nesbitt on the secure messaging app.

B reached out. The target's AMEX was used five minutes ago. A cash withdrawal at an ATM

A map link followed. KBZ Bank, Sao San Tun Road. Bishop clicked on it, his eyes widening. 'Jesus Christ,' he muttered, tapping the map. Madeleine looked up as Bishop quickly thumbed out a reply message.

We're in Taunggyi!! On it. Send updates

'Maddy, eat up,' he said, standing and throwing some notes onto the table. 'We have to go. Right now. Sophie's credit card just made a withdrawal from an ATM about three hundred metres from here. Don't worry about old mate across the road. We'll sort that out later. Let's go.'

Madeleine nodded and followed Bishop, sprinting after him as he ran west along the narrow and darkened street. She caught up with him as he turned right, then sharp left, emerging into a small alley lined with food carts and drink stalls, each lit by bright festoon lights. They ran on past shocked locals who pushed themselves back against the alley wall. Bishop stopped at the next intersection and quickly checked maps on his phone. Right! He ran off with Madeleine close behind.

The alley opened up onto a road, and traffic flowed chaotically up and down as Bishop darted across, weaving through cars, scooters and bicycles. Madeleine glanced back and could not see their tail – perhaps they had lost him in the mad dash through the alleys. She crossed and pulled up next to Bishop, who had suddenly stopped, looking intently forward.

'There,' he said, panting slightly. 'The ATM.' It stood on a darkened corner with only one small globe above it, throwing a weak cone of light over the grey concrete. People were walking the footpath, but no one was standing by the bank machine. Bishop checked his watch. 1942 hrs.

'About seven minutes since the card was used. Whoever did it has long gone.' He looked around, desperately hoping to see Sophie. He didn't.

'There's a CCTV on the ATM,' Madeleine observed. 'I can probably...' She was interrupted by Bishop's phone buzzing in his pocket. He drew it out and studied the screen. Nesbitt.

Used again 90 secs ago. Shopping mall. Across the road. Aung May Yu fishing store

Bishop didn't reply but spun on his heels. 'The mall,' he said, pointing. 'Just now. Fishing store.' He ran off across the road without looking, car and scooter horns sounding around him in agitation. Madeleine took a breath, timed her run, and followed.

27

THE TWO RAN through the open glass doors to the mall. It was spacious, well-lit and clean, if ageing and a little run down. A store directory stood by the main doors. Some stores were listed in English, but most were only in Burmese and Shan. Madeleine stepped up to it, running her fingers over the perspex screen.

'A fishing store, you said?' She tapped an icon of a soccer ball and a fishing rod. 'Aung May...?'

'Yu,' Bishop said. 'Aung May Yu.'

'First floor, up the escalator and right,' Madeleine snapped over her shoulder as she ran onto the escalator, taking the stair treads two at a time.

They hit the first floor at a run, skidding on the shiny tiles, and entered a corridor with shops and stores on either side. Groceries, clothing, electronics... fishing gear. Bishop slammed to a halt at the door and looked up. The faded sign said: *Aung May Yu, Finest Goods for Fishing & Sport*. He stepped in, his eyes flicking around the store.

The store was empty except for the male clerk standing behind the counter scrolling through his phone. Bishop cursed under his breath and joined Madeleine who stood outside, looking up and down the corridor as crowds of shoppers flowed around her like an incoming tide. Bishop rubbed his face.

'It's hopeless. We're chasing our bloody tails.' He stopped as a thought crashed in on him. 'It isn't Sophie. Why would she be buying fishing gear? Someone has her card and whoever *that* is probably knows where she is.'

'Could have found it in the street...'

'Could have, but no. Girl goes missing five hours east of here, girl's credit card is used. Too much of a stretch for them not to be connected.' Bishop paused in thought, then grabbed out his phone and tapped a message to Nesbitt.

Tell Bouchard NOT to cancel the card. We need to keep tracking transactions

He was about to speak when Madeleine slapped his arm.

'There!' she hissed. 'Through the crowd. The little man, tan baseball cap, green T-shirt. Fishing rod in his right hand.'

Madeleine started walking fast, elbowing her way against the flow of people in the corridor. Bishop squinted and spotted the man. He was entering a clothing store. *U Chit Tin Fashion*. He caught up to Madeleine, who stood outside the store, just to the left of the doors.

'We can't nab him here,' he said. 'I'll go in; you keep watch. When he leaves, we'll follow until we can take our chance to pull him.'

Madeleine nodded and eased herself further away from the door as Bishop stepped into the small store. He moved to a table of jeans only two metres from the man who had his back to Bishop and was flicking through a hanging rack of shirts. Bishop studied him.

The man's boots were black tactical lace-ups, dusty and well-worn, and there was a long strand of grass stuck in the laces of the right boot. His pants were khaki, faux tactical with cargo pockets, and his green T-shirt, torn at the left shoulder, had the words "My wife's Burmese – nothing scares me" screen-printed on the back. The tan cap had a small cloth badge velcroed to the backstrap. A stylised white tiger head. The man selected two shirts and moved to the counter. Bishop watched as the sales attendant rang up the purchase. The man reached into his back pocket and pulled out a single plastic card, unmistakably silver, with the words *American Express* written in bold black across the top. Bishop's heart thumped as he watched the man pay for the clothes and walk from the store. The man with the fishing rod and bag of shirts was their link to Sophie.

Exiting the store, Bishop watched as the man walked onto the escalators, with Maddy a few paces ahead of him. Three people back from the man, Bishop stepped onto the escalator just as his phone buzzed.

Another one. Two minutes ago. U Chit Tin fashion

Bishop looked back and smiled grimly to see the name of the clothing store. It was confirmed. The man, now boxed in by him and Maddy, had Sophie – or knew where she was. He felt his pulse racing as the three of them stepped off the escalators, through the mall entrance and out into the busy evening crowds on the road.

They had walked fifty metres, heading north, when the man stopped on the side of the busy road, pulled out his phone and made a call. Bishop tensed. Madeleine stopped twenty metres ahead and studied a jewellery display in a brightly lit shop window. Bishop turned to his left, his phone in his hand, and moved as if waiting to cross the road.

Before either could react, a silver Landcruiser, dust streaked down its sides, veered into the curb. The back door swung open, the man threw the fishing rod and bag into the back, jumped in and slammed the door shut. In seconds, the Landcruiser had sped off and down the road past a stunned Bishop, who quickly took a photo of the back of the vehicle as its taillights disappeared into the traffic.

He turned as Madeleine joined him at the curb. He was breathing hard, walking in tight circles. 'What a balls up!' he spat. 'We've lost him. *Fuck!*' He drew a deep breath, held up a hand and shut his eyes. 'Give me a minute...'

Madeleine stood silently, letting Bishop blow it off and gather himself. When he opened his eyes and huffed out a frustrated breath, she spoke.

'Did you get a good look at him?'

'Not his face. Just build and his clothes...'

'So that puts us back at the ATM. I need to break into the CCTV and pull down the footage so we can get a shot of him.'

'You can *do* that?'

'Of course I bloody can.'

'Impressive. But what's the point? Even with a photo of his face, how will we ever find him again? We were lucky tonight, and won't be again.'

'Luck comes and goes in this game. We both know that. Besides, it will be better to have some sort of ID on this guy, and you've got pics of the car registration, so if either, or both, come into our space again, we'll be on them.'

'Fair enough,' Bishop conceded. 'Okay, first thing's first...' He scratched under his chin and looked around. 'We seem to have lost our follower, but he'll pick us up again at the hotel, so we need to get back there, grab our gear and get out, losing him along the way. I've got an idea...'

~

Taunggyi is quiet at 0215. The streets were deserted except for the army patrols, and all was silent but for the occasional bark of a dog and the crow of an early-rising rooster.

They had returned to the hotel hours before and quickly thrown their gear together, then loaded their rucksacks into the back of the Hilux parked at the rear. Five minutes later, Madeleine had walked casually from the front of the hotel, and their watcher had moved from his perch across the road and followed her. Madeleine had walked the pre-determined route, gradually building her pace until she was in a light jog and had opened up a gap between her and the watcher.

Madeleine and her shadow were fifteen hundred metres from the hotel when the Hilux sped up beside her, the front passenger door open, and she leapt in. The utility roared off into the night, leaving the tail standing dumbfounded on the side of the road and minutes away from his scooter.

Now, under the shroud of a light drizzle, Bishop and Madeleine huddled in the shadowed confines of an alley. The KBZ Bank ATM sat just out of reach around the corner in the flickering light of the single, dim bulb. The echo of the troop truck faded into the dark as it passed, and time was bleeding away. Bishop picked up a brick fragment by his feet and hefted it once before throwing it out and up. The light bulb shattered with a pop, and the corner was plunged into darkness. Madeleine moved fast.

'Keep watch,' she whispered, her voice masked by the steady tap of the rain on tin roofs. Bishop nodded, his eyes scanning the dimly lit street for the returning glare of headlights. They had only minutes.

Madeleine crouched and unzipped the backpack, extracting a sleek laptop and a string of cables. Her hands steady despite the adrenaline coursing through her body, she connected an ethernet cable from the laptop to a discreet port on the bottom right of the ATM. Her fingers danced across the keyboard, firing up Wireshark to sniff out the network's traffic. Passwords and data flowed across the screen in an electronic waterfall, and she quickly isolated the CCTV's IP address.

'Got it,' she muttered, launching Hydra to crack the login. It never ceased to amaze her how many organisations were content to sit fat, dumb, and happy with default passwords, and her decision to chance that vulnerability was a gamble, but luck was on her side. Access granted. Her heart thumped, and her breathing quickened as she navigated the CCTV's storage directory, searching for footage time-stamped 1935 hrs the previous evening.

Files loaded, and video thumbnails flickered on the screen. The target's face appeared, a ghost in the machine. 'Got you, you bastard,' she muttered. Quick, precise clicks began the file transfers to an encrypted flash drive. Every second stretched, taut as a wire.

The distant rumble of a truck engine grew ominously louder as it approached the bend only metres away. 'Hurry, Maddy,' Bishop hissed, tension coiling in his voice.

The download progress bar on the screen crept to completion just as headlights danced across building facades and the troop carrier began to round the corner. 'Done,' Madeleine breathed. She yanked out the USB and executed a script to scrub her digital footprint, leaving the system as untouched as when she found it. No one would know it had been accessed.

Madeleine shoved her gear into the backpack and ducked into the alley. Bishop was already moving, and they vanished into the rain-drenched night as the troop truck rolled past the ATM. The glare of its headlights reached out into the night, searching but finding nothing.

28

SHAN STATE, Burma

They left Taunggyi just after dawn. Bogyoke Aung San Road wound east through lowland farming country, dotted with small townships, rice paddies, vegetable farms and golden fields of maize and millet. The heat outside was oppressive, and the threat of rain in the rolling, grey clouds raised the humidity to sauna-like levels. Inside the Hilux, it was cool and the cabin hummed softly with road noise as Bishop sped the utility along the road, encountering only the occasional car or truck.

They had decided not to visit the Global Horizons Field Office. Given the tail the previous day and what Bishop had discovered, they knew that doing so would have been to walk into a trap. They had always planned to go dark at some point, and that time had arrived.

After hacking into the ATM, Bishop and Madeleine checked into a small, anonymous boarding house on the city's outskirts to grab a few hours' sleep. Before Bishop finally allowed himself to rest, he opened his burner laptop and journeyed back into the dark web, looking for

CryptoKnight. After exploring several dead ends, he found the hacker and pinged out a message.

What have you got for me?

The cursor blinked silently, and Bishop stared at the screen, then CryptoKnight replied.

Are you sure you want to do this?

Yes.

Okay dude, it's your funeral. We're both dead if they track this. But I want payment first. Crypto. Twenty-five large. Into here.

A crypto wallet address appeared on the screen.

That will take me a few minutes.

You've got five then I'm gone.

Bishop was no stranger to cryptocurrency transactions; many of his sources used them and needed their payments to be highly secure. He double-checked his VPN was running, then, fingers skipping across the keyboard, he created a new wallet, the address a jumble of random characters. Completely anonymous. With a few clicks, he entered a peer-to-peer exchange, scanning listings from sellers. No one on this exchange would ever think of asking a question – it isn't how business is done. He picked a name, then paid with one of the gift cards he had loaded before leaving Singapore – operational funds weren't just folding stuff these days, although cash was still king. He watched the screen and, seconds later, his wallet balance updated.

With swift, practised movements, he sent the funds to a cryptocurrency mixer. The coins disappeared into a pool of thousands, blending and re-emerging clean. There was no way to trace them now. Bishop considered converting the Bitcoin to Monero for added security but decided against it. Speed was crucial. CryptoKnight was waiting, and the hacker would not hang around.

Bishop quickly copied CryptoKnight's wallet address, pasted it into the payment field, and added the hefty fee to ensure the transaction was processed instantly. One click and the payment was sent, vanishing into the blockchain's depths.

He exhaled slowly, the tension easing from his shoulders. No physical traces, no loose ends. He digitally wiped the laptop, deleting all traces of the transaction. Then he waited. Of course, CryptoKnıght could just take the money and run, but Bishop doubted it. Two minutes later:

This should get you started. Before you ask, I've sent the logs too – the file is legit. Nice doing business. But be careful, dude. You're playing with fire.

Two files were attached. Bishop watched as the hacker logged off. He hesitated for a split second before downloading the files. The first was the logs that showed when the file was accessed and copied, along with a screen recording of the extraction process. The accompanying document was genuine. Bishop opened it.

As Bishop read, his pulse quickened, and he realised he was holding his breath. The document was a heavily redacted report, but the visible parts were explosive. It referred to Global Horizons by name and linked the fake NGO to a series of US covert activities in Southeast Asia, including operations that were far from humanitarian.

'Cambodia, Burma, Laos,' Bishop said as he steered the Hilux along a narrow, winding street through a township before exiting back onto the main road. 'And all fronted by Global Horizons.' He shook his head. 'These guys really don't give a shit. It's like they're back in the 60s battling old Uncle Ho.'

Madeleine nodded. 'There's an argument the dominoes are still standing across Southeast Asia – they're just lined up differently.' She paused, deep in thought. 'It's hard to believe this would come out of Langley, you know, officially. It has to be a rogue op somehow...' *Jesus,* she thought. Her handler was going to lose his mind.

'Rogue or not, I don't care,' Bishop said. 'What I want to know is what it has to do with Sophie's disappearance.' He sighed, his eyes on the road ahead. 'It *has* to be connected. She worked for Global Horizons, Global Horizons is a CIA front, Sophie stumbles on something she shouldn't have, and she disappears...'

'The *CIA* disappeared her?'

'Them or one of their local partners. They never do this stuff on their own. They always use locals. You know: plausible deniability.'

Don't we all, Madeleine thought. 'Okay, that makes sense,' she said, gazing out the window as they passed a rice paddy, where a farmer and his ox slowly ploughed the shallow water. 'But who?'

'That's what we need to find out.'

'What about this contractor... Longbow? Could it be them?'

Bishop shook his head. 'I don't think so. They're heavy, and maybe their operators are involved somewhere, but I get the feeling they were just used by the Agency as an arms-length measure to set up Global Horizons. Again, "deniability". Anyway, the question is less "who" and more "where".'

'No. The question is, *what*. What did she see?' Madeleine added. 'Find *that* out, and we answer who and where.'

They settled into silence, each lost in their thoughts as the Hilux sped on. The bright sun sparkling into the cabin was suddenly fainter as they left the lowlands and began to climb a mountainous ridgeline through dense tropical forest. As they climbed, the road narrowed, barely two lanes now. On the uphill side of the road, rugged cliff faces towered over them, topped with a fringe of large trees, the cliffs themselves dotted with saplings that had managed to seed and grow on the sheer, stone face. On the downhill side, the road shoulder dropped straight down into a tangle of trees and dense undergrowth. A car going off the road here would never be found.

Bishop checked the rear-vision mirror and noticed no vehicles behind them for the first time that day. With a jolt, he also realised that not a single car had passed them going the other way for maybe half an hour. They were alone on the road, with nowhere to go but forward, and Bishop's skin crawled.

He checked the odometer, then the stopwatch on his G-Shock. They had been travelling for a little over ninety minutes and would soon descend the twisting road off the high ground to Mong Pawn

Bridge which would then give them another two and half hours to Narhkan. If everything went well, they would be off the road, the Hilux hidden, and in a hide by mid-afternoon. That would give them a few hours to get a look at the township before dark.

He picked up his phone from the centre console. 'No network,' he said. 'We'll be increasingly off the cellular grid the further east we go. We'll move to satphones from here on. Then our comms when we need to.'

Maddy nodded and pulled her satphone from the backpack at her feet, checking its charge.

'I wish I still smoked,' Bishop muttered as he negotiated the utility around a tight hairpin bend. Madeleine snorted a laugh. Two more tight bends and a long right-hand sweeper, and the Hilux broke from the shadow of the high-country canopy and into the clearing that marked the approach to the banks of the river and the Mong Pawn Bridge.

Madeleine sat forward suddenly in her seat. 'Bishop...' she said, her voice ringing in urgency.

'I see it,' he replied.

The Tatmadaw roadblock completely cut the road and barricaded both shoulders. Coils of loose barbed wire lay across the road behind yellow and black wooden barriers. Behind the barbed wire stood six soldiers dressed in green camouflage uniforms and matching chest rigs, each with three ammunition pouches across the front, and Kevlar helmets with matching camouflage covers.

Bishop saw the squad were all carrying the standard Tatmadaw BA-63 battle rifle – a clone of the H&K G3 – and all of the weapons were held in a ready stance as the Hilux slowly approached. Bishop turned his head to the half-right and spotted the sniper. The soldier was sitting on a paddy dyke, sighting the vehicle down the scope atop his 7.62 mm sniper rifle.

The soldiers looked like they had been expecting the car, and they were coiled tight in readiness. Bishop's blood chilled in his veins.

'Stay cool, Maddy. Our paperwork will get us through, and we'll be on our way soon.'

Madeleine instinctively reached for her right hip, but there was nothing there. Slowly, she raised her hands so the soldiers could see them.

A soldier stepped forward and raised his hand in a command to "halt". Bishop brought the utility to a stop. He reached up to the sun visor, pulled out their Letter of Introduction, sat it on the dashboard, powered down the windows, and slowly placed his hands on the steering wheel.

The soldier – Bishop could now see the two stars of a Lieutenant on his epaulettes – slung his rifle and drew a handgun as he approached the Hilux. His brown face was set, and his dark eyes glinted with menace. He stepped up to the driver's side window and looked in, studying the vehicle's occupants. His examination over, the officer pulled out his phone and tapped the screen twice, each time looking back at Bishop and Madeleine.

Bishop's heart sank. They had photos. That could only mean they had pulled down their immigration arrival images or those from the CCTV at the hotel. Someone had rumbled them, and whoever it was had connections. The soldier knew precisely who he was looking for.

The officer shouted a command in Burmese.

'English?' Bishop asked, his voice calm.

The Lieutenant shouted again, louder, and waved his pistol to the side.

'He wants us out, Maddy,' Bishop said quietly. 'Easy does it.'

The two stepped slowly from the Hilux, leaving the doors open, and raised their hands. Bishop had the LOI in his right and offered it to the Lieutenant. The officer shook his head and waved the paper away. Bishop glanced right and saw the sniper had stood down, cradling his rifle across his knees. Whatever was about to happen wouldn't require his skills.

He tried to offer the LOI again, and his movement was greeted with a crashing blow from the officer's pistol. The sharp bottom edge of the magazine cracked against Bishop's right temple and opened up a gash that ran blood into his eye. Bishop stumbled slightly but held his feet. He eyed the Lieutenant.

'We are aid workers,' he said, his voice level. The officer probably could not understand him, but if he kept his voice evenly modulated they might have a chance. Unless, of course, the decision had already been made. Bishop's gut clenched. 'We have approval from the Ministry... Narhkan.' He pointed east. A scream to his left jolted him, and he spun his head.

Maddy was standing with her shirt torn open, and one of the soldiers was roughly pawing her breasts, while his partner leered in anticipation. She slapped at the soldier and was backhanded across the mouth. Bishop took a step and felt another blow, this time to the back of the head, that dropped him to his knees.

That was the signal.

Four soldiers rushed forward and grabbed Madeleine and Bishop, yanking their arms and pinioning their hands behind their backs. Bishop looked frantically around. There was no one in sight. *What would it matter if there were?* he thought.

The soldiers marched the two off the road and into a bare field that ran down to the banks of the river. The sun blazed down on them, and the ground shimmered in the heat. Madeleine and Bishop stumbled on, their ankles rolling on loose rocks and boots scuffing ridges of old, ploughed dirt. They had walked fifty metres from the road when the officer called a command, and the group stopped. Two shallow graves had been dug, side by side, in the parched soil. They had been expected, and this was the end.

Madeleine was roughly shoved to her knees at the end of one grave, and Bishop received a blow to the back of his legs that dropped him to the dust. Kneeling at the end of the grave, he looked up. In the distance, the hills rolled away to the north, green and endless, and, above them, three vultures circled, their necks craned and heads scanning down at the figures below them. Bishop smiled grimly. They might be an endangered species, but the bastards always seemed to know when there was a feed on. Still looking up, he spoke.

'I'm sorry, Maddy. I really am...'

Madeleine sucked at her teeth and spat into the grave. 'Don't be.

It all comes to an end one day. Somehow. This is as good a day as any, I suppose.'

'Funny. I haven't got any last words...'

'Nor have I.'

The soldiers cocked their weapons behind the pair, but neither flinched, both looking to the bright, blue sky. To Madeleine, it looked like the sea off her beloved Capri, and she let her mind wander to the euphoria she felt when free-diving its depths. Bishop suddenly thought of his mother and sister, whom he had not seen in two years. It had been a rough start to life for them all, and he hoped they would be okay.

The sound of automatic weapon fire shattered the silence of the field.

29

BISHOP OPENED HIS EYES. He realised he was still looking skyward and could hear small arms fire. A lot of it, and it was getting heavier. Still on his knees, he spun around. Three of the soldiers were spread-eagled on the ground, their bloodied bodies rag-doll limp. The fourth soldier, and the officer, were firing furiously to their left at a dozen or more figures, clad in dark green, who surged across the field from the treeline, their weapons blazing.

Before Bishop could speak, Madeleine sprang to her feet, dust spitting up around her from the incoming fire, and kicked the officer in the side of the head, a savage blow that rocked his skull and felled him. In an instant, she leapt on the dropped handgun, spun it into her right hand and fired two shots into the officer's face.

Bishop was on his feet and moving the three paces between him and the last soldier when Madeleine spun and fired two more shots. The soldier dropped, the back of his head blowing out across the dust of the field. The firing slowly petered out.

Bishop looked back to the road and saw more of the green-clad figures moving around, gathering weapons and equipment from the dead at the roadblock. On the paddy dyke, Bishop could see the sniper sprawled head-down on the bund, the back of his shirt dark with blood.

Madeleine dropped the handgun and moved to stand beside Bishop as the assault line from the jungle fringe reached them.

'You okay,' she said, her voice as calm as if she were asking him for the time.

Bishop nodded. 'Okay. *Fuck*, that was close.' He scanned the arriving troops. 'Who are these guys?'

Madeleine shrugged. The assault line stopped a few metres away, and a young woman stepped forward, followed by a young man. To Bishop, they looked remarkably alike. The girl was dressed in jungle green, and the young man wore a black T-shirt under his chest rig. The young woman was beautiful – breathtaking, if Bishop had any breath to spare. Both of them wore cloth caps with the insignia of a fighting peacock on the front. The young woman smiled at them, her dark, almond-shaped eyes sparkling.

'I am glad to see you have been unharmed,' she said. Her English was excellent, better than Bishop's Nesbitt would have said, and London accented. 'My name is Swe, and this is my younger brother, Zaw. We are PDF, and you are both now my guests.'

Bishop knew the People's Defence Force. They were the armed wing of the National Unity Government, Burma's government in exile. Both organisations had been declared illegal by the State Administration Council – Burma's ruling junta – with the PDF also being designated a terrorist organisation. Immediately following the coup, the early, organic formations of people's defence had been poorly organised and even more poorly equipped. But now – if reports Bishop had seen were accurate – the PDF was well trained and were armed and equipped better than most small-nation armies. They were the implacable enemy of the junta and of the Burmese military.

Bishop smiled weakly, his nerves still jangling. 'I'm Bishop, and this is Maddy Carter. Your arrival could not have been better timed. We're in your debt.'

Swe shook her head as her brother collected up the weapons of the dead soldiers, calling forward two comrades to strip them of their equipment. She eyed the tall stranger. He was sweating, and his face was streaked with dirt, but he was a handsome one. She felt her heart race and a blush rise to her cheeks. Annoyed at her response, she pushed it down and spoke, her voice clipped. 'There is no debt here,' she said. 'If there was, it has been repaid with the bodies of these *Sit-Tat* pigs.'

Bishop nodded. He had heard of that term. The resistance in Burma strongly objected to the use of "Tatmadaw," the decades-old official name of the Burmese military. Given the acclamatory nature of the royal particle "daw" included in the name, Bishop knew that its use amounted to a whitewashing of the crimes committed by the armed forces and even risked emboldening them to continue their horrific abuses. *Sit-Tat* was simply Burmese for "military".

Watching Zaw at work, Madeleine stepped forward. She picked up the Lieutenant's handgun – a Myanmar Defence Industries MA-5, a clone of the Glock – and checked the load. She stepped to the officer's body and stripped off the holster, slipping into her waistband, then leaned over and opened his chest rig, pulling out two spare magazines.

'I'll keep this,' she said to Swe. 'If you don't mind.'

The young woman smiled and nodded. 'Be my guest. What is ours is yours.' She turned to Bishop. 'Would you like something? Please, take your pick. We have plenty of weapons.'

Bishop returned the smile but shook his head. 'No, thank you. I'll pass.'

Swe looked at him, her head cocked to the side like a small bird. 'You're a pacifist?'

'I'm an analyst.'

She laughed. 'I'm not sure I see the distinction, but, whatever...'

Swe turned and called out a series of orders, and her assault line fanned out across the field, heading back toward the roadblock. As she did, three large, canopied civilian trucks crossed the bridge from the direction of Mong Pawn and pulled up behind the roadblock. With a piercing whistle from Swe, the PDF troops began to climb aboard. Swe gestured to Madeleine and Bishop with her head and walked off after her troops.

Bishop turned and looked back. Zaw and his comrades were tipping the bodies of the Lieutenant and his four men into the shallow graves. They kicked some dirt over the corpses and then jogged toward the trucks. Bishop looked up. The sky was a brilliant cornflower blue, caressed by a few small wisps of clean, white cloud. He drew in a deep breath and watched as the vultures soared in.

30

YANGON, Burma

Bill Reilly was a CIA operations officer. He had been for thirty years. He had spent the last ten years in SAC – the Special Activities Centre – working on the Agency's most sensitive and secretive missions across Southeast Asia. He was good at what he did.

That was until he had been approached by the man who had pitched him the job. Reilly had bought into it instantly, despite it requiring a cover within the Agency that saw him removed from SAC for unspecified "disciplinary reasons" and posted to the embassy in Yangon in a junior liaison slot.

He hated what everyone thought of him now, and he hated the rumours more – the mighty Bill Reilly busted down for touching up an admin assistant or for being caught with his hands in the social club funds. But fuck them all. That just meant they had all swallowed the cover. Even his Station Chief had no idea. Only two men in Langley knew what he was doing and why. And he was proud of that.

But right now, he was furious.

Pacing the living room of the safe house, his phone in his hand, he drew a deep breath, struggling to control his rage. *Goddamn* it, how hard could it be?

Reilly had easily tied Downs' two visitors to the same two asking after the girl at the hotel, and a single phone call had delivered their immigration arrival details and photos. He had then checked into their background. The consultancy they worked for was the real deal, but, after a bit of digging, it was clear both of them weren't what they appeared to be. The Bishop guy was an ex-Commando, and the woman, Carter, was just as worrying – some sort of fucking Xena Warrior Princess. Something about Bishop ate at Reilly. A few more cross-checks, and a call back to Langley, had quickly revealed Bishop's ties to the private intelligence agency known as "the firm". It didn't take a genius to figure out why he and the woman were in Myanmar. They were on a recovery mission for the girl, and he couldn't let that happen.

Better yet, Reilly knew who ran the firm. They had crossed paths in Thailand back in the day, and they hated each other. He had smiled widely for the first time in days at that. It was fucking perfect!

Even though they had not gone to the field office in Taunggyi, Reilly had known where they were headed – the tip-off during a late-night phone call had given him that. He knew where Bishop and Carter were going, and there was only one way in. The photos had been sent to General Min, who had sent them out to his men along the route with a kill order. It should have been easy. He stopped pacing and raised the phone to his ear.

'So, you're telling me six soldiers are dead, and both of them have disappeared. Just gone.'

'That's what I'm telling you,' the other man on the call said. The connection was weak, dropping in and out. 'We don't yet know who did it...'

'Jesus *Christ*! Can you take a *guess*? It sure as hell wasn't the SSA. Sai is too smart to jeopardise what he stands to gain by taking a pop at a bunch of soldiers. *And*, you dimwit, he is *also* on the watch for these two. They're as much a threat to him as they are to the rest of us.'

Reilly paused and drew breath. It had to have been the PDF. It was bad luck – the worst – that they had decided to attack the army post at precisely the same time the two meddlers were safely in hand. He had said often enough over the years that he did not believe in coincidences, but he did now. This was the mother of all coincidences.

He couldn't be bothered explaining it all to his confederate – the asshole should have figured it out for himself. He lit a cigarette and took a slow, deep pull on it, feeling the smoke snag his lungs and the nicotine snap at his brain. It calmed him a little.

'Okay, listen up. I'll call General Min and organise a mobilisation across Southern Shan, looking for these two and the goddamn PDF unit they're probably hanging with. You speak to Sai and get the SSA out in the field between Mong Pawn and east to Namsang. Have them cover Highway 45 south to Narhkan and beyond.'

'On it,' the other man said. 'We'll set roadblocks everywhere.'

'Do that, but I want troops in the forest and fields. The PDF, and these two assholes, aren't likely to be schlepping along on the roads – especially after today. Beat the bushes, flush the fuckers out and deal with them.'

He paused, dragging again on the cigarette, spitting the blue smoke angrily into the room. He had a decision to make, and he made it quickly.

'And tell Sai to get rid of the girl.'

There was a pause on the other end. 'Can you be clear? What do you mean by "get rid of the girl"?'

'Kill her, goddammit. Kill the girl and hide the body where it won't be found...'

'They won't do that. The SSA won't kill her.'

'They'll do what I goddamn *tell* them to do...'

'Not this, they won't.'

'Explain.'

'Shan society holds women in high regard. Women are seen as the bearers of life and the guardians of family honour. Harming a woman would go against their deeply ingrained cultural values. These insurgents adhere to a code of conduct that places a high value on honour, and killing a female hostage would be an act that would shame the individual soldier and the group as a whole.'

'Even if she is a risk to everything we – *they* – have built?'

'Even then. I'll also add they are all Theravada Buddhists, so there's that as well...'

The walls of the safe house began to close in, and Reilly felt a headache coming on. He lit another cigarette from the butt of the one in his fingers. For the love of God! They were goddamn drug-running insurgents, and now, when it was all at risk, they had developed a fucking *conscience*? He drew a deep breath to calm the pulse that was thrumming at his temples.

'Okay, wise-ass,' he said. '*You* do it, and do it today.'

'That could be a problem.'

'Do what I'm *ordering* you to do! You're not getting squeamish on me, are you?'

'No. I'm just pointing out that I'm still on the border, in Loi Tai Leng, with Sai's work-up exercises. It will take me about eighteen hours to get there – maybe more if the weather is bad. I can be there late tomorrow.'

Reilly stubbed out the smoke and clenched his fist. *If you want a job done properly, do it yourself.* He turned his head, and his eyes lit on the mission bag in the corner of the room. He had to get a grip on this situation, and that meant he was going to have to get dirty.

'Okay, just get it done,' he said. 'I'll meet you in Narhkan.'

31

LAI KHA VILLAGE, Shan State, Burma

It was cool at night in the hills; a fat moon hovered overhead, and mist clung to the valley like a shroud. Firelight flickered on the faces of the group as they squatted or sat cross-legged in front of a large wood and bamboo *hlwè*. The house was raised on stilts, and village women prepared food beneath it while their children skipped and danced about. Crickets chirruped in the dark, and the occasional rustle of a forest creature skirting the village could be heard. The quiet murmur of voices, and the crackle and pop of the fire, was comforting. Safe.

Bishop accepted a cup of *lahpet*, sour tea, with a nod and sipped it. The earthy, umami taste warmed him, and he felt himself begin to unwind. He had been hyper-vigilant since their encounter at the bridge and the mad run through the hills to the village, but now, the tight-knit community atmosphere of the village and the low fireside conversation calmed him. He glanced over at Madeleine.

She was sitting on the ground across the fire from him, her hands in her lap, wearing a fresh shirt she had pulled from her ruck. She had bathed from a bucket, and the firelight shone in her hair, giving it a golden lustre. Two small girls stood behind her, gently touching her hair in fascination. Her face was calm, and her lips were arranged in a slight smile, despite the faint frown that crinkled her brow. She did that when she was thinking hard.

Neither of them had spoken much on the journey to the village, each processing their narrow escape from death, but Bishop knew Maddy Carter would quickly deal with that and move on. She was nothing if not mission-focused. Sipping again at the tea, Bishop suddenly realised that, while his shoulder ached – it always would – he had not felt a hand tremor or experienced the dreaded head fog in the past days. But he felt ill almost all of the time, and he knew why. He had not touched the pill bottle since leaving Yangon, and the withdrawals were almost too much to bear. But, all in all, he felt better than he had in months. Perhaps it was the adrenaline, the thrill of action, that had eased his symptoms. Perhaps it was the decision, finally, that he no longer wanted to live with the drug.

'Let us return to this girl,' Swe said, leaning forward to poke a stick into the fire. She was flanked by her lieutenants, all of whom were quietly cleaning their weapons and sipping small glasses of rice wine. 'You are sure she has not just walked off, but has been taken... possibly because she saw, or heard, something she should not have. In Narhkan.'

Bishop nodded. 'Exactly.'

'And, in Narhkan, whatever she saw or heard had something to do with this NGO... I have heard of them, by the way. You believe she stumbled on something the CIA is doing using Global Horizons as a front.'

'Again, yes.'

Madeleine sat still, her head lowered, as she listened. While Bishop had been washing, she had made a satellite call to her handler and had passed on an update. Her handler had been blasé about her brush with death, and she had come away from the call none the wiser. She was thinking that through when she heard the reference to the CIA. 'What we do *not* know,' she interjected, 'is what that could be. Any ideas?'

'None.' Swe tapped her lips with a finger, then turned and spoke, in Shan, to her brother. She and Zaw spoke for a minute or two, occasionally shaking their heads and shrugging as they debated Madeleine's question. Finally, Swe spoke, a smile curling the corner of her lip.

'You're the analyst here, Mr Bishop. What do *you* think?'

'I'm only guessing, but it makes sense it's something targeting the junta. A destabilisation operation, maybe.' He paused. 'After all, the CIA do like a bit of "regime change".'

Swe nodded. 'Possibly. But why the need for the NGO subterfuge?'

'They need to move something around the country without attracting attention,' Madeleine said. 'Weapons? The CIA supports *you*, the PDF, don't they?'

Swe shook her head. 'Not really. On the edges, a little. Some intelligence and the like. But we are proud of our organic roots. We have built what we are by ourselves. Our weapons are all taken from Sit-Tat, and, now, we have quite advanced manufacturing facilities of our own.'

'The SSA then?' Bishop asked.

'Again, possibly, but I do not think so. The Shan State Army has the weapons, and then some, for their current needs. That is especially so given things between them and the army have been unusually quiet in Shan for some months now.'

'Could they be planning something?' Madeleine asked. 'The SSA, I mean. Something big for which they need a new force, that has to be armed and equipped...'

'I don't think so,' Swe said. 'They have their hands full with establishing a state here in Shan, and they have no inter-state territorial ambitions...' She suddenly stopped and turned to her brother. Again, they spoke for a minute or two before Swe returned to Bishop.

'There *have* been rumours they have been building a force in Loi Tai Leng – their main headquarters on the border – for a while now. Just rumours, and I don't know why.'

Madeleine looked up sharply. The satellite photo of Loi Tai Leng. Was that why it had been included?

'As I say,' Swe went on, 'they don't need additional troops in Shan – at least not at this time. Maybe they are just looking to the future... who knows? Besides, were the CIA to be arming them, would they not do it through Thailand?'

Bishop shook his head. 'Unlikely. Thailand maintains formal diplomatic ties with the junta, mostly adopting a position of non-interference in Burma's internal affairs. The Thai government, particularly under General Prayut, has stressed stability and pragmatism in its dealings with Burma – particularly on issues of mutual concern like border security and economic ties. The Thais would be unlikely to be running guns – or permitting anyone *else* to do it – across their border to Burmese ethnic armed groups.'

There was a long silence as everyone digested this and picked away at the problem. None of them had any answers. Bishop broke the silence as he remembered something and pulled out his notebook and map.

'Swe,' he said. 'Are you aware of a camp at...' he checked the grid reference in his notebook and quickly found it on the map. 'Here.' It was the site of the anomaly in the forest canopy that Maddy had spotted during their brief in Bangkok. Swe leaned in and studied the map.

'Yes, I know this. It is hardly a secret. It is the Shan State Army's main drug lab in the state – well, at least in the south. It is their primary manufacturing facility.'

Bishop's eyes widened. The SSA was the largest producer of heroin and block opium in Burma, itself Southeast Asia's largest exporter of the drug. Was that what Sophie had seen? Had she stumbled on an SSA drug run?

'The army has done nothing about it? Why?'

Swe snorted in amusement. 'Because General Min is taking a cut. They all are at some level... but Min's is the largest.'

Bishop glanced across at Maddy. 'Okay,' he said, a germ of an idea taking seed in his brain. 'A drug lab. That's interesting.'

Just then, a line of village women stepped out from under the house, bearing trays loaded with dishes of food and began handing them out to the group around the fire. The fragrant smells of the spiced food were enticing, and Bishop's stomach cramped painfully as he realised he had not eaten for over twelve hours. They were silent for a while, Bishop and Madeleine, Swe and her council, as they ate. The only sounds were the fire, the muted conversation of the women, and the laughter of their small children.

After a while, Madeleine lowered her plate onto her lap. 'Let's get back to the girl,' she said. 'To sum up: she was probably taken in Narhkan, and probably because of something she saw. That something could be to do with Global Horizons' front for a CIA op. Maybe weapons, but if so, what and for whom? Maybe something else, but, if that's the case, what and why was it so sensitive the girl had to disappear?'

'If it's not the Agency, and it's the SSA, it could be drugs,' Bishop said, around a mouthful of noodles. 'We have to get to Narhkan. We won't know anything until we can get eyes on it.' He glanced across at Madeleine. 'I'll call Terry tonight and set up the drop.'

Bishop looked at the young resistance leader. While he and Maddy had been doubly lucky at the bridge – getting away with their lives then falling in with the PDF – they no longer had a vehicle after Swe's men had pushed the Hilux into the destroyed army post and fired it. It was also increasingly clear he and Maddy could not pull off this operation alone.

'Can you help us?' he asked. 'I know it's a risk...'

Madeleine spoke up. '*And* we need anything you can discover about what is happening in Loi Tai Leng.'

Bishop shot her a look. He couldn't see what that had to do with Sophie's disappearance; it was a distraction, but he decided not to question it in front of their hosts. He would speak to Maddy as soon as he got her alone.

Swe looked at her brother who sat silently, staring at the fire.

'Helping you is no more of a risk than we run every day,' Swe said. 'However, we have our mission and our own troubles. We are hunted by the Sit-Tat, from the ground and from the air, every day. My country is under the heel of the junta, and I cannot risk my people, nor can I shy away from our task.'

Bishop nodded. 'I understand, Swe. We will make it on our own. My thanks for...'

'*However*,' Swe went on. 'We *are* talking about finding a young woman and returning her to the arms of her family. So, I will make inquiries on the border, *and* I will give you a vehicle with my very best man.' She nodded and stood, the fire lighting her eyes so they glowed like coals in the dark.

'We will help you.'

32

With its distinctive postmodern style and tiered, angular form, the "Ziggurat" resembles those ancient Mesopotamian structures, and it stands proudly, almost arrogantly, on the south bank of the Thames. Although it is a landmark on the London skyline, the building is more widely known as the headquarters of the UK's Secret Intelligence Service, MI6.

The large office on the ninth floor faced northwest across the river. Outside, the late afternoon was dimming in a hazy sky, and a weak London sun whispered a tepid light through the expansive glass window. The room was well-lit and perfectly silent, shielded from outside noise by the secure glass and the walls' soundproofing. The desk, a pale timber, flat-pack affair, was cluttered with secure tablets, a coffee mug and a pile of cybersecurity reports. Two men sat in the room in uncomfortable modernist, leather sling chairs. One of the men, the older of the two, shot the cuffs of his shirt and checked his watch. He leaned forward with difficulty in his chair, the paunch of his belly straining his crisp white shirt.

'Bloody near half four,' he said. 'I could use a drink. Join me?'

The other man stood and walked to the window. Silhouetted

there, Nigel Harris adjusted his glasses with an index finger and glanced down at the river. Below him, passenger ferries and cargo barges cut their way through the choppy waters. He angled his head slightly.

'Thank you, no. Perrier isn't my... what do our fresh-faced boys and girls call it? My "jam". I'll wait until I can have a real drink.'

He turned his head back to the window. Below and to his left, Vauxhall Bridge was jammed with traffic lined up behind a red double-decker bus that had slewed across the road and was stuck into the crumpled side of a plumber's van. Impatient drivers milled about on the roadway as emergency services struggled to make their way through the chaos.

'It's a bloody mess,' C said, nodding down at the bridge as he handed Harris a Waterford crystal tumbler. 'I keep a bottle of The Macallan stashed in the sideboard. Privilege of rank.'

Harris nodded and sipped at the whisky, delighting in the flavours of dried fruits, sherry and wood smoke. 'I should come up here more often...'

C was studying the bridge. A fire engine had made it through the traffic, and its crew was working on securing the tilting bus. In typical Londoner fashion, the delayed drivers and pedestrians stood around in groups, idly chatting and offering advice to anyone in authority unlucky enough to pass by.

'Up here?' he said, then turned to face Harris. 'Play your cards right, and this will all be yours soon... You *are* the Director of Operations and anointed one, after all.'

'C. Don't be bloody stupid. You're the best DG the service has had in living memory. You've grasped the nettle of modern spying, whereas I miss the old days and don't even use a tablet. I'm younger than you, C, but I'm the dinosaur in this evolutionary tale. You will be here for years. I'm sure I will have moved on to a trout farm in Scotland, with two Red Setters and a housekeeper, long before you retire.'

The older man shook his head. 'It may have slipped past you, Nigel, but I am no longer a young man and, besides, the new government... A new broom sweeps clean.'

'But an old one knows the corners...'

'True, but our new Foreign Secretary is no friend of mine nor of the Service. When I first joined, he would not have passed vetting for his party's preselection, let alone now be our political master.' He sighed and shrugged, sipping from the glass in his hand. 'And the new PM... Well.'

Harris nodded and swallowed a mouthful of whisky. The new government was a mess, and he was sure both the Prime Minister and the Foreign Secretary would not last the term. The country reflected the government leading it, and it, too, was a bloody shambles. He sighed. Was it really worth it anymore?

'Well, let us hope you do not leave us anytime soon. We have work to do... I assume that *is* why you have invited me up.'

The Director General of MI6 turned away from the window. Behind him, the last vestiges of wan sunlight faded out, and street-lights flickered on. On the river, the five illuminated arches of Vaux-hall Bridge lit the dark waters. Watercraft navigation and decorative lights glinting in the dark gave the ancient Thames a festive air. C gestured back to the chairs, and the two men moved across the room and sat. The DG sighed as he leaned back in the leather.

'So, what is your girl saying?'

Harris chuckled. 'She would not like to hear you call her that.'

C nodded and picked at the frown on his forehead. 'I've read her military record, of course, and the two reviews she has had since joining us, but tell me more about her. Who is she? What drives her?'

Harris leaned back in the chair and crossed his legs. 'I can have her psych assessments sent up if you wish...'

'No need. Give me the Nigel Harris version.'

'Well, let me see.' Harris pulled at an ear lobe. 'She's pretty wild. Not erratic and certainly not unstable, just a little... wild. She reminds me of one of the Lost Boys in Peter Pan.'

C chuckled, and Harris went on.

'As you know, she's the only child of Major General Neville Carter. She grew up in quite an irregular household. No mother, home-schooled in the early years, father often away and she was raised, mostly, by Carter's gamekeeper. That independence of spirit has only grown over the years, so she can be hard to handle, but she's one of the very best agents I have ever had...'

'Should we take her on permanently? Make an honest woman of her...?'

'I don't think so, and she would probably refuse us if we asked. She likes the freedom offered a contractor, and we most *certainly* prefer to use her skills from a comfortably deniable distance.'

C nodded. 'Okay. So, steady and reliable, if a little fiery... sounds like my wife.'

Harris sniffed. 'Madeleine Carter has the skills and the righteous certainty to use them. That makes her an extremely valuable agent. But she's *no one's* wife. I shudder at the thought...'

C swallowed his whisky and moved to a small cabinet set in the office wall to pour another shot. He waved the bottle at Harris, who shook his head.

'So, what is she telling us?' C asked. 'Has she found anything to confirm our fears?'

'Yes and no. The NGO that the missing girl worked for is almost certainly a CIA front, and the girl has vanished as a result of stumbling on something. What that is, we do not, as yet, know. But it suggests the Cousins are up to no good in Burma, and *that* suggests that the fragments we have heard may have substance.'

'Nigel, a phoney NGO providing operational cover is far from what we fear might be in the winds...'

'I agree, but then there is this: Carter and this chap, Bishop, were both taken at an army roadblock and barely escaped execution. It is clear there was a connection between what the two of them have found so far and their targeted apprehension by the army. It's hard not to conclude our cousins were behind it.'

'What now? What have you told Carter? Surely not everything...'

'No, she has been given the bare minimum.' Harris paused as he sipped the whisky. 'Mind you, there *is* one other who knows about all of this.'

C pursed his lips. It was a curiously prissy expression. 'Yes. I spoke to the rebellious bastard only recently. He is not much changed.' C waved a hand. 'Back to young Carter. What does she *think* she's doing?'

Harris studied the fine-cut crystal glass, watching the amber body of the whisky shimmer in the light. 'She has been tasked with sniffing about at this point, but she's no fool. *If* they exist, she will quickly start putting the pieces together. She did pass us the rumour of a troop build-up by an EAG in the south, which is still very much that. A rumour. But if she *confirms* that, well...'

'We would have a corner piece of the jigsaw puzzle. Mind you, it's hard to build the puzzle when we don't have the box lid to tell us what the picture looks like.'

Harris swirled the remnants of the whisky around in his glass. It was dark outside and, from where they sat, the two men could make out the skyglow thrown up by the great metropolis. Not for the first time, Harris pondered the sliding doors in life, the twists of fate, that saw him sitting high above the city deliberating on vital secrets and dangerous operations, while the vast majority of London's nearly ten million citizens slogged away below, oblivious. Harris sometimes longed for oblivion.

'Have you given any more thought to requesting the additional resource?'

C shook his head. 'I'm hesitant to do so at this point. It will mean either bringing the Foreign Secretary and Defence Secretary into the tent, or lying to them...'

'We have *both* done that before...'

'True. But not this time. If we are right, there will be too much at stake. No, we will have to gather the evidence and brief them before getting approval to deploy the Reaper and any subsequent action. I'm quite sure we will get Delhi across the line, but we need something actionable for any of this to work. Have your girl sniff about more.'

Harris sighed. 'C, I do wish you would stop calling her that.'

33

As Bishop and Madeleine waited in the long grass, the first faint flush of dawn had yet to smear the night sky over the hills. It was dark, still, and quiet.

The clearing at the end of the dirt track was the right size, flat, and obstacle-free. Bishop had positioned an IR strobe on the upwind side and marked the clearing's boundaries with a series of green cyalume chem-lights. Two strips of white linen tied to a bamboo stake beside the strobe completed the preparations. The Landing Zone was ready.

Bishop raised his head and looked over his right shoulder. The battered old, dark-green Land Rover Series 3 was well hidden in the scrub, with Zaw behind the wheel, ready to power it out into the open the instant Bishop gave the signal. He lowered his head and checked his G-Shock. Three minutes if Terry was on schedule. Maddy was lying next to him, a small set of binoculars to her eyes, scanning back down the dirt track toward the main road. He tapped her shoulder.

'Why Loi Tai Leng?' he whispered. 'I mean, I get that satellite photo anomaly in the forest. Now we know it's a drug lab – but why some remote hill town on the border?' With the mention of the drug lab, Bishop's mind flicked again to the idea he had been developing.

Madeleine lowered the binoculars and turned her head.

'I don't know,' she murmured. 'But something tells me Loi Tai Leng ties into all of this.' *Something tells me it's what The Masters want to know*, she thought, although she wondered, yet again, why they had played their information requirements so close to their chest. 'A possible troop concentration on the Burma-Thai border? That's of interest...'

Bishop watched an ant brush his fingertips, bravely struggling a twig across the dry ground. 'Not to me, it's not. It's a distraction. Our job is here.'

Madeleine shrugged. 'It can't hurt to know what's going on there.'

'I don't see why, but okay. Just so long as...'

Maddy held up a hand. 'Shhh,' she hissed. 'Listen...'

Bishop tilted his head and cupped his ears. Sure enough, the familiar throb of a "Huey" drifted faintly to him through the dark. He checked his watch. 'Right on time,' he murmured. 'Get ready.'

The rising sun began to tint the sky a soft red as the night sounds slowly faded. The morning chorus of forest birds began, hesitant at first, then bursting into full-throated song as the new day heralded its coming. With it came the chopper. Flying low and slow on its finals into the LZ, it looked like a fat dragonfly skimming the surface of a grass pond. It slewed slightly to port as Tak made a final adjustment for the gentle breeze, then nosed into the LZ. With a flare, the chopper's skids contacted the earth and the aircraft was down.

Bishop waved at Zaw and heard the Land Rover start up as he and Madeleine rose to their feet and ran, bent low under the Huey's rotors. Tak sat in the left pilot's seat, his face obscured by the black visor of his helmet. He had kept the chopper's engine at full throttle and the aircraft was shuddering on the ground. Terry Dougherty was kneeling in the cabin, the doors open, throwing laden sandbags onto the ground. Dougherty grinned widely as the two ran up.

'*Fuck me*,' he shouted over the roar of the turboshaft engine. 'How much fun is this?'

Bishop slapped him on the shoulder. 'Is everything there?' he shouted back. Madeleine was grabbing the sandbags and hefting them back to the edge of the LZ, where Zaw was flinging them into the Land Rover's tub.

'All there, mate,' Dougherty bellowed. 'Everything you asked for. I bagged it up so you can throw it straight into your rucks. The bags with the red ties are your rations... a week's worth with heat bags for each.'

Bishop nodded. The heat bags were a good idea. Where they were going, fires, even small hexamine stoves, would be out of the question, so flameless ration heaters were the go. He leaned into Dougherty and pulled aside the headset, shouting in his ear. 'I'll be in touch. Stick to the comms schedule. If we get lucky, we could be ready for extraction in a few days.'

Dougherty gave a thumbs-up and toggled the mic on his headset. Bishop ducked away and sprinted across the LZ to the Land Rover. Zaw and Madeleine ran around the small LZ, retrieving the strobe, wind indicator, and chem-lights.

With practised ease, Tak gently coaxed the aircraft from the ground, the machine trembling slightly as it lifted into a hover. He pivoted the Huey on its axis in a deft manoeuvre, the tail swinging around elegantly until it faced the opposite direction. Then, dipping the nose forward, he accelerated swiftly. With a blur of motion, the engine's roar and thwop of the blades, the chopper skimmed low over the terrain, hurtling back the way it had come. Ninety seconds later, the aircraft was out of sight in the glowing red ball of the sun that had risen above the hills.

34

Major General Min Kyaw Ko walked to his office window, adjusted his uniform jacket, and looked across the division's parade ground. Below him, the scene was a hive of activity as his regiments prepared for their departure in the coming days.

Row upon row of dark green Nissan troop trucks and trailers lined the square, with mountains of stores and equipment piled next to each. Soldiers swarmed the area, carrying storage trunks, weapons crates and ammunition boxes. Behind the troop trucks, squads of soldiers lined up, each man with his ceremonial uniform in a bag that he would hang from the canopy frame inside. In long ranks on the far side of the square, and across the playing fields further beyond, sat the Type 85 and Type 90 Armoured Personnel Carriers. Mortars, field guns, howitzers, multiple rocket launcher systems, short-range air defence systems, radar units and unmanned aerial vehicles – all of it was lined up, being carefully inspected and prepared to move.

Min watched idly as a young soldier dropped a box of ball ammunition on his foot and, hopping around on one leg, received a kick in the arse from an irate NCO. They were young and had been rushed through training to fill the gaps left by recent losses, but they were ready. They were prepared for the task ahead, and General Min felt a thrill of anticipation shiver through him at the thought of what was to come.

More importantly, his officers were ready. Except for a handful of recently graduated Lieutenants, his officers were experienced, battle-hardened and capable. Above all, they were loyal. They were his men first and Tatmadaw soldiers second. He knew he could rely on them all to do their duty. Their duty to him. At the top of that tree of fealty sat his Second-in-Command, Brigadier Myat Nay Win. They had been together for many years, and Min placed absolute faith in Win's unquestioning loyalty. He was reliable and steadfast in his devotion to Min – the man had been tested repeatedly and had always proven solid. Being married to Min's eldest daughter since 2021 only helped to strengthen that bond. Min nodded to himself. He would be busy in the coming weeks, but he knew Win would conduct the operation well, ensuring it all went according to plan. Yes, they were ready.

Min moved back to his desk, loosened his jacket and sat, reaching for a packet of cigarettes and a gold lighter. Leaning back in the chair, he lit a smoke and closed his eyes. The recent phone call with the American had been... displeasing. Two foreigners – spies of some sort? – had entered the country and slipped through their fingers. They were looking for that damned girl.

Min grunted and drew on the cigarette. The girl did not bother him. Whatever she saw in that rathole township was of no conse-quence to him; it would not affect what he had set in train – things were too advanced to stop now. If what she had witnessed got out, it *might* affect his Dubai bank balance each month, and that was disap-pointing, but, with what was to come, that loss of income would be a drop in the ocean.

What bothered him more was those cockroaches in the PDF had murdered six of his men. He would make that ah-kway-ma, *bitch*, and her bandit gang, pay for that. It would be a welcome bonus if he netted the two spies into the bargain. To that end, he had ordered the deployment of an additional light infantry battalion and supporting assets into Southern Shan. They were to avoid contact with the SSA at all costs, but they were to burn every village and tear apart every town in search of the PDF. They were to use every means at their disposal, and they were not to hold back. He had been most clear on that point.

Min crossed the room and poured a Chinese whisky from a decanter on the office sideboard. He sipped the liquor and chased it with a drag on the cigarette as he looked at a large map on the wall. The map was pinned to a corkboard and marked with military symbols and written references from the Operational Order. He carefully traced a finger along the Blue Route through Naypyidaw's main thoroughfares, past the saluting dais and onward to the grand parade ground near the Presidential Palace.

After much lobbying at the War Office, Min had secured the prime positions for his regiments. They would lead and tail the parade, with other regiments interspersed throughout the Order of March. His regiments would be prominent to the generals of the State Administration Council. It was a great honour and it would send an unmistakable message. This year's parade would be truly memorable for him, his men, and the people of Myanmar.

Min looked back across the parade ground and the frantic preparations below him. Armed Forces Day, and the parade through the capital, was twelve days away. His advance guard would depart in two days. General Min had read Ancient History in his youth and knew this was his Rubicon. From the moment their wheels and tracks began to turn, there would be no going back.

35

NARHKAN TOWNSHIP, *Shan State, Burma*

The house had been abandoned for years. What had once been home to a large family, a place of grandeur and luxury, now stood broken and dark – foreboding. Its windows were shattered, and much of the tiled roof had caved in. The desiccated bones of a long-dead animal lay scattered on the front steps, barring entry to the lopsided and weathered front door.

The house was said to be haunted, and the people of Narhkan avoided it. Rumours had been flying around town recently of unearthly howls and screams heard from the old house, and everyone gave it a wide berth.

Mya stopped in the shadows of the small copse of trees and eased her old knees into a squat. The field was washed brightly by a full moon, which hung like an enormous celestial pendant light in the clear night sky. She could see the back of the house and, just beyond it, the old tin shack on the edge of the creek line.

Her eyes caught a sudden movement, and she heard a muted cough. Mya froze in place as she watched a man stand on the front verandah, step over his sleeping comrades, unzip his pants, and piss over the edge. The man was armed, and she was sure, even with her old eyes, that he was one of the gang of thugs who took Ma Sopee.

It had all been such a chaotic time. She still did not quite remember how she moved into the middle of the struggle, scooped up what had dropped from Ma Sopee's pocket, and then darted away to safety. She *did* remember hearing the gunshot and crouching against the side of the shop wall, terrified, her breathing coming in rapid pants.

That was eleven days ago, and it had taken her that long to pace the town methodically, working out just how far the men, dragging a screaming young girl, could have gone that night. No one paid the withered old lady any attention as she shuffled around the town – most thought she was losing her mind anyway. She had moved freely, without challenge, at one stage being given a lift from the highway back along the dusty road into Narhkan by two Shan State Army soldiers.

Now, she was sure she had found it. She settled deeper into the squat, her hands resting lightly on her knees, and waited.

The large copse of trees sat on a bend in the track, just east of Narhkan. It was thick and overgrown, and the small access track had long ago been barricaded with concrete-filled steel drums. No houses were near it, and the track past it was more of a footpad that had last seen traffic a week or more before. It was a perfect hide from which they could observe the river-flat land in and around Narhkan.

After taking the drop, the trio had raced up the highway from the LZ to the township. Zaw had driven slowly around the town, his right arm hanging casually from the open driver's window, while Bishop and Madeleine had lain hidden with their gear in the covered tub of the Land Rover. Finding the copse they had map reconnoitred the night before, Zaw had backed in, and Bishop and Madeleine had slithered out into the undergrowth, dragging their heavy rucksacks after them. Zaw had driven off to check in to a tea room beside the highway, just another traveller on a long journey.

Now, Madeleine and Bishop sat in the dark, sheltered by the hide, eating from MRE rations warmed through in heat bags. Bishop was scraping the bottom of his ration pouch for the last of the beef stew when Madeleine spoke.

'Are you okay?' she asked, her voice low.

Bishop looked up, the plastic fork paused at his mouth. 'Me? Yeah. Why?'

'You were using in Yangon...' she whispered. She held up a hand as Bishop began to reply. 'No, don't interrupt and don't lie to me. I know the signs. But I've noticed you haven't been for the last few days, and I've just figured out your comment yesterday about smoking. So... how are you feeling?'

Bishop dropped the fork into the empty ration pouch and scrunched the rubbish, dropping it into the hessian bag and stuffing it deep into his ruck. He had not been feeling well for days, but he had hoped to have kept it hidden from Maddy. He sighed. Time to level up.

'Madds,' he said quietly. 'I'm an addict – but you already know that – and I'm in withdrawals. I feel like shit. I'm not sleeping. I feel anxious all the time, my gut aches, my muscles throb, and the shoulder is killing me.'

'The brain fog?'

'Weirdly, that seems to have lifted. I feel like I'm thinking more clearly, but the cravings are a beast.' He shrugged. 'It's bloody hard, and I don't know if I can do it.'

Madeleine smiled and leaned forward to place a hand on Bishop's knee. This was the worst possible time for him to try and kick the habit – or was it? She felt sure she knew why he was doing it. He was putting himself through this, and handling it stoically, for the mission – and maybe also for her. The thought that she was betraying his trust ate at her.

'Have you still got the Oxy?' she whispered.

Bishop nodded. 'I do. But I'm saving it for when I might really need them – not because I *want* them. I'm worried my symptoms could return at any time.' He rubbed his eyes. 'To be honest, Maddy, I'm scared. I'm in constant pain, and my head isn't right – it hasn't been since that fucking RPG. I don't know if or when it will finally kill me.'

Madeleine leaned in close and kissed Bishop's cheek. 'You're doing well, and I'm proud of you. Now you've finally 'fessed up, we can deal with this together.'

Bishop broke a lopsided grin and scratched his cheek. 'What about your Italian stallion?'

'Well, he *is* better looking than you.' Maddy said, spooning some chicken chunks into her mouth. 'And richer. But you? You're more... me. You know?'

The two sat looking at each other, not wanting to break the moment. Each was acutely aware of something happening, but both knew now was not the time for whatever that was. Finally, Bishop broke eye contact and pulled his rucksack to his side.

'Twelve days since her last message to her family,' he said. 'So, maybe, eleven days since she disappeared.' He pinched the bridge of his nose. 'We don't even know she's here – she could be anywhere. If she's even still alive...'

'This was always the place to start...'

'My gut tells me she *is* here but I'm worried. What if she is back in Taunggyi? I mean that guy with her credit card...They could have stashed her there.'

Madeleine thought about that for a moment. 'If she *is* still alive, they will have her here or nearby. They wouldn't run the risk of taking her to the city. Too many eyes.'

Bishop nodded. 'I hope you're right,' he said, grabbing his rucksack. 'I need to send a SITREP to Nesbitt. He'll be champing at the bit, wondering what's happening. While I'm doing that, you get your bird up and see what you can see.'

Madeleine nodded, and they set to work.

Bishop crouched deep in the copse of trees, the moon-sketched shadows blending with the surrounding undergrowth. His breathing was steady and controlled as he unzipped his ruck, careful not to disturb the silence. The Inmarsat Explorer 510 emerged first, its rugged form catching a glint of moonlight. Next came the laptop and his cable bag. He scanned the area once more then, satisfied, began his setup.

With practised precision, he positioned the Inmarsat unit on the ground, adjusting the antenna to align with the satellite he knew would be overhead. The device hummed to life, a faint LED glow winking in the dark. He worked swiftly, connecting the satellite terminal to his laptop, fingers moving deftly over the keyboard as he booted up the secure communication software.

He waited, tension easing slightly as the connection stabilised and the comms interface appeared on the screen. He quickly drafted his situation report, detailing the previous day's movements, actions, and observations and finishing with an assessment of risk and future intentions. The words came easily, honed by years of similar reports, each sentence conveying the critical information Nesbitt and the firm would need.

The report finished, Bishop encrypted the message and initiated the upload. Seconds ticked by as the data was transmitted across the globe. He watched the progress bar, aware of every rustle in the trees, every distant sound. When the transmission was completed, he shut down the devices and packed them in his rucksack.

Maddy was on first stag, so he lay back, crossed his arms on his chest and was soon asleep.

36

THEY ARE IN THE UTE. His mum sits next to him, his baby sister in her lap, as he speeds out of town heading west. The driver's window is rolled down. Furnace-hot air blasts in, and the roar of rough road on rubber thumps at them. The boy takes his eyes off the ribbon of hot, grey asphalt and glances at the baby. She is asleep, her tiny hands balled in fists. Yeah, you'll need that. This life is shit. You'll need to fight just to get on. His mum looks out the window as the dry plains, parched and whitened by the harsh Queensland sun, speed by. A road sign. Toowoomba 60. I think I killed the bastard, he says. His mum doesn't answer. His hands grip the hot steering wheel. There is blood under his fingernails. If I didn't, I'll go back and finish the job, he says.

The inside of the big old timber Queenslander is cool and clean. A giant Poinciana spreads over the verandah. There are birds in the tree, and the front lawn is thick and green. There are women and little children everywhere. The boy is puzzled. The women are smiling, and the kids are playing happily. They are safe here, the big red-headed woman says, smoothing her crisp, white apron as she takes his sister from Mum's arms. Where will you go? The boy doesn't know. Far away. He kisses his sister on the forehead and pats her silky blonde hair. Mum hugs him. It is a fierce, desperate embrace. She kisses his cheek and smooths away a tear with her thumb. I'll be seeing you, she says.

The horse shies at the nip of the big fly on his neck, and the boy tightens the reins and grips his legs against the saddle. The herd of Brahman spread out before him across the red expanse of Nockatunga Station, lowing quietly as they graze the rough desert grasses among the stunted gidyah. The boy pushes back his hat and wipes his brow. The sun is brutal out here, two hours west of Thargomindah. He rolls and lights a cigarette and crosses his hands on the pommel of the saddle. He watches as a white Landcruiser drives up the bulldust of the track. Lights on the roof, blue and white checks down the side. The big Sergeant is beside the horse, and he looks up. You took some finding, son... Whyja wanna find me?... There's a warrant out for you; you nearly killed your old man... I wish I had... Fact is, he's in Boggo Road now for what he did... What he do?... Aside from beating up your mum, he knocked over the TAB in Miles. The boy drags on his smoke and spits. The big copper sucks his teeth. Yeah, well, there's been a computer glitch, and somehow that warrant has been wiped. Just thought you should know. The big copper smiles. Funny how I thought I seen you but I must have got it wrong. The boy nods silently. He looks around. The horizon looks far away today. Get a fresh start, the copper is saying. When you're old enough, get away and do something for yourself. Join the army; you'll do well there. The boy nods and kicks the horse into a canter, riding toward the sun and the lengthening shadows.

NARHKAN TOWNSHIP, Shan State, Burma

While Bishop slept, Madeleine had scanned the township and surrounding fields with the HISS-XLR thermal weapon sight. The world was an eerie grayscale mosaic of heat signatures and shadows. The moonlight washed over the area, casting a silvery glow on the terrain, but the weapon sight revealed far more. Trees and tall grass appeared as dark, jagged silhouettes, while the ground radiated a subtle warmth, showing as a pale grey expanse. Scattered rocks and boulders, retaining heat from the day, pulsed in varying shades of white. The occasional animal, a small rodent or bird, darted across the scene, leaving streaks of bright white as their body heat flared momentarily before disappearing into the brush. Beyond the town, a ridgeline cut across the horizon, a cold, dark line against the warmer sky.

She needed to see beyond her line of sight, so she began preparing the drone for action. She drew the Pelican Case from her ruck and opened it. Carefully, she took out the Black Hornet Nano PD-100, and snapped the lithium-polymer battery into the back of the unit.

Madeleine took a moment to study the object in her hand.

Resembling a tiny helicopter with a compact, streamlined body and two counter-rotating rotors, the Nano was a small and lightweight micro-drone developed for special operations, ideal for real-time reconnaissance without exposing the operator. Dark in colour to blend in with its surroundings and minimise its visual signature, the drone's nose housed a tiny camera system, including both optical and thermal imaging sensors. Weighing in at just eighteen grams, the Black Hornet was about the size of a giant insect – Madeleine thought it looked like a Hercules Beetle – making it easy to conceal and deploy in the field. Best of all, it flew in near silence.

She powered up the unit and switched on its controller before performing a pre-flight check on the drone. Rotors clear, no airframe damage, camera lens clean. Glancing up, she noted a break in the canopy, moonlight streaming in to light the legs of Bishop's sleeping figure. Moving quietly, she positioned the drone and pressed a small button on the controller. The Nano's rotors spun, and, with a faint hiss, it lifted from the ground and through the trees, where it stabilised and hovered forty feet above her. With a gentle push of the controller's joystick, Madeleine set the micro-drone off on its mission over Narhkan.

Mya did not wear a watch – she never had – but the moon's position in the night sky told her it was early morning. Perhaps around 2:00 a.m. She slowly eased herself to her feet, feeling the circulation rush warm back into her legs. She peered into the darkness. There was no movement in the house, and it was quiet but for the snores of armed and brutal men on the verandah.

Stepping carefully, she edged her way through the treeline to the back of the house. The tin shack sat rusted and dark only metres from her, the last gloss of the sinking moon burnishing its roof. She had taken three steps toward it when she heard a sound. Mya froze and held her breath. There it was again! A sob. Muffled, as if someone was covering their face with their hands.

Mya moved forward, stalking cat-like on her bare feet. The snores from the house continued unchecked.

Reaching the shack, the old woman edged up to its rear wall and squatted, leaning one ear against the warm tin. She could hear the sound clearly now. A woman was crying and muttering to herself. Mya took a deep breath and scratched the tin wall with a fingernail. Be soft, be a mouse, she told herself. The sobbing stopped, and she scratched again, then heard a shuffling from inside. She listened. Silence. Whoever was in there was crouched in the dark, listening too. Waiting.

'Ma Sopee,' Mya whispered. 'Is it you? It is me, Mya.'

She held her breath and shut her eyes, willing her spirit through the wall, commanding the silence to break. *Speak to me...*

'Mya?' A soft voice, weak and disbelieving.

The old woman smiled. She had found her! But her joy was short-lived. She could not get her out. Even if she could force her way into the shack, where would she go? Where would she take this battered and frightened young thing? Who would help her?

'Ma Sopee. Listen. You no alone. Mya is here. Must go think... but come back. Be courage...'

'Mya don't leave me,' Sophie Bouchard pleaded from inside her prison, her whisper insistent and her voice cracking. 'Please, I beg you. Get me out!'

The old woman hung her head. 'Quiet. I come back,' she said, then stood and flitted like a wraith back through the shadows into the treeline and away from the old house.

The controller's screen lit Madeleine's face as she watched the drone's progress. The township was silent. No one moved.

The first thing she had done was send the drone to the highway and work back towards the town, flying over the old sports field. It was empty. The Global Horizons trucks were gone, as were the tents and piles of stores, but the dirt road was streaked with wide tyre tracks. She quickly checked her notebook and adjusted the drone's flight path to head northeast to the project site. Pushing forward on the throttle, she accelerated the silent watcher, and, in moments, it hovered over the Global Horizons project site. That, too, was abandoned. The only signs anything had ever been there were a series of rutted tyre tracks in the dirt, some piping, and a broken wooden pallet.

Madeleine tapped the side of the controller while she thought. It added up. They were sure Global Horizons was a front, and *if* it had been involved in some way in the girl's disappearance, it figured they would pull out, likely crafting an excuse pointing to project delays or changes in priorities. She checked her watch. 0205. It looked like a bust, so she decided to bring the drone back, download the footage, and close up for the night.

As the Black Hornet spun around and headed for home, Madeleine caught sight of a lone figure, small and bent, hurrying away from the back of a darkened house. The figure's thermal signature was clear, as were the three prone figures on the verandah of the house. She spun the drone back for another pass. Her mind was racing, and she wanted to stay on station, but a quick check of the controller told her she needed to bring the unit in for a battery change. The drone was passing over the main street, on its way back, when a line of large vehicles entered the township and pulled up.

She stared at the screen. Five trucks, all in Global Horizons livery, had stopped in the centre of town, and the street was suddenly alive with armed men disembarking and unloading.

She leaned across and slapped a boot. Bishop was awake in an instant.

'What have you got?'

'Trouble,' Madeleine said. 'We've got company.'

38

THE BLACK HORNET returned to the gap in the canopy and slowly lowered itself to land in Madeleine's outstretched hand. She placed the drone on its case and snapped on a fresh battery as Bishop rubbed dirt into his face.

'I'm going to take a closer look,' Bishop said fitting a Thales compact tactical radio to his belt, connecting it wirelessly to an in-ear piece and throat mic. 'We need to know what's in those trucks.'

Madeleine nodded, fitting her own earpiece and mic as she quickly prepared the drone for its next flight. 'The last pass showed no sign of Global Horizons,' she said. 'They've gone, so I'll bet my fat bonus those trucks aren't carrying aid.'

Bishop tapped the throat mic. 'I'll set this to full duplex mode so it's on open mic... Have you got me?'

'Loud and clear.'

Bishop took a deep breath and checked his G-Shock. 'Okay. Get the bird back up, I'll need your eyes. Wish me luck.' With that, he stepped out of the trees and into the field, bent low and moving fast.

Narhkan had few streetlights, and the trucks were parked under the few there were. That was good. Bishop knew the men unloading the trucks would all have their night vision destroyed, which worked to his advantage. The township was darker as the moon began to set, and he stuck to the shadows, hugging the walls of houses and alley-ways, moving stealthily. He knew he was on the clock. Dawn was only two hours away.

'I need some directions, Madds,' he whispered.

Madeleine responded instantly. 'The bird's up, and I've got you. Keep going the way you are, and take the next left. A small alley. You're all clear.'

Bishop peered into the dark, turning his head slightly to engage his more powerful peripheral vision. He could make out the turn in the alley, and he stalked forward, straining his ears for any sound ahead. Over the rooftops, he could hear the voices of the men unloading the trucks, and the banging of crates.

'Can you ID where they store their load?' he said quietly. 'I'll have a better chance of getting into a storeroom than into the back of one of those trucks.'

'Standby.' Madeleine was back thirty seconds later. 'There are a series of lockups on the main street, just west of the little market. They are unloading into those. You won't get close... Wait!'

There was another, longer pause as Madeleine guided the nano drone over the rooftops of the main street and into the nearby side alleys. Bishop watched the seconds tick by on the G-Shock. *Come on!* Then Madeleine's voice, calm and low.

'There is a smaller overflow storage shed in an alley. No roller door, just a single wooden door that's been left ajar. I think they may be done with it and have moved on.'

'Steer me there.'

'Take the next right. A small alley. Don't miss it, or you'll be in the street. Move down twenty-five metres and turn left. The shed is on the left, about five metres in. No enemy in front of you – they've finished unloading and are hanging about the trucks. Looks like they're waiting for someone.'

Bishop acknowledged and moved off.

Seventy-five seconds later, he stood at the final turn and edged his head around. The alley was clear so, taking a deep breath, he rounded the corner and moved down, running his hand along the wall. Seconds later, he felt the open door and pushed on it. He stepped in, closing the door behind him and snapped on his small Surefire G2 torch.

'Holy Christ,' he muttered, the torchlight playing around the room.

'What?' Madeleine's voice urgent in his ear. 'I saw you enter the shed. What's wrong?'

'Weapons, Maddy. It's weapons. And if this small lock up is any indication, thousands of them.'

Bishop crouched by the nearest olive-drab storage box, flipped open the locking levers and raised the lid. Nestled inside foam inserts, separated by metal dividers, were new, lightly oiled M16A2 assault rifles. Side compartments of the box held loaded magazines and cleaning kits. Bishop moved to the next box and flipped up the lid. M4A1 carbines and more loaded magazines.

Smaller wooden crates were stacked high along two walls. Bishop saw they were stencilled with "5.56mm Ball M855" and quantity and lot numbers. He counted the boxes and did a quick calculation: ninety thousand rounds of ammunition.

Bishop moved the torch beam around the room. There were boxes of M67 Fragmentation Grenades and crates of M72 Light Anti-Armor Weapons. The men outside had stored enough weapons in just one small shed to equip a rifle company, and then some.

'Maddy,' he whispered. 'Weapons and ammo. It's all US manufacture, most of it in-service kit – tons of the stuff. Get some close-ups of the goons outside. They have to be SSA...'

Before Madeleine could answer, the door to the storage shed creaked open. Bishop spun around, the Surefire pointing into the surprised face of an armed man. Bishop moved fast. Before the man could recover, he yanked him into the room by his shirt collar, kicked the door closed, and lashed out with a headbutt that caught the man across the bridge of his nose.

The man sagged but quickly began to rise, his mouth wide to shout a warning. Bishop clamped a hand over the soldier's mouth and spun him around to position himself behind the struggling figure. The Surefire dropped to the ground, and the shed was plunged into darkness. Bishop wrapped an arm around his opponent's neck, locking it tightly in a chokehold. He grabbed the man's chin with his other hand, forcing the head sharply to the side and simultaneously jerked it upwards in one fluid motion. The savage movement snapped the soldier's vertebrae, severing the spinal cord, and the man crumpled silently to the ground.

'*Bishop!* What's going on?'

'Can't talk now. There's a dead guy in here with me... Give me two minutes, and I'll be heading back. Give me the all clear.'

Bishop fumbled around on the floor until his fingers brushed the small torch. He snatched it up and flicked it on. With the small torch between his teeth, he worked quickly but smoothly in the darkened shed. He pulled two M4 carbines from their crate, grabbed up a single-point sling each, fitted them, and slung one of the weapons over his back. He stuffed two grenades and eight magazines into his pants and shirt, fitting a ninth magazine into the housing of the carbine in his hands before pulling back on the cocking handle and slapping the bolt assist.

Madeleine's voice. 'You're clear. Move now.'

Bishop eased the door open and darted out into the alley, sprinting away from the storage shed and back along the route in. He knew Maddy was covering him, so he could afford the speed and the noise. He was about to turn a corner when Madeleine's voice sounded urgently in his ear.

'Figure right in front of you! Don't...'

It was too late; Bishop rounded the corner and ran straight into a little old woman who bounced backwards and fell at his feet.

39

As Bishop stood over the old woman, a white Toyota Landcruiser pulled up on the main street behind the last truck. The driver's door opened, and a man stepped out onto the road. He was dressed in faded tactical pants, scuffed boots, and a long-sleeved shirt, its sleeves rolled above the elbows. A tattered blue Chicago Cubs cap was pushed back on his head, and a Glock was holstered at his right hip. Staring at the line of trucks and groups of men milling about in the streetlights, he spat on the ground at his feet.

'Goddamn it,' he muttered before stalking off along the line of trucks. The small groups of armed men parted before him, their eyes averted. 'Aung Min!' He shouted. 'Where the fuck is Aung?'

A small man in jeans, T-shirt and running shoes stepped forward, flicking away a cigarette. 'Here, koh. Aung is here.'

The American pulled the ball cap off his head and rubbed a hand through his blonde hair. 'Dammit, Aung,' he said. 'Get these trucks outta here! The pickup convoy from the south is arriving any minute – they are just behind me.' He looked around. 'Is everything unpacked and ready to be cross-shipped?'

Aung nodded. 'Yes, koh. It is all unloaded and accounted for...'

'Good. Load the men up and get going.' The American pulled his phone from his pocket and began to tap a message into the secure app. He glanced up. 'Why are you still here, Aung? *Move!*'

Aung nodded and spun away, shouting to the men who quickly butted out cigarettes and clambered onto the trucks that roared to life, choking the street in clouds of blue and black exhaust. He turned back to his phone.

I'm here. Quicker than expected. Shipment will transit soon and be on the way. ETA 20 hrs. Where are you?

He waited for a minute then the reply message from Reilly pinged in.

They're in the township! The two mercs... just heard

WTF!! Here?? how do you know

I just do! Kill the girl and flush them out! I'm still about three hours away

Roger. I'll deal with the girl. We'll find them. I'll be waiting on the main road as you drive in

He looked up and ran to the first truck, banging on the side of the passenger door. The window wound down, and Aung poked his head out.

'Leave six men with me, Aung. The two we're looking for are here.' He looked up the street. 'Have them start a sweep from the east and work towards the highway. I want them alive, but kill 'em if you have to.'

Aung nodded and clambered down from the truck, shouting orders. Six men spilled from the rear of the truck, cocking their rifles, and ran off into the dark.

The man looked around quickly to get his bearings, and then jogged through the township toward the old house.

Bishop bent down, extending a hand to the old woman at his feet. 'Khao taw, mae phaw,' he said as he pulled her up, offering his apologies. The old woman shivered and stared at him with wide eyes. Bishop had to move, but first he needed to calm the old girl so she didn't shout a warning. He held up a hand and smiled. 'Mai sa baw?

Mya nodded, taking a step back. She was okay. She stared at the big man. He was taung kyi, a foreigner, but he did not sound like the others, and she had not seen him before. Unlike the others, he spoke Shan – terribly, but at least he tried. His eyes were hard, not matching the smile on his face. The weapon in his hand was relaxed and deliberately pointing away from her. He had come from the direction of the trucks, but instinct told her he did not belong to them. Was he the one she needed? Mya felt she had no choice, so decided to trust him.

She reached into her blouse and pulled out the mobile phone that she thrust into Bishop's hands. 'Ma lao! Ree law!' She said in an urgent whisper. 'Mai noi... mae nung bon jinggway... *Ree law!*'

Bishop frowned and shook his head. Then Madeleine's voice loud in his ear. 'Bishop, who is that? What's happening?'

'I ran into an old woman. I can't make out what she's saying. Something about a woman and the house of ghosts... I don't know. It's urgent, 'though. She's telling me to hurry.'

There was a moment's pause before Bishop heard the faint hum of the drone immediately overhead, then Maddy's voice again. 'That's the woman I saw earlier. I'm sure of it. She was moving away from a house at the rear of the village. It's about two hundred metres from you.'

The old woman was pulling at Bishop's shirt and gesturing behind her. She wanted him to follow. 'Ma Sopee,' she hissed. 'Ree *law!*'

'Christ,' Bishop breathed, looking at the phone before he pocketed it. 'It's her. Sophie. The old girl knows where she is...'

'If it's that house, it's guarded,' Madeleine replied. 'Three male figures are lying on the front verandah...'

'I'm going with her. Pick an RV on the highway, close to the house then contact Zaw and have him bring the Land Rover around. Can you manage both rucks...?'

'Of course I can!'

'Is there somewhere between me and you where we can meet?'

'A creek line. Trees and good cover. That's where I saw the woman. I'll meet you there in ten.'

Bishop turned to the old woman. He pointed down the dark alley. 'Lead on, grandmother,' he said, bringing the buttstock of the carbine into his shoulder. Mya nodded and, together, she and Bishop hurried off through the sleeping town.

~

Madeleine quickly retrieved the drone, packed it away and stowed it in her ruck that she cinched tight and threw onto her back. Next, she pulled a map from her pocket and checked it, her finger settling on a location on the highway two hundred and fifty metres west of the house. She messaged Zaw the instructions and secured her phone. Then she grabbed Bishop's rucksack and slipped her arms through it, positioning it on her front, before unholstering the dead Lieutenant's MA-5. With a last look around their hide, she stepped out into the darkened field and headed off toward the creek line and the rendezvous with Bishop.

She had taken less than a dozen steps when she froze, movement to her half-left catching her eye. She squinted into the dark. Faintly silhouetted against the headlights of the trucks, six men were moving toward her in an extended line.

'Bishop,' she whispered. 'We've got trouble. Something's up. There's a sweep going on. Six men heading east toward the hide. That makes them between you and me so move quick.'

'There looking for us,' Bishop replied. 'They know we're here. Moving now.'

Madeleine had moved another one hundred metres when a faint shadow, thirty metres away, passed her front. The shadow appeared in a patch of moonlight, and Madeleine saw the clear figure of a man, wearing a cap and holding a handgun, striding across the field toward the house. Standing perfectly still, she counted to sixty and then whispered.

'Bishop, we've got one more. Another man, walking toward the house. This one isn't Burmese. That makes four at the house now and six to our southeast.'

She heard Bishop's clipped response then stepped off, paralleling the man's path to take her to the creek line. Reaching the safety of the trees, she dropped to her knees, the weight of both rucksacks pulling her down, and waited. Three minutes later, Bishop and the old woman arrived. She shrugged out of Bishop's ruck as he squatted down beside her.

'All good?' he whispered, handing Madeleine a carbine and four loaded magazines.

Madeleine nodded in the dark, softly snicking home a magazine and silently cocking the M4. 'What's the plan?'

Bishop secured the two grenades into a side pouch of his rucksack, and looked out of the trees at the darkened shape of the old house only forty metres from them. They could both hear the sound of more trucks arriving into the township.

'We'll go with simple and elegant,' he said quietly. 'The forward edge of these trees is the Line of Departure. We have to take big packs with us. We go in fast through the front, neutralise everyone in the house, and take the girl. Then, meet Zaw and get to the LZ, where we'll call in Terry, Tak and the chopper. Back in Chiang Mai for dinner.'

Madeleine nodded again. 'Okay. Simple is best.' She nodded at the carbine in Bishop's hands. 'So can I now safely assume your "lover, not a fighter" phase has passed?'

'I'm not happy about it, Maddy, but it's the way it has to be. Needs must.' Bishop turned to the old woman, who was staring wide-eyed at Madeleine, and held up a hand. 'Stay here, grandmother.' He checked his G-Shock. It was 0315, and dawn was only a little over an hour away. He looked at Madeleine.

'Time to go,' he said and, together, the two raised their weapons and stepped out of the treeline.

∾

The sound of the chain rattling through the handle woke Sophie. She scurried back in the dirt as the rusty tin door creaked open and a figure stepped in, shining a light in her face. The figure crouched down and watched her silently, before hanging the torch from a nail and lighting the inside of the small shed. Sophie stared in disbelief.

'*David!*' She gasped.

David Sutton smiled. 'Hi, Soph,' he said. 'Surprised?'

She shook her head and coughed to clear her dry throat. 'Thank God! I... I can't believe it. I thought they *shot* you! How did you get away?'

Sutton scratched his chin. 'Ah, you see, here's the thing. I wasn't shot. It was a clever charade. The men who grabbed you – the men with that truck – they work for me.' He paused and turned his head at the sound of more trucks entering the township. The delivery convoy had arrived from the south. Good.

Sophie stared. 'They work for... Who *are* you?'

Sutton shrugged genially. 'Well, let's just say I'm not who you think I am.'

Sophie thought fast, her mind whirling. 'The truck. The opium and heroin... it's yours.'

Sutton shook his head. 'Not exactly. We are facilitating its movement and sale, the proceeds of which are going to something *much* more important. There is a much bigger picture here, Sophie. One you wouldn't possibly understand.'

Realisation dawned. 'You're US government,' Sophie said quietly. 'What are you *doing*?'

Sutton winced. 'Soph, can't tell you that.' He stood. The black Glock in its holster glinted menacingly in the torchlight. 'I'm not here to chat, Sophie. I'm afraid it's the end of the road for you. You are the evidence to at least part of what's going on here, and we can't have that getting out...'

Sophie held up her hands. '*No!* I won't say anything,' she said desperately.

'We can't take that chance...'

'My government will find out. They will *know*. They will find out what you've done... *Please!*

'Fuck the Canadian government,' Sutton said mildly. 'God-damned snow Mexicans. They'll learn nothing and, even if they did, do you think we care? They can't stop what's about to happen.'

Sophie sobbed. It was hopeless. She hung her head. 'If you don't care,' she murmured, 'and no one can stop you, what does it matter if you let me go...?'

Sutton shrugged and unholstered his handgun. 'Loose ends, Sophie. They're messy.'

He had taken a step forward when the sound of gunfire erupted behind him from the house. He spun around then, wracked with indecision, looked back at the woman cowering on the dirt floor. A voice in his head yelled *Shoot her! Do it now!* But the gunfight behind him grew louder. He needed to get in there. After quickly running the chain back over the shed door, Sutton turned and ran back to the house.

40

THEY HAD MOVED twenty-five metres at a fast walk, weapons at their shoulders, both eyes open over their combat optic sights. Bishop and Madeleine could see the house's verandah, and their sight dots danced across it like fireflies.

Twenty metres. Bishop's sight dot skipped across a hunched shape that suddenly sprang to its feet with a shout, raising its weapon. In the moonlight, Bishop caught a quick glimpse of a tan cap and he snapped off two shots. They went wide, splintering a verandah post, and the soldier shifted his point of aim. Before he could fire, Madeleine double-tapped her carbine, and the soldier stumbled back, slumping against the house wall.

By now, the dead man's comrades were awake and returning fire, rapid but unsighted shots spraying out into the dark. Bishop and Madeleine fanned out diagonally, putting round after round into the verandah as they closed in.

They sprinted up the stairs as the firing from the verandah suddenly ceased. Bishop turned left and kicked a weapon away from the body of one of the soldiers.

'One dead. *Clear!*'

Madeleine had turned right, her weapon still at her shoulder as she approached the other lying figure. She was standing above it when it suddenly rolled over; a handgun pointed up. Madeleine fired twice, and the body bucked then was still.

'One dead. Clear.' she said. She bent to check the third body against the wall. The soldier was dead, 'Two dead. All clear.' They dropped their big packs on the verandah, and Madeleine bladed her left hand, indicating that Bishop should enter the corridor that led from the front door of the house. Nodding, Bishop stepped in, the carbine at his shoulder. Madeleine entered behind him, her weapon covering over his right shoulder.

The firing from the front of the house stopped, and so did Sutton. He heard the voices as they checked and cleared the bodies on the verandah. Two of them, and one was a woman. It was the two who had come looking for the girl! He stood still against the door frame of the back room, listening as he peered into the darkened corridor. His ears rang, and he could hear nothing except the thump of his pulse. The house was silent as a tomb and just as dark.

He glanced over his shoulder and saw a doorway that led out of the back room and into the large sitting room at the front of the house. He knew the corridor ran along the wall of that room. They would be in that room. Or the corridor. Or both. He remembered the lesson at The Farm – movement was vital in Close Quarter Battle; stay fluid, keep moving forward. He had to make a choice and move. He chose the room.

Bishop's mouth was open to help the hearing in his ringing ears, and his head was slightly turned to use his peripheral vision in the pitch black of the house. He stalked slowly and silently forward. He knew Maddy was right behind him. They passed a doorway to their left that led into another room, and Bishop gestured with his head, feeling the subtle shift in the air as Maddy peeled off and entered the room. A second later, the silence was shattered by two shots, then two more. Bishop spun around and barged into the room.

Sutton had taken two steps into the room, his Glock raised and gripped steadily in both hands, when a form, darker than the rest of the room, stepped in from the corridor. Both eyes open, he fired along the line of his left thumb, extended just below the Glock's slide. Two shots exploded into the dark. He could not see their strike but immediately felt the sledgehammer punch in his right arm as the figure returned fire.

The Glock dropped from his hand, and he staggered backwards, grabbing at his bicep. Before he could react, the figure was on him, and lights exploded before his eyes as the stock of the weapon in the figure's hands crashed into his forehead. Sutton's eyes rolled back in his head, and the last thing he heard as he slumped to the floor, unconscious, was a woman's voice: 'Nighty night, arsehole.'

Bishop stepped in beside Madeleine. His left hand trembled, and he shoved it deep into his pocket. Maddy looked up as she changed magazines.

'That's four,' Bishop said. 'The house should be clear, but let's take a quick look.'

Madeleine nodded, and the two split up, quickly searching the remaining rooms of the house before meeting back at the prone figure. The man lay on his back, one arm out to the side, the other tucked under his body. Bishop winced as a spasm of pain lanced through his shoulder, then bent and flipped the body over.

'The girl isn't here,' he said as he patted the body down. 'Go check out back. We have to move quick. The others will be heading this way by now...' He stopped suddenly. 'Hello. What's this?' he said as he pulled an iPhone from the right back pocket of the body's pants. He waved the phone at Madeleine. 'Silly boy...'

Madeleine nodded. 'It will probably be encrypted if he is what we think he is.' She slung the carbine across her back and drew the handgun at her hip. 'I'll only be a minute,' she said. 'I'll meet you back here.'

With a last glance at Bishop, who was drawing a wallet from the unconscious man's left back pocket, Madeleine left the room.

Bishop squatted back on his haunches and pulled out the Surefire. Flicking the torch on, he hurriedly tipped the contents of the wallet on the floor and sorted through them. A Global Horizons photo ID in the name of David J. Sutton. $104 US in cash, and 110,000 Burmese Kyat – Bishop did a quick calculation: about $50US. A hotel parking stub from the Lotte Hotel in Yangon. A Delta Airlines 'Sky-Miles' American Express card in the name of D.J. Sutton, and a laundry receipt, hand-written in English, from "Chang's Golden Laundry", made out to D. Sutton.

Bishop held the receipt to the torchlight. Peering closely, he could make out the printed address of the laundry: Market Street, Loi Tai Leng.

'*Jesus*,' he breathed. The American had been in Loi Tai Leng, the headquarters of the Shan State Army – South, and the township they were *now* in was bursting at the seams with US weapons and ammunition. Why *was* Maddy so interested in knowing more about Loi Tai Leng? Was this whole thing just about weapons to the SSA?

He was about to toss the wallet away when the tip of a finger touched a small piece of paper deep in a side pouch. He quickly drew it out and unfolded it. His eyes widened as he read it. The paper was a receipt to Anthony J. Sutton for a rib-eye (medium rare), fries, creamed spinach, corn, two beers and a glass of Olivier Leflaive Meursault 2020. The address on the receipt was "J. Gilbert's Wood Fired Steaks & Seafood, 6930 Old Dominion Dr, McLean, VA."

Bishop knew "Langley" was a colloquial term for the CIA headquarters, but the building itself was located on Colonial Farm Road, also in McLean. It could all be a huge coincidence, but Bishop did not believe in God or coincidences. The unconscious man on the floor had to be CIA. Bishop was scooping the wallet's contents into his shirt pocket when he heard his name from the doorway behind him. Standing, he turned.

Maddy stood by the door in the shadows cast by the torchlight. Her face was grimy, and her blonde hair, pulled back in her trademark ponytail, was stuck with twigs and strings of cobweb. She was smiling, and a hand rested gently on Sophie Bouchard's shoulder.

41

MÖNG KYAWT, Shan State, Burma

The lead elements had taken five days to reach the tiny village perched high on the ridgeline in the dense forest of eastern Shan. They had arrived, weary but spirited, and, after leaving a small reception party, had pressed on deeper into the mountains, pushing ever eastward. The following day, General Sai Wint Maung, commanding general of Shan State Army – South, arrived in the village just ahead of the expedition's Main Body.

Two thousand men, and a heavily laden mule train of three hundred beasts, had left Loi Tai Leng six days before and entered the dense jungle that cloaked the mountainous terrain in the southeast of the state. That was the last time any of them had seen the sun, the thick canopy giving only a hint of filtered, green light that weakly lit their path along the narrow, twisting footpad.

The going had been slow, much slower than General Sai had planned. Instead of a long column of troops, he had opted to break his force into smaller company-sized groups that had set off at staggered times, the idea being that at day's end, when they halted for the night, the groups would still be separated. Inevitably, that had not happened. Delays, as fractious mules had refused to move or slipped off the narrow, root-twisted track, caused a concertina effect with the order of march jamming up at choke points and soldiers mingling. Poor communications had not helped the confusion, as the force's VHF radios struggled with the length of the column and the mountainous terrain.

General Sai sat beneath a spreading acacia tree and lit a cigarette as his command group busied themselves around him. Forest birds chattered and squawked in the trees overhead, but the village was quiet as its Pa'O inhabitants, their eyes dark and still, squatted by their huts and silently watched the soldiers moving through their hamlet. Sai sighed. It had not been an auspicious start, but that was to be expected – large troop moves were always chaotic at the start as the men and animals adjusted to march routine. He had expected as much, and they were still on schedule, thanks to the extra days padded into the plan.

He pulled on the cigarette, letting it burn down, and huffed out the clove-spiced smoke. There was still much that could go wrong over the next three weeks as the column pushed deeper east, crossing ridges, plummeting deep valleys, and forcing their way through the jungle. Three weeks until they were ready to cross the border. When that happened, the die was cast. He scratched his cheek as he watched a young soldier pat a mangy village dog, slipping it a treat from his meagre rations.

The plan was bold and dangerous. Carving out an enclave inside Mainland China was a terrible risk. Still, it was worth it if it united ethnic Shan populations across the border, appealing to the shared heritage and culture of a people divided by national borders. And then there were the commercial benefits.

Yunnan was a strategic location for the Golden Triangle drug trade, so by holding a position within China, the SSA would gain a crucial foothold in opium production and trafficking routes that reached further into Southeast Asia and China. The move would bypass border restrictions and checkpoints between Burma and China, making trafficking more efficient. Controlling a cross-border village would allow them to establish an even more effective underground network for smuggling opium and forced labour. The new income would be staggering.

Sai stubbed out his cigarette, stood and dusted off the seat of his pants. He bent and reached into his pack, pulling out a small packet of sticky rice balls and *nga pi*, dried fish. He carefully unwrapped the packet and scooped a mouthful of rice and fish that he chewed slowly. He watched as three mules, strapped down with ammunition boxes, were led through the village, small boys chasing after them, whooping in excitement.

He had always been a betting man, but this wasn't a cock fight or a game of *hsi kye*, dice. He was betting on his plan taking advantage of the political instability in Burma – and that was where that pig General Min Kyaw Ko came in. If General Min had stayed true to the agreement and played his part, Burma would be rocked by a tectonic interval shift, after which Min had undertaken to leave Shan State and the border region alone.

Muang wrapped the food package and carefully placed it back in his pack. He lit another cigarette. He was also betting that China's response would be measured. Given that China often took a pragmatic approach to border conflicts, this would be a calculated risk, especially if the SSA promised to manage the local ethnic Shan population without disrupting Chinese interests such as the Belt and Road Initiative projects.

He grunted and spat on the ground. But what did the Americans want? That, he still did not know. He knew the two foreigners were CIA – they could be nothing else – but what did they stand to gain by the protocol he and Min had signed weeks ago in Mandalay? Having General Min in their pocket would certainly advance American interests in the country and, by default, weaken Chinese influence, but Sai was sure there was more to it than that, and that itched at him. Not for the first time, a dark thought that he was being played rose to gnaw at him like a hungry rat.

With an effort, he forced the doubts down and shouldered his pack. Turning to his Operations Officer, he raised his arm and wound the air with a finger. 'Let's go,' he shouted. 'I want to be across Route 45 before dark.'

His order sparked a hive of activity as his command group leapt to their feet and furiously packed up behind him. Packs were hefted, radios crackled, weapons were shouldered, and the young soldier threw a last morsel to the dog. With a glance back at the next company group entering the clearing, General Sai cradled his rifle and left the village, stepping back onto the narrow path that led into the eerie gloom of the jungle.

42

Narhkan Township and vicinity 20°46ʹ22.1ʺN 97°53ʹ02.0ʺE, Shan State, Burma

Few words were exchanged. Bishop quickly double-checked the face of the young woman standing in front of him with that of the photo and, satisfied it was Sophie, he told the two women to wait as he ran back out into the verandah. He flicked the Surefire on and played its powerful beam across the boards. Finding the body he was looking for, he squatted down and rolled it over.

The man's new fishing shirt was soaked with blood, and the tan cap on his head had flopped to the side. Bishop saw the white tiger-head patch on the backstrap. He pulled the collar of the man's shirt aside and checked the label. *U Chit Tin fashion.* It was him – the one who had used Sophie's credit card. The man's mouth was open, and his eyes stared, glassed and sightless.

Bishop glanced up. Three beams of torchlight were playing across the field and heading their way, fast. Working quickly, Bishop rifled through the pants, wincing at the touch of urine and the stench of the shit. His fingers brushed a wallet, and he pulled it out. He flipped the wallet open and tipped the contents onto the ground beside the body, grabbing what he sought before turning around and running back into the house.

Madeleine and Sophie stood next to the unconscious and bleeding American, Madeleine's weapon trained on the body. Bishop approached, holding out a hand to Sophie.

'Your Amex card,' he said. 'We have to go. Right now!'

Bishop and Madeleine bundled Sophie out of the back of the house and west across the fields, the sun cracking the night sky behind them.

They stumbled in the half-light across the rutted ground for what seemed an age, Sophie in bare feet, before a vehicle's headlights flicked briefly on then off, fifty metres to their half-right. They spotted the Land Rover and veered toward it. Reaching the vehicle, Bishop shoved Sophie in the front seat between Zaw and Madeleine, then threw their packs in the rear tub. He then moved to the driver's side window.

'They're following us up, Zaw! The LZ. Let's go!'

Zaw shook his head. 'We cannot. There are Sit-Tat roadblocks everywhere on the highway – north and south. We can go back to Lai Kha. I know a way through the hills, but it will take many hours.'

Bishop chewed his lip. They could possibly find another LZ close to Lai Kha, but would Dougherty's old Huey have the range to get there? If it did, it would be much deeper inland, and the risk posed by ground-to-air would be greater. Maybe even too much to chance it. What then? They would have to walk out to the southern border and, in a straight line, that was over one hundred and twenty kilometres. So much for being back in Chiang Mai for dinner.

'Okay, get us to Lai Kha. We have to move. *Now!* We'll work it out from there.'

Bishop scrambled into the rear tub between the packs and slapped the cabin roof. Zaw gunned the engine and spun the wheel, sliding the pickup onto the highway and heading north just as gunfire broke out behind them.

∾

They had turned off Highway 45 after a five-kilometre dash, each moment filled with tension as they awaited a roadblock around every bend. Bishop heaved a sigh of relief when, just after dawn, they had turned off onto a dirt road heading northeast. He cursed as he bounced around in the tub, gripping the packs for support as Zaw threw the old Land Rover down the rutted and broken track. Checking his compass and map had been a challenge, but he quickly determined that they were heading in the right direction. If Zaw knew the tracks, they should reach Lai Kha in a little over three hours. If their luck held out.

As they rounded a bend, Zaw had slowed the pickup to negotiate a large pothole when a log lying across the road came into view two hundred metres up the track. Zaw braked the Land Rover and spoke quietly through the open driver's window.

'Bishop, don't get up. There is a roadblock ahead. Three SSA soldiers. They have seen us. What do I do?'

Crouching in the back of the pickup, Bishop swore under his breath and reached for the carbine.

'Drive on, Zaw,' he said. 'Slowly. Maddy...' he added. 'Keep Sophie down and get ready.'

Zaw dropped the Land Rover into first gear and crept forward, waving his arm out of the window and smiling. One hundred and fifty metres. Madeleine turned to Sophie.

'Get your head down. Behind my legs. And stay there. No matter what, do *not* sit up,'

Sophie silently did as she was bid, and Madeleine pushed her carbine between the seat and the door. Then, she checked the load in her handgun and lowered it into her lap. One hundred metres. Zaw kept waving and smiling, and the Land Rover crept forward. Seventy-five metres.

One of the three SSA soldiers stepped forward and held up his hand while his comrades moved around the log to get a clearer shot at the oncoming vehicle. Fifty metres. The two soldiers on either side of the log raised their weapons. Thirty metres, twenty... ten.

Zaw stopped the Land Rover and switched off the ignition. The soldier with his hand up saw Madeleine through the windscreen and frowned. The only sound on the dusty track was the ticking of the pickup's hot engine and the loud rasp of cicadas. The man walked slowly forward, his boots crunching in the gravel.

Madeleine held her breath. She had seconds left. The man studied the front of the Land Rover as he moved down the side of the vehicle, and then he was at the driver's window. He was about to speak to Zaw when he saw Sophie crouched under the dashboard. An instant later, he spotted Madeleine's carbine and the handgun in her lap.

He jumped back with a shout, fumbling to raise his rifle, but Madeleine was quicker. She snapped up the handgun and fired two shots that took the soldier in the face, blowing out the back of his head in a spray of blood and brain. The instant she fired, Bishop was on his feet in the tub, the carbine at his shoulder, firing rapid shots into the roadblock.

The first two rounds took the soldier on the left, and Bishop swung his aim as the last soldier fired a round into the front of the Land Rover. Bishop's next two shots took the soldier cleanly in the chest, and he slumped over the log like a broken puppet. Madeleine was out of the pickup and running forward as Bishop vaulted to the ground to cover her.

'Get the bodies into the bush,' Bishop shouted. 'Zaw, get the truck around this bloody log.'

He and Maddy each grabbed a body at the roadblock and dragged them into the low scrub that lined the track; then Bishop ran back to the body of the man lying spreadeagled on the track beside the Land Rover.

'Bishop!' Madeleine yelled, holding up a handheld radio. 'Get his comms... It'll be useful to have ears on these guys.'

Bishop tore the radio off the front of the dead man's chest rig. Grabbing the body under the shoulder harness, he manhandled it off the track and tipped it over the edge into an overgrown culvert. Zaw gunned the engine and slowly drove the vehicle around the end of the log, the right side wheels leaving the road and tipping precariously on the shoulder.

In moments he was around, Bishop and Madeleine both leapt into the vehicle, and Zaw stamped his foot down. The Land Rover responded, and they roared away, a plume of dust tailing out behind them.

43

Lai Kha Village, Shan State, Burma

The sun was high in the sky, beating down on the village and its inhabitants. There was no breeze, and everything sat still and flaccid in the oppressive heat. Zaw steered the Land Rover around two dogs rolling in the dust and parked it under some trees on the edge of the village. The three companions eased their way stiffly from the vehicle, and Madeleine helped Sophie out, sitting her in the shade with a bottle of water from her pack.

'Stay here,' Madeleine said, patting the girl on the shoulder. 'Just rest up. We'll be with you soon and get you cleaned up and fed. You're safe now.'

Sophie looked up and spoke the first words she had uttered since leaving the locked shed. 'Thank you. I can't believe...' Her face crumpled, and she collapsed in a wave of tears and choking sobs.

Madeleine studied her briefly, then walked back to the Land Rover and pulled the packs onto the dirt. She looked up at the sound of a shout from across the small, dusty village square.

Swe ran down the stairs of a house, her eyes alight. With an effort, she pulled herself up to walk calmly to the small group in the shade of the trees. Stepping up to Zaw, she smiled and wrapped her arms around him.

'Little brother,' she said. 'Welcome back.'

Zaw smiled in return and hugged his sister. 'It is good to be home,' he said. He indicated Bishop and Madeleine with a nod of his head. 'It was very close,' he whispered, 'but these two do not hesitate. They are killers.'

Swe examined the two foreigners as they bent over their rucksacks, unpacking and re-ordering their gear. She could see the cold professionalism in them as they wordlessly went to work. *Killers indeed*, she thought. It was a shame they would have to leave – especially the handsome man with the deep brown eyes. She could use them both in her band.

Turning, she called out to a small group of women sitting under a house, watching the proceedings with interest. The women rose to their feet and moved to Sophie, taking her by the hand and gently leading her to a house where she could wash and rest. Swe watched her go, then walked to the Land Rover and leaned against it as she spoke.

'I did not think you would find her, but you did.'

Bishop lowered his pack and looked up. 'Swe, I did not think we would either.' He shrugged. 'We got lucky, that's all.'

Swe glanced back at her brother and then eyed Bishop for a moment. 'Is there anything I should know?'

Bishop nodded. 'There are three dead SSA in Narhkan and another three on a track about twenty kilometres from here. Zaw took us the long way around, and we backtracked a lot. It should confuse the scent for a while.' He held up one of the radios and switched it on. A crackle of static came from the handheld. 'We hid the bodies and took their comms. VHF, so the fact we're not hearing anything is good – it means they aren't close enough for transmission range.'

Swe chewed her lower lip. 'We need to get you out of here, and we will probably have to move ourselves. Once they pick up your tracks, it won't take them long to find the village. And once *they* know where we are, so will the army.'

'I'm sorry, Swe,' Bishop said. 'We couldn't go to the LZ and had nowhere else to run. We've led them to you.'

Swe took Bishop's hand. 'It does not matter,' she replied with a shrug. 'It's the way of things – we are always on the move. We have other places we can go, even more remote than this. But I will be sorry to see you go.' She sighed. 'What matters is that we leave before the villagers suffer for our presence. I'm worried the army will find us first – there has been much activity in the district over the past few days.'

Bishop gently disengaged their hands, his heart thumping, and pulled the map from his pants pocket and unfolded it. He spread it out on the bonnet of the Land Rover and ran a finger across it until it came to rest on a forested ridgeline.

'We're here,' he said. 'Right?' Swe nodded, and he went on, tapping the map again. 'This large, cleared area, about a kilometre southeast of here: is it still there?'

Swe looked at the map and nodded. 'Yes, I know it. It is there. It is an old garden. The village has left it in fallow this season...'

'So, no bushes or trees? Clear to the ground?'

'Yes. You are thinking of a Landing Zone?'

'Exactly.' Bishop turned to Madeleine who had subtly elbowed Swe aside and was leaning over his shoulder, studying the map. 'What do you think, Maddy? Good LZ.'

Madeleine nodded. 'It is, but it's another, what, hundred-odd klicks inland. Can Terry's busted-arse chopper make that range?'

'More like one hundred and twenty,' Bishop replied. 'I think they can make it but it will be right on limits. And we'll have extra weight now Sophie's with us. It's a bit dicey. Maybe Tak can fit that external tank he mentioned...'

'When can you extract?' Swe asked.

Bishop scratched his ear. 'Hard to say. It will be up to our friends in Thailand and how ready the chopper is. Twelve hours earliest, I would say – maybe more. But we will leave here at dawn tomorrow and lay low by the LZ – that way, we are one less problem for you.' He turned to Madeleine. 'Maddy, can you go and see to Sophie? Stay with her and...'

He suddenly stopped. 'Jesus, I forgot!' Rummaging around in his pants cargo pocket, he pulled out the phone the old woman had given him. 'Sophie's phone... I forgot to tell you about it in all the excitement. I'll get it charged up, then we can give it to her. There might be something we need to see on it.'

Madeleine nodded. 'And give me the other phone you took from the house. I'll have a go at breaking into it.'

Bishop handed over the American's phone, and Madeleine briefly examined it before slipping it into her pocket. 'I'll go and see to the girl, then I'll clean both weapons,' she said and walked off across the sun-beaten village square with Swe in tow.

Zaw caught Bishop's eye and nodded. He grabbed his small pack from the back of the Land Rover.

'I am glad it worked out, U Bishop,' he said. 'It has been fun. But you are a threat to everyone here. You need to go – the sooner, the better. For all of our sakes.' He nodded one last time as if satisfied he had spoken, then walked away into the village.

Bishop watched him go. They had Sophie, but at what cost? How many now would suffer because of what he and Maddy had done? How many more lives would be lost to get the girl back to her family? He shook his head. They weren't home yet – not by a long way – and there was work to do. With a grunt, he hefted his rucksack and dragged it under an old acacia tree.

It was hot, and the sun was high in a cloudless, kerosene-blue sky. Nothing moved around the village; the only sounds were the din of cicadas and the occasional lazy cluck of hens as they pecked through the dirt under the houses.

Bishop squatted in the shade of the acacia tree and pulled the Inmarsat terminal from his rucksack. His left hand trembled, and he clenched it a few times before snapping open the antenna and positioning it carefully on the tripod. The display flickered to life, showing the signal strength as he adjusted the angle and checked his field notebook to confirm the satellite coordinates. Next, he connected the terminal to a small solar power pack, ensuring it would stay charged under the brutal sun, and the modem hummed to life as it linked to the satellite overhead.

Bishop watched as Madeleine returned and picked up both the carbines, pulling a cleaning kit from a pouch on the side of her pack.

The Inmarsat held the connection steady, and Bishop connected his laptop and entered the BGAN –Broadband Global Area Network – interface to establish the link. The screen prompted his encrypted login credentials and, with a few swift taps, he was inside the firm's network.

The metallic clacking of weapon parts echoed through the silent village as Maddy cleaned both carbines. Bishop checked his notes. There were holes – they have still not answered the final question of "why?" – but this report would be explosive when it reached Nesbitt's inbox. He scanned the horizon briefly and began to type.

44

Narhkan Township, Shan State, Burma

Reilly had a foot on the bottom step and rested an arm across his knee. It was late morning, and the sun was high in the sky, blurred with smoke haze that covered everything in a mustard yellow tone. He felt the back of his neck burning and the sweat running in rivulets down his back. He spat in the dirt and eyed the man leaning against the wall, holding a balled-up T-shirt to his right arm.

David Sutton was pale, and he bit at his lower lip – both in pain from the wound and deep embarrassment. Reilly looked down again at the three bodies lying on the verandah. He sighed.

'I see you found them... So, what the fuck happened?'

Sutton grimaced as he shifted his weight. 'It was the two Brits,' he said. 'They came out of the dark. I was at the back of the house when I heard the firing. I got two rounds off, but one of them – the woman – hit me with a lucky shot...'

'Lucky, my ass. The only "lucky" is that she didn't put it in your face. Go on.'

Sutton drew a breath. 'When I came to, they were gone, and so was the girl.'

Reilly nodded. 'No shit. We'll talk later about why you didn't deal with the girl.'

Sutton stirred, his eyes flaring. 'I goddamn was! I was about to do it when the gunfight broke out. Shit got kinda busy at that point...'

'Look at me, boy,' Reilly growled. Sutton looked at him. 'It might have been busy,' Reilly said, 'but it wasn't so bad you couldn't have put one in her head before you charged in all Lone Ranger. Now she's fucking gone.' He wiped his brow with a handkerchief from his pocket and sighed. 'When was all this?'

'Not long after I messaged you. I figured I'd wait until you got here...'

'Good of you,' Reilly said, his voice dripping with sarcasm. He shook his head. 'We have to assume they saw the weapons.'

'They did,' Sutton winced. 'Aung realised he was missing a man and went back to look. He found him in a storage shed, his neck broken. The shed was full of weapons and ammo. An M4 and grenade box were open. Two carbines, mags and some grenades were missing.'

Reilly sucked at his teeth. 'Jesus Christ! Who *are* these fucking people?' he hissed, although he already had a pretty good idea. He walked up the stairs into the shade of the verandah. 'This isn't good. They've got the girl, and they've seen the weapons. When she tells them what *she* saw, that's a pretty simple two and two for them to put together.' He thought for a moment. 'You didn't tell her anything, did you?'

Sutton averted his eyes. 'No, we barely spoke... But she's seen me.'

'Jesus H Christ!' Reilly said, gritting his teeth. He pressed the tips of his fingers against his temples, rubbing small, tight circles as if trying to knead away the tension building in his skull. His jaw tightened, and a sharp exhale escaped through his nose.

'What a cluster fuck,' he said finally. 'I'll be damned if I'm telling Langley about this,' he said. 'We have to find these two and the goddamn girl and deal with them once and for all.'

He pulled a pack of cigarettes from his shirt pocket and shook one out. Lighting the smoke and dragging on it, he jutted his chin at Sutton's shoulder. 'How bad is it?'

'I think it's a through-and-through. The bleeding has slowed a lot, but I need to get it looked at.'

Reilly nodded. 'Well, they've got a three-hour lead on us, and we have no idea which way they were headed. I'll run you up to Namsang and get a doc to patch you while I try and work out just what the fuck is happening.'

Sutton shifted once again. He lowered his head. 'It gets worse, Bill.'

Reilly squinted at him. '*Worse*? How, on God's green earth, can it get worse than it already is?'

'They frisked me when I was out. They took my wallet...'

'Big deal. It'll be clean, won't it? Just the usual wallet litter?'

'I think so... but they got something else, Bill. They took my phone.'

Reilly turned around and looked up at the pale sky. It was a nightmare. It had to be! He clenched his eyes and prayed to wake up. But when his eyes opened, he was still standing on the verandah, looking down at three dead bodies. He turned back to Sutton, struggling to keep his voice even.

'Your *encrypted* phone? Your work one...' Sutton nodded, and Reilly went on. 'Why the *fuck* were you carrying it?'

'Fuck you, Bill! You're carrying yours. Aren't you!'

Reilly was, as it happened, he always did, but fuck this guy. He jabbed a finger at Sutton. 'Back off, son. You don't want me angrier than I already am.' He dragged hard on the cigarette and spat out the smoke in annoyance. 'Okay,' he said. 'Let me think.' He rubbed his eyes. 'The phone is encrypted – its NSA-grade, hard-ass encryption. These two assholes might be some Wild Geese shit, but they won't have the tech, or the know-how, to crack the phone. Even if they get into the device, they won't be able to open the vault.'

'Call Langley and have them reach out and wipe it...'

Reilly shook his head. 'No can do. The devices were prepped at Fort Meade,' he said, referring to the National Security Agency's headquarters in Maryland. 'Langley doesn't know about them and, even if they did, they don't have the keys. The only way we can do this is for me to call the NSA, explain what happened and request a wipe. I ain't doing that...' he waved a hand across his face as if to wipe away the issue. 'No, it should be okay... they won't get in. Anyways, between us, Tatmadaw and the SSA, we'll find these fuckers pretty damn quick and end it.'

Reilly looked out across the field to straighten his thoughts. *Get a grip, Bill,* he told himself. Min was on the way to Naypyidaw, and Sai was heading east to the border. It was all still in place and going to plan. That's all that mattered, and all his boss and their backers in DC cared about.

Reilly bent down and gripped Sutton's left hand. The bloodied T-shirt fell away as Sutton struggled to stand. Reilly stepped back and turned for the stairs.

'Stay here,' he said. 'I'll get the Toyota and bring it around then we'll get to Namsang for treatment.'

Sutton smiled weakly. 'Thanks, Bill.'

Reilly eyed him like an angry bear. 'Don't thank me, boy,' he gnarred. 'I'm not talking about you. I need a drink.'

45

The sun had reached its zenith and was slowly sinking to the west as the late afternoon bird chorus sang it to rest, but there was still heat in the air as Bishop, Madeleine, and Sophie gathered under a tree. Bishop had invited Swe and Zaw to the meeting, but they had declined, telling him they had much to organise for their withdrawal from the village in the coming days.

Madeleine sat with her rucksack open at her feet and the American's phone in her lap, while Bishop opened his field notebook, checking his notes and occasionally glancing at the map spread out in front of him. Sophie sat across from them, clean and in fresh clothes, wearing a pair of sandals. She was still and quiet. She had a distant look on her face, and her eyes were blank and unfocused, the thousand-yard stare of someone who had just undergone an immense trauma. Bishop looked up from his notebook.

'Sophie, drink some of your tea. It will do you good.'

The girl sipped delicately at the mug in her hand. Her hands shook. 'You killed those men at the house and the three men at the roadblock. In cold blood,' she said, her eyes wide. 'Why?'

Bishop lowered his notebook and looked at the young woman. 'If we hadn't, we would all be dead now...'

'You don't know that...'

'Trust me. We would have all been killed minutes after being dragged from the car.'

'Why do you do it? The work you do...'

Bishop thought about that for a moment. 'I'm good at it,' he said. 'All I've ever been good at, really... and it pays very well.'

'You're a *mercenary*,' Sophie accused. 'You and men like you are everything that is wrong with this country. With the *world!*'

'You have an opinion; I respect that. And you're right – Burma is unlikely ever to know real peace. Maybe I *am* a mercenary, just a different job title. But you should thank your lucky bloody stars that Maddy and I are here doing the job we do.'

Sophie frowned, suddenly uncertain. 'I hate what you do,' she said. 'It goes against everything I believe, but... but I'm grateful. Really.'

Bishop nodded. 'You have every right to be angry and confused. You've been through a lot, and it's not unusual for you to be a little disassociated from reality right now. But know this: you *are* free and safe with us. We will get you home. I promise that.'

Madeleine leaned across and patted Sophie's knee. 'Are you ready, love,' she said. 'We don't have much time, and there is a lot to go through...'

Sophie drew a deep breath and smiled hesitantly. 'Ready,' she said. 'I still can't believe I'm free. It's... it's like a dream.'

Bishop leaned over and handed Sophie her iPhone. 'The old lady in the township gave it to me not long before she led us to you. I've charged it up, but there's no signal. After this, I'll get you on the satphone to your father so you can speak with him. Would you like to do that?'

Sophie blinked back tears and shook her head. 'No. No, I don't think I can. Not right now. It would be too hard.'

'Okay. There's no need – just whenever you're ready. I've reported back to my boss and he will have told your parents you are safe and well but unable to communicate now. Maybe later, hey?' Sophie nodded and bit her lip.

Bishop went on. 'So, this is called a "debrief". I will lead you through everything that happened from when you arrived in Yangon to when we picked you up. It might be a bit scary, having to relive it, but it's important you remember everything you can and tell me.' Bishop studied the girl for a moment and exchanged a quick glance with Madeleine. 'So, let's start, shall we?'

For the next forty minutes Sophie told them her story, Bishop and Madeleine occasionally interrupting quietly with a gentle question. She told them of her arrival in Yangon, her stay at the Lotte, her induction into Global Horizons, and her initial training, followed by the long trip to Kyethi and the Advance Field Office. She told them of meeting David Sutton, who had been kind, if a little awkward, and of her arriving at Narhkan and starting work in Stores and Admin.

'Did you see or feel anything out of place up to that point?' Bishop asked.

Sophie paused, her head tilted to the side in thought. 'Not really. Although David was often away from the project, which struck me as odd, given he was the project lead. "Running errands", he would tell me. He would be gone for about twenty-four hours before he returned.'

'Okay. Let's move on,' Bishop said, making a note. 'What happened that they would take you and cover up your disappearance?'

'The truck arrived.'

'Truck? Tell us about it.'

So Sophie told them about the broken-down Global Horizons truck limping its way into Narhkan and of Mya leading her to it. 'There was no one around, so I climbed in the back. That's when I saw it...'

Bishop leaned forward and Madeleine, listening intently while she picked her fingernails, looked up. 'Saw what, Sophie?' Bishop pressed gently.

'The back of the truck was loaded with wooden pallets. On the pallets, covered by canvas tarpaulins, were piles of opium blocks and bags of white powder. There must have been tons of the stuff. I took some pictures.'

Sophie looked down and powered up her phone. She unlocked it, quickly flicked through her photos, and passed the phone to Bishop. He studied the phone, flicking from one photo to the next. They were clear, focused and date-stamped. A pallet loaded with blocks, each wrapped in brown wax paper and stamped in red ink with a logo. Opium. The next was a pallet stacked high with heat-sealed plastic bags containing white powder. Bishop did not need a test kit to know it was heroin.

He passed the phone to Madeleine, who examined the photos and whistled softly.

'That's just one truck,' she said. 'And we have to assume it was part of a much larger convoy. Is it any wonder they had to take Sophie out of the picture?'

Sophie sipped her tea and watched the two in front of her. It was as if they had forgotten she was there. Each was absorbed in the discovery. She watched as Bishop drew a Pelican Case from his ruck-sack and pulled out a sturdy-looking laptop, quickly connecting the phone and transferring the photos to a folder on the desktop. The woman, Madeleine, was watching the Australian as he worked. She had a frown on her face, and she tapped a finger on her chin. Madeleine looked to be deep in thought but then, she too, leaned over and dragged across her rucksack and pulled out a laptop.

Bishop handed the phone back to Sophie as Madeleine spoke to him. 'I'm going to break the Yank's phone. It shouldn't take long.'

Bishop nodded and, as Madeleine set to work, he spoke. 'So, we have opium and we have weapons, both being shipped in and out by the same means – Global Horizons' trucks – and Global Horizons is a CIA front.' He shook his head. 'Jesus, it's Iran-Contra all over again. Drugs for money for weapons. The question is for who and why?' He turned to Sophie. 'Any ideas? Did you see or hear anything else?'

Sophie shook her head. 'No. Nothing. Just the drugs, then they took me. It was David.' She shuddered. 'He said I had seen too much, and he was going to kill me moments before you arrived. The shooting stopped him.'

Bishop looked up as Swe crossed the village square and joined the group, sitting beside him. She momentarily dropped her hand to his knee and smiled.

'Do you mind if I join you?' she asked.

Bishop held her hand and smiled back. 'Not at all.'

Bent over her laptop, Madeleine snorted quietly. *Making cow eyes at him again*, she thought. It was enough to make her throw up. As Bishop took Swe through what they had discussed, Madeleine began to work.

First, she connected the captured phone to her laptop using a Cellebrite Universal Forensic Extraction Device. The screen lit up, but a familiar block stopped her cold – an NSA-level encryption prompt. This wasn't your average lock; it was fortified with layers of defence, meant to hold off even the most determined attempts. Madeleine frowned, knowing she couldn't just bash her way in without risking a wipe.

Switching tactics, she opened the Cellebrite software and selected the advanced extraction mode. After a few keystrokes, the device's firmware was scanned. The NSA's encryption protocols are designed to resist traditional exploits, so she decided to run a modified boot-loader – a program that manages the device's startup sequence and security. It was a risky move, but it would bypass the initial passcode.

The screen flickered, and she waited, her heartbeat in sync with the blinking cursor. Finally, the system hooked in. Cellebrite's tools started dissecting the phone's file system, avoiding the outer encryption shell by accessing it through a lower-level debug mode. It was a backdoor – one she doubted the NSA ever expected to be used in the field.

Bishop and Swe talked on, Madeleine only half hearing them as she concentrated on her attack. After a tense five minutes, the extraction software found its way through, pulling raw data from the depths of the device.

Madeleine sifted through app caches and temporary files before finally striking gold: an encrypted partition labelled "archive_docs." Documents started populating her screen – PDFs, Word docs, and spreadsheets. She opened a PDF and briefly read it. It was a contract and a scope of work. Bishop was right: it looked like Longbow Defence Solutions had been used to set up the NGO structure, nothing more. But it was the audio file dated six weeks before that made her pause.

Cellebrite's built-in decryption tools struggled momentarily, but they eventually cracked the code, revealing a series of voice recordings. Madeleine played the first file, and the words spilled out of the laptop speaker.

Bishop, Swe, and Sophie stopped talking and leaned in to listen. The recording was a conversation between two men, one of them American, before a knock on the door, and a third entered. Then two names: Min Ko and Sai Maung.

'That's Major General Min Kyaw Ko, commander of Eastern Command,' Swe said. 'And Sai Wint Maung, commander of SSA-South.'

Madeleine hit pause on the recording. Bishop spoke. 'Sophie, is the American Sutton?'

'No. Definitely not. That's not his voice. An older man. I don't know him...'

Bishop nodded, and Madeleine hit play. Rustling sounds as the three men are seated, and the conversation begins in earnest. The meeting lasts over an hour, and the four around the laptop sit silently, listening. Bishop makes quick notes in his notebook.

The four sitting in the dirt under the tree were staggered by what they heard. It was an agreement between General Min of the army and General Sai of the SSA, facilitated by the American. An agreement for Min to launch a coup on Armed Forces Day and take control of the State Administration Council after killing the junta's leader. The SSA would support Min's ascendancy and, in return, the new leader of the country would not take action over an SSA incursion into Mainland China, led by General Sai, to seize and hold an enclave close to the border. Min also agreed to step away from Shan and award the state full autonomy as an ethnic Shan heartland.

Frustratingly for Bishop and Madeleine, several references were made to the United Nations and an "invitation", but the specifics were not discussed – although, at one point, the American could be heard saying he would draft a protocol document, which Min and Sai would sign. Finally, the meeting ended and, after the two men had been separately escorted from the room, the recording ended.

The four sat in silence for minutes, digesting what they had heard. Madeleine continued to tap away at her laptop and the down-loaded classified files. Finally, Bishop looked up, an eyebrow cocked.

'Talk about your smoking gun,' he said. 'But what do the Americans get out of this, and what is the "invitation"?'

Madeleine held up a hand. 'Hang on... Nearly there.' She made a few more strokes on the keyboard and studied the screen before looking up with a grim smile.

'That recording was just loading the chambers... *This* is the smoking gun. It's a copy of the protocol document, signed by Generals Min and Sai. Are you ready for this?'

Bishop nodded. And Madeleine continued. 'They expect the SSA incursion to elicit a firm military response from China...'

'No shit...'

'...threatening Burmese sovereignty. After taking power, Min will address the UN and invite the US to send in troops to expel the Chinese, then secure Southern Shan State and the eastern border. These fuckers are going to start World War Three.'

'But China and Russia will veto,' Swe said. 'It won't work.'

Bishop shook his head. 'The US won't give a shit. They took action despite a veto for Kosovo – although that was technically a NATO mission. And Syria... arguably also for Iraq. It will be a unilat-eral action on the back of a request from the host nation.'

Swe stared, her eyes widening in realisation. 'Oh, hell!' she said. 'I meant to tell you... we found out what is happening at Loi Tai Leng. General Sai has left with a heavily armed force of around two thou-sand men. He is moving east, through the mountains. He must be heading to the border with China. They left six days ago.' She covered her mouth with her hands. 'It has started.'

Bishop thought quickly. 'In that terrain, it will take a force that large about thirty days to reach the border. We've got, maybe, three weeks.'

The sun had almost set, and the village was cast in a warm gloaming as villagers moved about, preparing cooking fires and the evening meal while a gang of dusty, raucous children played soccer in the square. A light breeze played with the trees, and a gentle rustle of leaves hissed across the early evening sky. Bishop shook his head in disbelief, then rubbed his face.

'The US will have a puppet government in Burma, will control trade routes west into Bangladesh and India, and south into Thailand, Cambodia and Malaysia, and will have built a wall against Chinese influence in most of Southeast Asia.' He shook his head. 'Beijing won't take that. It will mean war.'

46

THE LINE FILLED with a faint hiss of static, the occasional digital crackle cutting through as the call connected. The firm's satellite phones and smartphones were well encrypted, so Bishop was comfortable making the highly classified call. What he had to tell Nesbit could not wait for an email situation report; the Old Man needed to know what they had discovered, and he needed to know now.

'It's been a while since I have heard your dulcet tones,' Nesbitt said through the white noise. 'I assume this is urgent?'

Bishop adjusted the position of the Iridium 9555 against his ear. 'It is. Are you sitting down?'

There was a brief pause. 'I am now.'

'As you know, we have the girl. She's alive and well – if a little traumatised. We're in a village called Lai Kha.' He read off the lat-long. '*But*, there's more. We've got to the bottom of her kidnap. We've stumbled on something big...'

'Don't tease, dear boy,' Nesbit said, his voice calm. 'My pen is poised, so go ahead.'

'The CIA is behind everything. Using their phoney NGO, they are running drugs for the SSA and arming them with US weaponry with the proceeds. I guess that's not startling. *But* we have hard evidence the Agency is behind something far more disturbing...'

Bishop spent the next ten minutes detailing the protocol, the planned coup and the SSA incursion into China. He finished by telling Nesbitt that Armed Forces Day was only five days away and that there were, at best, twenty-one days before Sai reached the border. There was silence on the line when he finished. Finally, Nesbitt spoke.

'It will be war.' Nesbitt stopped, and Bishop could almost hear him thinking. After a long pause, Nesbitt said: 'It *can't* be the Agency more broadly – it has to be a rogue operation. A bunch of hawks at Langley and in Congress. Of all the crazy schemes they've hatched over the years, this takes the cake. I doubt it's a wide group in the know, but, I *guarantee* it's officially sanctioned at a very high level,'

'Surely not...'

'The president *has* to be in on this. He's the biggest hawk of them all, and he's plummeting in the polls – a handy little shooting war always delivers a bump for the incumbent. I know it's long before your time, but just look at Maggie Thatcher and The Falklands.'

'Ancient history has always fascinated me... I wouldn't have picked you for an anti-Thatcherite.'

'I'm not,' Nesbitt relied. 'I was there on Tumbledown with the battalion. I believed *then* we were there for the right reasons and I still do. Anyway, let's return to the present dilemma. The War Powers Resolution gives the president the ability to deploy troops without a formal declaration of war by Congress, but there are conditions and there *is* Congressional oversight. He needs the numbers in Congress to carry it, and there are any number of new-age Neocons he can call on to deliver them. He will get his deployment and, with it, US force projection hard against the Chinese border.'

'So what now?'

Nesbitt paused. 'It has to be derailed somehow – but that's beyond even *our* impressive capabilities, so the best I can do is pass it on.'

Another pause. Nesbitt was tossing something around in his

mind. Bishop could sense it. He turned and looked back into the village. It was dark and the air was thick with the enticing smells of food cooking over wood fires. He caught sight of Madeleine walking down the steps of their billet and turning away from the light of the village toward the jungle. Swe was sitting on the stairs of her house, talking to Zaw, and Sophie was squatted in the dirt, playing with two small children and a rattan ball. It was a peaceful scene, but all Bishop could see in his mind's eye was a vision of charred bodies in the ruins of the village. Fire and ash.

Nesbitt's voice broke his nightmare reverie. 'Email me the evidence. I'll send it on to someone senior I know in the Agency – that should start an investigation that, hopefully, flushes out the wolves. I'll also leak it to a chum of mine at *The Times* – that way *The Wall Street Journal* will pick it up; they're both News Corp-owned.'

'And the SSA column. How do we stop *them*...?'

Yet again, Nesbitt paused before he answered. 'I haven't a clue. If Langley accepts the evidence, maybe they'll do something about that, but I doubt it. I imagine they'll bury it. They will want to distance themselves from the plot and prevent any US reaction to the crisis. The next thing the world will see is the US Ambassador making dismayed rumblings at the UN, as the Chinese counter-attack and throw out the incursion.

'So the cross-border attack will go ahead...'

'Maybe...'

Bishop swore softly and then agreed to send the evidence immediately. He was about to end the call when Nesbitt spoke again.

'Oh, I was going to email you, but as I have you, your sister called...'

'Did she say what she wants?'

'She did not, but she did say to tell you "the bastard is back".'

Bishop drew a breath and stood very still. He should have killed him all those years ago. The old man was back and harassing his mother and sister. He had been out of jail for years but had left them alone – until now. That was not news he wanted to hear, especially with him in the jungle, over seven thousand kilometres from outback

Queensland where his mother and sister lived. He terminated the call
and ran a hand through his hair, his heart pounding.

With an effort, he put aside thoughts of his family, and turned his
attention to the situation he and Madeleine were facing. He had been
involved in some heavy dealings over the years, but *nothing* came
close to the seriousness of the game they were now playing, and the
odds against a win had never been worse.

He strode back to the house he shared with Madeleine for his
laptop and Inmarsat to send the files and photos to Nesbitt. He was
on the stairs when, in the quiet of that part of the village, he heard
Madeleine's voice, low and urgent, in the bush. He froze on the small
footpath.

'So, that's what you've been looking for, isn't it?' Madeleine was
saying. 'The SSA invasion of China, don't be coy... Why didn't you tell
me?... *Confirmation* bias? Are you kidding me right now?... Well, you
fucking know now, don't you... You should have told me... No, of
course not! I haven't said anything... And don't give me the old King
and Country bullshit...'

Bishop didn't move as Madeleine stood with her back to him, the
satphone to her ear. She listened for a long minute then spoke again.
'I agree. You're right not to trust the Cousins, so the back-channel to
Beijing makes sense... What next, then?... It may have escaped your
attention, but the fucking clock is ticking... No. I understand. None
taken... Well, if I'm not in the tent, I'll sign off and leave it to you and
The Masters... No, *sir*, of course, I bloody...'

Bishop moved fast, and before Madeleine could react, he stepped
up behind her and snatched the phone from her hands.

Madeleine yelled. '*Bishop!* No, for fuck's *sake!*' Bishop held her
away with a hand and raised the phone to his ear.

'Who is this?' he said.

Six and a half time zones away, Nigel Harris sat in his office over-
looking the Thames. It was late morning, and the day was grey and
gloomy for the time of year. He looked to the ceiling and drew a deep
sigh. *Fuck!*

'Mr Bishop, I presume...'

'I asked who's speaking,' Bishop said, his voice tight. He glanced at Madeleine who was standing in the dark, her arms loose at her sides and fists clenched. Her eyes flared with anger.

'My name is Nigel, Mr Bishop. I am Madeleine's employer.'

'Her *employer*? She doesn't have a...' Suddenly, a lot of things made sense. 'Wait, are you Six?'

'Now *that* I can't tell you, but I *will* say that our interests intersect in what you are doing out there. Hence Madeleine's current brief.'

Bishop thought fast. It could only be one thing; it couldn't be the girl. 'The coup or the China incursion?'

'Well, as you appear to have got the jump on Madeleine – quite unusual, that – I suppose I can feed you. Just a little, mind you. The coup is of *some* interest, but we tend to take a pragmatic view of such things. Whichever uniformed thug sits in the big chair in Naypyidaw does not bother us. That is, of course, unless we could convince them to hand power back to the people of Burma, and I *very* much doubt our Mr Min is about to do that. No, I think you'll agree that it is the very real threat of war on the Burma-China border that is of interest. I should say of *concern*...'

'What are you going to do?'

'Again, that's not something I care to share with you.'

'Maddy will tell me...'

'No, Mr Bishop, she won't. She does not know, and even if she did, she would not tell you.'

Bishop paused. There was only one thing that mattered to him. 'You know why we're here. Is any of this going to interfere with my getting the girl home?'

'Provided you can stay ahead of those currently hunting you both, I should say not.'

'Right, we're done here then. One last thing: leave Maddy alone.'

'She is in this voluntarily, so I rather think that would be *her* choice, old boy, not yours.'

'I'll make it mine.'

In his office, Harris paused and gazed out of the window. Christ! Now it was raining. Bloody London spring weather. 'And how will you do that, Mr Bishop,' he said, his voice dropping all pretence of bonhomie. 'I caution you not to do anything rash. I take a very dim view of people harming my agents. If you do, I will find you, and we *will* kill you.'

'Fuck off, Nigel,' Bishop said and stabbed at the phone, ending the call. He looked up at Madeleine who remained frozen in place. He tossed the satphone to her and she snatched it out of the air. Bishop sighed.

'How long, Maddy?'

Madeleine chewed the inside of her mouth for a moment. 'Since you phoned me about the job – I had to call it in. It's procedure.'

'Procedure for whom, Maddy?'

'MI6 agents... I've been a contractor for some time now.'

'When were you going to tell me?'

'I can't tell anyone I'm Six, Bishop. You know that...'

'Not *that*, Maddy, for fuck's sake! When were you going to tell me you've been playing me all this time and reporting back to fucking Nigel in London? When were you going to trust me, as I've trusted you every step of the way...?'

'It's my job, Bishop,' Madeleine shouted, 'and my job has rules. Surely you, of all people, understand that!'

Bishop shook his head. '*Fuck*, Maddy! We were nearly executed together. Remember that? Even then, not a word. How many times since Bangkok have you told me not to bullshit you? And all that time, you were leading me by the nose, manipulating me.'

'Oh, grow up! I've *killed* for you, Bishop. I've done everything you've asked on this hair-brained adventure, and fuck me if we're not standing here with the girl free and safe.' Madeleine tossed her head. '*Manipulating* you...? Please!'

Bishop moved to walk past her and stopped. 'All your little side questions about shit that had nothing to do with the job, about Loi Tai Leng, all make sense now.' He shook his head again in disgust and began to walk off. Madeleine reached out and took him by the elbow.

'Bishop, come on... Let's talk about this. It's not as bad as you're making out.'

Bishop shook off her hand. 'Don't Maddy. I'm already pissed off but you don't want me angry. You'll regret it...'

Maddy laughed. 'You haven't got it in you, Bishop. And we both know I'd knock your teeth so far down your throat you'd be opening your fly to clean them.'

'Don't bet on it, Maddy,' Bishop growled and stalked off, leaving his partner standing in the dark, cursing under her breath.

47

THE MEAL HAD BEEN STRAINED. Bishop ate silently, scowling deeply, while Swe tried to engage him in light conversation. Madeleine kept her eyes down, concentrating on the food in her bowl, only occasion-ally looking up to ask Sophie if she was okay or needed anything. Zaw had just sat between them all, looking about in amusement as he ate plate after plate of food and drank cup after cup of *khao niew lao*, Shan rice wine.

Bishop placed his half-empty bowl on the ground and stood. 'I'm turning in,' he said abruptly. 'Goodnight.'

Zaw grinned. 'Lovers' tiff, Bishop? So sad. Now my sister has the chance she has been seeking...'

'*Zaw!*' Swe hissed. 'Be still.'

'Bishop doesn't love anyone, Zaw,' Madeleine said, picking her teeth with a small twig. 'He's incapable of it.'

Bishop stared hard at her, a look of hurt crossing his face, and walked slowly up the stairs of their darkened house. Madeleine watched over her shoulder as the door closed and a hurricane lantern was lit to cast a golden glow inside.

~

The house was dark, and Bishop felt the movement at the door. She was quiet; he'd give her that. He rolled over on the rough stretcher bed, an arm behind his head.

'You might as well come in, Maddy. You have to sleep somewhere.'

Madeleine leaned against the door frame, her shapely figure silhouetted by the fire outside. She didn't move. 'I'm sorry, Bishop,' she said quietly. 'That last comment about being incapable of love. It was out of order. I was being childish. I didn't mean it...'

In the dark of the house, Bishop's voice sounded tired, resigned. 'No, you were right. I *do* feel that I'm incapable of loving anyone. I always have, I think. Since I was a kid.' He suddenly thought he was going to vomit – the withdrawals had been bad the past two days – and he coughed to clear his throat.

'Don't say that,' Madeleine said softly. 'You're just tired, and this op has been bloody difficult. Terry told me in Chiang Mai that you were the original warrior monk – maybe that's it; you're just too dedicated to your work to let love in.'

'He's got a big mouth, that bloody Irishman.' A pause. 'I thought I loved my mother, but maybe I just pity her. Perhaps I love my sister, but we haven't seen each other in so long...' He swore softly. 'Look, enough of this!' Bishop winced to feel his left hand trembling. He sat up and swung his feet to the floor. 'So where do we go from here, Maddy?'

Madeleine stepped into the house and crossed the room to sit beside him on the stretcher. 'I could use a smoke right now,' she said, smiling.

Bishop chuckled. 'Maybe we should both take it up...'

Madeleine nodded. 'Yeah, maybe. Look, no more secrets, I promise you.'

'What about next time?'

'Will there be a next time?'

'Who knows? It's a scary and dangerous world out there, and there's always a need for people like us.'

Bishop could feel the warmth radiating from Maddy's leg pressed against his, and the scent of the oils from her bath lingered in the air. He pressed back slightly, and she didn't move. His chest tightened, and his breathing quickened.

Madeleine turned, meeting Bishop's gaze. His eyes were dark, and he was so close. He hadn't washed since their return to the village, and he carried the scent of sweat and earth. It was the smell of a man, raw and intoxicating. Her lips parted, her heartbeat racing – a call to arms.

They had been here before, years ago. It had come out of nowhere when they had crossed paths in Geneva – she working with Swiss intelligence on a case, and he ironing out the details of a ransom payment with a private Swiss bank. Neither had told the other what they were doing. It had been a torrid forty-eight hours that had ended as quickly as it started.

Now, they sat still and silent, studying each other in the dark, each acutely aware of the other's closeness. Then, as if in mutual agreement, the moment was gone.

Bishop slid away slightly as he spoke. 'So, tell me what's happening? What have your masters – that's what you called them – got planned?'

Madeleine stood and began to pace the room. 'I don't know. He wouldn't tell me unless I was involved. Which I'm not. Whatever it is, it's way above my pay grade and probably my security clearance.'

'It's going to have to be a strike, wouldn't you think? That would do it. You mentioned Beijing when you were on the call to old mate in London...'

'Six will back-channel into Beijing and tell them what's afoot. His Majesty's Government won't say a word officially, but the nod to Beijing will be on. The Chinese will probably move troops to the border to disrupt any border crossing ...'

'And combine that,' Bishop added, 'with a targeted strike. It would stop everything. Dead.'

Madeleine shrugged. 'Yeah, maybe. I don't know anyway, so it's not worth losing any sleep over. Greater minds than ours, and all that...'

Bishop was about to reply but he stopped as, out of the dark, came three faint, but clear, sounds. *Thoomp, thoomp, thoomp.* Years of training kicked in and he started counting as he grabbed his gear and threw Madeleine's rucksack at her. He pushed her to the door.

'Mortar primaries! They've found us. *Get out!*'

They were halfway down the stairs when the three mortar bombs crumped into the ridgeline, just north of the village in three synchronous explosions of high explosives, shrapnel and dirt.

'Six seconds,' Bishop yelled. 'The baseplate is about two klicks away.'

They ran down the stairs and into the village square. It was a kicked ants' nest of activity as villagers and PDF soldiers ran about grabbing possessions, equipment, animals, and small children. Swe ran to meet them and shouted at Bishop.

'They have found...'

Thoomp, thoomp, thoomp.

Bishop looked around. 'They're adjusting,' he said to Swe and Madeleine. 'The fire is being observed and directed... *Wait!*'

The three bombs struck home, this time just to the south of the village. 'The bastards are bracketing us. The next shot will be in the centre of the village. We *have* to move. Swe... which way? North or south?'

'South! Off the ridge toward the gardens and your LZ. Then we fan out and head for the river. Cross that and we're back in the jungle. We can then head southeast to another sanctuary village in the hills.'

Bishop looked around. Madeleine held Sophie by the arm and gripped the panicked young woman tightly. The rest of the village was in chaos, with people running in all directions, stricken with fear and leaderless.

'Give the order Swe!' Bishop barked. 'Get these people moving!'

Thoomp, thoomp, thoomp... Thoomp, thoomp, thoomp.

'Here it comes! *Maddy! With me!*' Bishop turned and, cradling his carbine, lumbered off under the weight of his pack, across the square and onto the narrow footpad that led off the ridgeline from the village, south toward the river and the LZ. The six mortar bombs struck home three seconds later, crumping into the centre of the village in a catastrophic wave of fire and metal, bringing death and mutilation to anyone standing there. And dozens were.

Stumbling in the dark down the steep side of the ridge, half sliding and half falling, Bishop heard another sound that chilled him. It was a sound he knew and had never forgotten. It was a pop and hiss as white phosphorus rounds thudded in, and the phosphorus ignited and spread. The sound was followed instantly by unearthly screams of agony and horror as the phosphorus stuck to flesh and burned white hot, unquenchable.

He stepped to the side of the track as villagers and soldiers hurried past. Madeleine turned, but he waved her on. 'Keep going, Maddy. Stay with the group.' He looked back as Swe emerged in the middle of the terrified mass streaming down the hill.

'Keep them moving Swe!' he shouted. 'Lead them on and don't stop. They will follow this up with a ground assault. It's move or die.' Zaw was behind his sister, and Bishop shouted again. '*Zaw!* Get to the back and make sure there are no stragglers. Push them forward and leave no one behind!'

Zaw nodded and ran back toward the burning village as mortars continued to fall, decimating the tiny hamlet and any living thing still there. Swe moved to Bishop, her face grim and set. Bishop gripped her shoulder.

'Keep moving. We'll achieve a clean break, then push the civilians on while we find ground to establish a Rear Guard. We need to delay them while the villagers get away.'

Swe nodded, stumbling slightly as an elderly woman, laden with a basket of chickens, pushed past. 'I know just the place. It is a small hill about a kilometre from here. Its rear is protected by the river, and one flank is secure against a cliff face. We can hold there.'

Bishop slapped her on the back. 'Good job. Lead on, Commander – I'll be right behind you.'

Swe saluted briefly then moved off down the track, pushing villagers ahead of her and helping young children and the elderly with a gentle word and steadying hand. Bishop looked back toward the village. The screaming had stopped and it was eerily quiet. All he could see over the top of the ridge was a faint red-orange light. The stench of roasted flesh, thick with the chemical tang of burnt cordite and the pungent, acrid smell of phosphorus, wafted through the forest on a light breeze.

48

LATE THE PREVIOUS AFTERNOON, the SSA had found the three bodies hidden off the track after the roadblock failed to respond to calls. The local unit had called it in to the military, and the district Battalion Commander, recalling his orders directly from General Min, had phoned Reilly to tell him.

In Namsang, nursing a glass of bourbon, and with Dutton in the local clinic, Reilly had pulled a map from his pocket and spread it out on the bar top. He knew where they were. He traced a finger across the map, locating the position of the roadblock, then moved his finger in a circle, by the scale taking in about twenty kilometres of rugged terrain.

The Battalion Commander had told him they had received intelligence a PDF unit of twenty-five strong was hiding out in the hills in a remote village called Lai Kha. That tallied with what he had been told. Reilly's finger zig-zagged on the map until it came to rest on the tiny hamlet, less than forty minutes away by road.

He knew the PDF was sheltering them, and the village was only twenty klicks in a straight line from the roadblock incident. Nestled in a river fork, high on a ridgeline, Reilly noted. Steep sides to north and south, with a more gradual slope to the west. He had picked up his phone and dialled the Battalion Commander, quickly giving the soldier his instructions.

'And don't start without me,' Reilly had said. 'Under no circumstances. I want to be with the assault.' Reilly would not be armed, and he wasn't stupid enough to actually go in with the assault element, but he would move behind the Reserve from where he would have a good view of the attack. All that mattered to Bill Reilly was that he was on hand when the three fugitives were either killed or captured. Hell, but it would be good to be in at the kill of those two. And the girl, of course. *Goddamn*, they had been a nuisance.

The Battalion Commander agreed and hung up the call. Reilly then took a minute to reflect on what was ahead. He smiled, happy at the plan and confident that this would finally end it, before downing the remainder of the bourbon and walking to the Landcruiser.

The ground crunched underfoot. The white phosphorus had baked and fused it, and any organic matter on it, so that it crackled and broke with every footstep like hard toffee. Except it wasn't. Burning houses and trees lit the night as Reilly tied an army sweat rag around his nose and mouth, but the stink still got in – a witch's brew of chemicals, charred flesh, and boiled blood. He looked around the destroyed village, watching the soldiers clearing what remained of it, shadows against the light of the fires. Tripping on something and dropped to one knee. He reached out instinctively with his hand to break his fall, and looked back over his shoulder.

The lower half of a tiny torso, burnt beyond recognition, twisted and misshapen, lay at his rear-most foot, his boot stuck in the charred corpse. With a cry of alarm, Reilly sprang to his feet and shook the remains off. He was breathing heavily behind the sweat rag, and his gorge rose, acid-bitter, as he looked at his right hand. It was covered in a sticky black substance that he instantly knew was clotted and burnt blood.

Unable to hold himself back, Reilly dropped to his knees and whipped away the sweat rag, vomiting again and again until his stomach heaved painfully, wanting more but empty of anything to give.

Still on his knees, Reilly looked up and saw he was not the only one sickened by the hellish scene. A number of the soldiers, young conscripts, were doubled over and retching their hearts out at the horror of the charnel house that had once been a vibrant rural hamlet.

Reilly stood and wiped his mouth with the rag as orders were shouted around the village. The soldiers quickly regrouped and moved off the ridgeline, cautiously descending the dark, jungle-lined track in pursuit of their enemy and those who supported them. Reilly joined the staggered file patrol, tucking in behind the Company Commander and his signaller.

Every step was filled with tension. The soldiers, their eyes and weapons scanning the dark jungle on either side of the track, expected an ambush at any moment. None came, and fifty minutes later, as dawn was breaking, the lead platoon broke from the treeline into a clearing, on the other side of which stood a small, lightly wooded knoll. Small arms fire immediately burned in from the hillock, and the platoon went to ground, crawling and scrambling their way into some sort of cover to return fire.

Just inside the treeline, Reilly lay down beside the Company Commander who was studying the knoll through a set of small binoculars. With the binoculars still to his eyes, the officer spoke.

'They are on that small hill. Maybe twenty of them. Hit is hard to see in this light. One hundred and twenty-five metres. Their rear is protected by the river, and one flank is secured against that cliff. That hill and cliff will take too long to move around, so we must attack from here...'

'A frontal assault, Chief,' Reilly whispered. 'That's a ballsy move.'

The officer lowered the binoculars and regarded the foreigner with disdain. He really did hate them, but orders had come from the top, so who was he to question?

'We do it all the time,' he said, his face unreadable. 'They are a ragged bunch of terrorists, and we are an infantry rifle company. We outnumber them over five to one, and we are better trained...'

Reilly wasn't so sure about that. 'The mortars...?'

'Not available. They are a battalion asset and have been re-tasked. Also, we are now out of range of the baseplate.' He pointed to their right. 'I will put a platoon in fire support on that paddy dyke – the approach to it is mostly covered from this direction. Two platoons will assault from here.' He turned again and looked at the big foreigner. 'I suggest you remain here – do not engage in the assault.'

Reilly nodded. 'I wasn't planning to, Captain. I'll just chill here in the bleachers and watch you guys win the glory.'

The officer grunted something unintelligible and then barked a series of orders. Out in the open, the soldiers began to slither around, forming three rough lines, one for each section, while the platoon behind the Captain shook out into their assault line, still deep in the treeline. The third platoon broke off and began their run, under cover, around to the paddy dyke. Desultory fire from the knoll continued to pepper the company as they prepared and the Captain smiled.

'Their response is weak. They are probably low on ammunition and will be armed with poor weapons – everyone knows the PDF are just a street gang.'

Reilly was going to comment but decided against it. He was feeling increasingly uncomfortable about the outcome. He wriggled backwards a little as the Captain watched his fire support take position. Without another word, the officer blew two sharp blasts on his whistle and, as the sun rose, his troops climbed to their feet, shouting and firing as they charged forward.

Bishop and Madeleine lay on their backs on the reverse slope of the knoll. Around them lay most of Swe's force – over sixty men and women – while a mere twenty were positioned on the knoll's lip in the trees, firing half-heartedly at the soldiers to their front.

Bishop raised his head and looked across the river. Guided by five of Swe's men, Sophie and the surviving villagers had crossed the river and fled into the forest, disappearing from view as they climbed the steep ridge that ran east from the river bank. Their destination was a small village high in the hills, some seven kilometres away, and it was the Rear Guard's job to hold their ground long enough to give the refugees time to make a clean break to safety.

He lay back and took a slow pull on the cigarette between his lips. It had been eleven years since he had last smoked, and he was enjoying it. Madeleine did a double-take as the exhaled blue smoke drifted over her.

'Where did you get that?'

Bishop ashed the cigarette and drew on it again. 'One of Swe's boys gave me a pack. It helps clear the taste of death from my mouth – and I'll be damned if the nicotine doesn't seem to be doing some good to my head.'

'It's your bloody lungs I'm worried about.'

Bishop grunted. 'Maddy, there is a Tatmadaw rifle company about to assault this position, and we could well be dead in the next thirty minutes. Lung cancer isn't on my list of worries right now.'

Madeleine grinned. 'You're right,' she said. 'Give me one.'

Bishop tossed her the packet and a box of matches, and watched as she lit up and dragged hesitantly at the smoke. Madeleine coughed then spat on the ground.

'Shit! That's bloody awful...'

'Yeah, but so good, right?' Bishop reached into a pocket of his pants and pulled out a grenade. 'I've only got two, so this one's yours.'

Madeleine took it and stuffed it into the cargo pocket of her tac pants. 'You're a prince,' she said with a smile. 'Are you ready?'

Bishop nodded. 'As I'll ever be...'

'Here they come!' Swe shouted as heavy automatic fire broke out to their left front, thudding into the slope of the knoll before it found its range to rake along the skyline. Bishop and Madeleine moved with the sixty soldiers around them, crawling up the reverse slope and filling the gaps on the firing line. Their weapons snapped into their shoulders, and rapid, aimed shots poured into the advancing line of soldiers.

On Bishop's immediate right, an MA-15 machine gun– a clone of the German MG3 – opened up, followed by another from the centre of the line. The heavy 7.62 mm bullets ploughed into the assaulting line of troops at the Rapid Rate – nine hundred rounds per minute. The rounds scythed through the assault line and further back into the Reserve. Soldiers were bundled aside, torn to shreds in a welter of blood and gore as the machine gunners went to work. Their Number Twos rapidly flipped feed plate covers and slapped in new belts as the ferocious rate of fire devoured the rounds, and 7.62 mm link tinkled into hot piles in the dirt beside the gunners. Meanwhile, a third machine gun, an FN MAG58 on the left of the knoll, played back and forth across the paddy dyke, suppressing the attacker's supporting fire and bringing death to any man foolish enough to look up long enough to take a sight picture.

The assault line began to waver, and the defenders on the knoll sensed a shift. The machine guns dropped back to the Sustained Rate – two hundred rounds per minute – but the fire was still devastating. Meanwhile, the modern, well-maintained small arms of Swe's unit blazed away. Empty magazines were ejected and dropped to the ground to be quickly replaced, as the defenders fired round after round into the confused and demoralised conscripts, now only thirty metres to their front.

Bishop was firing rapidly, shifting the aim of his carbine from target to target, and every round struck home, dropping a soldier. The carbine suddenly stopped and Bishop glanced down. Empty magazine! He ejected the mag and slapped in a fresh one.

'Second last!' he yelled to Madeleine on his left.

She snapped off two rounds, taking a crawling soldier, desperately seeking cover, in the top of the skull. 'I'm on my last! This is going to be tight!'

Gunfire cracked like lightning as eighty weapons spat rounds in quick taps and bursts, punctuated by the heavier, rapid thudding of the machine guns pouring fire into the advancing enemy. The incoming fire from the assault, and its fire support, was vicious, and Swe's troops began to take casualties.

A thick, shimmering haze rose to their front – dust kicked up by the firing and the relentless heat from the barrels. The attacking soldiers blurred in and out of view, distorted by waves of heat and the chaos of gunfire. Dirt and debris erupted from the ground, turning the field into a hot cloud of dust and churned earth. Shadows moved in the distance, but the lines were unclear, obscured by the fury of the firepower.

The smell in the air was pungent and sharp – burnt propellant, hot metal, and the earthy tang of upturned soil and blood. Each round fired thickened the fog that carried the acrid scent of battle – sweat mixed with the biting odour of gun oil and the heat of weapons – that stuck in throats and seeped into everything.

Bishop raised his head slightly and peered through the battle haze. In moments, he found what he was looking for. Fifty metres away, a single soldier was lying on the ground, waving his arms and directing the assault. He lay next to a man carrying a radio. The company commander. Bishop shouldered his carbine and sighted carefully. He drew a deep breath, then slowly exhaled as he squeezed the trigger.

The officer turned his head, his mouth open in a shouted command. Bishop's shot cracked across the gap, and the M4 round sliced into the helmet's edge at the temple. The officer's eyes went wide, and his shoulders lifted before his body dropped, his helmet punched to the side. The attacking force's commander was dead.

~

Reilly watched the battle from the safety of the treeline, a growing feeling of disquiet rising in him as the defenders on the knoll decimated the assaulting force. *Decimated* was the wrong word, he thought. One in ten, be damned – they were being massacred.

Perring through the dust and haze, he spotted the white guy on the knoll and saw him take the shot. He saw the company commander killed and stared in disbelief as the last of the assault group broke and streamed back across the field as the PDF's fire continued to take victim after victim. He counted the survivors as they crashed into the treeline and away up the narrow footpad into the jungle. Thirteen. Unlucky number.

Reilly turned his head and watched as the platoon in the support fire position tried in vain to disengage. Two PDF machine guns mercilessly cut them down as they stood and attempted to flee the shelter of the paddy dyke. In less than a minute, the entire platoon was down and still, except for one man who crawled through the paddy, screaming and holding the blue rope of his guts with a bloodied hand.

Jerking his attention back to the knoll, Reilly watched PDF troops advance off the hill in disciplined lines, leapfrogging forward to clear the battlefield. Single shots rang out as they dispatched the wounded, moving ever closer to Reilly's hiding place. Time to go. He rose slowly into a crouch and moved deeper into the trees until he found the track. With a last glance back, he broke into a lung-burning run up the hill, side-stepping pieces of abandoned equipment and a wounded man sitting crying against a tree.

The track seemed to go on forever, and he feared he may have taken a wrong turn, but then, suddenly, he burst out of the bush and back into the destroyed village. His Landcruiser and safety lay only four hundred metres to the west, so he set off at a jog, stumbling and tripping on the torn and root-tangled track along the ridge. As he ran, a bitter voice sounded in his head.

That was an almighty clusterfuck, Bill, and it's got your fingerprints all over it. What the fuck were you thinking?

'Get a grip, you maniac,' Reilly said in reply. 'Nothing's changed. Min and Sai are on the move, and nothing will stop them now.'

You think? What about those two Marvel Characters and that girl? Fuck, Bill, were they even there? They can stop you...

'They were there, goddammit, I saw them! And they can't stop shit,' Reilly yelled into the hot and silent forest. But as he ran on, his heart thudding painfully and his lungs burning, a black beast of fear and doubt crawled from its den and began to chew at his brain.

49

SHAN STATE, 20°57'50.4"N 98°01'44.2"E, Burma

The refugees had stumbled into the village at dusk and had gathered in a frightened group as they looked around them at the devastation. This village, too, had been targeted by Sit-tat and, now, all that remained were the burnt-out husks of houses and bodies scattered everywhere in the blood-pooled dirt. They were exhausted – the elderly and the children especially – and five of Swe's troops were carrying wounds, three so severe the soldiers were not expected to survive.

Two of Swe's men stood protectively on either side of Sophie. Bishop and Madeleine dropped their rucksacks at their feet and emptied a box of ammunition onto Bishop's map to reload their magazines.

Swe pulled her brother aside. 'Get everyone out of here and bed them down in family units on the edge of the village. No cooking fires. Post sentries, and I want the three guns manned all night on a picket. Have the medic and the Moh Yao, *healers*, to see to the wounded.' She looked around. 'And have the bodies gathered and shown what little dignity we can.'

Zaw nodded and ran off to see to her orders. Swe turned to the three foreigners. She nodded at Madeleine and took her hand. 'Thank you, Maddy. You were a tigress today. I can't ever repay what you have done for my people...'

Madeleine nodded curtly. 'No thanks necessary, Swe. We just helped where we could.'

'Just so. But my thanks, nevertheless.' Swe turned to Sophie. 'Are you alright?'

Sophie, still wide-eyed with shock, nodded. 'I'm okay,' she whispered. 'Just tired and ... and sickened.'

'It is the way of this war that is tearing my country apart. One becomes hardened to it after a while, but it is never easy – especially when it is the innocent so often targeted. Bishop...' Swe said, turning her head. 'Walk with me.'

The two moved to the edge of the destroyed village. The sun had set, and the jungle fringe was impenetrably black. The smell of rotting flesh hung in the air, cloying at the back of their throats. A light breeze rustled through the dense canopy. Bishop could barely make out the tiny figure standing in front of him.

'What will you do now?' he asked, his voice a soft murmur against the night sounds of the forest.

'We will keep moving. We cannot stay here. The army is everywhere, and they will find us again.'

'Where will you go?'

'I do not know.' Swe's voice cracked with the strain and the horror of it all. 'Somewhere.'

The forest was thick with the ceaseless hum of crickets, like a thousand tiny clockwork gears whirring in the darkness. An Indian Nightjar sang its repetitive churring call into the night. 'You won a great victory today, Swe...'

'Yes. My six dead for their eighty-seven. The arithmetic is good, but that is six dead from my larger family – and the dozens killed in the village. And let us also not forget that every one of those eighty-seven soldiers we killed was a poor conscript who did not want to be there, and certainly did not want to die for the junta. Yet they did.' She sighed. 'Yes. A victory.'

Bishop did not reply. Swe went on, stepping in close and looking up into his face.

'I did not want to mention it, but I must. I know you... well, I know *of* you. You have been here before, haven't you?'

Bishop closed his eyes. He had always supposed it might come up, but he didn't imagine it would be like this. But Swe *was* Pa'O. Without a word, he nodded.

'My uncle,' Swe said softly. 'He is Pho Saung... you would call it "shaman". I remember the tale he told of you – "Bisso", the big foreigner who helped the Pa' O. Trained the Pa'O National Liberation Organization. Fought with them. He called it a turning point, an omen. He said your path would cross ours again in a time of great struggle and change. And so it has come to pass.'

Bishop had a hundred answers to that, but none he could voice, so he stood in the dark, waiting on Swe.

Eventually, she spoke, her voice firmer now. 'I want you to stay...'

'Swe, I want to stay...'

'*But* you must call your friends in Thailand and get out. Get the girl out to safety. You do not belong here. This is our fight, and we must win it on our own.'

'Or die in the attempt?'

'Yes. That. In all of our hearts, death is preferable to living under tyranny. What is it you say in the West: Better to die on your feet than live on your knees?'

'Emiliano Zapata, a revolutionary. Like you in many ways – just don't end up like him. The generals got him in the end.' Bishop sighed. 'But, you're right. My job is to return the girl to her family. We will be leaving just as soon as I can arrange it.' He paused. 'You know, you can come with us,' he said quietly. 'Get yourself and Zaw to safety – you would enjoy life in Singapore.'

Swe smiled in the dark. Bishop could not see it, but he heard it in her voice. 'Is that a proposition...?'

'I don't know,' Bishop whispered. 'It could be...' He felt the soft warmth of her hand take his.

'As much as it would please and honour me to join you somewhere where we could live a life, I cannot. My life is here. My people are here, and so is my duty.'

Bishop cleared his throat, then pulled out his map and switched on the Surefire. He spread the map on the ground and crouched beside it. His left hand trembled as he pegged the map with small rocks at each corner. 'There are a lot of cleared areas marked on this... are they accurate?'

Swe tapped the map. 'All of these garden areas are still there. You can land a chopper in any one of them. Pick the closest once you get out of these ridges and valleys – it will take about three days to walk out of here. I will send Zaw with you.'

Bishop studied the map again, folded it, and placed it back in his pocket. He needed to arrange the extraction, and the feeling of other unfinished business lay heavy on his mind. 'I have a call to make,' he said as he moved back toward his rucksack.

'We move at first light,' Swe said into the dark at his retreating back, tears coursing her cheeks.

∾

Bishop looked up. High up on a large hill at the centre of four intersecting ridgelines, the canopy was open, and the night sky above him was clear. It was a deep purple dotted with pinpricks of light, and the stars glittered like shards of glass on dark cloth.

His plan for the drug lab had crystallised over recent days, and he was now certain what he would do. But he would not tell Madeleine until it was too late. She would be angry, no doubt about it, but he knew she would understand and, eventually, forgive him. First, he needed to pass on his shopping list to Terry Dougherty.

He powered up the satphone and adjusted the antenna to ensure a clear line to the satellites passing overhead. He brought up the quick-dial menu and tapped Dougherty's contact, then held the handset to his ear and waited. The connection was made in moments, and Bishop could hear the ringtone. He pulled out his notebook and switched on the Surefire torch. Dougherty answered almost instantly. Bishop smiled. The big Irishman must be sitting on the phone.

'You've been quiet,' Dougherty said. 'Glad you're alive...'

'Grid Reference for the extraction LZ,' Bishop replied bluntly. 'Prepare to copy.'

A brief pause, then Dougherty's voice. 'Send.'

Bishop read off the six-figure grid reference, a method of locating a position in a grid square on a map with an accuracy of one hundred metres. He gave Dougherty the date and time for the extraction.

'Stand by,' Dougherty replied, and Bishop could hear him place the phone down as he unfolded and laid out a map. One minute later, Dougherty was back on the call.

'That's pretty deep in country,' he said. 'It's beyond the Huey's limits. You've got the girl?'

'Yes. So, three pax and our two rucks.'

'Tak and I will fit the external tank and strip out the cabin to lighten the load. Fuck, Bish, it will be a close-run thing.'

'Just be there, Terry. Things are hot here. It's our last chance to get out. Now, write this down – I need some stores.'

Dougherty was silent as Bishop read from a brief list in his notebook. 'I can get all that,' Dougherty said. 'See you in three days. Go steady, Your Eminence.'

Bishop ended the call, powered off the satphone, and stowed it in his pack. He looked back up at the night sky. He was weary beyond words, but one last push would do it. 'Just seventy-two hours,' he said quietly. 'That's all we need. Please give it to us...'

As usual, when a man stands alone in the jungle and speaks to the sky, there was no answer. Bishop hefted his pack and walked into the treeline to catch what sleep he could in the four hours left of the night.

50

'ZAW, BACK!' Bishop shouted as he fired three rounds at the men advancing from tree to tree, firing as they moved. Madeleine lay on top of a screaming Sophie and fired as Zaw spun about and, dodging left and right, ran past them. He ran on another ten metres and slid onto his belly, the MA-1 assault rifle at his shoulder, firing rapidly to cover Bishop's withdrawal.

Bishop rose into a kneel to better see their attackers, and friendly fire cracked past his head, tearing chunks out the trees and felling a man in dark green tiger-stripe camouflage, a bright orange neckerchief at his throat. Bishop double-tapped and another man stumbled forward, skidding on his face in the jungle mulch.

The four had left the relative security of the hilltop camp only two hours before and had been moving for an hour when they heard a faint whistle off to their right. The two SSA radios – one on each of Madeleine's and Bishop's pack straps – burst into chatter. Another whistle answered further away and to their left. Madeleine turned to Bishop.

'They're not close, but they are flanking us.'

Bishop nodded, stepping carefully through the forest tangle. 'We stay on this bearing for another klick; then we'll hit the valley and bear east. We should get in front of them by the time they come off the ridge. Keep moving.'

Madeleine did not respond; there was nothing to say. She gripped Sophie's hand tighter and drew the girl on as they pushed through the thicket and emerged into clearer, primary jungle. They increased their pace, Zaw scouting out front, then Madeleine and Sophie, with Bishop bringing up the rear. The whistles continued to sound, shrill and threatening in the jungle quiet.

Bishop had turned to check their rear when he spotted a flicker of orange moving through the trees toward them. He instantly dropped to a knee and fired three rapid rounds as eight men materialised out of the jungle green.

'SSA!' he shouted. '*Move!*'

Bishop stood and ran back, grabbing Sophie as he passed Madeleine, who had rolled off the girl and was pouring fire into the advancing men. Bishop ran on, dragging a screaming Sophie with him in a stumbling run past Zaw, who quickly changed magazines before resuming his fire to cover Madeleine. The five remaining SSA soldiers lay prone, and then, on command, all rose as one and advanced, firing from the hip.

Madeleine heard the dead click of the bolt on an empty chamber and rolled over on her side to change magazines. No time, they were too close! She flipped onto her back and reached into her tac pants, pulling out the heavy, spherical shape of the M67 grenade.

Holding the grenade in her right hand, she ran a finger of her left hand through the ring pull and yanked out the pin, extending her left hand and briefly checking the pin to ensure it had been pulled. She looked back over her shoulder one last time at the advancing men. Dirt sprayed into her face as rounds thudded in around her. Zaw and

Bishop were firing rapidly. Madeleine swung back her arm and
lobbed the grenade.

The safety lever sprung off as the grenade sailed through the air
and thudded into the ground in the middle of the tightly packed
group of attackers. Two seconds later, it detonated and one-hundred
and eighty grams of Composition B explosive shattered the grenade's
casing, sending deadly steel fragments cutting through the air.

Two SSA soldiers took the brunt of the blast and were eviscer-
ated, one dying instantly while the other lay squirming on the
ground, screaming in agony as blood dripped thick and hot from the
leaves of the trees. A third soldier had taken a single piece of fragmentation between the eyes and sat, dead, against the bole of a large
Taukkyan tree, a look of surprise on his face.

Madeleine hugged the ground as the fusillade from Bishop and
Zaw ripped and cracked above her, striking the remaining two men
who sat stunned on the ground. Their lifeless bodies tipped back into
the leaf mulch. Bishop was instantly on his feet, sprinting past
Madeleine to the bodies.

He approached the mortally wounded man and fired a single shot
into his head, cutting off the screams. It was suddenly quiet among
the trees as Bishop quickly inspected the rest of the bodies. Satisfied,
he moved back to Madeleine, who was standing and changing magazines on her carbine.

'You okay?' he panted.

Madeleine nodded. 'I'm okay. Another close one, huh?'

'We have to keep moving. The other two groups will have heard
all of that and will be closing in. We'll change our line of march and
head more obliquely left down into the valley. The other groups will
be converging on this location, so if we do that, we should be heading
diagonally away from them.'

Madeleine pulled back on the cocking handle of her carbine, and
slapped the bolt assist, as she scanned the battlefield. The trees were
pitted and scarred, and their foliage was shredded. Five bodies lay on
the ground in grotesque death poses, with three further back in the
jungle. The stink of opened bowels and blood hung heavy in the air.

Turning about, she suddenly froze. Zaw knelt thirty metres away, his weapon slung over his back. He was tearing Sophie's shirt open.

'Bishop...?' Madeleine whispered.

Bishop turned and followed her stare. He knew instantly what had happened. He and Madeleine ran up to stand beside Zaw. Bishop dropped to his knees as Madeleine opened her rucksack and pulled out a large red medical kit. Sophie looked up at Bishop.

'Am... am I going to die?' she asked, her voice quavering.

Bishop shook his head, forcing a tight smile. 'Not on my watch, kid. You'll be fine.'

Sophie's face was pale, her lips dry and cracked. Blood seeped steadily from the wound in her left side, pooling on the torn remnants of her shirt. Another dark stain spread below her left knee, where her shattered tibia jutted at a grotesque angle beneath the skin. Madeleine dropped to her knees beside Bishop, snapping on a pair of latex gloves.

'She's losing blood fast,' Madeleine muttered, her tone clipped but calm. 'Side wound might've nicked the spleen. If it did, we've got a slow bleed. Infection will be a problem no matter what.'

'How bad's the leg?' Bishop asked, his eyes darting between the wounds.

'Shattered tibia," Madeleine said, shaking her head. 'We'll splint it, but she won't be walking anywhere.'

'And if it's her spleen? Bishop pressed, his voice low.

'Three days to evac? She'll need antibiotics now, or sepsis could kill her before the blood loss does.' Madeleine glanced up, her gaze sharp. 'We need to keep her hydrated, keep moving, and pray nothing ruptures.'

Bishop's jaw tightened. 'Then we don't stop.'

'Zaw, get the trauma gauze,' Madeleine barked, already cleaning the side wound with antiseptic wipes.

Bishop steadied Sophie's shoulder, murmuring reassurances as she whimpered under Madeleine's firm touch. Zaw handed over the gauze, his eyes darting to the jungle beyond the bodies.

'We don't have much time,' he said, his voice tense.

Madeleine pressed hemostatic gauze into the wound on Sophie's side, her hands quick and practised. She paused to uncap a small bottle of iodine solution, tilting it over Sophie's leg.

'This'll sting,' she warned.

As the liquid hit the open wound, Sophie's scream ripped through the jungle. Bishop reacted instantly, clamping a hand gently over her mouth to stifle the sound. 'Easy, Sophie,' he whispered, his voice steady but strained. 'Breathe through it. You've got this.'

Bishop pulled a green whistle from the trauma kit, cracked the vial inside, and shook it briskly to activate the pain-relief vapour. He brought it to Sophie's trembling lips, his voice firm but calming. 'Breathe in, Soph. Deep, slow breaths – it'll help.' Sophie coughed weakly, then managed a shaky inhale. Her panicked gasps eased as the Penthrox began to work, her body slackening slightly, though tears still streaked her pale, sweat-slicked face.

Her muffled cries subsided into soft, hitching breaths, and Bishop leaned closer, his hand shifting to her forehead as he wiped the sweat away. 'You're tougher than you know. Just hang on.'

Madeleine worked fast, packing the wound with haemostatic gauze and securing it tightly with a pressure bandage. Sophie hissed in pain, her eyes rolling back momentarily.

'That'll hold,' Madeleine said, moving to the tibia next.

She shifted to Sophie's leg, pulling the SAM splint from her kit. 'Zaw, hold her steady,' she ordered, her voice sharp. Zaw crouched at Sophie's side, bracing her thigh as Madeleine carefully aligned the fractured tibia.

Sophie moaned, her head rolling against Bishop's knee. 'Stay with me, Sophie,' he murmured, his hand still resting on her forehead.

'This is going to hurt,' Maddy warned, wrapping the splint tightly around Sophie's lower leg. She secured it with strips of elastic bandage, her bloodied fingers moving quickly and efficiently. The hot jungle air was thick, and the sounds of their pursuers could be heard in the near distance.

Sophie winced and bit her lip, tears welling again. Bishop

clenched his jaw, his free hand steadying her knee as Madeleine tied off the final bandage.

'That's the best I can do,' Madeleine said, sitting back on her heels and wiping sweat from her brow. 'She won't be moving it, but it's stable enough for you to carry her.'

Bishop adjusted his pack and rifle, then crouched to lift Sophie. With a deep breath and a groan, he hoisted her over his right shoulder in a fireman's carry, careful to keep her injured side exposed. His right shoulder screamed at him, and a bright light flared behind his eyes. Sophie whimpered as he stood, her body limp against him.

'Let's move,' he said grimly, glancing toward Zaw. 'Keep your eyes sharp.'

51

BISHOP STUMBLED DOWN THE SLOPE, tripping on exposed tree roots and sliding in the damp mulch. His body screamed for relief as Sophie's weight, an unbearable weight pressed into his shoulders.

The jungle heat was oppressive and clung to him as Sophie's unconscious body slumped around his shoulders, her limp arm swaying loosely over his back. Every agonising, weary step was a grim reminder of their predicament. Sophie's clothes were wet with gore and stuck to Bishop's neck. A putrid stench as Sophie soiled herself rose with each breath of the humid air. Heavy with ammunition and equipment, his rucksack dug into his lower back with every step over the brutal terrain.

Madeleine followed in silence, her eyes fixed ahead, her own heavy pack a torment, dragging at her. She was exhausted, the toll of the last forty-eight hours etched in her sunken cheeks, her steps uncertain over the uneven ground. Despite her fatigue, she watched Bishop carefully, ready to step in if he faltered, but she knew better than to ask again. She had tried, gently offering to share the burden, her voice quiet with exhaustion, but each time Bishop had shaken his head.

'No,' he had grunted, his voice tight with the strain. 'I'll carry her.'

And so, he did. He carried the wounded girl every excruciating kilometre through the jungle, the steep hills and valleys blurring together in an endless green hell. His shoulders burned from the weight, muscles on fire as Sophie's body grew heavier with every step. Her skin, once smooth and fair, was now ashen, with a sickly sheen of sweat and faint blotches spreading across her cheeks and neck. Flies swarmed around her wounds and in the folds of her clothing. But Bishop kept moving. He refused to let her go.

In his fevered mind, Bishop was carrying not only Sophie but also his sister and mother. Carrying *them* to safety, to a place he would find for them. One day. He should have killed that bastard...

There was no let-up at night. As darkness fell, they slumped to the jungle floor, limbs shaking with exhaustion. There was no fire – they could not risk it – and the insects descended on them in swarms, biting through their torn clothes and leaving angry welts on exposed skin. Sophie muttered through her fever as she slipped in and out of consciousness. The rasping bark of a distant leopard sent a troop of macaques into a frenzy, and Bishop barely slept, twitching at every sound in the blackness, his body wracked with withdrawal.

The pain in his shoulder was relentless, a constant throb beneath the agony of his opioid cravings. His head pounded, vision blurring as nausea rolled through him in waves. Every nerve in his body was on fire, demanding relief, but none was to be had. The little white bottle sat deep in his pack, and he refused to touch it. All he had now was the raw, gnawing ache in his bones.

Madeleine endured the nights in silence, her hand occasionally brushing Bishop's arm in the dark – her only way of reminding him she was there – as she tended the wounded girl. It was late at night, when both the jungle and her spirit were darkest, that Bowdyn would come to her, his thick northern accent gentling her along. *You've done harder, lass. Much harder. Just put your head down and push on. Your Da and me, we're right proud.* At night, she would cry out to the old game-keeper in her mind, but she rarely spoke to Bishop other than to whisper a word or two about Sophie's deteriorating condition. There was nothing to say. They both knew the score.

By the second day it was clear they had evaded their pursuers, and they dared to relax their level of vigilance. They needed everything now just to survive the trek. Bishop's legs had weakened beyond anything he had ever known – beyond Commando Selection, beyond the long marches in Afghanistan. The green-clad hills rose steep and unforgiving before him, and his breath was ragged in the choking humidity. His arms burned from Sophie's weight, and his shoulder felt like it was tearing apart.

Sophie's fevered muttering and soft cries were clawing at his resolve, each broken word cutting deeper into his mind, a wound he couldn't shake. Hour by hour, his withdrawal symptoms worsened – dizziness, cold sweats, and a pounding headache that split his skull. Each step was agony, but he forced himself to keep moving, driven by a promise he had made, a vow that Sophie would make it home, no matter the cost.

Madeleine, although exhausted, took up position behind him, nudging him forward whenever he staggered. She bore the weight of her pack with quiet determination, although it was clear the strain was getting to her. They hadn't eaten properly in days, and the little water they had left sloshed hollowly in their hydration packs as they moved further and further from the river. She stole glances at Bishop's face, watching the lines of pain deepen as he fought through wave after wave of withdrawal. The desperation in his eyes was unmistakable. But still, he pressed on.

The jungle became their world – a dank, green hell where heat, decay, exhaustion, and pain all blurred into one unending ordeal. Their clothes were ragged, and their skin was smeared with dirt and blood. Hunger gnawed at their stomachs, but the thirst bit deeper, making every breath a dry, throat-burning rasp.

When they finally dropped to the ground on the second night, too spent to speak, the jungle hummed around them, indifferent to their suffering as they dressed Sophie's wounds and coaxed her to take the last of their water. Insects chirruped and whined, and unseen forest animals scuttled by on the hunt, or being hunted. Bishop's shoulders throbbed mercilessly, the weight of Sophie's body never leaving him. But he knew, in the silence, that he wouldn't let her go. Not yet.

52

NAYPYIDAW, Burma

The Myanmar Army Headquarters, also known as the War Office, is a modern, heavily fortified complex in a secure, restricted zone in the capital. The area surrounding the building is meticulously maintained, with wide roads, manicured lawns, and strategically placed security installations. Army HQ is the most secure location in Burma, protected by multiple layers of security, including blast-proof windows and reinforced walls, armed guards, surveillance cameras, biometric access controls, and frequent patrols. No one got in, or out, without the correct authorisation.

Major General Min Kyaw Ko, commander of the army's Eastern Command, stood on the wide, granite stairs leading to the main entrance and lobby, beyond which, deep in the heart of the building, lay the Operational Command Centre. He tilted his head back and looked up at the massive, multi-story structure, a modern concrete and glass edifice. He smiled grimly. Today was the day, and now was the hour. The hard metal of a handgun pressed insistently on his hip, as if in reminder of what lay ahead.

He turned around and ran a critical eye over his bodyguard. Each man of the detachment had proven their loyalty to him time and again, showing their willingness to kill or die for him. Their hard faces were unreadable, and their eyes, always moving, flicked about assessing any possible threat to their charge. General Min nodded at the sergeant detachment commander, a man who had been with him for over a decade and received a nod in return. Yes. They were ready, and they would stand by him.

His 2IC, and son-in-law, Brigadier Myat Nay Win, checked his watch. 'It is time, sir,' he said. 'Are you ready?'

'I have never been more ready, Myat. The people of Myanmar call to me, and I shall answer. Is everything in order? Things will escalate very quickly once it is done.'

'The regiments are all in place, sir. We are ready to move here and on Communications Command; on the airport, the radio station, Presidential Palace, and Parliament; on internet exchange points and telecommunications hubs, police headquarters, and on the railway and major road networks connecting to Yangon and Mandalay.' Brigadier Win smiled at his father-in-law. 'All is ready, father. Your destiny awaits.'

General Min nodded once. He turned and strode up the stairs and into the spacious lobby of the headquarters. Soldiers snapped to attention, and the General and his bodyguard were guided quickly through security without further checks and into the building. The corridors were brightly lit, and General Min noted they were deserted – there was not a soul in sight. He wasn't surprised. After all, this was a secure, high-level meeting between the commander of a major military command and the Commander-in-Chief, Senior General Min Aung Hlaing. The corridor stretched ahead, echoing with the sounds of military boots on the cool tiles.

The group rounded a corner, and Brigadier Win approached an unmarked door. He gripped the handle. 'In here, sir,' he said as he twisted the handle and swung the door open. Min stepped in, then halted in the middle of the room.

'What is this?' he barked. 'Where is the Chairman?'

Win and the sergeant entered the room, the sergeant closing the door. The room was empty except for a single chair against the wall and a CCTV camera in one corner of the ceiling. The floor was bare, polished concrete, and General Min noticed with a shudder that the walls were sound-proofed.

'The Chairman will not be attending, sir,' Win said, removing the handgun from the general's holster. He glanced up at the camera. 'However, he is watching proceedings.'

General Min was no fool. He knew what was about to happen. What he could not understand was *who* was about to do it.

'You...?'

Win nodded. 'Yes, father. Me.'

'But... why? How...?'

'I have always been the Chairman's man – since before he took over in February 2021. He has known of your plans from the very beginning. Did you really think you could keep something like this a secret? That you could just march in here on the eve of Armed Forces Day and assassinate him?' Win shook his head. 'As to why, let us call it "patriotism"... We do not want the Americans here.' He shrugged. 'Then, of course, there is my promotion into your seat in Eastern Command, not to mention the very handsome sum paid into my Zurich bank account.'

'You are my *son-in-law*,' General Min barked. 'My *family*!'

'A necessary subterfuge. Your daughter will be safe, as will your wife – however, sadly, my marriage will come to an end shortly.' Win smiled faintly. 'It is a shame. I had grown to like her.'

General Min caught the sergeant's eye. 'Sergeant! Kill this man. Do it *now!*'

The soldier did not blink but quietly turned and left the room, closing the door behind him. General Min sighed. It was a long, deep sound of resignation. 'My men...' the general said, looking at Win.

'Will all be unharmed. The regimental commanders and other senior officers will, however, be dealt with. They are being rounded up now and will not live to see Armed Forces Day tomorrow.'

'What will you tell them? My wife and daughter...'

'Nothing. They will mourn you, of course, but this is an occupational hazard for senior officers in today's Myanmar. They know this.'

General Min pointed a finger. 'Do not think this will not happen to you one day.'

'Perhaps. But that is a problem for then. Now, sir, take a seat.'

General Min straightened his shoulders and adjusted the jacket of his dress uniform. 'I will stand like a man. I will look you in the eye as you do it, and may your soul bring you endless torment.'

'I very much doubt that,' Win said, drawing his handgun. 'But as you wish. Standing.'

Without hesitation, he raised the pistol and fired two shots into General Min's chest. Blood instantly blossomed on the front of the general's jacket, staining the ribbons of his decorations, and he dropped to the floor. Brigadier Win walked to stand beside him and looked down into the general's eyes as they began to cloud. He took careful aim and fired a shot into General Min's forehead. It was done. With a last look up at the CCTV camera, Brigadier Win holstered his automatic and left the bloodied and silent room.

53

Shan State, 20°55′33.8″N 98°02′51.5″E, Burma

They were in the treeline, just on the edge of the field that was to be the extraction point. They had placed no LZ markings - exhaustion and security worries had prevented the usual procedure for a field helicopter landing. Instead, they lay in the shade, breathing heavily and willing themselves to recover from the ordeal of the past days.

Bishop lay next to Sophie. She was conscious and breathing rapidly. The wound on her left side had begun to smell the night before and showed clear signs of infection. It oozed pus, and the puckered skin around the dressing was tight and red, hot to the touch. The leg wound was not much better. Madeleine had one hand on Sophie's shoulder as she mopped the girl's brow with her dampened sweat rag.

Bishop had not spoken a word in six hours, other than a brief satphone call to Nesbitt advising him of their location and the pending extraction. Madeleine watched him closely. It was clear he was suffering through another bout of withdrawal. But his left hand had stopped trembling, and his eyes looked a little more focused, perhaps even brighter.

Madeleine, too, had not spoken for hours, and she cleared her parched throat. 'We made it,' she croaked.

Bishop, staring fixedly out into the field, just nodded.

'You know,' Madeleine went on, 'you still have the meds. Why not take one now? It will ease the symptoms and the pain...'

Bishop turned his head to look at her. 'That's ironic,' he rasped. 'You, of all people, suggesting I should take the drugs.'

'I'm just worried about you. That's all. One dose will help you...'

'And set me back to the start,' he snapped. 'After all I've been through to shrug the fucking thing.' He rubbed his eyes and shook his head. 'I'm sorry. I know you're just trying to help. But I'm nearly through this. The last few days have finally broken the back of the Oxy's grip on me... I think. I can feel I'm coming out the other side.' He looked back across the field and turned his eyes to the sky. 'I just need to rest for a bit.'

'We'll both rest soon. Once we're on the chopper.'

Bishop did not reply. Instead, he checked his G-Shock. 'They're late,' he murmured. 'Nearly forty minutes. Something's happened...'

'Fuel shouldn't be a problem. If something *has* happened, it will be...'

'Ground-to-air. Yeah. That's what worries me.'

They lapsed back into silence, watching the field as they slapped at midges and mosquitos that had risen from the damp mulch on the ground. It was an agony of uncertainty as both played through the worst cases in their minds. Had the chopper even left Chiang Mai? Did it have the fuel payload to make it? Had it been shot down as it crossed the border? Bishop could not communicate with the aircraft, so they had no idea of knowing what had happened. And so they waited.

Deep concern had risen in Bishop, and he was checking his watch again – fifty-seven minutes late – when he stopped and tilted his head. Nothing. Then, faintly in the distance, the familiar thwopping of the twin blades of a Bell UH-1 Iroquois. He squinted his eyes, scanning the pale, kerosene-blue sky and tapped Madeleine.

'Here they come,' he said. 'About bloody...' he stopped suddenly as he caught sight of the Huey. 'Fuck...' he whispered.

The Huey was flying lower and slower than it should have been, a thin trail of smoke washing away in its wake. The aircraft was unstable as it staggered its way toward the LZ. It was tilted slightly up and was wobbling unsteadily, crabbing through the sky as Tak struggled with yaw control, while also dealing with what was obviously reduced engine power. As it got nearer, Bishop and Madeleine could hear loud vibrations from the tail rotor as Tak fought the damaged aircraft into the LZ. As it approached the field, the Huey's descent was slow and deliberate, as Tak used a longer, flatter approach to compensate for reduced control and power.

Bishop and Madeleine rose to their knees and watched anxiously as the chopper limped in. They could see now that the aluminium skin of the aircraft's fuselage was pock-marked and torn, pieces of it flapping in the wind to add to the din. The perspex canopy was shattered over the right-hand pilot's seat. They saw Tak look down, his face obscured by the black visor of his helmet. Dougherty was in the cabin, leaning out and watching the ground. It looked like they would overshoot the LZ, but at the last possible moment, Tak dropped the battered airframe the last few feet, and it thudded into the dry field.

Madeleine and Bishop looked at each other. 'Fuck, indeed,' Madeleine said. 'This isn't good.'

Bishop stood and gently lifted Sophie onto his shoulders and staggered out of the treeline toward the chopper, his carbine slapping his legs on the end of its sling. Madeleine followed him, her pack on her back and dragging Bishop's by its top handle. They reached the Huey, and Madeleine dropped Bishop's pack and turned around to cover their rear.

Bishop stepped up to the open and stripped-down cabin. Terry Dougherty just stared at him. There was nothing to say – it was obvious things had gone badly wrong. He reached out to help Bishop gently lay Sophie on the cabin floor.

Bishop pointed at the chopper. 'What happened, Terry?' he shouted.

Dougherty pulled off his headset and jumped out to stand beside Bishop, yelling in his ear. 'Fucking ground fire about five klicks in from the border. We took shrap from a Type-87 then got raked by heavy machine gun fire.' He shook his head. 'Sure, and I don't know, but judging by the sound it made when it pinged us, and the size of these fucking holes, it had to be a Russkie KPV. Thank fuck they didn't hit the external tank. Jaysus, but it was close! It's like they knew we were coming...'

Bishop waved Madeleine into the aircraft and watched as she mounted and secured her rucksack. 'Can you make it back, Terry?'

'Yeah,' Dougherty shouted. 'We can. If we're not shot out of the sky. But we've taken tail rotor damage and the engine has been hit – the fuel lines and engine casing, I think. We've got fuck all power and even less lift.' He grabbed Bishop by the shoulder. 'We can't take all three of you. The girl has to stay.'

Bishop shook his head. 'That's not happening,' he yelled.

'Look at her, Bish! She's going to die anyway. None of us get out of here if she comes.'

Bishop poked his friend hard in the chest. 'And if she were your daughter, Terry...?'

'She's fucking not,' Dougherty yelled back. 'And I'd like to think I get out of here in one piece so maybe I *can* have a daughter one day.'

'You can be a heartless bastard sometimes, Terry,' Bishop shouted. 'But I've got a solution for you. Have you got the items I asked for?'

Dougherty reached into the cabin and pulled out a heavy hessian sack. He handed it to Bishop. 'All there. But I have to ask: what the fuck is it for? Your job here is done.'

'Unfinished business, Terry,' Bishop shouted as Tak furiously waved at them to hurry – they had to get off the ground now, or they never would. 'It's my solution for you. You are to take Maddy and Sophie back to Chiang Mai. Get Sophie stabilised. Then get her to Bangkok.' He passed Dougherty a slip of paper. 'Nesbitt's details. Contact him, tell him what has happened, and he'll make arrangements to get Sophie into care in Bumrungrad Hospital.'

'And you?'

'I'm staying,' Bishop shouted.

Madeleine looked up sharply and shouted over the roar of the chopper's damaged engine. 'You're *what*...? No, you're not...'

'Maddy,' Bishop hollered. 'I've got something to do. You stay where you are. Terry, I'll be in touch. Get out of here! *Now!*'

Dougherty looked at his friend. Whatever the mad bastard had planned with the contents of that sack, he knew then he might never see him again. He nodded and slapped Bishop on the shoulder. 'I'll have beers on ice for when you get back,' he shouted and clambered aboard, nodding at Tak before he gently tied Sophie down with cargo straps.

The Huey whined and shuddered, then slowly, shakingly, lifted from the ground. Bishop grabbed the hessian sack and his pack and started to run back off the LZ toward the shelter of the trees. Behind him, a rucksack thudded to the ground, followed immediately by Madeleine, feet and knees together, rolling. Dougherty leaned out of the aircraft shouting, but his words were whipped away as Tak wrestled the Huey around and began to climb, heading south toward the Thai border.

Maddy sprinted across the field and charged into the trees, catching up with Bishop as he crouched at his rucksack, his back to her.

Bishop turned, his eyes widening. '*Maddy!* What are you *doing* here...?'

'Don't "Maddy" me, you utter bellend!' she hissed. 'You're here, so I am too! The question *is* just what the fuck are *you* doing?'

There was no point in arguing. Bishop tipped the contents of the hessian bag onto the ground, and Madeleine stared dumbfounded at the pile of rations, 5.56mm ball ammunition, C-4 explosives, wireless electric detonators and the small, dark green box of a remote firing system. As he stuffed the stores into his rucksack, Bishop looked up, his face grim.

'I'm going to destroy that drug lab.'

No sooner had he spoken than gunfire broke out to their rear, and a section of Burmese Army soldiers surged out of the jungle and across the field toward them.

54

Reilly stood at the window and snapped open the shutters. Bright light burst into the dark room, and dust motes sparkled and danced in a golden luminosity. He slipped on his sunglasses as he looked out of the old casement window.

Across the road, Yangon City Hall shone white in the sun, and, opposite it, the golden stupa of Sule Pagoda glittered amid the busy traffic roundabout of Sule Pagoda and Maha Bandula Roads. The Pagoda was both a two thousand year-old Buddhist shrine and the focal point for the protests of the 2021 Spring Revolution – neither of which facts impressed Reilly. All he saw, as he gazed from the second-floor window, was a shrine to both an Indian beggar and a failed pro-democracy movement.

He turned away from the window and lit another cigarette. He had been chain-smoking for much of the morning, and his mouth was dry and tasted like the bottom of a hamster's cage. Sutton's phone call two hours before had been a shock, and the Station Chief had been calling, but Reilly had not picked up. He poured a bourbon and checked his watch. Ten more minutes until he made his run.

'You're an asshole, Bill,' Sutton said the moment Reilly answered his phone. 'Leaving me in that goddamned clinic in Namsang...'

Reilly looked around the open-plan office at the back of the large complex that was the US Embassy on University Avenue Road. There had been a time when he had his own office... He lowered his voice. 'Did you die? No, you didn't, so you can thank me later. I had things to do and needed to return to Yangon...'

'Were those "things" the massacre of a Shan village followed by the destruction of an entire army rifle company...? Before you ask, I know about it – I *do* know things, Bill.'

Reilly swallowed, the memories of the child's body, the stench, and the blood and gore flooding back. He had seen some shit in his time, but never... 'I was after the girl and her two heroes. We had them bottled up...'

'But you didn't get them, did you. My guy inside the battalion called me. Jesus Christ, Bill! An *entire* rifle company...?'

'It doesn't matter,' Reilly hissed, covering the phone with one hand and leaning over his desk. 'It's all too late. Armed Forces Day is today, and Min is about to...'

'Min is dead, Bill. His security detail assassinated him yesterday.'

Reilly sat back in his chair, the phone limp in his hand, his heart racing. For a moment, he thought he would vomit on the desk. Dead? Min? Holy *Christ!* It was the end of everything. He thought fast. Sai was on autopilot, right now, heading for the Chinese border with an invasion force, and there was no stopping him. Now, with Min dead and the plans for the coup in the toilet, there would be no address to the UN, no invitation to Washington, and no US troops on the ground in Myanmar.

What there probably would be, however, were Chinese troops, mad as hell and with no one to stop them. Then, what? Thailand? Bangladesh? More immediately, how long before Tatmadaw's secret police connected the dots that led right back to him?

Reilly swallowed a chunk of his lunch that had risen in his throat. Maybe there was a way out, he thought desperately. Maybe...

'Listen,' he whispered. 'We keep our heads down. The girl and those two assholes won't get out of the country, and no one can trace any of this back to us. General Hlaing and the junta command will be busy pulling apart Min's leadership group and smiling for the adoring fans on Armed Forces Day. Sai is still days from the border, so we can tip the Council off that we have stumbled on plans that...'

'You haven't seen the papers today, have you? Haven't been online?'

'No...'

'I suggest you do. *The Wall Street Journal*. The front page, and a two-page exposé in the centre pages. It's all about a CIA operation in Myanmar to run drugs for guns, using a shell NGO to sponsor a takeover of the country. It's also about the kidnap of a Canadian national. The limey press has got it, too. *The Times*. They have photos and documents.'

'Your goddamned *phone*, you dipshit! They broke it...'

'Christ knows how, but that's fucking irrelevant now, Bill, don't you think? It's all out there, and pretty soon, arrests will be made back home, and Senate Committees will convene. We're screwed.' Sutton paused. 'I'm getting out. I'm going to head for Haiti and lay low for a while; then Christ knows what – Langley will be hunting us once we're connected. And you better believe we'll be connected pretty damn quick. Maybe you...'

Reilly hung up the phone and cradled his head in his hands. It really was the end of everything. The only hope he had now was protection from the man who tapped him for the job in the first place. He shook his head. Christ, what was he thinking? The asshole would be standing in front of the Senate in days with his right hand raised, and would throw him under a bus in a heartbeat.

No. He had to get out, and he had to get out now. He grabbed his phone and keys off the desk and stood, snatching his jacket off the back of his chair. *Move, Bill! Leave now!* As he stepped away from his cubicle, he glanced across the room and saw two figures through a glass partition into the next corridor. The Station Chief, flanked by an armed security guard, was headed his way.

They hadn't seen him, and Reilly walked quickly in the opposite direction, his head down. He turned a corner and lucked out when an elevator opened in front of him. He dragged a young consular officer out and stepped in, hammering the button to the Ground Floor. The doors hissed closed, and the lift dropped. In seconds, Reilly walked into the secure area at reception guarded by a US Marine, tapped the security door with his ID card, and exited into the public waiting area. Five steps later, he was outside and heading to the main gate on University Avenue Road. In three minutes, he was in a black and yellow taxi, heading to the safe house on Sule Pagoda Road.

Reilly sipped the bourbon. He had not used his phone in hours, so he had no way of knowing, but he hoped the girl and her two heroes had been killed at the LZ ambush. Christ, how he hoped that had happened! He checked his watch again. Five minutes. He would arrive at Yangon International with his perfectly counterfeited diplomatic passport, be quickly ushered through formalities, and board the flight just before the doors closed. He was cutting it fine, but he had done this before.

He knew where he was headed – it was a nice enough place and, best of all, a man could disappear there – but first, he would make a large transfer to his bank in Hong Kong, followed by a series of cash withdrawals from ATMs at his next two stops.

There was no returning now – not ever. He would miss his wife and the house they were going to build in the hills of Wyoming, but anything was better than doing fifteen to life in Leavenworth. He swallowed the remnants of the bourbon. It was time. He picked up his backpack and leather overnight grip, and walked to the door. He did not look back as he left.

55

It had taken them four days of hard marching to get there, but it had not been as arduous, nor as agonising, as their flight across country following their contact with the SSA patrol.

After a brief firefight at the LZ, their steady, aimed shots cutting down the six of the soldiers before they made it across the field, they had managed to break contact. They had checked each other for wounds, shouldered their packs and quickly moved off on a bearing that took them back into the hills and the jungle. Back into the security of the forest at a ground-eating jog. Hours later, they had slowed and force-marched until they reached a spot on top of the first large hill southeast of the LZ. There, they had rested – drinking from their replenished hydration packs, eating a rehydrated meal, and sleeping.

Sharing the night piquet duty, they slept the sleep of the dead, deep and undisturbed for seven hours. As the day's first faint light filtered through the jungle canopy, they cleaned their weapons and did running repairs on their clothes and gear. Bishop opened a muesli bar for himself and tossed one to Madeleine. She tore it open and took a bite.

'So,' she said around a mouthful of fruit and nut. 'Not a bad plan, overall. Get there, set up an OP from the high ground just north of the camp, watch the routine, count the numbers, assess their readiness, and then I create a diversion while you slip in and blow the place to kingdom come. I like it...'

'Thank you,' Bishop said quietly, rubbing a lightly oiled cloth over the bolt carrier of the stripped-down carbine, before re-assembling the weapon and loading it.

'The only thing we haven't discussed is how we get out,' Madeleine said.

'I have a plan for that too.'

'Care to share, Napoleon...?'

'There is a small beach on the river, immediately east of camp. That will be the LZ. Terry will take three hours to get there, so I will call him two hours before we start the raid. That gives us time to get the job done, and not have to loiter around before he arrives.'

'Slight wrinkle, there, 'though. Assuming they made it back, what if that old clunker isn't airworthy in time? We're royally screwed then.'

Bishop shook his head. 'Those old Huey's were built to take a lot of punishment. Besides, I called Terry last night while you were sleeping. They made it back okay and have already repaired the critical damage. They are working on refining it over the next twenty-four hours. I have every faith...'

'Admirable sentiment. Let's pray you're right.' Madeleine finished the muesli bar and stashed the wrapper in her pack. She pulled out her handgun and dropped the magazine as she looked at Bishop. 'And Sophie...?'

Bishop sighed. 'They pumped her full of antibiotics in Chiang Mai and cleaned the wounds. She'll be in hospital in Bangkok later this morning. From there, it will be on to Montréal. Nesbitt is arranging all the papers, and Bouchard is sending his private jet.'

Madeleine was pushing rounds into the magazine of her handgun. She spoke without looking up. 'She's going to live, Bishop. You did everything you could,' she said. '*We* did, but especially you. You never let up on her...'

'Yeah, well. It wasn't enough.' Bishop checked his G-Shock. 'Nearly 0530. Saddle up and let's go.'

Three days later, after a hard but uneventful trek, they arrived at their observation post after briefly doubling back on a broad hook to check they had not been followed. Once they were satisfied they were where they needed to be, they sat and watched for an hour before stealthily moving forward on their stomachs, pushing their packs in front of them. After slithering in, they quickly camouflaged their observation position and, the hide established, settled in to study the target beneath them, a little over three hundred metres away.

A low, rumbling chorus of frogs pulsed from the shadows, each croak and reedy trill a ripple that drifted through the late afternoon, layered like the slow beats of a drum in the stillness. Madeleine lowered the M25A1 stabilised binoculars and made another pencil annotation in her notebook. She rubbed her eyes, feeling the grit chafe under the lids.

'That's another rotation right on time,' she said quietly, checking her watch. 'Like clockwork, these boys.'

'What do you think?'

'I think it's doable. A total of eight armed men – we have to assume some halfway decent level of training, but probably lulled by their untouchable status.'

'You're right. They don't expect anything to happen. I get the feeling the guards aren't there to keep intruders out, but to keep the workers in.'

'You notice they don't seem to have any team leaders? It all looks like the security just happens organically – some weird process of osmosis. They won't expect anything, so they'll lose their heads when we go in hard and fast.'

'Makes sense. Booby traps and early warning?'

Madeleine shook her head. 'I can't see anything. You?' Bishop shook his head, and she went on. 'If they have any set, they're not checking them. I just don't get that kind of vibe from this lot. I mean, shit, they guard a bloody drug lab that they expect to be left alone.'

'What about the lab workers?'

'They aren't a worry. They'll panic and run at the first loud noise. No, it is the security det we need to be concerned with. To be honest, I'm not that concerned.' Madeleine looks back over the camp. 'But we are going to have to deal with them. All of them. I'm not overly fond of hot extractions, so we can't have any of them left to take potshots at us as the chopper flies in.'

'Agree.' Bishop paused and checked the field sketch in his notebook. 'What about the layout? The storage of the chemicals is too confined. No Materials Safety Data sheets here. One slab, maybe two, and the whole joint will go off in a chain reaction...'

'And you have six slabs.'

'I do. I'll get in, rig and blow the place, no problems. But it's all down to your distraction. You have to draw the crabs and deal with them.'

Madeleine nodded. 'Consider it done. I'll want that grenade you've got secreted somewhere about your person and most of your ammo.' She handed the binoculars to Bishop. 'Your stag,' she said. 'I'm going to grab forty winks. Don't do anything stupid.'

Bishop smiled, raised the powerful binoculars, and studied the camp. After two days, he knew the layout and routine intimately, but you could never have too much reconnaissance.

Makeshift shelters and camouflage netting, the cookhouse and mess, the tarpaulin-covered shed holding large plastic drums of chemicals, and the lab itself. A long hut, open-sided, where a dozen men, gloved and masked, work the production line. Flammable chemicals are everywhere. That's good.

He panned the binoculars across the camp, slowly counting. Four uniformed and armed men stood at their posts. They were alert and watchful, poised for action but looking in, not out. Bishop nodded. That confirms *that* theory. They were alert in the middle of the day, fresh on shift, but they would not be at 0400. The night shift would be tired and thinking about bed, and the men he could see would be half asleep, still fuddled with the early morning rise.

He nodded again, satisfied. Tomorrow morning it was, then.

56

TEZPUR AIR FORCE STATION, Assam, India

The airbase was nestled in a lush green belt of the northeastern state, dominated by the picturesque backdrop of the Eastern Himalayas. The Brahmaputra River ran nearby, and the rolling foothills of Assam, terraced with tea plantations, rose northwest from the runway's end. Tezpur is a small but historically rich town that showcases a mix of traditional Assamese culture and Indian modernity – but this was no quiet stroll through a plantation, testing and savouring the tea.

The MQ-9 Reaper sat, dull grey and slender, in a reinforced concrete hanger positioned away from the other hangers and the hectic routine of the runways. An inner cordon of armed Indian Air Force airfield defence guards – *Garud Commando* – surrounded the hanger. A section stood post, statue still, in the sweltering heat of Assam in March, while another section patrolled the perimeter of the hanger.

Inside the hanger, a crew of shirtless RAF aircraft mechanics and armourers swarmed the Reaper, preparing it for flight in the hot-house atmosphere. With its bulbous head, eleven-metre length, and a wingspan of almost double that, the UAV looked like a giant, other-worldly bug, and the men busying themselves around it treated it like that – with care and a good deal of wary respect.

Nigel Harris stood in the ineffectual shade of the hanger and watched the activity around him. His shirt stuck to him, and sweat ran free over his face, sliding his glasses down the bridge of his nose. Ordinarily, as Director of Operations, he would have controlled the operation from London, delegating a more junior officer to the field role. But this particular op was too important and too secretive for anyone but him to manage. C had been most insistent on that point. So, he now found himself sweating it out in India – a place he had never much liked, as exotic as it was, having spent most of his career in the cooler climes east of Berlin.

The deep-throated roar of a flight of Sukhoi Su-30MKI fighter jets blasted over Harris. He turned to watch the sleek fighters clear the runway and pull into a steep climb, doubtless flying off on a combat air patrol of the northeastern border with China.

China. The previous day, he received a call from C, during which he was briefed that General Min was dead and, with him, the plotters' coup aims, thus presumably the subsequent planned deployment of US troops. But the problem remained the inevitable Chinese reaction to an invasion of their territory. The goalposts, it seemed, had shifted.

A week before, C had made a back-channel call to his counterpart in the Second Bureau of the Chinese Ministry of State Security. He had been politely thanked for the information and for the steps that would be taken to prevent the incursion from Burma – China, he had been assured, would do nothing about that. But C had been left in no doubt as to Beijing's response should an "armed gang invade China." They would respond with all force at their disposal, C had been told, and they would not stop at the border.

Harris swigged warm water from the plastic bottle in his hand. By their best estimate, the Shan State Army column was three days from the China-Burma border. They were then expected to immediately cross into Yunnan and converge on a target somewhere in the Xishuangbanna Dai Autonomous Prefecture. Harris felt his stomach cramp – the remnants of a particularly nasty stomach bug he had picked up at the Officer's Mess two days before. He felt hot and uncomfortable, but it was more than the weather and the gastro. World War Three would start in three days if he failed.

Harris checked his watch. The Reaper would take off shortly on its first mission. During the planning phase, they had decided it was vital to mission success – and later deniability – to employ "spoofing" tactics to deliberately mislead radar, signals intelligence, or satellite observation systems regarding the aircraft's true identity, origin and intent. After consulting the cleared flight crew, Harris had instructed them to use Transponder Manipulation.

Although the Reaper's ADS-B transponder would usually be disabled during such a classified mission, Harris directed that they temporarily enable it with a false civilian aircraft identification, mimicking a non-military aircraft's flight path. Using a false callsign, they would transmit the Reaper as a commercial cargo plane.

The first mission was to be a photo reconnaissance of the column to identify its precise location and order of march. From there, the targeting team would work out the UAV's attack profile and run it by Harris for approval before the green light from headquarters in the UK.

Walking deeper into the hanger, Harris dropped the water bottle in a cut-down forty-four-gallon drum. He pushed on the heavy door of the Ground Control Station, a portable, windowless unit in a fitted-out shipping container that housed the mission's operations room. Cool air-conditioning swept over him as he stepped into the darkened interior, lit only by an array of LCD screens in an eerie red light.

A man and a woman, both in flight suits, were seated in front of what looked like a simulator cockpit. The UAV's Pilot and Weapons Officer. The drone pilot turned in his seat and pointed over his shoulder.

'We have secure comms with London and with RAF Command in High Wycombe. The headset is on the desk, sir. It's fifteen minutes to launch, so if you have any last thoughts, now is the time.'

Harris nodded. He fitted the headset and toggled the press-to-talk switch. 'No changes, Squadron Leader. We proceed as briefed.'

57

0355 hrs. Nothing moved in the camp below them. The jungle was deathly quiet, but for the light chirping of crickets as the night animals began to settle in readiness for the dawn. On the spur line above the camp, their faces blackened, Bishop and Madeleine sat beside each other, leaning against their bulky rucksacks, their carbines across their knees.

The camp was lit by festoon lighting, and a diesel generator chugged in the dark. The cook fires were out, and nothing moved. Bishop raised the HISS-XLR thermal weapon sight and scanned the area away from the lights. A night shift guard moved past the lab, then sat with his back against a tree. Further through the camp, Bishop could just make out the thermal signature of another guard standing with his back to them. There were two more somewhere, but Bishop was sure they, too, would be at a low ebb, longing to hand over to the day shift in an hour.

He lowered the sight and checked his G-Shock. 0358.

'I can't believe I'm doing this,' Madeleine said in a low murmur. 'It's completely outside my job brief...'

'*Which* job?'

'Both of them, really. Especially London. They tend to get itchy with any side hustles.'

'Well, fuck them... but I appreciate it.'

'You bloody should, Bishop. Christ, but you'll owe me after all this. *If* we get out.' Madeleine shook her head in the dark. 'Have I said I can't believe I'm doing this...?'

'It's because you love me, isn't it...'

'Don't fucking kid yourself, chum.'

Bishop smiled and checked his watch. 0400. 'Time to move, Maddy. You have fifteen minutes to get into place before I go in.'

'I'll be there in ten.' She reached out and punched Bishop lightly on the shoulder. 'Good luck.'

Bishop nodded and set a timer on his G-Shock. He watched her move silently, as stealthy as a cat, down the slope and through the bush, contouring to another piece of high ground on the other side of the camp.

He clenched and unclenched his left hand. It had not trembled for days, but the fist clenching had become a habit, a pre-action ritual. He shifted in the dirt to move the weight of the hessian sack, for which he had fashioned a sling that now hung over his left shoulder. Everything he would need was there, and he would have quick access to it once he got into the camp. He checked the fourteen pieces of pre-cut duct tape stuck to his shirt sleeve – twelve to use, two spare. He did not want to lose any of them.

0405. Time crawled glacially forward. It always did before a raid, before the shooting started and time suddenly seemed to speed up, minutes eroding in seconds. Bishop let his thoughts run. The chopper would be fifty-five minutes out – Terry had sworn he would be there, and Bishop knew he would, or die in the trying.

Where was Sophie now? Was she recovering? Would she ever truly recover from what she had been through? He would be blamed for the girl's injuries. Not by Nesbitt, but Bouchard would point the finger. Why wouldn't he? *You did nearly get his girl killed, after all. There's no dodging that.* There had been so much death, so much destruction, to get the girl out, and Bishop knew the mission would haunt him. He wasn't sure how he would process it. The small, white bottle in his pocket seemed to nudge his leg at the thought.

Barcaldine would be bloody hot right now. Mum probably didn't have aircon in whatever shitty little place she was living. He really should have killed the old man when he had the chance. He would next time. And there would be a next time...

The timer buzzed on Bishop's watch. 0415. He stood and moved off, heading straight down the spur toward the camp. His eyes were on the brightly lit drug lab, only two hundred metres away.

He stalked slowly forward, his carbine at his shoulder, slowly scanning ahead with his eyes. One hundred metres. He stopped and lowered himself into a crouch. Any second now...

From one hundred metres away, to his left and across the camp, came the sudden eruption of automatic small-arms fire as Madeleine opened up into the camp. It was like poking a stick into a wasps' nest. The guard shift, suddenly alert, began calling to each other and moving toward the firing. Bishop watched as the sleeping day shift crawled blearily from their shelters, pulling on boots and doing up pants, fumbling with their weapons in the dark.

Madeleine's fire went on, now rapid single shots, as she sought to conserve the ammunition she had – all of hers and most of Bishop's. Bishop listened closely. It sounded like she was moving about, firing from different positions to confuse the guards. The day shift guards had now organised themselves, and they ran off into the dark, seeking their comrades. Bishop moved.

Crouched low, he fast-walked into the camp and slid into the chemical store. The chemical drums were stacked high and jammed close. Perfect. He reached into the sack and drew out a slab of C-4, then reached back in, pulled out a small black plastic box, and flipped the lid. He gently extracted a wireless electric detonator that he slowly inserted into the explosive block. Tearing two pieces of duct tape from his sleeve, he gently but firmly taped the detonator in place and then positioned the C-4 slab between two large drums in the centre of the stack.

The firing went on outside. Maddy wasn't letting up, and now the guard force had joined in, having zeroed in on her position. Things would be getting hot for her, Bishop thought, as he repeated the process with another C-4 slab, this time laying it in between two drums at the end of the stack and close to the jerry cans of diesel the camp used for the generator. *They really are making it easy!*

Before he left the stockpile, Bishop took out the remote firing system and synced the wireless detonators by assigning all the charges to a single frequency for simultaneous detonation. Finally, he armed the two detonators by pressing a button on the handheld transmitter, which sent a signal to prepare the dets to fire on command. Satisfied, he ran into the drug lab.

He had stepped into the brightly lit work area of the lab when he heard a strangled shout to his left. He spun around and saw one of the guards, a young man wearing a bright red baseball cap, scrabbling with his slung weapon. Bishop leapt forward, drawing the fixed-blade combat knife at his hip.

The young man stepped back and tried to swing his weapon up, but Bishop was on him. He grabbed the guard by the collar of his shirt, pulled him in with a single, hard tug and drove the blade upwards into the guard's chest, exploding his heart. A small brass locket on a thin metal chain dropped to the dirt, and the guard was dead before his body hit the ground. As Bishop turned back to the lab, his boot crushed the delicate keepsake underfoot.

He quickly prepared and synchronised the last four C-4 slabs and positioned them throughout the lab. That done, he reached into his pants pocket and pulled out the small, white bottle. He looked at it briefly, gave it a rattle, and then placed it beside one of the charges. He looked down at it one last time, then held the remote firing system steady as he armed the remaining charges before tucking the transmitter into his shirt and running out of the lab toward the gunfight.

Bishop had not moved more than thirty metres when the loud crump of a grenade ripped through the dark in an incandescent explosion of heat and shredded metal. He picked up his pace and suddenly came up on the rear of the guard's line. With a quick glance at the muzzle flashes, Bishop knew Madeleine had done her job.

Only three guards remained. They lay on the ground, firing into the thicket from where Madeleine's own muzzle flashes were sparking the night. He shouldered his carbine and snapped off six rounds, two into each guard. The firing abruptly ceased.

In the sudden quiet following the gunfight, Bishop could hear shouting and confusion from inside the camp as the workers tried to gather themselves and flee the scene. He turned around and looked back. None were coming their way, so he called into the bush.

'*Maddy,*' he hissed. 'With me. Let's go.'

Madeleine burst from the dark and ran up beside him.

Bishop looked at her. 'Christ, you look like you've been dragged backwards through a bush.'

'I've been busy, you twat. You don't look so hot yourself... All set?'

Bishop nodded. 'I'm going to blow the lot. Get on the ground.'

Madeleine flung herself to the ground and shielded her head in the crook of an elbow as Bishop dropped beside her. The weight of their packs pushed their faces into the dirt. Bishop pulled the remote firing system from inside his shirt, then fired all six charges simultaneously with the press of a single button.

The roar of the explosion, only fifty metres away, was deafening, and the shock wave swept over them instantly, pummelling them and pounding their senses. A giant red-orange fireball erupted into the night sky, swirling and snarling like a live beast that sucked the air from the forest and dragged at their lungs.

As the last of the fireball rolled away into the night sky, debris from what was left of the chemical store and the drug lab began to rain down on the camp, and on Bishop and Madeleine as they cowered in the dirt. After what seemed an age, and a last loud clang as a steel drum came to ground, Bishop stood. He checked Madeleine was behind him and headed east into the jungle toward the river, forty metres away.

∾

Terry Dougherty leaned out of the chopper's cabin, the wind buffeting his face. The Huey flew low and fast as Tak expertly banked it left and right, following the river's line as it wound through the steep and thickly vegetated terrain. The sun had begun to rise, but it was still dark at river level, although grey shapes were starting to emerge, hesitantly, as if the jungle was uncertain about stepping into the day. Dougherty had always marvelled at Tak's expertise as a pilot, and flying at high speed, at ground level, on Night Vision Goggles, was no mean feat. He whooped aloud at the exhilaration of it.

The entire flight, and the hour or two preceding it, had been what Dougherty would describe as "fair interesting." *Ah, sure,* he thought, *it has been grand altogether.* If more than a little puzzling. Bishop must have known about it, so he would ask him. No time to ponder that now, as Tak said 'one minute,' over the intercom and gently adjusted their line to take them down the centre of the brown, fast-flowing torrent. Dougherty leaned further out and peered into the gloom.

Ahead lay the strip of beach on which knelt two figures, weighed down by large rucksacks. Tak gave the Huey a little left rudder, and the chopper slid smoothly to the left as they came in fast, adjusting their approach before lining up for the landing. The rotors beat at the air, thumping an echo up the narrow river gorge, as Tak pulled back on the cyclic, flaring the old chopper to slow their speed, then adjusted the collective to ease them in. The skids hissed across the sand, and they were down.

Dougherty gave Madeleine and Bishop a thumbs up, calling them into the aircraft, and watched as they stumbled across the sand toward the Huey, lugging their heavy packs by the top straps. They looked like shit. Ragged and gaunt, covered in filth, and their eyes, sunken in their cheeks, were glassy with exhaustion. He reached out and took Madeleine's pack, then Bishop's, laying them out on the cabin floor and strapping them down as his two passengers clambered aboard. Dougherty indicated two headsets. Bishop and Madeleine donned them and toggled the intercom.

'Loud and clear,' Dougherty replied. 'All set back here, Tak,' he said. 'Let's go.'

Madeleine pushed herself against the bulkhead, its metal surface scuffed and dented from years of hard use. She grabbed a yellow canvas Jesus Handle to prevent her from sliding as Tak pulled back on the collective. The Huey rose fast. Tak kicked the right rudder, and the chopper spun like a top before he dipped the nose, and they roared off back down the river.

58

THEY WERE FLYING ALMOST DIRECTLY into the sun. Not long after they had taken off, Tak had banked the chopper hard to the left and climbed to make it over the top of a ridge. He had not changed direction since then. Puzzled, Bishop tapped Dougherty on the shoulder and pressed the intercom.

'We're heading northeast,' he said. 'We should be going south. Where are we going?'

Dougherty faced him 'I thought you knew,' he replied, his voice tinny through the headset. 'Your man Nesbitt arranged it...'

'Arranged what?'

'The transit through China and Laos, of course. You didn't know?' Bishop shook his head, and Dougherty went on. 'Bloody good idea. We were worried about another two flights over the border from the south – especially after the reception they gave us last time – so we jumped at it when your man contacted us and told us he had arranged a transit through Yunnan.'

Bishop looked stunned. 'Nesbitt. *Nesbitt* made arrangements for you to transit through China?'

'Yep, including a refuel, if you can believe it.'

Bishop looked at Madeleine, who just shrugged. 'Terry, where are we going now?' Bishop asked, deeply suspicious.

'Back into China, mate. A wee flyspeck called Manguo Village...'

Bishop turned again to Madeleine. 'You know anything about this?'

Madeleine shook her head. 'No, but I have a feeling London does.'

Bishop frowned. London? 'Terry,' he said. 'Are you telling me Nesbitt arranged for us to fly through Chinese and Laotian airspace to get back into Thailand? That's impossible...'

Dougherty grinned widely. 'Maybe, Bish, but he fucking did it.' He scratched his chin. 'The only problem is we have to surrender this old girl when we land in Manguo, but then, apparently, the Chinese are flying us all back to Chiang Mai.'

Bishop shook his head. This was insane. *Nesbitt* lined up the People's Liberation Army, and the Laotians, to give them a covered run out of Burma. How did he do that?

A thousand kilometres away at Tezpur Air Force Station, Nigel Harris rubbed his eyes as he stared at the screen that projected the high-definition video images from the Reaper's Multi-Spectral Targeting System. A troubling niggle of doubt itched at him. Flying at twenty-five thousand feet, at a speed of just over three hundred kilometres an hour, the Reaper had been airborne for three hours and detected nothing. His guts clenched painfully, and he was about to run for the bathrooms when the drone pilot spoke, his voice calm in the manner of all pilots.

'Sir, we have an aircraft below us. At about eight thousand feet, on a heading of sixty-seven degrees. Stand by, bringing it up now.' There was a pause as the video zoomed in on the aircraft thirteen thousand feet below the Reaper. 'It's a helo. Military, but no markings.'

Harris leaned close to the monitor as the low-flying aircraft came into sharper focus. It was the Bell UH-1 Iroquois C had told him to expect. Harris smiled. *Very well done, Madeleine.*

'Carry on, Squadron Leader,' Harris said. 'Nothing to see here. In fact, we did *not* see it...'

The Pilot did not blink. He had worked with spooks before, and this was a particularly delicate mission, so nothing would surprise him. 'Acknowledged, sir. Nothing to see here.'

59

WITH THE EXPLOSIVE *revelations coming out of Myanmar this week, questions are being asked of the President. What did he know, and when did he know it? How high up does this alleged plot go? What is the role of a shell aid organisation – Global Horizons – and how is a major US defence contractor involved? Finally, why is the United States behind the possible invasion of Chinese territory at a time when the world is sitting on the brink? All questions that, hopefully, will be answered once the Senate Select Committee on Intelligence begins its hearings in a week. But one thing we do know: this is shaping up as a political scandal of epic proportions. And now, back to you in the studio, Wolf...*

Welcome to BBC World News. The time is 4.00 p.m. GMT. In a statement today from 10 Downing Street, the Prime Minister said that he was dismayed by the apparent American involvement in an attempted coup in Burma and fears of an armed incursion into sovereign Chinese territory – both of which are alleged to be part of an operation conducted by the CIA. The statement went on to say that the United Kingdom had no involvement in the original plot nor in any subsequent operations involving either Burma or China. The Foreign Secretary, in a rare statement about the UK's spy agency, also said today that MI6 were aware of the situation but was not involved in any way. It's just not something we do, he said...

CryptoKnıght lit a smoke and opened a can of 7Up. His darkened studio was lined with screens, burner laptops, and smartphones, all connected to the Dark Web and all under different handles, using a variety of secure apps and VPNs to mask his presence. He used data obfuscation tools and custom scripts for automated identity-switching that helped ensure his metadata appeared inconsistent, disrupting pattern analysis attempts. It was as secure as he could be.

And yet, he was nervous.

The document he sent that dude had lit a fire that was now burning around the world, and he was beginning to regret asking only twenty-five K for it. The Agency, and their cyber-pals at Fort Meade, would be scouring the planet for the source of the leak because, no matter the outcome here, they would want to plug it. Permanently.

There was already talk of a possible presidential impeachment, and political scalps were stacking up around the Beltway after the Department of Justice launched a probe parallel to the CIA's internal inquiry. The FBI and a fistful of other federal agencies were involved, and it was only a matter of time before the Suits came knocking.

The dude he sold the files to was good – very good – but CryptoKnıght had partially controlled the forum in which they met and had used a Man-in-the-Middle Attack to intercept the data exchanged in the session. Although most of the dude's IP information had been masked, CryptoKnıght had a few files stashed for insurance. He dragged on the smoke and huffed out through his nose. Yeah, good to have that.

He had covered his tracks so well that even the faintest traces had vanished, leaving nothing but virgin snow behind. That set him apart from the rest. From douches like those glorified data thieves, Manning and Snowden. Manning might have lifted state secrets, and

Snowden exposed systems he barely understood, but they were mere leakers – amateurs who took information as bluntly as smashing a glass to steal the jewels underneath. *But I'm a fucking craftsman, man.* One who slipped in and out undetected, weaving through firewalls with the precision of a surgeon. CryptoKnıght didn't just grab data; he mastered it, bending it to his will. But that hadn't stopped the sleepless nights lately.

Maybe it was time to cash in a wad of Bitcoin and ghost out to the Bahamas for a while. He could use some sun.

Melissa Downs was cried out. She had been living in a funk since the news broke, alternating between fear, guilt, and bottomless depression. She hadn't eaten in days. Every time she tried to sleep, she was plagued by nightmares that woke her in a sweat, her heart racing with anxiety. And she cried. Endlessly.

She swallowed the last of the vodka in the glass and poured another before walking into the bathroom, where she plugged the bath and turned on the taps. Sitting on the bath rim, she lit a cigarette and took a deep swallow of the chilled spirit. What had she *done*? How did it get to this?

When Reilly first approached her, she had resisted his overtures, but he was persistent and convinced her it was her patriotic duty to serve her country. She still believed in the dream that was America, didn't she? She would be doing the President a personal favour that he would not forget. And, after all, did she not want to bring democracy to the people of Myanmar? Aren't they the ones she had spent a career working for?

In the end, she bought it, and that was the start of the nightmare as week by week, month by month, the depth of the conspiracy revealed itself in all its shocking detail. Then the Canadian girl was taken, and, although they had never discussed it in so many words, it was clear she was to be killed. That was the last straw for her, but by then, she was in too deep, and there was no getting out. She swal-

lowed again from the vodka and guffawed drunkenly. No getting out –
at least not alive.

Standing unsteadily, she slowly undressed and stepped into the
hot bath. She eased herself down and closed her eyes in relief as she
brought the cigarette to her lips and took a long drag. She finished
the vodka in two big gulps. Feeling numb now. That was good. She
had Googled what to do next.

Carefully, Melissa Downs placed the empty glass on the bathroom floor and dropped the cigarette into it. Then she took up the
fresh razor blade and watched as the bathroom lights glinted off its
vicious edge before she opened her veins and lay back, waiting for
death.

60

Morale was high, and General Sai Wint Maung was happy. They were all tired and, due to the lean rations on the long march, had all lost weight. Their uniforms hung in loose bags, many torn and rotting, but the men laughed and joked around him as they ate their evening meal.

Sai's force had concentrated in a defensive position only fifteen kilometres from the border – just a day and a half march – and they could sense the end of their trial. They itched for the action to come. Every man in the column was confident of their abilities and secure in the knowledge that they would cross the border uncontested and force-march to their target. They would get there before the Chinese could react in that remote corner of Yunnan, and, once there, they would be harder to remove than a jungle tick.

The sun was setting, and it bathed the jungle around Sai and his men in a soft light that comforted them as they prepared for the night routine. It relaxed them after a month in the dank, green forest. General Sai picked a piece of dried fish from his teeth and flicked it into the dirt as he lit a cigarette. His headquarters staff busied themselves, and runners moved in and out, carrying messages to the unit commanders around the position. It was all professional, orderly and, to Sai, imbued with a deep sense of purpose.

And there was a purpose. A united ethnic Shan population in an independent, transnational state extending beyond national borders would secure the future of the Shan for generations to come. Then there was the money. Billions of dollars of drug income flowing into the state's coffers and his own pockets. General Sai drew on the cigarette and let the smoke trickle slowly from his nostrils. He smiled and looked up at the clear evening sky. It was perfect, and it would work.

Thirty thousand feet above General Sai and his men, the Reaper prowled. Its sensors had picked up the large thermal signature of the two thousand men camped in the forest, and its advanced optics had a clear view of the position.

As the sun began to set, the UAV banked away to come in for another run the length of the ridgeline on which the SSA column sat. At that altitude, it made a low, vibrating thrum. The sound was steady and relentless, mechanical and cold. Its sleek, predatory silhouette stretched gracefully against the deep, endless blue of the upper sky, and sunlight glinted off its metallic body that shimmered as if in excitement.

Two GBU-12 Paveway II 500-pound bombs and four AGM-114 Hellfire missiles were securely mounted beneath its wings. Their shapes were cold and menacing, hanging beneath the great bird like talons, ready to strike and cleave its prey.

In the Tezpur Ground Control Station, Harris spoke into the headset microphone. '*Overlord*, this is *Vortex*. We have a clear visual, and the target has been positively identified. You can see its location on screen.'

Eight thousand kilometres away, a man spoke in the Operations Room of RAF Command in High Wycombe.

'This is *Overlord*, *Sunray* speaking. Yes, on screen. That target area is two kilometres from the village of Wan Ha. Its northernmost line of troops is fifteen hundred metres from the village. It is too close.'

Harris frowned. 'This is a precision-guided weapons platform, *Overlord*. You know that. Fifteen hundred metres is a long way. It's a good five hundred metres outside the GBU's danger radius...'

'Don't presume to tell me my job. The Paveway's larger blast and fragmentation radius make it risky within fifteen hundred metres of a populated area....'

'We can't do the job with the Hellfires alone.'

'You shall have to. I will *not* authorise use of the GBU. I'm not going to have the deaths of civilians on my conscience.'

'You're lucky you still have one,' Harris spat. 'I've seen your orders, and they are clear that we use all means necessary to destroy this threat. The safety margin is satisfactory. You want to appease your precious conscience, do that, but hang up your bloody uniform and go march in the streets with the rest of them...'

The two RAF officers in the GCS glanced at each other, eyebrows raised. The radio was silent for a long moment, then:

'This is *Overlord*. *Sunray*. You will not, I say again, will *not* engage with the Paveway. Acknowledge.'

Harris was about to reply when the drone pilot turned in his chair.

'Sir, there is activity in the centre of the target. It looks like they are preparing to move.'

Harris stared at the video. What appeared to be the command group was standing and packing up their gear. The column's lead element, east of the command group, was also on its feet and beginning to shake out. Harris knew he had to make a decision and make it quick. It was do what they had come here to do – and destroy his career – or sit back and watch the start of a world war play out on the screen.

He switched to intercom. 'Squadron Leader, you may arm and prepare to fire *all* weapons.'

'Sir, I can't. *Overlord*...'

Harris moved to stand behind the Pilot and leaned over his shoulder. 'Squadron Leader,' he said, his voice calm, measured. 'You know why we are here. The mission will fail if we do not employ the *whole* payload. You know what that failure will mean...'

'I do, sir, but...'

'I am the Field Command. The village is outside the danger radius, and I take full responsibility for this decision. I have ordered you, so you're in the clear. Work up the attack profile and tell me when you're ready.'

The Pilot and Weapons Officer sat side by side in the dimly lit room, their screens flickering with data feeds. They nodded and went to work, the Pilot skilfully flying the Reaper on its sweeping pass over the target while the Weapons Officer armed the weapons and readied the attack.

The Reaper held steady at thirty thousand feet, cruising in circles above the target's location. The Pilot nudged the controls, bringing the UAV onto its final approach. Below, the column of troops clustered in the jungle in their unit groups on either side of the jungle track.

'Coming down to fifteen thousand feet,' the Pilot said, glancing at the telemetry. He eased the drone into a gradual descent while the Weapons Officer prepared the payload.

'Target confirmed,' the Weapons Officer reported, aligning the laser designator onto a large group of personnel in the centre of the position. The GBU-12 bombs were primed, tightening the death grip on the distant column of troops.

Harris' headset was suddenly loud in his ear. '*Vortex*, this is *Overlord*. What the devil are you...'

Harris switched off the comms as the Weapons Officer locked the laser on the first target. 'Laser hot,' she confirmed. The beam was invisible but precise, painting the target with pinpoint accuracy. The Pilot levelled the Reaper off at fifteen thousand feet.

'Attack ready,' the Weapons Officer said, her voice steady. 'Permission to fire?'

Harris paused for the briefest of moments. 'Fire.'

'First bomb away,' the Weapons Officer called, releasing the GBU-

12. The drone bucked slightly as the payload dropped. The Weapons Officer immediately shifted focus, lighting up the secondary target with the designator. 'Second bomb away.' She armed the Hellfires, taking a deep breath before squeezing the trigger. 'Missiles away,' she said, voice taut.

Free of its load, the Pilot banked the drone gently, already climbing back into the safety of altitude and the return to Tezpur.

Far below, unseen by the drone's telemetry, the farmer moved out of the forest and toward the tiny hamlet that housed three families and their stock. The world's most advanced sensors – or perhaps just the Mark I human eyeball monitoring them – had failed to detect it, but it was there. His young son walked by his side. His wife and daughter would be waiting at the door to greet them after another day of labour in their small field in the hills. He did not like the look of all the soldiers so close to his home, but he was sure they would soon move on. He smiled down at his son and looked up into the clear evening sky, wrapped in hues of red and purple as the sun began to set. Far above, his eyes caught the glint of something as the sun's last rays bounced off it.

The screens in the Ground Control Station, London, and at High Wycombe flickered with high-definition clarity. As the GBU-12s detonated, a rippling shock wave expanded outward, flattening the nearby forest and sending debris skyward. The infrared optics captured the intense heat bloom, bright white flashes that faded to reveal two charred craters. Moments later, the Hellfires struck home in rapid succession, their smaller blasts punching through men and animals, scattering wreckage and bodies in a hideous wave of flesh and bone.

Harris let out the breath he had been holding. The destruction was terrible, and the death toll would be astronomical. Very little would have survived that maelstrom of metal and high explosives in such a concentrated area – and those that had would no longer be a viable fighting force. The threat had been eliminated.

He leaned forward and switched the communications back on. 'This is *Vortex*,' he said quietly. 'Target destroyed, mission complete.'

'This is *Overlord. Sunray* speaking. What have you done? I'll have your hide, *and* your career, for this.'

Harris sighed. 'You're welcome to both. *Vortex*, out.'

He looked around the dimly lit room and watched for a while as the two RAF officers quietly and professionally carried on their duties. Their mission would not be complete until the Reaper was safely back on the ground. Harris' job was done – and with it, probably his career.

It would be up to London to handle the inevitable repercussions of the strike once the Cousins realised who had done it. Not that there would be any – after a few stern words, this sort of thing just quietly disappeared into the god-awful mess that was geopolitics these days. He realised his stomach was no longer clenching. But he did need a stiff drink.

61

It was warmer today than when they had last met. The spring sun shone brightly, and a light breeze ruffled the waters of the Tidal Basin, whispering through the cherry blossom that was in full bloom, the delicate light pink-white petals thick in the trees. But it was not a scene that the middle-aged CIA officer enjoyed – if he even saw it. He had other, more pressing, issues on his mind. And he felt physically ill.

He knew from the start he shouldn't have gone along – and yet he had. He was sure he could still not provide a convincing answer if he were asked why he had done that. And he *would* be asked. Patriotism? One last hurrah before retirement? Disenchantment with the way things were done these days? Or was it revenge for the promotion that should have been his, but had gone to a thirty-something girl with big tits and a degree in Comparative Literature from Cornell? He turned to the granite bench and sat, staring back out toward the Washington Monument.

It had been a little of all of that, he supposed. But whatever the motivation, it had been the wrong thing to do, and now he would pay for it. His retirement would look a whole lot different from what he and his wife had imagined. Lost deep in thought, he did not notice the younger man slide in next to him on the bench.

'You're losing your touch,' the young man said. 'I could have had you any time in the last ten minutes...'

The older man turned his head. Dressed in a well-cut, navy suit with a US flag pin at the lapel, a crisp white shirt, blood-red tie, and high-shine black shoes, the young man next to him looked like every political operative schlepping around DC these days. The older man hated him.

It wasn't just that the arrogant young asshole had dug this hole for him; it was more than that. It was what he represented – he was the 'New Way', the modern CIA, and the older man hated that more than anything. He smiled grimly. The good news was the slick little jerk would go down with him. Hell, they might even get to share a cell.

'It's all over,' he said, getting straight to the point. 'General Min's dead, and now the attack force has been blown to pieces before they even got to the border. We're screwed.'

The younger man pulled a handkerchief from his jacket and brushed the toe caps of his shoes. 'Yes,' he said, studying his reflection in the shiny, black leather. 'It's awkward...'

'*Awkward?* It's a fucking disaster. We have lost our man inside the regime, the one who was going give us the keys to South Asia, and now there's no casus belli. No armed incursion into China means no Chinese reaction.' The older man snorted. 'Awkward. Jesus!'

'I'm aware of the geostrategic situation,' the young man replied tersely. 'It's why we did this in the first place. Myanmar offers a land corridor linking the Indian Ocean to China and, by extension, to South Asia. We needed that.' He carefully folded and repocketed the handkerchief. 'Which brings us to the destruction of Sai's column.'

'How so?'

'I've been looking into it. It's interesting.'

'Does it change anything?'

'Not for General Sai and his people, but it does give us something we can work with. Maybe...'

'And that is what, exactly?'

'Chantilly,' the young man said, referring to the location of the National Reconnaissance Office. 'Their infrared satellites picked up the thermal signature of the strike. They analysed Blast Radius and Fragmentation Patterns and concluded they were caused by laser-guided bombs and precision-guided missiles. They dug a bit deeper, and the analysis identified the detonations as consistent with GBU-12 and Hellfire munitions.' The young man sucked his teeth. 'It wasn't us, so it had to have been the Brits.'

'Holy shit,' the older man breathed. 'So they've known about it all along?'

'Probably not, but they've certainly known about it long enough to put together a strike.'

'Yeah, but why? Why take the risk?'

The younger man shrugged. He didn't know. 'Post-colonial guilt? Keep things quiet in Good Old Burma? Maybe. More realistically, they figured out what was happening and didn't like the odds of a shooting war on the border. They certainly managed to convince the Indians of the need to maintain the status quo, and Delhi would have baulked at the thought of Chinese troops just across the border from Bangladesh.' He paused and sniffed the air. Damn, it was a nice day. 'For all I know, the Brits even told the goddamn Chinese.'

'You think?'

'Shit, *we* would if it served our purpose. Why wouldn't they?' The young man thought for a moment. 'The problem is, we have enough circumstantial evidence on the strike to use if necessary, but nothing definitive.'

'What difference would it make?'

'None that I know of. Right now. The President *could* use it as a distraction... after all, we've done nothing. It was the Brits who breached another nation's sovereignty, killing hundreds of its citizens. Still, some proof would be useful. It's always good to have a loaded gun in the locker if we need it. London can be such a pain in the ass.'

'They always have been. What about the aircraft? It had to have been a Reaper.'

'Probably, but no proof. They must have masked the flight. All the NRO could pick up, at that time and location, was a chopper – an old Huey – and a civilian cargo plane en route from Yangon to Kunming.'

'The documents? The press is all over this like a dog on a steak...' He didn't mention the girl. Neither of them knew she had escaped – Reilly had never told them.

'Everything that points to us, even the documents the media have, can be refuted...' The young man waved a hand in the air. 'Spun away into yesterday's news.

The older of the two turned his head and watched as a young mother jogged by, pushing a stroller. People like her were everywhere in D.C. They knew how the place operated; they just didn't want to know *what* was happening. Like fucking sheep, all bleating to be governed harder. Just keep me safe, but don't, for the love of God, tell me how – do *that*, and I'm going get outraged and hit my socials.

He sighed. It had all gone to shit. Nothing had gone right, plus Reilly and Sutton had disappeared. As if reading his mind, the younger man spoke.

'We have to find those two clowns, Reilly and Sutton and deal with them. And that woman from Global Horizons. No testimony from those quarters will take a lot of wind out of the Committee's sails.'

'Don't look at *me*! I'm under surveillance. I can't scratch my balls without being recorded and photographed.' He turned around. 'Hell, they're probably out here right now.'

'Relax. It's in hand. The woman will be handled any day now. Reilly and Sutton might be a harder nut to crack, but we'll find them.'

'What about Longbow? They set this up for us ...'

'They won't talk. Too many fat contracts at stake. Besides, some of the shit they're up to elsewhere would see their entire management team and board jailed if it ever got out. No, we won't have a problem there.'

The older man frowned. This hole was getting deeper and deeper. 'In other news, U.S. Marshalls were at my home yesterday. I've been subpoenaed to appear before the Senate Select Committee.'

The young man nodded. 'Me too.'

'*And* I've been stood down pending an internal inquiry – the Director has gone ape shit.'

'She hasn't got to me yet. I imagine she will...'

'You're taking it all very well.'

The young man shrugged. 'Well, I'm not happy about it – and I *am* going to burn that fucker Reilly to a pile of ash – but we'll dodge this...'

'Just how the *fuck* do you figure that? And please don't give me "Presidential Directive". We're road kill to the Whitehouse. There is no way on God's earth the President, or his Chief of Staff, will do anything but deny any knowledge and throw us to the wolves. Hell, they already *have* – why else would we have been subpoenaed? '

'You could be right. But bitching about it changes nothing. *If* we appear before the committee, we'll start by invoking national security and operational secrecy.'

'Jesus! That won't fly...'

'*Then,* after that, we plead the Fifth to avoid self-incrimination. The committee will follow up with an offer of limited immunity to compel our testimony because it's central to unravelling the extent of the "scandal".'

'Do me a favour: don't parenthesise that. It *is* a scandal, a goddamned big one, and you and I are right in the middle of it.'

'Which is why we'll get immunity to testify.'

'So that's your plan. We push for immunity, then dump the lot?'

The young man shrugged. 'I haven't decided yet. It all depends on what's best in the long run...'

'For the country?'

The young man laughed. 'No. For me, of course. I might refuse to testify and take the fall. It will go to trial, but, at worst, I'll get a suspended sentence, a couple of years of probation and community service while I wait for the convictions to be vacated. Then reinstatement and promotion.'

The older man looked at him, stunned. 'Are you *insane*? It won't work like that. It *never* works like that...'

'It did for your old buddy Ollie North. Remember? His convictions were vacated after an appeals court ruled that *his* Congressional testimony, which had been given under a grant of immunity, might have influenced the trial.'

The young man stood and looked down at the other man on the bench. Jesus, these old guys! What happened to them? They used to rule the world. Southeast Asia, Latin America, and the Middle East. They did what they wanted when they wanted. Fucking full speed ahead, and damn the torpedoes. Now they were just a bunch of senile old pussies, wetting their incontinence pads and worrying about scratches on their fucking Oldsmobile.

He smiled. 'Leave it to me. Do you honestly think I wouldn't prepare for this eventuality? Because I did. Every time I spoke to the Whitehouse. I have what we need, and you can be sure this will all go away. Very soon. Just lawyer up, and keep your mouth shut.' He pointed a finger at the seated man. '*Do* that, or you go on the list with the others.'

Without another word or a backward glance, the young man walked off along the jogging track, whistling a low tune to himself. The older man sat on the bench and watched him go, shivering despite the warmth of the day.

62

The midday sun blazed, and the streets were alive with a throbbing, chaotic pulse. The narrow, uneven footpaths were jammed with people pushing in every direction, their faces glistening with sweat. Street vendors were shouting over each other, hawking everything from fried plantains to small, hand-carved trinkets, their voices sharp and insistent, mixing with the blast of car horns and the cough of motorcycle engines.

David Sutton left his safe house near the docks in Portail Léogâne, a rundown area filled with small, ageing apartments, storage facilities, and shipping yards. It was the kind of place where an outsider could keep a low profile. He jumped a *tap-tap*, a colourfully painted minibus, on Boulevard Harry Truman which ran along the waterfront. The sea was on his left as he moved southwest to Martissant.

The district was a known "no go", ruled by the violent *baz*, gangs, that plagued the city, but what the Station Chief had told him made the meet in Martissant a necessary risk. *We've been running operations down here that don't add up*, the Chief had said. *You're on a list. But come in, we'll get you clear of this.* How had they known he was in town?

Sutton had demurred but the Chief had pressed. *Meet an asset where we won't be seen. It's secure, and off-the-grid. It will be a quick in and out job, then you're in the clear.* Sutton knew it was a risk, but the opportunity to clear his name and come in from the cold was too tempting to pass up. Besides, the Chief was an old friend, so Sutton had agreed, and now he was sweating his ass off in the back of a tap-tap.

The smell through the open windows was thick and dizzying – a heady, swirling blend of diesel fumes, dust, and the unmistakable scent of cooking oil hanging in the hot and heavy air. An occasional breeze teased with the faint scent of salt from the nearby sea, but it was quickly swamped by the rank odour of garbage piled up on the street corners, buzzing with flies and heaving with maggots.

Children darted about, chattering and begging, their voices bright in the cacophony. The tap-tap screeched to a halt, and its passengers tumbled out. The driver shouted the names of distant neighbour-hoods, his voice hoarse, and people pushed forward, a tangle of limbs and voices as they jostled for seats.

Sutton stepped off the bus and pulled his battered blue baseball cap down low over his eyes. He tried to shrink his tall, lanky frame, but it was hopeless. He had immediately been spotted as an outsider, and there were eyes on him everywhere. He quickly got his bearings and moved off into the markets in search of the meeting location.

As he stepped away from the kerb, a *chimè*, gang member known as "ghosts", slipped in behind him and another shadowed him from the rooftops. Still more fanned out in the crowds, loping along like wolves, a loose cordon that boxed their target in.

Sutton spotted the narrow alley ahead, leading from a cheap hardware store. He turned into its shadowed, rubbish-strewn interior. The walls were grimy and smeared with Creole gang graffiti. Broken glass crunched underfoot. It was quieter in there, and the smell of the streets had dropped away, only to be replaced by the stench of urine and rotting meat. A dark figure stepped away from the wall and approached, his hands open and in clear sight.

'Blue Rivers,' he said, giving Sutton the agreed password.

Sutton nodded. 'Red skies.' He moved toward the man.

The Haitian was sweating, but everyone did in Port-au-Prince. Sutton moved closer, and the Haitian's hands dropped to his sides, a smile creasing his wide face. Something was wrong. Sutton sensed it, and a premonitory shiver coursed through him, his skin tingling in response to the unseen threat. The Haitian's eyes started to dart left and right. They glanced over Sutton's shoulders. Sutton spun around. The alley was clear, so he began backing out, keeping his eyes on the approaching Haitian.

Sutton turned at the sudden sound behind him as a rusted box trailer was dragged across the alley entrance, blocking it off.

'I have a message from the office,' the Haitian offered. 'From the Chief. Calm down, man.'

Sutton spun around and began to run, building up speed to hurdle the trailer. He was three paces from it, and tensing ready for the leap, when he heard the cracks and felt the savage punches in his back. He was thrown forward and landed, face down, in the broken glass and puddles of piss. *Funny*, he thought. *No pain*. Just a gentle numbness that was washing over his body like the water of a warm bath.

The Haitian stepped up beside him and looked down.

'Pa gen sove pou ou jodi a, *There's no saving you today,*' he said quietly and fired a single shot into the back of Sutton's head.

It would be a robbery gone wrong, another statistic lost in the haze of Port-au-Prince crime, the truth buried in Martissant's dusty streets.

63

Naples, Italy

ITA Airways flight AZ 1263 pulled into the gate at Naples-Capodichino International and came to a halt with a slight bump of the brakes. Madeleine unbuckled her seatbelt, and the Business Class steward opened the overhead locker, handing down her Luca Faloni overnight bag. Its caramel-brown leather was battered and scuffed, a testament to her many short-hop jobs over the years.

In the terminal, Madeleine walked quickly through the crowds, her bag slung over her left shoulder. Minutes later, she stepped through the glass doors and immediately spotted Matteo leaning casually against his latest Ferrari, a 599 GTB. Matteo's tanned face lit with a brilliant white smile as he saw her.

Madeleine kissed him lightly on the cheek and dropped her bag in the luggage compartment of the Ferrari, then slipped into the tan and black leather interior. As Matteo pulled the sleek red vehicle out of the airport, the car's low, guttural hum filled the air, adding to the early morning sounds of the city. Madeleine shut her eyes. The last thirty hours had been bloody awful.

∾

Madeleine sat in a third-floor interview room, her overnight bag at her feet. The room was brightly lit and windowless. The furniture was minimalist and functional. There were no more two-way mirrors in the rooms – there was simply no need, with the array of cameras and microphones that covered every angle of every room in which a debrief was held. She crossed her legs and tapped lightly on the tabletop with a fingernail. It was SOP to make them wait. It put the wind up them before an Inquisitor enters. It was never one's own handler. It was always someone specially trained to question, pry, and trip up. Get to the truth at all costs, and they were good at what they did. Madeleine had met them before.

The door opened, and a small, middle-aged man walked in. He was wearing a rumpled brown suit and a weary expression. Sellotape held an arm of his glasses together, and he had a shaving nick on his throat. The absent-minded professor types were the most dangerous, and Madeleine tensed.

The Inquisitor turned to a fresh page on his yellow legal pad and clicked the top of a ballpoint pen. He opened the file he had placed on the table and slowly flicked through its pages. Madeleine caught a glimpse of a photograph of her and Bishop together. They were eating a meal in a small restaurant. The sign said "Pa-Oh Kitchen," and the boy in the background was wearing a faded AC/DC T-shirt. She didn't move, but her heart rate accelerated. The watcher in Taunggyi. *He was one of ours.*

'Miss Carter,' The Inquisitor said without introduction. 'You know why you are here. Just procedure, but you will tell me everything about your most recent mission, no matter how seemingly insignificant. I shall lead you on this guided tour, but you will be the one to point out the sights. All of them.'

Madeleine knew Nigel was watching and listening.

'Is not brevity the soul of wit?' she said. 'Nigel has my report.'

'I do appreciate a Shakespearean quote, I really do. Not many of the young ones can do that these days.' He sniffed the air. 'Let me respond with another fitting quote: "A kind of confession in your looks, which your modesties have not craft enough to colour." I am saying, of course, that I can hear the truth behind your actions and intentions. I can see beyond your words and know more than they reveal. But I'm sure you know that. Shall we start?'

So, Madeleine started. She told the Inquisitor everything she could recall. Everywhere she went, everyone they met and what they said. She was telling The Inquisitor about arriving in Yangon when he said:

'You forgot to show me Mr Dougherty's weapons bunker. Let's have a look now, shall we?'

Madeleine had long ago ceased to be surprised at what the Service knew and how they knew it, but she had intentionally left that out. That would be a black mark. So she led The Inquisitor down the stairs into the concrete-lined room and showed him everything there. They moved on.

As she described their capture at the army checkpoint, The Inquisitor interrupted again. 'Let's briefly skip forward to the firefight on the knoll,' he said.

'You don't care to know about my near-execution at the hands of the Burmese military…?'

'We will get to that. But the firefight. That's quite the tale.'

'It's true,' Madeleine replies.

'I don't doubt it. How many rounds did you fire?'

'I wasn't counting.'

'And did you hit any targets? Kill anyone?'

'Of course I bloody well did. It's what you employ me to do.' *Calm down, don't let him get to you.*

'And you had earlier shot and wounded a CIA officer.'

'I didn't know he was at the time, but I would have done it anyway. He was shooting at *me*…'

A note on the yellow pad. 'When did you first know that Mr Bishop was a drug addict?'

She paused for a split second, but it was too long. The Inquisitor looked up.

'At our first meeting,' she said. 'I have always known.'

'Yet you carried on a relationship with him.' The Inquisitor wasn't asking a question. He continued to write.

'Yes. We fucked. Like rabbits. He was the best I've ever had, and, believe me, I have had a few.'

The Inquisitor didn't blink. He nodded, wrote again on the legal pad, and, for the next two hours, Madeleine talked. And talked. The Inquisitor backtracked her now and then, revisiting something she had told him, but her answers were the same. They were the truth, so why would they vary? Finally, after they land in China and are ferried back to Thailand, The Inquisitor sat back.

He was slipping the pen into his jacket pocket when he stopped and clicked his fingers as if a sudden thought had come to him.

'Why did you let Bishop listen in on your call with your handler? The night he took the satellite phone from you...'

'I didn't. He came out of nowhere.'

'So, you admit you failed to take satisfactory precautions before making a classified call in the field...'

Madeleine looked up into the CCTV camera that faced her. 'Nigel. What the fuck is this? A debrief or a disciplinary hearing?' She turned back to The Inquisitor. 'He jumped me. I thought he was somewhere else.'

The Inquisitor stood and gathered up the file and legal pad.

'That was a grave error of judgement, Miss Carter. But that will be all. We're done here.' Then he left the interview room. As the door clicked softly behind him, Madeleine hung her head, angry and exhausted.

The drive from Naples had been quiet. Madeleine had been silent, and Matteo had spoken only a little, trying to coax her to open up. She had barely noticed his efforts. Her mind was still in the thick Burmese jungle, and she could feel the suffocating heat. The sound of gunfire echoed in her ears. The images she was trying to block out – the broken bodies, Sophie's agonised screams, and the relentless torture of their escape – pressed on her, their weight leaving her tense in her seat.

She and Matteo had navigated the twisting roads of the coastline beneath a clear blue sky and warm Italian sun, Matteo handling the Ferrari like the professional driver he was. Eventually reaching Porto di Sorrento, they saw the unmistakable silhouette of the Ferretti 580 bobbing gently in the marina's waters. The yacht, Madeleine knew, was waiting to take her far away from everything Burma had left her with – and far away from The Masters.

An hour later, standing at the back of the boat, looking across the glittering waters off Capri, Madeleine's thoughts were skittish and fractured. She struggled through her pre-dive calming and breathing exercises, essential for staying focused in the deep blue, eventually giving up on them. She knew she shouldn't, but, with a final look back toward the island, she drew in three deep breaths, tapped her watch, and dived in.

At only thirty feet, she started to stress but pushed deeper, finning erratically and too fast. Her lungs screamed, and at forty feet, she felt the first flush of panic and nearly exhaled. She bit down on the urge and immediately inverted, swimming with all her might to the surface. Her vision began to grey. Seconds later, she burst clear to suck in a deep breath with a tortured gasp.

The late afternoon sun was in her eyes, and she was confused. She could not see the yacht. She spun in a circle and spotted the aft swim platform only metres away. Matteo stood there, bent over, holding out a hand. She struck out for the ship and threw her long fins onto the platform as she grasped Matteo's hand, and he pulled her clear of the water.

Matteo stood beside her as she panted, drawing oxygen back into her system. He did not speak but moved close to reassure her with his presence. He gently rubbed her shoulder, then turned and climbed the stairs to the flybridge, where the skipper sat at the upper helm, gazing into the setting sun.

Madeleine heard Matteo's footsteps pad away. She leaned back and pulled her dive bag across. She unzipped the bag and drew out her phone. The last twenty-four hours – particularly being thrown to the Inquisitors by Harris – had confirmed the doubts in her mind. She knew what had happened in Burma – everything The Masters had cooked up and dropped her in – was par for the course. It was all part of the Great Game; it always had been. But she also knew she no longer wanted to be a pawn on the grand Machiavellian chessboard. After so long, she was sick of it and what it was doing to her.

With a deep sigh, she opened the secure app and tapped the contact labelled "Gardening Service." Madeleine stared out to sea. It was flat and calm, moving from light blue to dark azure and purple as the sun's rays lifted from it. After three rings, the phone answered.

'Nigel,' she said. 'I'm out.'

64

ILFRACOMBE, *Outback Queensland, Australia*

Bishop had not waited. After only twenty-four hours back in Singapore, where he had slept and rehydrated, he had taken the eight-hour overnight flight to Brisbane. He had arrived in Barcaldine late the same day and had spent the evening with his mother and sister.

Their small weatherboard rental sat on a quarter-acre block, its front verandah shaded by the spreading branches of a large gum, and a sprinkler had hissed on the thick front lawn, its spray throwing up glistening jewels into the late afternoon sun. It was a nice little place, Bishop had thought. Certainly a big improvement on the shithole he had grown up in. It was the first time Bishop had seen them in two years and there had been much to talk about.

Now, he pulled the Hilux off the road and into the gravel driveway of the pub. He pulled on the hand brake and switched off. It was quiet in the small outback town. The Landsborough Highway stretched gun-barrel straight toward Longreach, the setting sun seeming to sit on the rough road surface like a giant red eye. An occasional road train roared by, heading east, and flocks of galahs gambolled and squawked on the powerlines and in the gums of the park.

Bishop stepped from the vehicle – no need to lock it out here – and walked the shaded concrete terrace to the open door of the front bar. The bar was busy with the late-afternoon crowd of locals washing the dust from their throats with schooners of beer. A grey nomad couple sat quietly in the corner, keeping to themselves as they chewed slowly on a pub meal.

No one looked up as Bishop walked in – people were friendly out here, but they didn't like to get in your face. He pulled up a stool at the bar, facing the door, and ordered a beer. He checked his watch. If he were right, the old man would be in soon to drink himself into his daily stupor. Bishop was right. Fifteen minutes later, he glanced over the rim of his beer glass as a figure shambled into the bar.

The old man was skinny, a faded shadow of the muscled brute he had been twenty-four years earlier. A sun-bleached khaki work shirt hung on his frame; the sleeves rolled up his spindly arms, which were inked with blurred jail tattoos. The belt on his black work shorts was cinched to the last hole, and the shorts bagged over his skinny hips and stick-thin legs. He walked with a limp, throwing his right leg out as he rolled into the bar.

The old man sat on a bar stool with his back to the door, facing Bishop down the length of the bar but not seeing him. He ordered a double rum and coke as Bishop studied him. His teeth were browned and gappy, and his eyes were rheumy. His hair was unkempt, grey and greasy. A long scar stretched from the top of his neck and over his jaw to just below the corner of his mouth. *I did that, you bastard.*

The old man was pathetic, Bishop thought with disgust. How could he have ever been so scared of him? He slowly finished his beer, then, his eyes straight ahead, walked past the old man and out of the bar.

∾

The new moon cast almost no light. In the cloudless outback sky, stars and planets shone with striking clarity. Beyond the lights of the pub's front verandah, the landscape was dim, grey and uncertain. The contrast between the vast, dark land and the brilliant starlit sky was stark. Bishop waited.

The last of the locals had left half an hour before. At 9:00 p.m. the old man, the last to leave, stumbled out. He was unsteady on his feet as he looked up and down the highway before weaving his way into the dark. Bishop gave him a slow count of sixty and then started the Hilux.

The skinny shadow staggered on and off the footpath, blind to his surroundings, as Bishop crept the vehicle close behind him. Seconds later, the old man reached the street corner, and Bishop gunned the engine, flicking on the powerful LED light bar as he swerved the ute across the drunk's path. The old man held a hand up to his eyes as Bishop leapt from the cab and grabbed him, spinning him around and snapping a cable tie onto his bony wrists.

The old man squeaked like a bludgeoned rat as Bishop bundled him into the tub of the ute, climbed back behind the wheel, killed the lights, and drove off slowly, heading south. He crossed two intersections, dark and quiet as the town slumbered, and turned right onto Leichhardt Street. One minute later, he turned left and pulled over, switching off the engine.

Road gravel crunched under Bishop's boots as he moved to the rear of the ute and dropped the tailgate. He grabbed the old man by the ankles and dragged him out, dumping him to the ground with a thud. Bishop bent down, pulled the old man to his feet and half-dragged, half-marched him through the cemetery gates.

The small, well-maintained cemetery was dark, with only the faintest light reflecting off the white headstones. Nothing moved or made a sound. Bishop dragged the old man into the middle of the field and dropped him beside a grave. The old man groaned as Bishop squatted beside him and slapped his face.

'If you shout or scream, I'll cut your throat where you lie.' Bishop said, his voice quiet, matter of fact. 'Do you know who I am?'

The old man wriggled on the ground. 'I can't see your face,' he slurred. 'Is that you, Gino?'

'Not Gino. Who's he?'

'Bloke I owe money.'

'You'll wish it *was* Gino, you bastard.'

Some vague memory, or a sudden understanding, came to the old man, and he turned his head and spat into the dirt.

'Is that you, *boy*?' he snarled. 'You finally come back, have ya? How the *fuck...*'

Bishop backhanded him then, rocking the old man's head. He leaned in close to the old man, the stink of body odour and rum washing over him. 'We're not having a conversation, you and me. You're a heartbeat away from death right now. I'll talk, and you listen. Are you listening?'

'It *is* you! Fucken get on with it, then. You were useless as a kid. Weak as piss, prob'ly still are. *Christ*, how I hated you. You and that slut of a mother of yours....' The old man howled as Bishop drove a fist into his mouth, shattering the remaining top teeth.

The old man groaned. 'I take that back. You gotta bite to you now,' he mumbled through split lips. 'That's good... You know where you got that?' He burbled blood over his chin and spat a wad onto his shirtfront. '*Me! I* did that for you. You should be fucken *thankin* me, boy!'

'I said no talking.' Bishop reached into his back pocket and drew out a lock knife that he snapped open. He positioned the tip just under the old man's left eye and pressed. The old man howled again, and a small stream of blood, black in the night, trickled down his face.

'One more word, and the eyeball comes out. That'll hurt, but not anywhere near as much as it will once I get to work on the rest of you.' The old man's eyes were as wide as saucers. He nodded, gritting his broken teeth, blood flowing over his lips.

Bishop went on, his voice cold, remorseless.

'I thought I had killed you when I hit you with that shovel. It would have been better for everyone if I had. Instead, I've dreamed for years of the ways I would do it. But here's the funny part: I decided not to. I *was* content with leaving you in the past, something rotten, like roadkill. That changed when I heard you were back, stalking Mum and Rosie.'

Bishop pressed the knife a little deeper, feeling the steel grate against the bone of the old man's eye orbit. The old man bit his lip and whimpered.

'It ends here,' Bishop whispered malevolently. 'You foul, drunken cunt. Right here. But I'm not going to kill you. Not tonight. You get to stagger back to whatever rock you crawled from under. *But* if you *ever* go near Mum and Rosie again, and by "near" I mean within a five-K radius, I'll find you, and I will take you apart, piece by piece, until you beg me to finish you. Is that clear?'

The old was shivering, and he nodded dumbly. Bishop slapped his face again and twisted the tip of the knife.

'Don't doubt me, you piece of shit. Your death will be slow if I ever have to come back. They'll be picking up bits of you from here to bloody Townsville.' In a sudden, violent movement, Bishop flipped the old man onto his front and cut away the cable tie before rolling him back.

'You got a watch?' he asked.

'A what?'

'A watch. Have you got one?'

The old man nodded.

'Show me.'

The old man slowly raised his left hand. Bishop grabbed it and slammed it down on the stone edge of the grave, gripping it tight. Without a word, he pulled the forefinger aside, placed the knife blade across the last knuckle, where the finger joined the hand, and pressed. The old man shrieked then, long and high. Bishop pressed harder, blood flowed, and the heavy, razor-sharp blade cut through the bone with an audible pop. The finger fell into the dirt.

Bishop leaned down to the old man's ear. The old man was panting, blood flecking his lips, as he grabbed his mutilated hand.

'You're not dead tonight. But take this as an important message.'

Bishop stood and looked up at the clear night sky. It was limitless and beautiful. Somewhere in the dark, a pair of curlews screamed. He kicked the old man hard in the ribs, driving the toe of his boot in and hearing the fragile bones crack.

'Remember what I told you. Five kilometres,' he said quietly as he turned and walked from the cemetery.

65

Bishop stopped and looked into the shop window. Expensive watches sparkled and shone in the display, but he didn't look at them. He stared back over his shoulder in the reflection, looking for the tail he had sensed for over an hour. He did not know where it had picked him up, but he knew it was there.

Crowds moved up and down Orchard Road, laden with bags from the high-end stores in the iconic shopping belt. Traffic moved politely along the broad avenue. There were faces everywhere, but none that Bishop could see looking at him. No one figure standing still, no one moving in on him.

The uncomfortable feeling nagged at him as he moved up Orchard Road and turned left into the MRT entrance. Weaving through the commuter crowd, he walked quickly into the subway and scanned through the turnstile with his EZ-Link card. A sleek train stood at the North-South Line platform as he stepped off the escalator.

Walking swiftly, he boarded and moved to the side of the door, looking back at the platform. Seeing nothing, he grabbed a handle strap as the train moved rapidly out of the station, south to City Hall, where he changed trains to the East-West Line, heading to his destination at Tiong Bahru.

Ten minutes later, he stepped out of the MRT and headed east along Tiong Bahru Road to his apartment on Eng Watt Street. He checked his six as he walked but saw no sign of a tail – he was confident he had shaken it back at Orchard. He picked up speed, walking swiftly through the humid late afternoon, headed for home. He checked his G-Shock. Perfect timing. He was nearly home and would do a quick change, pick up the bike and head out for dinner and a cold beer.

Reilly paid off the taxi and stepped out onto the road. He watched as the rider dismounted from the blue SuperSport motorcycle and moved down Crawford Lane, pulling off his helmet. Slipping on a pair of Aviators, Reilly stepped back into the shade of a large Rain Tree – known locally as *Pukul Lima* – and sat on the public bench beside an old man reading a copy of *The Straits Times*.

'Nice day for it,' Reilly said, leaning back against the bench. The old man grunted and continued reading.

This guy had been hard to find, Reilly reflected. Hard to find and even harder to track once he had. Reilly had picked him up by putting his photograph out to a network of informants who worked across the city-state – bartenders, waitstaff, doormen, and even hookers. A doorman at The Fullerton had tipped him off to his target's preference for drinking along Boat Quay and that he parked his bike near the OCBC Centre, where his office seemed to be. Once he knew the area, Reilly had tightened the net, and from there, the pieces had all fallen into place. And now, here he was.

Reilly watched as the target sat at the restaurant and ordered. It was... fucking *awesome* to be so close to him after all this time. He gave it a minute or two before he was sure the target had settled in, then made his move.

～

Bishop placed his full-face helmet on the red plastic chair beside him and zipped off his leather jacket. The early evening humidity was thick, and his T-shirt stuck to him. He felt hot and greasy as he glanced inside and signalled for a beer, then picked up the table menu and began to read.

Low-cost public flats surrounded Tai Hwa Pork Noodle, a family-run restaurant known as one of the city's exceptional hawker stalls. It served the best street food in Singapore, and its *Bak Chor Mee* – a minced meat noodles – had been awarded a Michelin Star a few years earlier. Yet, the owners steadfastly refused to up their prices, more as a nod to the low-income residents around them than anything else.

All in all, it was a favourite of Bishop's, and he visited regularly. The ice-cold Tiger beer arrived, and Bishop ordered his meal. Bak Chor Mee, and *Guo Tiao Tang*, Rice Noodle Soup.

Mr Tang Chay Seng, the hardworking owner, cook, and waiter of the food stall, smiled and thanked Bishop before walking inside to prepare the food. He liked the big gua nang, *foreigner,* who always ate alone. He was polite, quiet, and unassuming, *and* he ate like a horse, which was good for business.

Bishop sipped his beer and glanced idly around. The restaurant had one or two other diners scattered about, and the place was quiet. He sat back, relaxed, in his chair. As he did, he noticed a man crossing the road and headed toward the restaurant. Tall, solid build, middle-aged. Sunglasses, crew-cut. A polo shirt tucked into shape-less, beige, straight-legged pants. Khakis. American.

With a jolt, Bishop realised the man was looking directly at him. The man crossed the restaurant terrace, a clean, checkered pattern of concrete slabs edged with green grass, and stopped at Bishop's table.

'Mind if I sit here?' Reilly said, a sardonic smile on his face.

'I do.'

'Always nicer to have company at dinner,' Reilly observed, sitting. 'Don't you think?'

'I don't. Who are you, and what do you want?'

Reilly smiled. 'C'mon, Mr Bishop. Don't be coy. I thought it was time we met and had a little... what do you Aussies call it? A "chin wag".'

Bishop leaned forward on the table. 'Mate, you have exactly ten seconds to tell me who you are and why you're here, or I'm going to shove this beer bottle down your throat.'

Reilly chuckled. 'You know, I do believe you would do that. You're certainly capable of it.' He lit a cigarette. 'You don't get to know my name, but I *really* wanted to meet you. Let's just say we have a... *had* a... mutual connection recently.'

'What are you talking about?'

'Myanmar, buddy. Ol' Burma... The Golden Land.'

Bishop stared at the American, the pieces quickly falling into place. 'You're Sutton's boss. The man who negotiated the protocol.'

'In person.'

'Is he dead? Sutton?'

'Not to my knowledge. He's on... sabbatical.'

'Well, whoever you are, you're a rogue CIA officer on the run.' Bishop sipped his beer. 'Are you armed?'

Reilly spread his arms. 'Of course not. Public place, safe and orderly Singapore. That would be just plain *wrong*.' He clicked his tongue. 'You know, it's because of you I'm currently... between jobs.'

'Fuck, mate. I'm sorry we messed things up for you...'

Reilly gritted his teeth. 'One of these days, smartass, the goddamned Chinese are going to pour over the border into Myanmar, and the good Lord knows no one will do anything about it. Not the UN, and least of all the Brits. *Then*, the world will wish there had been one of Uncle Sam's good old Airborne Divisions there to stop them. But it will be too late.'

Bishop shook his head. 'Is that what they teach you in CIA School? *That's* your understanding of the region's geopolitics? Everything you did, all the lives that were lost, was based on a fallacy. It was a Neocon wet dream. All you ended up with was another Bay of Pigs – only less successful. Don't you guys ever learn? *Jesus!*'

'Wake up and smell the coffee, Bishop. We're the only thing standing between you and a goddamn re-education camp!' Reilly took a deep breath and gathered himself. He re-arranged the smile on his face. 'Anyway, you really threw a spanner into the old works, you and that broad of yours. Kudos to you.'

Bishop laughed bitterly. 'You know, it's typical. In the end, you were brought down by bureaucracy. By the Agency's pathological need to document everything. Without that protocol file, there'd be nothing to pin any of this on anyone.'

Reilly took a quick hit on the cigarette, letting the smoke roll out slowly, and shrugged. 'There's still nothing to pin on anyone, Bishop. C'mon man! You know that...'

The food arrived at the table, and both men sat back in their chairs, eyeing each other like hunting dogs on a pig. Mr Tang laid out the meal and placed another beer by Bishop's elbow.

'Would your friend like a drink?' he asked with a smile.

Bishop didn't take his eyes off Reilly. 'No, thank you, Mr Tang. He won't be staying.'

Mr Tang nodded and walked off. Reilly rapped the table with a knuckle. 'I hear the girl was wounded, and she's now back in Canada. Doubtless, readying herself to take the stand. Shame.' Reilly cocked his head and stared at Bishop. 'You know, she might yet not make it into court. That would be a waste, wouldn't it? I mean, after all your heroic deeds, and all – you and those PDF rats.'

Bishop stared at him, resisting the urge to leap across the table and smash the beer bottle over his skull. 'You were there, weren't you. The firefight by the river. You were with the Tatmadaw rifle company.' He snorted in derision. '*Jesus*, you must have run like a scalded cat to get away from that lot. Too hot for you, was it? After murdering all those civilians...'

'Fuck you, Bishop,' Reilly snarled. 'You smug asshole.' He leaned conspiratorially across the table. 'Here's a newsflash for you, buddy. You ready? I knew. All the goddamn time. I knew where you were and what you were doing – sometimes even knew before you did it.'

Bishop eyed Reilly. It was like a game of poker. Reilly was all in and was expecting Bishop to fold. The American was unreadable, and Bishop's skin tingled. 'You're lying.'

'Am I? You calling my hand? Bottom line, Bishop: you and that gal of yours were lucky. More than once. Four times to be exact. Dumb fucking luck.' Reilly sighed dramatically. 'I should have had you, but I guess that's the game, huh?'

Bishop sat silently, his mind working overtime, sifting and selecting pieces to lay in order. Pieces of the puzzle that began to connect. Reilly dragged again on the smoke.

'I guess you'll find out at some point,' he said. 'I can't wait for that to happen. I'd love to be there...'

Bishop sipped the beer. He was deeply concerned. 'You'll do fuck all, mate. Right now, you're being hunted by the entire US intelligence community – you know, the *good* ones – and when they find you, we both know they would prefer to avoid the embarrassment of a trial. And then there's whoever put you up to that Burma debacle in the first place. They'll be keen to see you never speak. Face it, you're a dead man walking.'

Reilly shrugged. 'Maybe, but I wouldn't bet on it. I've got plans...'

'Look how the last lot worked out for you.'

'... and those plans will see me very much alive and moving into a comfortable retirement.'

Bishop had had enough. 'The minute you leave, I'll be on the phone with the RSO at the US Embassy reporting this little chat. You won't get out of Singapore.' He readied himself. 'And you're leaving right now...' He leapt to his feet, throwing back his chair, and stepped around the table.

Reilly's hand slipped under the hem of the polo shirt, and Bishop caught a glimpse of the Glock as it disappeared under the table. With nowhere to run, Bishop sat, his hands on the table.

'I lied about not carrying,' Reilly said quietly. 'It's pointed right at your balls, so calm the fuck down.' He picked up the cigarette with his left hand and dragged on it. 'As to me getting out of here... you know better than that. *Fuck* the Diplomatic Security Service.'

He waved his hand and snorted. 'Goddamn DSS – travel advisories and vaccinations. Assholes. No, not only will I get out of this joint – fucking Chinatown by the Sea – but we'll meet again, you and me. Fact is, ace, my plans – my *interests* – involve you. I'd go so far as to say you were central to them.'

Bishop frowned. What the hell was he talking about?

Reilly grinned wickedly. 'That got you, didn't it?' He dropped the cigarette and ground it out under his heel. 'That's two for two, and you're just *dying* to know what the hell I'm talking about...'

'I couldn't give a flying fuck.'

'Oh, but you do.' Reilly waggled a finger. 'All in good time, compadre. Until then, I want you to do me a favour: don't go changing. Can you do that for me?'

Bishop felt his heart clench. Something about the American, sitting there eyeing him like a pit viper, unnerved him. He had met his share of loose individuals in his time, but this one was genuinely deranged, and he felt a prescient shudder of doom. The man sitting opposite him had him off balance, and Bishop was unfamiliar with the sensation. He did not like it. The American pushed back his chair and stood, the handgun held loosely at his side. Bishop coiled, ready to spring at him.

Reilly stepped back and threw ten dollars on the table. 'Sit there and don't do anything stupid, pal. Have a beer on me. You look like you could use it.'

He flipped a mocking salute and turned. Stepping onto the road, he fired two shots into the engine of Bishop's bike and kicked the machine over. As people ran for cover and chairs flipped over, Reilly turned and pointed at Bishop.

'I'll be seeing you, Bishop,' he said. 'Watch your back.'

66

THE AIR WAS thick with the city's tropical warmth, and there was the hum of bustling traffic at the intersection of Bras Basah and Beach. The streets were alive with a mix of people – local and tourists – each on their own journey through the busy downtown area.

Bishop turned right and moved purposefully past the iconic Raffles Hotel on his left. The hotel's colonial architecture, with its whitewashed walls and grand verandas, was an oasis of calm elegance in counterpoint to the frenetic pace of life around it. The aroma of roasted meats, spice-laden dishes, and fresh tropical fruit filled the humid evening air, reminding him that he was nearing his destination.

After a few more steps, he spotted Purvis Street on his left, a small road lined with quaint shophouses. He stepped into the shadows of a doorway and studied the street. The atmosphere there was more relaxed. It was a slice of old Singapore nestled amidst the modern cityscape. And it was quiet, especially mid-week. That was why he had picked it for the meeting.

Bishop's eye settled on an outside table a short distance along Purvis Street. It was in front of an old, family-run restaurant, the last of the famed Hainanese eateries on the street. Nesbitt was already seated there, his legs crossed at the knee as he sipped a beer. Bishop leaned back into the dark and lit a cigarette.

Three days before, and one day after his confrontation with the crazy American, Bishop had gone to the office. He was still on the ten-day leave Nesbitt had given him after the mission, but he wanted to tie up the post-op admin. He had gone in early, logged on, printed the forty-page report, slipped it into a manila folder and dropped it on Nesbitt's desk. He was leaving the office when the elevator door swished open, and Nesbitt stepped out.

'What are you doing here? You're on leave...'

'I am. Just dropping the report off on your desk. I couldn't relax until that was done.'

Nesbitt smiled. 'Ever the professional, old boy. Well done. What have you been up to – apart from beavering away on the report?'

Bishop shrugged. 'Nothing much.' It was a lie, of course, and Bishop could see that Nesbitt knew that.

'Well,' Nesbitt said as he moved past Bishop. 'Fuck off and enjoy your break.' He moved down the corridor. 'As for me,' he said, 'I shall plough through your magnum opus... I can't wait to read about your exploits. Especially how you shot that company commander...'

Bishop paused, his finger reaching for the elevator button. He turned and watched Nesbitt enter his office and close the door. Bishop's heart raced, and he felt suddenly hot. His muscles tensed, and a knot formed in his stomach. Taking a deep breath, he stabbed at the elevator button. The doors opened, and he stepped in.

Dragging on the cigarette, Bishop looked up Purvis Street. As he had hoped, it was quiet, with only a few people moving its length. He glanced up and spotted the Land Transport Authority CCTV camera. It was on Beach Road at the Purvis Street junction aimed away toward Middle Road. Perfect. He knew there were no other cameras along Purvis. It was another reason he had picked this place.

Grinding the cigarette out under his boot, he pulled the folds of the dark, lightweight gym hoodie a little higher up the back of his neck and adjusted the peak of his cap lower over his eyes. He quickly checked up and down Beach Road and stepped out of the doorway.

Nesbitt looked up with a smile as Bishop approached the table. Bishop dragged the chair out with his foot, sat and lit a cigarette. He eyed Nesbitt silently, waiting for the older man to speak. Nesbitt could also play that game, but he gave in after topping his beer glass from the frosted bottle of Tiger on the table.

'I didn't know you smoked,' he said.

Bishop ashed the smoke into a tin ashtray. 'I've just taken it up. Seemed a good idea at the time.' He turned in his chair and signalled the waiter for a beer. He smoked quietly, tapping a finger on the table. The beer hit the table in moments, and Bishop spoke after a long pull at the cold bottle.

'You've read the report?'

'I have. Quite the time you had over there.'

'You could say that.'

'Bloody good job, by the way.'

'If you say so.'

'I do. You and young Maddy did a stellar job under very difficult conditions.'

'Thank you, *sir*.'

Nesbitt sighed. 'Oh, for Christ's sake, Bishop. What's on your mind? You're behaving like a surly teenager.'

'I want to know what I was really doing in Burma.'

'You were finding and rescuing the girl.'

'Sure, we rescued her, but all that effort for a lost girl... Strange, don't you think?'

Nesbitt ran a hand through his hair. Bishop was suffering post-op come down from the mission – that much was clear – but Nesbitt did not need to be a mind reader to know what Bishop was actually on about.

'The job to find the girl was real,' Nesbitt said. '*She* was real...'

'But there was something else, wasn't there? Something London wanted while I bumbled around bloody Burma.'

'Why do you say that?'

'You couldn't have organised that transit through China and Laos, but London could have. Not *our* London. MI6. They organised it because you suggested it after hearing from Terry about our extraction plans. And they did it with Beijing's approval and assistance, because they were already working with Beijing to take out the Shan force on the border. Weren't they?'

He pointed a finger at Nesbitt. 'You set me on something much more important than the girl. Without me knowing it. Something your mates in London desperately wanted to know. It was the same thing Maddy was working on.' He dragged on the cigarette and huffed out the smoke before stabbing it out in the ashtray. 'Shit, everyone was working on it but me.'

'What do you want me to say?' Nesbitt demanded. 'That it was all a waste? I bloody well won't say that!'

'What about all the bodies? All the people that died along the way? Doesn't that mean anything to you?'

'Frankly, no. It might be a Grey War, fought in the shadows, but it *is* war, and people die. What you did had meaning for the Bouchard family, and the broader outcome probably saved millions of lives. *That* would not have happened without your mission.'

'And there we have it... You're Six too, aren't you? Fucking spooks everywhere... And the firm is a front. A sham.'

'No, and no. The firm is a real business, beholding to no one and no agency. As for me, yes, I *was* in the Service for some years. Out here, as it happens. But I am no longer. However, I *am* close. C is an old colleague of mine. He reached out to me early in the piece, when they first heard rumblings coming out of Burma. As you were going in to find the girl, I contacted him, told him and volunteered our help. I knew you would pick Madeleine Carter for the team.'

'So did they, as it turns out.' Bishop lit another cigarette. 'The fact remains, you didn't tell *me*, did you? I bet you bloody well passed on everything I had found to London, though. I was risking my fucking *life*, and you couldn't trust me enough to bring me in.'

'For Pete's sake, Bishop. Of course I passed it all on. And, it's not about "trust"; it's about the need to know. You did *not* need to know. That's the way things work. You bloody well know *that*...'

'I'm still cleared...'

'Not to that level, you're not. So you feel slighted, do you? A bit miffed that I didn't let you in on a juicy secret that Maddy knew and you didn't?' Nesbitt finished his beer and signalled for another. 'What do the kids call it these days...FOMO?' He shook his head. 'There are no Sharing Circles in the intelligence game. No consideration of morals or ethics, no friends, when the world is on the brink of war. It's called "Realpolitik", son. Look it up.'

'I was played for a fool. By everyone.'

Nesbitt picked up his glass of beer and drank deeply. 'Look,' he said, his voice softening. 'You got her out. You found her, you saved her life, and you returned her to her parents. Not many could have done what you did.'

He toyed with the beer glass, turning it around in his hand, seemingly lost in thought.

Along Purvis Street, a car spluttered and backfired loudly as its owner tried to start it. The street was nearly deserted. Traffic noise from Beach Road rumbled as cars and buses roared by. The restaurant was quiet, with only four diners sheltering inside in the air conditioning. Raising his beer with his left hand, Bishop slipped the other hand under the hoodie.

'I was played,' he said. '*You* played me.'

Nesbitt looked up. 'What the devil are you talking about?'

'I met someone a few days ago. An American. I didn't catch his name.'

Nesbitt sat stone still, silent.

'It turns out,' Bishop went on, 'that he was the one behind the entire plot. The Protocol.' Bishop dragged on his cigarette. 'You're right, what you said... No consideration of morals or ethics, no friends.'

Nesbitt swallowed. 'Get to the point.'

'Okay. He told me he knew everything we were doing and that we were lucky. Four times, to be exact. That's what he said. That got me thinking. They took us at a roadblock and fucking near executed us, they were on us in Narhkan the night we found Sophie, they miraculously found us in Lai Kha, and again the day we extracted Sophie from the LZ. Four times. Each time we barely scraped out.' He waved the cigarette in the air. 'Luck.'

'*They* were lucky,' Nesbitt said. 'They were hunting you, and they stumbled on you. It happens...'

'Not like that, it doesn't. The point is, you knew we were in Taung-gyi, and each of the following times followed a SITREP I had sent to you. No other times, no other coincidences. Just my texts from Taunggyi and those three SITREPS. And they found us each time...'

'Are you saying I betrayed you? To this nameless American? Don't be bloody ridiculous...'

Bishop shook his head and dragged on the cigarette. He flicked the tip into the ashtray. 'I thought I was. Being ridiculous, I mean. But there was something I hadn't told you. Something not in any report back to you.'

'And that would be...?'

'The shot I took that killed the company commander during the firefight at the knoll. I never mentioned it. But you did. Three days ago, in the office.'

Nesbitt's shoulders slumped, and he seemed to sag in the chair like a deflated balloon. He rubbed a hand over his mouth and chin. Bishop waited. Finally, Nesbitt drew a deep breath. Up the street, the car farted and banged as the driver worked the ignition.

'His name is Reilly,' Nesbitt said. 'Bill Reilly. He's a CIA Operations Officer with a thirty-year career behind him. We crossed paths a few times years ago.' He shrugged. 'He was very good at what he did – one of the best, actually. But he was always a loose cannon on deck.'

Bishop shifted, his hand moving slightly under the hem of the hoodie. 'And you betrayed us to him. Why?'

'I didn't set out to. I had no idea what he was up to – that he was behind the girl's disappearance. I haven't seen or heard from him in over ten years. Somehow – I suppose it's unsurprising – he broke your cover and then placed you back with the firm. He contacted me...'

'That doesn't answer my question. Why?'

Nesbitt pinched the bridge of his nose. 'He has photos of something I did many years ago. Something I'm deeply ashamed of. I was ...'

'I don't want to fucking know. Get to the point.'

'He placed you, knew I was running the firm in Southeast Asia, and blackmailed me. Inform on you and the mission, or have the photos sent to the regiment, the office in London, Six, and the British tabloids.'

'So you gave us up for some dirty pictures... You put our lives in jeopardy to save your own skin?' A thought occurred to Bishop. 'Sophie. What if she had been killed? The contract would have gone to shit...'

Nesbitt sighed. 'No. The contract bound Bouchard to pay regardless of the outcome. Including the bonus, so long as he got her body back. Either way, it was a minimum forty-five million US for the firm. And Christ knows we need it...'

'What do you mean?'

'We're in trouble. Regulatory inconsistencies, banks putting the squeeze on. The firm's bleeding money – including a million of my own. A scandal involving me would have killed it.'

'Was there a sweetener...?'

'Reilly promised four million US if my information led to your capture... or death. It would have gone to the firm, if that makes any difference.'

Bishop dragged on the cigarette and ground it out in the ashtray. He drank deeply from the beer bottle. The restaurant door opened as the last of the diners walked out and made their way, laughing and talking up Purvis Street.

'Did you tell him about the pending attack on Sai's column?'

Nesbitt chuckled bitterly. 'No. Last ditch attempt at redemption, I suppose.' He looked into Bishop's eyes and shivered. They were as black and cold as a witch's heart. 'What are you going to do?'

Bishop slipped his hand out from under the hoodie. He gripped a Walther PPK, fitted with a Gemtech Aurora suppressor, and slid it under the table. The car finally started and stuttered its way down Purvis Street toward them.

'You know what I'm going to do,' Bishop said, his voice low and cold. 'I'm not letting you walk away from this.'

Nesbitt nodded and sat a little straighter in the chair. 'You know, I looked on you as a son... Make it quick.'

The car began to pass them, its backfire ripping into the quiet street like fireworks.

'I've never had much luck with fathers,' Bishop said and fired.

The .32 ACP round punched through the cheap laminate table and entered under Nesbitt's chin, blowing out the top of his head. His eyes snapped wide as his body rocked back in the chair, his head lolling to the side.

Bishop slowly replaced the Walther and stood, picking up the empty beer bottle. He used his T-shirt to take thirty dollars from his wallet and dropped the notes on the table. With a final glance around, he walked up Purvis Street toward North Bridge Road, tossing the beer bottle in a rubbish bin as he passed.

EPILOGUE

Mong Pat Township, Shan State, Burma

The fire mission from the 105mm howitzer battery splashed in on the west and east of the township in violent eruptions of high explosive and fragmented steel, that destroyed trees and decimated the crops.

The ground vomited dirt and rock into the sky, and the air was thick with a bitter, metallic tang, oil blended and overlaid with the rich, deep smell of the dark earth. From the north, crossing the road from their assembly area, a wave of Type 85 Armoured Personnel Carriers rumbled in, their 12.7mm heavy machine guns blazing. The APCs' smoke grenade launchers thudded off rounds, and the attack was quickly concealed in a thick, rolling wave of acrid smoke.

The carriers roared to a halt in a spray of dust and dirt. Their rear doors opened. In moments, each vehicle had disgorged thirteen assaulting troops that fanned out on either side of their carrier and advanced.

The delicate peace in Shan had ended weeks before with the reported death of General Min, and his successor, General Win, had taken the fight to the Shan State Army with a brutality that surpassed even the worst excesses of the Burmese military. After an acrimonious split during the chase for the Canadian girl, troops of the People's Defence Force and Shan State Army had come together and now fought side by side, desperately trying to stem the offensive against overwhelming odds.

'*Back to the monastery!*' Swe yelled above the battle din, firing repeatedly toward the advancing enemy. She dropped to a knee to aim at an army officer peering around a corner. She squeezed off a shot, and the officer's head exploded, his helmet flying off and clanging against the steel door of a burning shop. Swe watched as her brother sprinted by, dragging an SSA soldier with him, the soldier's bright orange neckerchief soaked dark with blood.

The soldier died on his feet, and Zaw dropped the body to herd the withdrawing soldiers through the township toward the large monastery at its southern end. They would make their stand there. Swe stood and fired again before spinning around and following on, her bodyguard of two men and two women clustered around her like a protective wall.

Swe suddenly stopped in a narrow street and swept her arms out to each side. 'Form a line here,' she shouted. 'Delay them as long as you can, then fall back to me in front of the monastery.' Her bodyguard looked at her and nodded. They all knew what the order meant. She ran on.

The township was burning, and smoke choked the furnace-hot air. Everywhere, bloodied and crumpled in the rubble-littered streets, lay the shattered bodies of civilians, PDF fighters and SSA soldiers. Gore dripped from the ruins of houses, and blood ran down walls like the claw marks of a great beast. Swe stumbled and tripped, then struggled to her feet, panting in exhaustion and rising panic.

Heavy fire and a series of muffled explosions echoed down the street as the four men and women left behind as a delaying force were bundled aside by the battalion that had entered the township. The army was methodically, mercilessly, fighting its way through the shattered town, street by bloody street.

Swe stopped and turned. A section of ten soldiers rounded a corner, their gun group on the ground providing fire support as the assault group ran on. She was about to run for cover when she was punched aside, a tremendous blow like a mallet hitting her in the right hip. She dropped with a scream, gripping her leg. Her hand came away wet, and she watched the fountain of bright red arterial blood arcing into the dust through her torn trousers. She groaned in despair, raised her rifle to her shoulder and fired at the advancing soldiers.

Her magazine empty, she rolled to her side and was fumbling in her chest rig for a reload when she felt the grab-handle of the rig tighten, and she was dragged to her feet. The pain in her hip was excruciating, and she screamed again.

'*Lean on me!*' Zaw shouted as covering fire cracked over his head from a barricade, felling two of the attacking soldiers. 'The monastery is only fifty metres away. *Move!*'

Swe shook her head. Stumbling, she pushed weakly on Zaw's chest. She looked into her brother's eyes, red-rimmed but dark and comforting, as a burst from a machine gun struck home, shredding them both where they stood. Brother and sister died instantly, their torn bodies collapsing together in a final embrace, as still more troops poured into the destroyed town, and swept across Shan State, bringing fire and death.

AUTHOR'S NOTE

I spent a lot of time in Burma between early 2017 and the end of 2020, and paid a short "visit" in February 2021 in the immediate aftermath of the coup. Myanmar, or "Burma" as it used to be called, has one of those histories that pulls you in – it's a complex web of cultures, politics, and turmoil.

After shaking off British colonial rule in 1948, the country found itself in an intractable political mess. A military coup in 1962 started a long stretch of authoritarian rule that isolated the nation and kept it economically stunted for decades. Ethnic conflict has simmered (and sometimes raged) as various ethnic groups, like the Shan, Kachin, and Karen, have been pushing back against a government that has often ignored or repressed them.

In 2011, it looked like things might turn around. A semi-civilian government introduced reforms, and people began talking about Burma's "democratic transition." But the military never fully let go, despite the General Election of 2015 and the first real taste of civilian-led government. In February 2021, they launched another brutal coup, and everything, as they say in the classics, went to hell. Since then, the Burmese people have been stuck between a rock and a hard place, trying to survive a brutal regime while the world mostly watches on – and sometimes doesn't.

What's remarkable is the degree to which the people have fought back. People's Defence Forces (PDF) sprang up around the country, many made up of young people – like Swe and Zaw in this story – villagers, and former soldiers, taking up arms to resist the junta's control. Some of these groups are local militias – like Swe's unit – while others are larger alliances of ethnic armed organisations that have been fighting for autonomy for decades. Each PDF unit varies widely in strength and structure, but they all share one thing – a determination to resist the junta, often at great personal risk. These fighters are up against an incredibly well-armed and ruthless military, and their struggle is far from over. In February 2021, I planned and conducted an evacuation from Yangon – a dangerous and stressful time – but, it pales to insignificance compared to what my Burmese friends were, and still are, up against.

The country is now trapped in a brutal cycle of conflict. Villages have been burned, families displaced, and the economy – never robust to begin with – has been destroyed. Burma today is a story of survival and defiance, where the stakes couldn't be higher, but the resilience of Burma's people is inspirational. They've shown the world what courage and determination look like, even when the odds are stacked against them.

Swe and Zaw are real people, brother and sister. However, I have changed their names in this book to protect them and their families. They were killed in Hsi Hseng, Shan State, by the Burmese military in January this year.

You may have noticed I've chosen to call the country "Burma" throughout this book rather than "Myanmar" – except where it is relevant to character. This isn't a casual choice – it's a reflection of the history and the ongoing struggle of the Burmese people. The name "Myanmar" was adopted by the military regime in 1989, a move that wasn't supported by a democratic mandate. Many people, including opposition leaders and various ethnic groups, continue to use "Burma" as a reminder of the country's fight for genuine representation and democracy.

In using "Burma," I'm acknowledging that the current military regime doesn't represent the people's wishes. "Burma" serves as a reminder of the country that so many are still fighting to reclaim – a Burma where people might one day be free to choose their leaders, their future, and even their country's name.

Like many of the locations of my novels, Burma has some interesting naming conventions. Most people don't have last names. In fact, names are usually just one to three syllables, often chosen by consulting astrology or based on qualities the family wants to see in their child. You won't find family names or any hints at ancestry. There are honorifics, though: "U" for older men, "Daw" for women, and "Ko" for young men.

"Khun" is another Burmese honorific, but it's typically used among the Shan ethnic group rather than in broader Burmese society. In Shan culture, "Khun" is a respectful term for men, somewhat similar to "Ko" in Burmese. Burmese names tell a personal story rather than a family one – something I found fascinating among my friends in Yangon, and dizzying when trying to keep track of my characters!

Reilly and Sutton, and their two masters in Washington, are bad guys. Or are they? I'm not sure even I know. But they *are* examples of what happens when accountability breaks down in intelligence agencies that operate in a unique grey zone of legality and ethics, balancing a mission that sometimes requires pushing conventional boundaries to protect national security.

To paraphrase Machiavelli, do the ends justify the means? If a goal is morally important enough, is any method to achieve it acceptable? Reilly, Sutton, and the two mysterious gentlemen in Washington seem to think so. It's a challenging topic of discussion over a bottle of red.

Unlike the average citizen, intelligence officers often find themselves in situations where they have to work around or beyond accepted norms – because, quite simply, the nature of their job frequently demands it. Yet, they don't operate in a vacuum. Despite their leeway, they must still be accountable to the government and, by extension, the public. Their actions are scrutinised through oversight committees, policies, and checks meant to hold them responsible, even if their methods must sometimes stretch the boundaries of what's typically acceptable. The need for secrecy and the demand for accountability, is a tough line to walk.

My thanks to the men and women I know in our intelligence communities – and the many tens of thousands I don't – who live and work in the shadows to keep us safe.

Finally, while I have tried to be as accurate as possible in all aspects of this novel - much of it drawn from my own experiences - it is a work of fiction and of imagination, so mistakes, doubtless, have been made. Last, I admit to, occasionally and slightly, altering aspects of geography, climate and streetscape. In my defence, I only did so where I felt it enhanced the story and allowed me to neatly tie up a narrative point. For that, I apologise to my Burmese friends and beg their forgiveness.

A.C. Edwards
Brisbane, 2024

ACKNOWLEDGMENTS

Writing is a solitary occupation – but, to paraphrase the proverb, it takes a village to raise a book. As ever, there are so many people I want to thank, but special acknowledgement must go to the following.

First, Dr Connor Simpson, the brilliant young ER doctor who took time off during his wedding preparations in Spain to step me through Bishop's battlefield injuries and subsequent addiction to Oxycodone. In the interests of full disclosure, Connor is like a second son to me, and I could not be prouder of him.

My good friend, mentor, and author, Tony Park – the legitimate heir to Wilbur Smith and teller of fantastic African adventure thrillers – who, despite his own pressing editorial and publishing commitments, took the time to read an advance copy of this book and give me his honest opinion and advice. I'm immensely grateful for that and for all the late-night phone calls.

To "Pips", who did a mighty job proofreading the book in what little spare time she has. I thought I had picked everything up, but I hadn't. I hope, together, we got it all.

To my friend who still works in Burma – he knows who he is – who spent hours on Signal with me, taking me through his assessment of what is happening in the country today.

ABOUT THE AUTHOR

A.C. Edwards brings unparalleled authenticity to the thriller genre, drawing on his extraordinary career as a former policeman, paratrooper, and Special Forces officer. Serving in the Australian Army, Andrew operated extensively across Southeast Asia and the South Pacific, with attachments to the Malaysian and Indonesian armies and other high-stakes operational deployments, retiring at the rank of Major.

Beyond the military, Andrew worked as a security adviser across SE Asia, a close-protection specialist for High Net Worth individuals, and a Security Contractor in the Middle East and Afghanistan. Most recently, he served as Regional Security Director for Asia Pacific at a multi-national company. Now, Andrew channels his wealth of experience into crafting gripping, action-packed thrillers full of military precision and nail-biting suspense.

Born in Singapore, Andrew has spent much of his life across Asia Pacific, shaping his unique global perspective. He now divides his time between Hong Kong and Brisbane, where he lives with his wife, a spirited dog, and a rescue cat.

facebook.com/acedwardsauthor

instagram.com/acedwardsauthor

www.ingramcontent.com/pod-product-compliance
Lightning Source LLC
Chambersburg PA
CBHW020330180626
46812CB00001B/127